OUTSIDE EDEN

A Selection of Recent Titles by Merry Jones

The Harper Jennings Series

SUMMER SESSION *
BEHIND THE WALLS *
WINTER BREAK *
OUTSIDE EDEN *

THE NANNY MURDERS
THE RIVER KILLINGS
THE DEADLY NEIGHBORS
THE BORROWED AND BLUE MURDERS

* available from Severn House

OUTSIDE EDEN

A Harper Jennings Mystery

Merry Jones

This first world edition published 2013
in Great Britain and in the USA by
SEVERN HOUSE PUBLISHERS LTD of
19 Cedar Road, Sutton, Surrey, England, SM2 5DA.

British Library Cataloguing in Publication Data

Jones, Merry Bloch.
  Outside Eden. – (The Harper Jennings series ; 4)
  1. Jennings, Harper (Fictitious character)–Fiction.
  2. Evil eye–Fiction. 3. Women veterans–Fiction. 4. Iraq
  War, 2003–2011–Veterans–Fiction. 5. Tel Aviv (Israel)–
  Fiction. 6. Suspense fiction.
  I. Title II. Series
  813.6-dc23

ISBN-13: 978-0-7278-8264-6 (cased)

All Severn House titles are printed on acid-free paper.

Severn House Publishers support The Forest Stewardship Council [FSC], the
leading international forest certification organisation. All our titles that are printed
on Greenpeace-approved FSC-certified paper carry the FSC logo.

MIX
Paper from
responsible sources
FSC
www.fsc.org   FSC® C018575

Typeset by Palimpsest Book Production Ltd.,
Falkirk, Stirlingshire, Scotland.
Printed and bound in Great Britain by
MPG Books Ltd., Bodmin, Cornwall.

To Robin, Baille and Neely

Acknowledgements

Deepest thanks to:

Rebecca Strauss, my agent at McIntosh and Otis;

the team at Severn House, especially Rachel Simpson Hutchens, my editor;

Adi and Gal Ben Haim and the many other Israelis who helped me get a sense of life there,

Robin, Baille and Neely, who helped me trek around Israel for research;

Supportive fellow members of the Philadelphia Liars Club, including Jonathan Maberry, Gregory Frost, Solomon Jones, Jon McGoran, Kelly Simmons, Marie Lamba, Dennis Tafoya, Don Lafferty, Keith Strunk, Keith DeCandido, Ed Pettit, Steve Susco and Chuck Wendig;

My encouraging friends and family, most of all, my first reader and beloved husband, Robin.

Harold Clemmons had been cheated. Suckered. Scammed. Duped.

Even worse: his wife had been the one to discover it. She'd gone online, totaling their credit card expenses, and boom – there it was. A charge for two hundred dollars. And he'd caught hell about it. Dot had kept him up the whole damned night, listing all the treasures she could have bought for the money if he hadn't simply signed it away. Even now, as he approached the gate of the shuk, he could still hear her.

'Didn't you even look at the sales slip? You just signed? Genius. They could have put down ten times the amount – they could have put down anything they wanted. Why don't you just wear a sign saying, "I'm a chump; cheat me. Take my money!"' Dot's voice had a piercing, nasal twang that jangled his skull, reverberated in his mind. 'So where is it?' She'd stared at him, her hands on her hips.

It took a moment for him to realize that 'it' was the receipt for the purchase. He had no idea where the thing was, hadn't paid attention. They'd been in a crowded street in the teeming marketplace of Jerusalem's Old City, and she'd bought souvenirs for what amounted to less than twenty dollars. Was he supposed to have kept track of every receipt for every paltry purchase she made? How was he supposed to have known the guy was going to rip him off? Dutifully, to appease her, he'd gone through his wallet and miraculously he'd found the thing. Sixty-eight shekels.

But Dot had been unrelenting. She'd gone on and on, calling him everything she could think of – irresponsible, careless, foolish, soft. Saying that he was an easy mark, that he all but invited people to take advantage of him, that it was the same back home. That he didn't command respect, let alone fear. Sometime after two in the morning, he'd pretended to be asleep, while in reality he'd lain awake, simmering. Mad at the vendor, mad at Dot. Mad enough that, as soon as the sun came up, he'd gotten up and showered, gone downstairs to breakfast, leaving Dot asleep, mouth wide open, but at least silent.

As soon as the shops opened, Harold entered the Jaffa Gate,

passing through the tall white granite walls into the Old City. He hurried past security guards and busloads of tourists, rehearsing what he would say to the vendor, if he could find him. Practicing standing tall and looking fierce like a man not to be messed with. At some point he stopped, getting his bearings, not sure exactly where he was. He walked along a main street, saw endless rows of shops. Clusters of travelers and shoppers. Schoolgirls in plaid skirts – but wait. Their uniforms looked Catholic or maybe Greek Orthodox. Definitely not Muslim. So he must have wandered out of the Muslim section, away from his vendor.

Harold changed direction, wandering the labyrinth of intersecting paths in the shuk, surrounded by booths displaying their wares. Sandals, jewelry, water pipes, scarves. Fragrant spices. Aromatic toasted nuts. Fresh fruits and flowers. Hundreds of booths, but not the booth he was looking for.

The morning was warm, and Harold's shirt was already damp. He went up an alleyway, around a corner, around another. Every display seemed familiar, identical. Vendors called to him: 'Come, sir. Buy a gift for your wife.'

'I have excellent souvenirs for you to bring home. Anything you like.'

'Come in. Take a look – just for one minute.'

Harold kept moving, grinding his teeth, determined to find the culprit. Turning left, then right, he found himself in a dank and shadowy passageway that came to a dead end. Harold stopped. He was wet with sweat, breathing too hard. Needed to slow down, cool down. Wiping his brow, he retraced his steps to the wider alley and continued searching the booths, hearing the clamor, seeing the monotony of trinkets, T-shirts, brass camels, brocade elephants, wallets, candlesticks, sun hats, harem pants. How was he to find the vendor he was looking for?

In fact, he almost didn't. He walked right by it, probably more than once, but finally, he saw them: Big brown eyes, too big for their bony face. Dark hair clipped almost to his scalp.

The thieving vendor.

Harold pushed past a hanging carpet, bumped a rack of dresses, and entered the tiny shop.

The vendor smiled broadly as if he'd never seen him before. 'May I help you?'

Harold stood at the small wooden board that served as a counter, shoved a display of beaded necklaces and charm bracelets to the side, dumping out his sack of key chains and scarves. He stood up tall and narrowed his eyes. 'I'm returning these . . .'

'Sorry?' The vendor's eyes widened, his hands raised, palms up.

'I bought these from you yesterday . . .'

'I don't know. I see many customers.'

'Well, I know. You sold me this stuff.' Harold's voice sounded thin. His pulse pounded, face sweltered. Sweat rolled down his back. 'And you overcharged my—'

'But why would you return these things?' The vendor picked up a key chain, examining it. 'Nothing is wrong with the merchandise.'

'Seriously? It's crap—'

'*Crap?*'

'And you charged me sixty-eight shekels for it, but you billed my credit card—'

'Only sixty-eight shekel? For all this? Well, you must have bargained well. That was an excellent price—'

'No – that's not the point.' Harold felt flustered, wiped his forehead. 'Point is you overcharged me—'

'But all our sales are final. So what I can do for you, because I want you to be happy, is to let you exchange this—'

'No, I don't want to exchange anything. I want my money back.' Harold sensed people standing behind him, watching. Fine. He'd let others know what was going on in this place. 'You charged my credit card two hundred American dollars – that's a lot more that sixty-eight shekels.'

The vendor looked astonished. 'This is not possible – show me the paperwork.' The vendor scowled, crossed his arms.

Harold presented his receipt.

'This says sixty-eight shekels.' The vendor pointed to the number.

'And I was charged six hundred and eighty.'

'No, sixty-eight. See?'

'But you charged my credit card—'

'How can I be sure?'

Harold took his phone out, began punching up the credit card information his wife had obtained the day before. He heard the people behind him moving, watching, listening. Good. If he embarrassed the vendor enough, maybe he'd get his refund.

The vendor didn't wait. He waved his hands. 'Either way, it's between you and your credit card company. It doesn't involve me.

Anyway, we don't give refunds. I'll tell you what; look around. Find something you like. I'll give you a good price . . .'

'Nothing doing.' Harold squared his shoulders, trying to look powerful. 'I want you to refund my credit card!'

'Is there a problem, Ahmed?' Someone bumped Harold from behind; someone else stood beside him, shoulder to shoulder.

Harold turned. Three beefy men with dark shining eyes stood in an arc around him.

'No, no problem,' the vendor said. 'This man simply can't make up his mind what to buy.'

Harold was surrounded. The vendor in front of him, a man to his side, two others blocking his exit.

'What will it be?' The vendor smiled, gestured at the wall of brass figurines. 'How about a lovely chimpanzee? Only six hundred and eighty shekel.' He lifted one, held it out.

Harold turned slowly, facing the three newcomers, looking from one to the other. Finally, head down, he stepped toward them. They didn't move. He was alone, outnumbered in the crowded, cubby-holed shuk. If they wanted to, they could make him disappear, never to be seen again. Never return to the hotel; never again see Dot or his mother in Ohio.

'Excuse me.' He turned to leave, managing to look the largest one in the eye.

'Wait,' said Ahmed, the vendor. 'You forgot your chimpanzee.'

Harold looked at him, at the brass ape, then at the men blocking his way.

'Only six hundred and eighty shekel.' Ahmed began wrapping the thing up.

Harold's face burned; blood roared in his head. He was trapped. He reached into his pocket, took out his credit card. Handed it to Ahmed, who processed the purchase and handed the package to Harold, smiling. 'Enjoy your ape.'

Harold turned to go, faced a wall of large, smirking men.

The biggest one waited a beat, then stepped back, clearing the way. Harold rushed out of the booth, down the passageway. At the corner, he looked back, saw the men following him. He kept going, hurrying. Pushing past shoppers, going deeper and deeper into the shuk, becoming completely lost. Sweat poured down his face; he didn't bother to wipe it away. It trickled down his nose, off the tip. He kept moving, trying to get away, running up a staircase, down a narrow lane, around shoppers, through a small courtyard. Finally, rounding a corner, he came to a shadowy, abandoned area where the booths were all shuttered. He stopped, looked back, didn't see the men. He stepped back, peeked around the corner. Saw nobody. He'd lost them. Probably they were back with Ahmed, laughing at him, dividing up the money from the dumb American they'd chased away and ripped off. Twice.

His face got red again. He could feel it, hot and pulsing. But never mind. All he wanted now was to get back to his hotel. He thought of Dot, what she'd do when she found out he hadn't gotten a refund – that, instead, he'd dropped another 680 shekels. Harold gathered his breath, trying to figure out what to tell her, and realized that he'd have to find his way out of the tangled paths of the shuk before he could tell her anything. Why had he ever set foot in the cursed place? He should have left it alone, let Dot rant and scold. But no, he'd had to be a hero, had to show her what a tough guy he was. How he could fix it. He regarded the package in his hand.

The chimpanzee was an insult, a symbol of his humiliation. He looked for a trash can to throw it away, then saw two people approaching. They looked American; one wore a T-shirt and jeans, the other a plastic raincoat. Odd, since it was hot and there was no chance of rain. But Harold was elated; the two would help him find his way out of this godforsaken maze. He walked toward them, and they smiled, came closer.

'Excuse me,' he said. 'Are you American?'

'Yep.' The shorter one grinned, and the one in the raincoat walked right up to him. Invading his space.

By the time he saw the knife, it was too late. The shorter one stood back, blocking his escape. The taller one raised the knife and ran the blade across his throat. Harold collapsed. Falling, bleeding, he had three final thoughts.

The first was that he was about to die.

The second was that he had no idea who these people were or why they were killing him.

The third was that he wouldn't have to tell Dot about the extra charge on the credit card.

All around her, women prayed, their heads bowed and covered. Some stuffed pieces of paper into small cracks and crevices between rocks. Harper Jennings stood at the Western Wall of the Old City in Jerusalem, holding her hand flat against a stone block in the structure. It felt rough, sturdy, solid. Ancient. It had kept its place for over two thousand years, outlasting invaders, empires, cultures, gods. Harper pressed her fingers against it, less interested in the bustling women around her than in the inanimate wall, its past. Who had cut the stone, hauled it, placed it there? And what had it seen – worshippers, warriors, centuries of change? How many other hands had touched it? Millions? Her hand on the stone, Harper felt connected to all of them, a chain of hands and shadows of hands, linked by a rock through ages.

But Harper couldn't linger. Hagit had the baby, and she didn't know Hagit very well. Following the practice of the other women, she moved away from the wall without turning her back to it, a sign of respect. When she was sufficiently distant, she looked around and saw Hagit and Chloe, holding hands, waiting for her.

Harper went to them, swept Chloe up, got a joyous squeal.

'Did you put in a prayer?' Hagit nodded at the wall.

'A prayer?'

'In the cracks. Didn't you see? People put prayers on paper and leave them in the wall.'

'I saw them.' Harper tussled Chloe's curls. Kissed her warm round cheek.

'I'll wait.' Hagit held out a pen and scrap of paper. 'Go – put it between the stones. Write down a prayer and leave it there. It's supposed to be like a . . . a what do you call it? A mailbox? No – like FedEx for God.'

Harper laughed.

'Even if you're not religious, it wouldn't hurt . . .'

'It's okay.' Harper looked back at the wall, the women gathered against it, the divider between them and the men on the other side. The men were praying, their shoulders covered with shawls, their heads with kippahs or black wide-brimmed hats.

Hagit watched her, disapproving. Shorter than Harper, she was plump, probably fifty, her unruly hennaed hair struggling to get free of a silver barrette. Harper wasn't sure who'd hired her. Maybe the organizers of Hank's symposium; maybe the Israeli Ministry of Foreign Affairs. But someone had hired her, for the moment they'd checked into their hotel, exhausted from the almost twelve-hour flight with a baby who'd had no desire to sit still or be quiet or sleep, Hagit had shown up with credentials and taken charge, telling Hank and Harper to rest, that she'd watch little Chloe. From then on, for the last two days, while Hank, Trent Manning and their international colleagues attended their meetings, Hagit had been Harper's helper, babysitter, tour guide and constant companion.

'Down, Mama.'

Chloe was restless, wanted to move. Harper sat on a ledge at the edge of the courtyard and set her down. As soon as her little feet hit the ground, Chloe took off, demonstrating her recently acquired ability to scurry. Hagit at her side, Chloe forged ahead, crashing into a gaggle of women before wobbling and grabbing a hemline to steady herself.

Harper ran over to apologize, but the owner of the hem was already crouching, chatting with Chloe. 'Aren't you a big girl, running all by yourself?'

'She's beautiful.' One of the hem owner's friends grinned at Hagit. 'What's her name?'

Hagit frowned, shook her head, no.

'Her name's Chloe.' Harper stooped to open Chloe's fist and free the fabric of the skirt. 'Let go, honey. Sorry – she's not interested in walking, only in running. And she doesn't have good brakes.' She helped Chloe to her feet.

'How old is she?'

'Fourteen months.'

'Only? She's agile for fourteen months. And so adorable.' The third woman grinned.

'Look at those curls!' The first woman cooed.

'And a charmer.' The second one beamed. 'Look at the twinkle in her eyes.'

Hagit mumbled something; her frown deepened. 'She's a baby. Nothing special.' She grabbed Chloe's hand and led her away.

Nothing special? Harper bristled at the remark, made an awkward, apologetic shrug and wished the ladies a good day. Then she chased after Chloe, who'd pulled her hand from Hagit's and sped off again across the courtyard, shrieking.

Harper caught up, her eyes never drifting from her child. Hagit had been approved by Israeli security, but Harper had never had a babysitter before, hadn't trusted anyone but Hank to watch the baby when she wasn't there. Consequently, Chloe had spent much of her first year in a sling attached to Harper's body, going mostly everywhere with her. But now, Chloe was becoming a little girl. She could walk, was starting to talk. She needed more independence, more people in her life. Hagit provided a first step in that direction. So Harper forced herself to let Hagit help with Chloe, but she watched them like a mama lion, lurking nearby.

When Chloe tumbled again, this time reaching for a stray cat, Harper ran over and scooped her up. She fastened the wiggly twenty-two-pound bundle into her sling, trying to get her to hold still long enough to tie it. Soon, Chloe would be too big for this mode of transportation, but for now, it offered a means of control.

Hagit watched, arms crossed, still frowning.

'What?' Harper eyed her.

'What do you mean, "what"? Those women. Why did you allow that?'

'Allow what?' Harper had no idea.

Hagit lowered her voice, looked around. 'The Evil Eye.'

Harper tilted her head. The *what*?

'They drew its attention to the baby.'

Harper shook her head. 'Sorry. I don't know what—'

'You heard them. Saying she's beautiful and a genius and so on? Kenahara. Harper, the Evil Eye is always watching. When attention goes to someone, it goes, too. It's dangerous to say a child is pretty or clever or somehow better than the rest. Why would you let them say such things, inviting trouble? You have to say a Kenahara.'

'A what?'

'Kenahara. It means "No Evil Eye".'

Harper shook her head. 'Wait, you're saying it's wrong to call a baby pretty?'

'Not just a baby. And not just pretty. You should never point out good luck or success. Attention like that – praise like that? It's like a phone call to the Evil Eye – you might as well send him an invitation. Ask him for trouble. Come with me. Hurry. There's still time.' Hagit grabbed Harper's arm and, rearranging the diaper bag on her shoulder, led her into the shuk.

The light changed as soon as they stepped inside. And so did the mood. The solemnity and awe that surrounded the Wall vanished. Suddenly they were in a teeming bazaar, closed into a dimly lit narrow corridor streaming with people. On all sides were overstocked booths, their goods spilling into the passageway. Vendors with dark shiny eyes beckoned and called, 'Come and look.' 'See what I have for you.'

The air was hot, dense. Crowded with smells: flowers, sweat, incense, spices. The cologne of a passer-by. Something pungent. Something decaying. And there was such noise – a steady undercurrent of shuffling and voices, bits of conversations in many languages. Commotion.

Harper moved along, Chloe snug against her in the sling, Hagit's hand gripping her elbow. She had a feeling of being caught in a current, being swept along. And her senses were on high alert, as if the waters held danger.

But Hagit seemed unfazed. She led them along, turned into one alleyway, then another. Harper fought waves of claustrophobia, glimpsing displays of motley wares – clothing and trinkets, hookahs and pashminas, pomegranates and rugs. Shoes and flowers. Roasted nuts.

'Mama. Go.' Chloe kicked Harper's sides, a rider spurring on a horse.

Hagit finally stopped at a booth displaying finer items: watches, silver and gold jewelry. Leaving Harper at the entrance, she stepped inside, stood at a display case. The vendor greeted her, offering help.

Hagit peered into the case and pointed. 'That one. And that one.'

'Certainly, you have excellent taste.' The salesman smiled, unlocked the case. Took out two necklaces with hand-shaped pendants, one tiny enough for a small child's neck.

Hagit said something in another language – Hebrew or Arabic, Harper wasn't sure. The man looked shocked and offended; he replied, shaking his head, no. An argument ensued. Eventually, Hagit put the necklaces down and turned to leave; the vendor grumbled and waved her back; Hagit took out her wallet.

'Mama.' Chloe kept kicking. 'Down.'

'Not now,' Harper said. 'It's too crowded.'

'DOWN.' The word was loud and shrill, and delivered to Harper's ears with simultaneous heels to the hips. Chloe had definitely outgrown the sling. Time for a stroller.

'Stop kicking.' Harper grabbed Chloe's feet, pictured herself with two matching heel-shaped bruises. She stepped out of the shop, looking up the aisle for a booth that sold strollers, but Hagit came back and fastened a chain around Chloe's neck.

'Wear this always.' She stood behind Harper, talking to Chloe.

'What is it?' Harper looked over her shoulder, couldn't see.

Hagit held up the larger one, showing Harper a gold, not inexpensive, charm before hanging it around her neck.

'These are *hamsas*,' Hagit explained as she fastened the chain. 'Protection.'

Protection? 'Good-luck charms?'

'No. Not to bring good luck. Just to keep away bad.' Hagit pulled her away from the booth, back into the crowd.

Harper went along, fingered the charm, its hand-shaped woven gold. Even if it were just a superstitious symbol, it was a generous gift. 'Thank you, Hagit. You shouldn't buy us—'

'Wearing the five fingers will hold off the Evil Eye. Wearing the *hamsa*, plus saying Kenahara – say it.' She stopped walking and faced Harper, waiting. Blocking the passageway.

People bumped into them. Pushed their way past.

'Kenahara,' Hagit repeated. 'Say it.'

Chloe kicked, impatient.

'Kenahara.' Harper obeyed, eager for Hagit to lead them out of the shuk.

'Good. The world is full of evil, Harper. Believe me. You have to take whatever precautions you can.' She held up the ornate, ancient-looking *hamsa* around her own neck. 'Now, come this way.' She led them round a corner into another narrow but less crowded corridor, along another aisle of booths that all looked the same.

Somewhere up ahead, a man was yelling in English.

'It's crap!'

As they moved along, the voice got louder.

'You overcharged me . . . refund my credit card . . .'

Harper strained to see who was yelling, saw a red-faced, balding man in khaki shorts and a sweat-stained green polo shirt, surrounded by Middle Eastern men.

'. . . want my money back.'

The vendor's voice was low, but he was shaking his head. Refusing. The other men closed in around the American, menacing.

Instinctively, Harper took a step forward, to help him.

Hagit grabbed her arm. 'What are you doing?'

'He's outnumbered . . .'

'It does not involve you.'

'He's an American. And he's alone. I can't just watch . . .' But she stopped mid-sentence. What was she doing? Chloe was on her back. Was she really going to step into the middle of an altercation with the baby there? She held Chloe's feet to stop them from pounding her.

Hagit was still talking. '. . . in the Muslim section, not my part of the shuk. Let them alone. They will work it out. He can call a security officer or a policeman if he wants.' She pulled Harper away from the man with the complaint.

Harper turned to look back at him. He was sputtering, his face crimson. Still arguing, even as the men closed in around him.

'He'll be all right; don't worry about him. Most merchants here are honest enough.' Hagit forged through a cluster of tourists. 'I shop here. I buy my spices and fruit. Fish. Flowers. Only one thing: here, I wouldn't use a credit card.'

Really? 'Because they cheat?'

Hagit tugged Harper's hand, turned a corner. 'Let me just say evil can dig in its roots anywhere and can take on many forms. Smart people know that. Kenahara.'

By the time evening arrived, Harper was exhausted. She'd lost a night's sleep because of the seven-hour time change and had run around with Hagit and Chloe ever since. Chloe, however, didn't seem the least bit tired. Harper hoped a bath would relax her but, as she sponged warm water over Chloe's back, Chloe slapped the water, splashed and jabbered energetically.

Maybe a lullaby would help. Harper began to sing. 'Hush little baby, don't say a word. Mama's gonna buy you—'

'No!' Chloe raised her little arms, sending water flying, drenching the front of Harper's T-shirt. Okay, maybe Harper wasn't the best singer, but she hadn't thought she deserved a soaking. Enough bath time. Harper pulled the plug, lifted Chloe, wrapped her in a towel. Chloe wriggled and squirmed to get free.

'Down, Mama. Down.'

And as soon as Harper set her on the bed to dress her, Chloe slid off and scampered through the suite, giggling.

Harper dropped onto the bed, seeing no point in chasing her. Chloe was delighting in her freedom, her new ability to scamper on two legs. Sooner or later, she'd tumble; then Harper would step in and grab her. Meantime, she sat, holding the diaper, amazed at how fast Chloe was growing, how much she'd learned in just fourteen months. Chloe ran, overtired, overactive, zooming from the bedroom into the sitting room and back. When Harper reached for her, she sped away. Finally, just as she was about to get up and give chase, Harper heard a key in the lock. Men's voices. Thank God: Hank and Trent were back.

The moment that Hank stepped into the suite, Chloe stopped

running. Her entire demeanor changed. Suddenly, she was sweet, coy. Angelic. 'Daddy.' She sucked three of her fingers, eyeing him.

Hank, of course, was smitten. He reached for her and swung her high into the air, kissing her tummy, squeezing her. Returning her to the bedroom and handing Chloe to Harper with a peck on the cheek. 'Needs diaper,' he commented, as if Harper hadn't noticed.

Harper marveled at the way Chloe took possession of Hank, curling her little body into his arms, claiming him with her confidence. Staring at him with rapt adoration as he unbuttoned his shirt and took off his shoes. Harper grabbed the opportunity to fasten Chloe's diaper and slip on her pajamas.

'Trent's here.' Hank headed for the sitting room, stopped and looked back. 'Hoppa. You okay?'

'Just tired.'

'Good.' He picked up Chloe and stepped out the door.

Good? Never mind. He must not have been listening; must be tired, too. In the sitting room, ice clinked. Snippets of conversation floated around. They were talking about the symposium. Harper tried to listen. Chloe vied for attention, squealing and interrupting, but Trent talked over her, complaining about tensions – or was it factions? He was saying that politics shouldn't play a part in their discussions. Hank's opinions were harder to discern; his speech was still affected by an old brain injury, and he spoke in short phrases, his words sometimes out of order. He seemed to agree with Trent, but Harper couldn't hear because Chloe was jabbering, then Trent said something about depletion.

Their work was fascinating. Hank and Trent were among thirty-four scientists participating in a multinational symposium on the region's water issues – specifically, on the deterioration of the Dead Sea and the potential consequences of its drying up. As geologists, they'd joined eminent hydrologists, ecologists, other-ologists and delegates from the US, Jordan, Egypt, France, Israel, Russia, Great Britain and she wasn't sure where else. Their task was to combine efforts and propose workable solutions for the future of the area's water.

While Hank and Trent talked, Harper went to drain the tub. She picked up Chloe's clothes, folded the towel. Went back to the bedroom. The men were still talking, but Chloe was oddly quiet.

'Then what are people supposed to drink?' Trent's ice cubes jangled. 'Forget the agricultural and industrial issues – we're talking about sixty percent of Israel's water and seventy-five percent of Jordan's. And the Palestinians—'

'Know that,' or maybe, 'No that,' Hank interrupted, annoyed. 'But conse. Quences are. Of salt water, Trent. De. Salination. Might con. Tami. Nate.'

'Obviously. But damn it, something has to give. The sea is disappearing a meter a year because its source, the Jordan River, is being grossly overused. It's depleting to the point of crisis. And you heard what Dr Habib said. His country is willing go to war over water—'

'Must fix, Trent. But not. Ruin. Ground water. And environ—'

'Expedience is key, Hank. Something must be done soon if not sooner. It's not just Israel and Jordan. It's Syria, Lebanon – the whole region is at risk.'

At risk? Over water? Harper stiffened. She'd known that water was precious in the area, but she'd had no idea how urgent the situation was. She tossed Chloe's clothes into the laundry bag, peeled off her soaking T-shirt, pulled on a fresh one.

'. . . Water has to come from somewhere. No one is saying that desalination is ideal; we all know the risks – environmental damage from foreign algae and minerals and so on. But, short term, I don't think there's an alternative—'

'Yes, are choices—'

Harper went into the sitting room, eager to hear more. But as soon as she came in, the conversation stopped. Hank and Trent turned to her, silent. Wearing twin silly smiles.

Why had they suddenly stopped talking? Ever since the accident that had caused Hank's aphasia, he'd welcomed her to join conversations. In fact, he often relied on Harper to help him articulate his thoughts. But now, he regarded her stiffly, as if she were intruding. And Trent was uncharacteristically mute. Normally, he wouldn't shut up, especially when he was drinking Scotch. So what was going on?

'Hi, Harper.' Trent finally stood, offered a hug.

Harper returned it, noticing that Chloe was sleeping soundly in Hank's arms.

She took a seat beside Hank on the sofa. 'So. How were the sessions today?'

Trent said, 'Stimulating,' as Hank said, 'Disappoint. Ing.'

Harper looked from one to the other. 'Really?'

'It's staggering to have so many experts together.' Trent looked at his drink. 'Everyone's a chief – no Indians.'

'Us, too.' Or two? 'Chiefs.'

Beyond that, Hank and Trent seemed unwilling to discuss the meetings, even superficially.

'It's complicated.' Trent sat on an easy chair. 'Very delicate.'

'Cultures,' Hank said. 'Countries.'

And then they were silent. Trent drank Scotch. Hank took Harper's hand. Trent cleared his throat.

Nobody spoke.

Harper tried another topic, asked about Trent's wife. 'Have you talked to Vicki?'

Trent answered. 'Yes. She's fine.'

More silence.

'The babysitter seems nice,' Harper finally said.

'Great.' Hank nodded too much, smiled too broadly. 'Good. To hear.'

Trent downed his drink. Hank crossed and uncrossed his arms.

'Okay. I'm out.' Harper stood, lifted Chloe out of Hank's arms.

'She's okay. With me. Sit—'

'I'll put her in the crib and leave you guys alone . . .'

'Have a good night.' Trent hurried her along.

'Hoppa.' Hank stopped her. 'We. Can't tell you.'

She frowned. 'Can't tell me what?'

'We were cautioned against discussing our work with others. Even our spouses.' Trent got up, poured himself more Scotch. 'Only the final report is to be revealed.'

Hank finally met her eyes, looked sorry. Or worried?

Harper told them that she understood, that it was no problem, and she carried Chloe into the bedroom, hearing their conversation resume behind her.

'So do you think Habib was just posturing? Making empty threats? Or was he serious about war?'

Harper stood beside the crib. Oh God, was that why the symposium had been sworn to secrecy? Because war was imminent? She heard the buzz of flies, bursts of rifle fire. No. Quickly, gently, she laid the baby down, covering her even as men screamed and a white flash carried her into the air. Harper felt herself fly . . .

No. She bit down on her lip, causing piercing pain that grounded her in the present. The flashback faded, but she remained shaken. She'd seen war, still bore the scars. Didn't want to see another. And, more importantly, she didn't want her child to. Ever. She gazed at

Chloe, touched her curls, her cheek. Promised to do anything in her power to keep her safe.

Trent's voice rose. 'Maybe Habib's just a bully. Threatening war gives him clout . . .'

'True . . .'

Harper grabbed the remote, turned on the television, drowning out the voices from the next room. She didn't want – couldn't bear – to hear any more.

Leaning back against the pillows, Harper winced as she bent her war-damaged left leg. All the walking she and Hagit had done had strained it, plus her shoulders ached from carrying Chloe. But what a day it had been. Wandering the Old City of Jerusalem, seeing the ancient structures. History was alive here; the entire country was layered, civilization built on top of civilization. The archeologist in Harper couldn't wait to explore, but the rest of her was spent. Thank God Chloe was finally asleep. Harper gazed through the slats of the crib, marveling at the child's ability to sleep so soundly, untroubled, trusting that she'd be safe and taken care of.

If only Harper could be worthy of that trust. She gazed at Chloe, chest tightening, eyes filling. For the last fourteen months, every nerve of her body had been on constant alert, every muscle on duty around the clock. Even in sleep, she remained vigilant, listening. On guard. Ready to respond to any cry, any need. She doubted she'd ever truly rest again.

The television show was in Hebrew. Some kind of drama. Harper picked up the remote, found a rerun of CSI in English. She looked at the screen, then back at Chloe. Watching the rise and fall of the baby's chest, she slowly became lulled by its rhythm, closed her eyes and drifted.

Dozing, she was only vaguely aware that the program ended and the news came on. A female anchor spoke with a British accent, and Harper dimly noted the flow of her voice, but not her words. Maybe it was the mention of an American citizen that roused her. Or maybe the reference to the shuk. But Harper was awake enough to hear that a murder had occurred, and that the body had been found in the shuk's Muslim section. And she opened her eyes in time to see a photo of the victim.

Harper blinked, focusing. And sat up straight. No question: it was the man she and Hagit had seen earlier – the one who'd wanted his money back.

Harper stared at the screen, remembering him, how he'd insisted on getting a refund. How he'd accused the vendor of cheating him, even as the vendor's friends had surrounded him – and how Hagit had stopped her from stepping in.

Now the guy was dead? Oh God. The vendor and his friends – had they killed him?

Harper hopped out of bed, not sure what to do. But surely she had to do something, talk to someone, to the police. First, she'd tell Hank.

She opened the door to the living room, expecting to see Trent and Hank still talking. But Hank was in there alone, sipping Scotch, staring intensely at the wall.

Hagit had brought a stroller, borrowed from her neighbor. 'She's too big for the sling. You'll hurt your back.'

And that was that. No discussion. In a heartbeat, Chloe graduated from riding around on Harper to being wheeled around in her own vehicle.

Harper hadn't argued. She hadn't slept much, disturbed by Hank's ominous, brooding silence. She'd tossed in the darkness, wrestling images of the shuk, of murder, of dried-up rivers, of war. No sooner had she dozed off than Chloe had awakened and begun yammering to herself in long, incomprehensible sentences dotted with actual words like Daddy, Mama, No, Car, Okay, Go. For a while, Harper had lain with her eyes closed, half-awake, listening. Hearing the baby talking, Hank's shower running. Somebody knocking at the door. Wait, what? Oh God. Harper had jumped out of bed and hurried to let Hagit in. And hadn't stopped moving since.

'I think that's them.' Hagit nodded toward two men walking across the hotel lobby. They were casually dressed for detectives: short-sleeved shirts, khaki pants. But they walked with authority, seemed military. Probably had been; in Israel, everybody served.

Hagit stood, walked over to them, spoke to them in Hebrew, brought them over to Harper and Chloe.

The shorter, thicker one held out his hand, shook Harper's. His skin was dry, the contact quick. 'I am Marake'ah Ari Alon; this is Marake'ah Mishneh Barach Stein.'

Harper blinked. 'Harper Jennings. Nice to meet you, Marak – sorry, can you repeat that?'

Hagit shook her head. 'Why do you use Hebrew?' she scolded the men. 'He's Inspector Alon. This is – what is it? Deputy inspector? Or sub-inspector? Anyway, his name's Stein.'

'Inspector is fine. And sub-inspector.' Alon's eyes twinkled, but only for a moment. Like his handshake, the twinkle was short-lived. 'So, shall we go somewhere private?' He led them to the front desk; the clerk escorted them to a small conference room.

Alon sat at the head of the table, eyes piercing Hagit, then Harper.

Chloe wiggled, trying to climb out of the stroller. Harper lifted her to her lap, where she kept squirming and complaining.

'So. Last night, you called police to talk about the murder in the shuk. What do you want to tell us?'

Chloe slid off Harper's lap and scampered under the table. Harper didn't try to stop her, but she was distracted, bending over to make sure Chloe was all right, reaching out to prevent her from bumping her head.

'She's okay,' Hagit scolded. 'I'll watch her. Talk to the police.'

Harper felt her face heat up; the babysitter had just chastised her. But she let it go and concentrated on describing the argument they'd witnessed. She told the inspectors about the three men who had closed in on the victim. About her feeling that the man was in trouble, that she should intervene. She raised an eyebrow at Hagit, who quickly looked under the table to check on Chloe.

'And you?' Alon turned to Hagit. 'Do you have something to add?'

Hagit shook her head. 'Only when he left, they followed him. The three men.'

Alon and Stein exchanged glances. 'You saw this? How long did they follow him?'

Hagit shrugged. 'I didn't see.'

'Did they go east? West? North?'

Again, Hagit shrugged. 'All I saw was that they walked right behind him. They were laughing. I thought they wanted to scare him.'

Alon took some photos out of an envelope. 'Were any of these the men you saw?' He handed them to Harper, who checked under the table before looking at them. Chloe was standing now, chattering softly, gripping Sub-Inspector Stein's calf. Harper didn't scold her; he seemed unbothered.

There were about ten photos. Among them were four that she recognized: the vendor and the three men who'd taunted the American. She showed these to Alon, who shuffled the pictures and gave them to Hagit. Hagit picked out the same faces.

Sub-Inspector Stein leaned back, sighing. 'Maybe you already know about the shuk, Mrs Jennings. But I'll tell you anyway. The shuk is divided into sections. Jewish, Muslim and Armenian Christian. Each section has its own businesses. And its own sense of pride. These men you identified are all Muslim shopkeepers. All of them were seen bothering an American Christian who was later found murdered in the Muslim section. Let me tell you: this event can raise tensions. And, by the way, the Muslim shopkeepers don't like to be bothered by Israeli police.'

'Of course that doesn't stop us from bothering them when we need to.' Alon leaned forward, elbows on the table. 'We've already questioned the operator of the shop, Ahmed Kareem. Let me ask: are you sure that the dispute you heard was about a refund only? Nothing else?'

Hagit and Harper looked at each other. Neither remembered anything else.

'We didn't hear everything, but what we heard, we told you.' Hagit ducked her head again to look for Chloe. Seemed satisfied to see her clutching Stein's leg.

'Mr Kareem insists he's shocked by the murder, but he also says he's innocent. He says he remembers the victim – his name was Harold Clemmons. But he says he never saw him after he left his shop. The witnesses agree.'

Really? 'Nobody else saw the men follow him?'

'Well, the problem is, even with the crowds that were there, the only other witnesses we've been able to find are the three men you've identified. All of them work in the shuk. They run the shops beside Kareem's. And they insist that, after he left the shop, they never saw Mr Clemmons again.'

'But I saw. They followed him.' Hagit crossed her arms, emphatic.

'Even if they did, we have no evidence to show they harmed him.' Alon showed his empty palms. 'Certainly not enough to make an arrest.'

Chloe let go of the sub-inspector and began running wobbly laps around the conference room.

Alon smiled. 'How old?'

'Fourteen months.' Harper beamed.

'Oh, no. And she's running already? She's going to be a hell-raiser.' His eyes sparkled.

A hell-raiser? Really? Harper's back stiffened, indignant.

'Oh, boy. You're in for it,' Stein added.

'She's trouble on two legs.' Hagit nodded. 'Stubborn, too.'

'She is not stub—' Harper began, but she stopped mid-syllable, interrupted by Hagit's fierce glare. Harper glared back, but said nothing.

The inspectors stood, thanked them for their help, said they might be in touch again, and left.

Harper was still annoyed about the comments. Her baby was stubborn? Trouble on two legs? Really? Pointedly ignoring Hagit, she lifted Chloe, popped her into the stroller and knelt to fasten the seatbelt.

'You're not trouble. You're a good girl.' She kissed Chloe's cheek, noticed the gold necklace with the tiny *hamsa*. And recalled Hagit's reaction to compliments.

Oh. Harper thought she understood. The detectives and Hagit hadn't meant to insult Chloe; they'd been saying the opposite of what they'd meant. Everyone except Harper had understood: compliments were to be inverted, delivered as criticism in a deliberate attempt to avoid – or at least to confuse the Evil Eye.

What hogwash. Ridiculous.

Harper pushed the stroller into the lobby filled with strangers, trying to remember the magic word Hagit had taught her. Ken something. 'Kenahara?' she remembered.

Whatever. It was all foolishness.

The killer couldn't stop sweating. Had crouched for hours, out of sight, waiting for the body to be discovered, watching the gathering crowd, the consternation. The corpse being carried away. And then, emerging from shadows, merging into the crowd, the killer had pretended to be shocked like the others standing there, gawking.

The assistant stood too close. Whispering. Whining about the location, that they'd messed it up. That the body shouldn't have been in the Muslim section. That their mistake would have repercussions.

But the killer wasn't worried. The death had been clean and pure. Surprise had washed over the man's face. Then indecision for just the slightest of moments before he'd lost his will and surrendered to his fate. The knife had sailed across his neck almost of its own accord, severing flesh and spilling blood. Fulfilling its purpose.

The man hadn't even struggled.

But the assistant kept sputtering about the section of the shuk. Harping on about the mistake. Squawking. 'He was a Christian. He wasn't supposed to die in the Muslim section. That wasn't the plan.'

'Enough!' the killer finally snapped, looking around, making sure no one was listening. 'We'll balance it out.'

'How? We can't exactly rearrange the shuk. It was supposed to be done in the Jewish section—'

'Don't you think I know that?' The killer's eyes narrowed, nostrils flared. 'Look. It's done. And instead of finding fault, you'd be wise to praise our accomplishment. It's not your place to criticize.'

The assistant met the killer's eyes, saw their dagger-like gaze, and backed off, looking away.

The killer kept glaring, unable to relax. As if there wasn't enough to worry about, the assistant was becoming a problem. Maybe a liability. Maybe the knife would like to sail across another neck, too? Meantime, sweat kept dripping down the killer's forehead. Into the killer's eyes. Even in the morning, even in the shadows, the air of the shuk was sweltering. How was it possible to think in such conditions?

But thinking was necessary. Because the assistant was right. They'd gotten lost in all the tangled passageways, and the murder had been in the wrong section. Now, they'd have to make it right, somehow restore the balance. And they'd have to do it soon. Time was passing, and the deadline approaching fast.

Harper stood beside Hank, sipping white wine. She wasn't in the mood for a cocktail party. She hated getting dressed up, despised high heels, especially because they bothered her left leg. Beyond that, she didn't know anyone but Hank and Trent, and they were busy chatting up their international colleagues. And she had no interest in light conversation. She wanted time to herself. Time to think about her day.

After their talk with the inspectors, Hagit had taken her sightseeing. They'd seen the Temple Mount, where King Herod the Great rebuilt the Second Temple, where the Dome of the Rock now stood. And the massive square-cut stones of the Old City, held together not by mortar, but by their sheer weight. Heaps of those huge stones, once part of the walls, lay scattered on the ground, knocked off by the Romans in AD 70. Then she'd seen a labyrinth of partially reconstructed Byzantine dwellings and mosaics, and the open-air dig site of the ancient City of David. Angular pieces of a second-century BCE construction, dubbed 'the First Wall' by Josephus Flavius. And a sloping, stepped structure, probably a support for a palace or fortification, dated to the tenth century BCE – the time of the Israeli kings David and Solomon.

Harper had looked into a partially restored house dated from the seventh century BCE, and had seen dozens of bullae, clay seals used for documents, with personal names still impressed on them in ancient Hebrew script. She'd been absorbed by the tour, rapt, lost in time and past millennia. Picturing the enthusiastic archeologists who'd unearthed these pieces of history. The ancient Hebrews and Byzantines who'd built them and wandered the streets of white stone. The Roman soldiers who'd ravaged the massive city walls.

Hank took her arm.

'So nice to meet you, Mrs Jennings.'

Oh dear. Apparently, she'd been introduced to someone, had no idea who he was. Hadn't been paying attention. Hank wandered off, leaving them.

'And you.' She managed a smile. Sipped. It was a local wine. Light, not too sweet.

'Your husband says you're an archeologist.'

Really? When had he said that? 'I just finished my degree . . .'

'Well, you certainly will find plenty to occupy you here.' He had a warm smile. A neatly trimmed silver beard, matching wavy hair.

'No question. I'm already overwhelmed.' Harper couldn't help it. She needed to talk to someone about where she'd spent the day, what she'd seen. 'It was a tease, though, seeing the City of David excavation.' She realized she might be boring him, ought to stop. 'I wanted to join the dig.'

'Well, if you really want to work on a dig, there are many in progress, all over the country. Most are hungry for volunteers. Especially for a volunteer with your training and enthusiasm.'

Harper eyed him, sipping more wine. Who was this man? How would he know about digs? And was he serious? Could she actually join one?

'Dr Berkson . . .' A stout man grabbed his arm, tugged him away.

'Excuse me.' He nodded to Harper as he left.

Harper stood alone, heard the stout man make introductions. 'Professor Slatoff, this is Dr Berkson of the Israel Antiquities Authority . . .'

The Antiquities Authority? Really? Harper stared. The man was in charge of registering every dig in the country. And he'd said she could work on one.

But he was probably just being polite.

Besides, she had Chloe with her – what was she thinking? She couldn't go off on a dig. What was wrong with her?

Harper stood alone among the eminent scientists and prominent statesmen, fingering her *hamsa*. She looked around for Hank. Saw him standing in a group, nodding at someone's comments, attentive and comfortable. Apparently unembarrassed by his aphasia. Not needing her to help him speak.

Trent was also occupied. She heard his laughter, turned to see him in a jovial cluster.

Harper sipped wine, replaying the name: 'Dr Berkson of the Israel Antiquities Authority.' She checked her watch; the cocktail hour wasn't even half over.

If she waited, she might have time to wander over and casually ask Dr Berkson some questions, just to satisfy her professional curiosity. To find out more about the country's ongoing digs. Harper stepped over to the bar, exchanged her empty glass for a full one, eyeing Dr Berkson from afar. Waiting for a chance to approach him.

After all, it was a cocktail party. Why not engage in light conversation?

Fadil Kasim walked the darkened pathway through the shuk, tired and hungry. Hoping Kalila would fix him a proper meal, despite the late hour. He'd stayed late at the shuk, restocking his shop. Doing inventory. Cleaning up. Postponing going home, where Kalila and her pout would be waiting. He doubted she'd have forgiven his harsh words that morning. She was not of a forgiving nature. She'd be silent, looking away when he addressed her. Keeping a distance. Making him angry all over again. Kalila was an expert; she knew how to aggravate him. That morning, she'd done everything possible to grate his nerves. Letting the children loose, interfering with his sunrise prayers. Speaking in that shrill tone. Her voice pierced his brain, it really did. How was he to bear it? Nagging about this. About that. Certainly, any man would react as he had – or worse. He was right to insist on peace in their home. And if she couldn't comply . . .

Wait. What was that up ahead? Was someone lying in the street? On the ground? Fadil hurried through shadows, calling out, '*Ahlan?* Hello?'

The form didn't answer, didn't move, but Fadil heard a groan. He stopped for a moment, wondering about his own safety. He looked behind him into the dark passageway. No one was there to help. And if this person had been attacked, the attackers might still be there. He himself could come to harm. Maybe he should go find a guard.

Ahead, the person let out another moan, louder. What had happened? A heart attack? A robbery?

'*Akhi, hal anta bikhayr?* Are you all right?' Fadil asked.

'Help me.' The voice was weak.

Fadil lost his hesitation, rushed to assist. It wouldn't do to let a sick or wounded person lie alone in the street. He reached the stranger and knelt, looking in the dim light for a wound. He leaned over, asked, 'What happened?'

When something darted up at his face, he dodged reflexively, but didn't identify it even when pain sliced the side of his face. His instincts kicked in, triggering his flight response. Before he could register the fact that he'd been wounded, let alone how, he was on his feet again, running through tangled alleys, racing through dark and narrow passages, bleeding, panting. Trying to evade the person chasing him. He sped past shuttered booths, up steps, around corners. Finally, he ducked into a cul-de-sac and stood silently, listening for footsteps. Hearing none, he stayed there, catching his breath, assessing his condition. Processing what had happened.

His cheek stung where it had been cut, but he'd moved quickly, avoiding a deeper wound. Who had done this? Why? His heart wouldn't slow down. But he couldn't stay there, had to keep moving. Fadil stepped out of the cul-de-sac, back onto the path. Realized that he'd run to the Christian section, was close to the school. Not far from the gate. He started for a main street, but a figure stepped in front of him, blocking his way, swinging an arm in front of him. Fadil spun around, running, vaguely aware that something was wrong. Blood? Spouting from his neck? What? His legs wouldn't obey him. He sank to the ground, trying to yell, emitting frothy gurgles. His face hit the cobblestones. Confused, he struggled to understand his situation, but unable to accept the truth, he kept proposing alternative explanations until he faded, and the truth didn't concern him any more.

Hank seemed distracted. He was looking at something on his laptop and holding Chloe, who leaned against his chest, perfectly content. 'Baby. Okay to bring?'

'There's a daycare at the kibbutz where we'd be staying. Apparently, all the young kids stay there in the daytime. I'd be done working at one thirty, so I'd be there all afternoon and night. And Hagit said she'd go with us and watch Chloe while I'm at the dig.'

Hank's scowl deepened. 'You already. Asked Ha. Git?'

Harper took a breath. 'I did. Because I didn't even want to suggest anything to you unless I could work everything out.'

'When talked?'

Why was that important? 'After the cocktail party. I called her.'

He looked down at Chloe, put his free hand on her head as if already missing her.

'It's not like we'd be gone long. And it's only a few hours' drive away.'

'Okay, good. Go.' He closed his computer, carried Chloe to the sofa and sat, holding her small foot in his big hand. Reciting, 'This little. Piggy. Went to. Market . . .'

Was he avoiding the conversation about the dig or just playing with Chloe? Harper wasn't sure.

'This little. Piggy. Stayed home.'

Harper watched her husband and baby, their comfort with each other. They cuddled. They played. They gazed at each other with adoration. They'd never been apart for a day since Chloe's birth, and now, Harper was talking about separating them for ten.

'And this little. Piggy . . .' He held her pinkie toe.

Chloe started giggling, tensing with anticipation.

Hank raised his hand, repeated, 'This little. Piggy . . .'

Chloe laughed harder – so hard, she almost choked.

'This. Little piggy. Ran all. The. Way. Home.' Hank's hand tickled its way from her toes to her tummy. He was laughing; she was shrieking with joy. How could Harper interfere with that? How could she even think of taking Chloe away from Hank, if only for a few days? She couldn't. It was heartless.

She went into the bedroom to respond to Dr Berkson. He'd asked for her decision as soon as possible, since the other volunteers were already arriving and would be attending an orientation meeting the following day. She wondered how experienced they were. Where they'd come from. How many there would be . . .

But what difference did it make? She wasn't going. She couldn't. Dr Berkson had been generous to find her a spot on a dig, but he'd understand. She was an archeologist, but she was also a wife, a mother. She had to put her family first.

Her laptop was on her nightstand. She opened her email and

reread the details about the dig site, Tel Megiddo South. It was fifty miles north of Tel Aviv in the Jezreel Valley, a fertile area of farmland and vineyards, on the site of a former prison. The excavation was at an early stage, extended from more developed sites at Tel Megiddo and Tel Megiddo East where twenty-six layers of ruins had already been discovered, including stables, a Bronze Age fortress, a third-century church . . .

Harper stopped reading. She couldn't bear it, ached to be part of it. And why couldn't she? Why should she turn down a rare opportunity like this one, a chance to practice her profession? To gain first-hand experience, uncovering who-knew-what structures or relics.

Besides, it wasn't as if Hank was spending time with her and Chloe. Since they'd arrived, he'd seen the baby before bedtime exactly once. And today was the first time he'd been with them for breakfast. His time was completely taken up by the symposium. If she accepted the offer and worked on the dig, he'd barely know the difference.

Even so, accepting didn't feel right. The only reason Hank had asked her to come along was that he hadn't wanted to spend weeks apart from her and Chloe. Harper closed her eyes. Laughter pealed in the living room. Harper clicked the 'respond' button and wrote an email, thanking Dr Berkson for finding her an active dig and explaining that, due to her family's needs, she'd be unable to volunteer there the next day.

She stared at the screen, disappointed. Pictured the dig site, sections of five-meter squares ready to be excavated. History waiting underground, undiscovered, resting in layers of time. She imagined buried walls, maybe entire buildings . . .

No. Never mind. She wasn't going. Instead, she'd stay where she was for the next two weeks, wandering around the city with Hagit, hoping to catch glimpses of Hank between sessions of endless politically sensitive meetings that he couldn't discuss.

Someone knocked and Harper heard the door open in the next room. Heard Trent come in, announcing that it was time to go.

Hank stuck his head into the bedroom. 'Hoppa? Going. See you. Later.'

She looked up. Said nothing.

'What?'

She shook her head. Clearly, he didn't have time for a discussion. 'You're mad?'

'Why would I be mad?' She crossed her arms, looked away.

Chloe ran in, grabbed her leg. 'Mama!'

'About dig?' He came into the room. 'Told you. Do it. Go. Yes.'

Did he mean it?

He stepped over, pecked her cheek. 'Ten days only. Good. For you. Do it.'

Really? Harper couldn't tell. He was hurried, in motion. Lifting Chloe for a quick kiss. Heading for the door.

Trent called, 'Arriba, Hank. Step on it,' as Chloe waved, 'Bye bye, Daddy.'

The door closed. Chloe picked up her stuffed monkey, nuzzled it and sucked her fingers.

Harper looked back at the computer, hesitating. Did Hank really not mind? Would Chloe be okay at the kibbutz nursery?

Chloe climbed on her lap, and they sat for a while before she revised her response to Dr Berkson, asking if she could join the group after orientation. In a couple of days.

Apparently, Hagit had mixed feelings. 'You can see lots of history without going on a dig. Why do you want to go to an old prison? We can take day trips from Jerusalem. To the north. To Eilat. All over.'

She went on about visiting the ruins of Massada, Caesarea. 'I can take you. We can look at the silver mines from King Solomon's times. We can visit ruins of Canaanites and Philistines. Byzantines. The past? It's all over the country. Whatever you want.'

Harper wanted to see all of it. But looking at what others had discovered wasn't the same as discovering things herself. She didn't expect Hagit or anyone else to understand. Finding history, uncovering it was like time travel, like detective work. Like having personal contact, even relationships with people and civilizations long gone. Harper thought of time as a decaying, eroding force that layered everything in dust. She saw current structures, even high-rise buildings, as future ruins, as fodder for digs of future millennia.

Hagit was still talking. 'I suppose it's different in America. To you history is what, two centuries? Three? Here we think in thousands of years, not hundreds.'

Hagit chattered on as they strolled with Chloe along the shops on Ben Yehuda Street. Not much was open yet, so they wandered back to the Old City under a relentless sun. Entering the Jaffa Gate,

Harper tuned Hagit out, thought about the murdered American. Wondered if Inspector Alon had found out more about his killer.

'Mime,' Chloe called.

'What?'

'Mama. Mime.'

'She wants water,' Hagit said. 'It's *mayim*,' she corrected Chloe's pronunciation. 'Ma-yim.'

'You're teaching her Hebrew?' Harper was stunned. Chloe hadn't even learned English yet.

'Why not? A few words.'

Harper pulled a bottle of juice out of her bag, handed it to Chloe.

'What do you say?' Hagit stooped beside the stroller, facing Chloe. 'Tell us. To—'

'DAH!' Chloe grinned.

'That's right.' Hagit nodded. '*Todah.*'

'That means "thank you"?'

'Yes. *Todah.*'

Harper frowned. Wasn't sure how she felt about Chloe becoming so verbal in a language she didn't understand.

They walked on among groups of Christians making pilgrimages along Via Dolorosa where Jesus carried his cross to his crucifixion. They were heading for the Church of the Holy Sepulcher when a bunch of uniformed schoolgirls stampeded out of an alleyway, nearly knocking them over. The girls were breathless, incoherent. Wide-eyed. Frantic. Hagit went to them, quieted them, gathered them together away from passing tourists. Asked them questions. A tall girl cried. A chubby one held her stomach, looking green. All of them talked at once, pointing into the alley.

Hagit spoke to them in reassuring tones, touched their shoulders, their heads. Harper hadn't understood their words, but she recognized the fear in their voices, the shock in their eyes. Other children flashed to mind, other eyes filled with terror. She heard sniper fire and men screaming. Saw a boy with no face . . .

'Come with me.' Hagit yanked her toward the alley.

'What's happened?' Harper went along, pushing the stroller. Where were they going? Was it safe? Should she take the baby and run the other way? 'Hagit?'

But Hagit hurried ahead. 'This way.'

The schoolgirls fluttered behind them, following like baby ducks.

Tourists clustered, curious, and closed in behind the girls. Harper looked back and saw a wall of people, so she pressed on after Hagit, who strutted into the alley, leading a parade.

First, she saw feet.

The passageway was stone on both sides, sunless and barely wide enough for two people to walk side by side, but there were gaps where the walls weren't as close. Doorways. Small nooks.

The feet projected out of one such nook. They were dusky and sandaled. Definitely male.

Harper stopped, recognizing the stillness of death. 'Who is that? What did they tell you?'

Chloe held her bottle up. She was done with it. 'Mama.'

Hagit kept going, waving Harper forward.

Harper took the bottle. Watched Hagit's backside. Behind her, the alley was clogged with people. Ahead, Hagit stood, staring down at whoever owned the motionless legs. Harper felt trapped, had nowhere to go.

Reluctantly, she rolled the stroller forward. Was she really taking her baby to see a dead body?

'Hagit,' she frowned. 'This is no place for Chloe.'

Hagit didn't budge. She stared down, mumbling syllables in Hebrew.

Turning the stroller so it faced the schoolgirls, Harper moved closer to the body. Followed Hagit's gaze.

The man appeared to be Muslim. He was young, maybe twenty-five. He'd been laid out flat, as if on display, his head bent to the side, revealing a deep slash in his neck. His shirt was covered in blood. Harper fought images of other bodies, other ghastly wounds. She closed her eyes, pinching her arm, twisting the skin and focusing on the pain, forcing herself to remain in the moment. When she opened her eyes, she noticed an odd cut on the victim's forehead. Carefully, Harper stepped over his legs, stooped to get a better look at his face. And saw an image carved there. At first, she thought it was a number six. But no. Her viewpoint was crooked. The carving wasn't a six; it was the letter C. The shape of a crescent.

The killer watched, invisible among the gawkers. Standing among others felt safe, but it didn't stop the memories. The morning's events kept replaying, over and over, beginning with the wondrous moment

– distinct and seemingly unprovoked – when the selected one had sensed his death, taking off, running through the silent narrow streets. Evaporating into shadows. The assistant had lagged and gotten lost, but the killer had followed the scent of fear all through arches and around corners, staying with him as he'd darted in and out of sight, nearly disappearing into the pink glow of dawn. He would have escaped, too, if not for the desperate slap of his sandals against the stone walkways and the blaring beat of his panicked heart. Finally, cornered, he'd hidden in the cul-de-sac, helpless as a lamb.

Cowering and winded, his back against the wall, he had offered no final struggle. He'd merely raised his palms, arguing or maybe pleading softly in his language, his eyes saddened by his fate. The blade had risen and swept down, silencing his voice in a clean and glorious moment. Praise the Lord, blood had been spilt in His name, according to His will.

The killer stayed in the crowd, buffered and invisible, watching the shaken schoolgirls in their uniforms. Realizing that there would be criticism for the killing. But who could have anticipated that the prey would run so swiftly, so far? Who could have prevented his desperate sprint to the Christian section? Surely not the assistant, who'd gone in the wrong direction altogether, useless and lost. The killer, though, had stayed with him. Had raised the knife and swept it down. Praise the Lord.

A small round woman with startling hair emerged from the passage, leading the school children away, yammering in Hebrew. Another, a short blonde pushing a baby stroller, asked in English for everyone to step back to make room for the police. Her voice projected an air of calm authority as if accustomed to dealing with death. Or with nervous crowds. In English, she told people that there was nothing to worry about. A man was dead, but they were in no danger. Amazingly, mumbling among themselves, the people believed her, quieting down.

The killer moved back with the others, easing away, leaving the scene before the police arrived. Walking slowly, in pace with the crowd. Maybe there would be no consequences for the error. Maybe the successful kill would be celebrated despite its location. The killer stiffened, doubtful, and continued along the Via Dolorosa, uttering prayers for forgiveness and searching for an acceptable excuse.

*   *   *

Police officers arrived, cordoned off the area. Inspector Alon and
Sub-Inspector Stein appeared moments later. Chloe was cranky
and restless; it was past lunchtime and her nap was overdue.

Word of the murder had spread through the shuk; onlookers
crowded the small intersection, jamming up the surrounding alleys.
Alon had Stein interview the schoolgirls who'd found the body. Hagit
translated for Harper when Alon asked the crowd if anyone had
information about the crime. No one responded. Even so, he told
them all to give their contact information to the officers and disperse.

Then he turned to Harper. 'I didn't expect to see you again so
soon.'

'Nor I you.' Harper lifted Chloe out of the stroller, asked Hagit
to help her with the sling. 'Do you need to talk to us?'

'Mama. Go.' Chloe kicked her ribs, but back in her old familiar
sling, she quickly quieted, snuggling against Harper's body, eyelids
drooping.

'Sorry. She's hungry and tired.'

Alon glanced up the passageway toward the body. 'Who discovered him? You?'

'No, the children did.' She indicated the girls gathered around
Sub-Inspector Stein. 'They took us to the body.'

'You know him?' He looked at Hagit, then Harper.

Neither did.

'Should we? Who is he?'

Alon crossed his arms, frowning. It was late morning. His shirt
already was stained with sweat. 'His identification says his name
is Fadil Kasim.'

Chloe hung limp, asleep. Heavy in the sling.

'Two murders in two days.' Hagit's tone was harsh, as if it were
Alon's fault. 'Both here in the shuk. What's going on?'

'I'm not sure.' Alon squinted into the sun, scanning the area. 'A
Christian was killed in the Muslim section. Now, a Muslim in the
Christian section.'

Harper wasn't sure what he was implying. 'Are you saying . . .
Do you think it was revenge? A killing to avenge a killing?'

'Not exactly.' He led them away from the passageway where the
body was being examined. 'Can we sit for a moment?'

Harper looked around. Saw nowhere to sit. Alon headed for a staircase across the courtyard. Took a seat on the steps. In the shade. Away
from the crowd. Hagit parked the stroller, sat one step below him.

'Your visit doesn't seem to be going as planned, Mrs Jennings. I hope you don't have a bad opinion of our country. Actually, compared to cities in the United States, our crime rate is quite low. Homicide is not usual for us.'

'Of course it's not.' Again, Hagit was scolding him. 'What happened to security? Where were they?'

'Hagit, please.' Harper sank onto a step. She was hot, her left leg ached, and she was upset about the murder.

'Please what?'

'Stop scolding the inspector. It's not his fault.'

'No, Hagit is right. This was a failure of security. The second failure in two days. It shouldn't have happened.' Alon paused, looked from one to the other. 'Look. I'll be direct. I already know a good deal about you, Mrs Jennings.'

He did? 'Sorry?'

'I know why you are here: Your husband is participating in the Dead Sea symposium. I know that you are an archeologist, that you might join a dig in the Jaz—'

'Wait.' Harper sat straight. 'How do you know all that? Why . . .?'

'Not to worry.' Alon smiled slightly. 'Security only. But I also know that you have a distinguished military background. That you are a decorated Iraq war veteran. Because of all this, I have some faith that I can trust you.'

Harper said nothing. She felt invaded, exposed. What else did he know about her?

'And me?' Hagit asked. 'What do you know about me?'

'About you?' He laughed. 'I know enough. You've been cleared to work for the symposium. I know your career history.'

Her what? Harper blinked at Hagit, whose expression was unreadable.

'What I also know is that you both had contact with the victim of yesterday's murder, and that you both were on the scene at today's.'

Hagit's nostrils flared. 'So? Are you implying that we have some connection with the killings?' She continued rapidly in Hebrew, but Alon interrupted.

'I said no such thing.' Alon met her eyes. 'All I'm saying is that you both have an interest in this situation. So, because of what I know about you, and because you might be of some assistance, I'm going to tell you something that you can tell no one. It stays among us. Okay?' He paused, waiting for them to agree before he went on. 'You both had a good look at the body, right?'

Harper and Hagit exchanged glances, nodding.

'So you saw the neck was cut, like a slaughtered animal.'

More nods.

'And you also saw the mark on the forehead?'

'Yes. A letter C,' Hagit said. 'What does it mean?'

Alon leaned closer, his voice low. 'What I'm telling you goes no further. Both bodies had a mark. Yesterday, the victim was a Christian. He had a cross carved into his forehead. This one is Muslim and has not a C, but a crescent. Only the police on the scene and the investigating officers know about these marks. The press was never told about the cross on the first victim, so we are convinced that—'

'The same person committed both murders.' Harper finished his thought.

Alon let out a sigh. 'It appears so.'

'Damn.' Harper took hold of Chloe's foot.

'It's too soon, of course, to say for sure. But still, we have to consider the possibility. We might be dealing with a religiously motivated serial killer in the shuk.'

Harper's lunch looked delicious: falafel, deep-fried balls of chickpeas and herbs, served with yogurt, spices and fresh vegetables in pita bread. She stared at her sandwich, without appetite, unable to stop seeing the dead man lying in the alley, the stunned eyes of the children who'd found him. To stop recalling other violent deaths, other stunned eyes.

'You're not eating.' Hagit frowned. 'Why not?'

Harper didn't answer. It wasn't Hagit's business whether or why she ate or didn't. Besides, she didn't want to discuss the killings. Not today's or yesterday's or those from the war or any others. And certainly she didn't want to dwell on Inspector Alon's casual observation that, aside from the killer, they were the only people connected to both of the murders in the shuk.

No, she didn't want to talk about any of that. Instead, she cut tomato slices into bite-sized chunks for Chloe's plate, adding them to pieces of falafel, pita bread and cucumber.

'What do you say?' Hagit put a hand on Chloe's arm. 'To—'

'Dah!' Chloe grabbed more food.

'That's right. *Todah.*' She sighed, turned to Harper, lowered her voice. 'It's the Evil Eye. All that attention – I knew it would bring trouble.'

'That's ridiculous.' Was Hagit seriously suggesting that the murders in the shuk were related to – if not the result of – Chloe getting too many compliments?

'Kenahara.' Hagit nodded. 'It wouldn't hurt you to say it . . .'

'Fine. Kenahara. But get real, Hagit. Those men are dead. We can say anything we want; nothing can help.'

'Well, it won't hurt, either. Go ahead. Say it again.' Hagit waited.

'Kenahara, okay?' Harper looked around the sandwich shop. People were talking, eating, drinking. At the next table, two men were arguing, each leaning forward, waving a finger at the other. Chloe stuffed food into her mouth.

'So what's bothering you? The murders? Or maybe the crescent and the cross?' Hagit would not let up.

'Neither.' Both, actually. 'I'm thinking about the dig.' She hadn't been, but she was now.

Hagit eyed her skeptically. 'What about it?'

'Can you be ready quickly? I'd like to go tomorrow morning.'

Hagit kept watching her. 'Of course.'

'Mama. Mo?' Chloe pointed at the plate of falafel. 'Peez.'

Harper cut some more pieces.

'The dig won't help, you know.'

'What?'

'It will go with you. You can't hide from it.'

Harper kept cutting.

'You can wear a *hamsa* and say "Kenahara", but once you have its attention, it will follow you—'

'Hagit, stop—'

'Whether you want to believe me or not.'

'—with your silly superstitions and magical expressions. These murders have nothing – not a single thing – to do with us or your stupid Evil Eye.' Harper's voice was too loud, her tone too harsh. As she put the chunks onto Chloe's plate, she saw the baby staring at her, open-mouthed, about to cry. And, as Harper leaned over to comfort her, she realized that Chloe was not the only one staring.

The men at the next table had stopped arguing and were eyeing her. As were the couple at the table on the other side. In fact, Harper felt eyes on her from all directions. Her face heated up. She hugged Chloe, smiled and told her everything was all right. Kissed away her single, bulging tear.

Hagit waited until the baby was quiet. 'Have a few bites of your sandwich,' she advised. 'If the Eye is watching, you don't want to let it see you suffering. It feeds on suffering. If you're upset, it will celebrate by bringing you more trouble.'

Harper blinked. 'Bullshit.'

Hagit was undaunted. She finished her own sandwich, wiped her mouth. 'Are you finished?' she asked Chloe.

Chloe grinned proudly, lifted her hands for cleaning.

Hagit cleaned them and Chloe's face, lifted her into the stroller. 'Go. Mama.' Chloe waited. Hagit pushed the stroller toward the exit.

Harper stood, picked up her bag and began to follow. Then she stopped, went back to the table. Gulped down a bite of her sandwich. Then another. A third. She washed them down with lemonade. It wouldn't help, but it certainly wouldn't hurt.

Hank filled Harper's wine glass. They were at a restaurant, just the two of them. Seated in a corner, away from others. On a date. Alone for the first time since they'd left home.

The table was covered with half-eaten salads – baba ganouj made from eggplant; tahini from sesame seeds; hummus from chickpeas and garlic; roasted eggplant; roasted peppers; chopped cucumbers and tomatoes; yogurt with dill. Pickled vegetables; falafel. And lots of pita bread.

Hank's attention was on the food. He dipped bread into this plate and that, spilling onto the table. Dropping bits of bread into the serving bowls. He ate steadily, without talking, as if the food were consuming him, not the other way around.

Harper watched with growing annoyance. Why was Hank so preoccupied with his appetizers? Why so silent? Was she less interesting than a pickled beet?

'So. I've made arrangements,' Harper broke the silence. He might not want to talk, but she did.

Hank cut off a piece of eggplant, lifted it onto his plate. Glanced at her, listening.

'I'm going to join the dig.'

Hank didn't look up. 'Good.'

Good? 'It sounds fantastic. The site is relatively undeveloped; it's called Megiddo South. Probably I'll just be doing grunt work. But still, I'll be in at the early stages. Kind of like taking wrapping paper off a gift.'

He chewed eggplant, watching her. She couldn't read his expression.

'We'll stay at a kibbutz near the dig. While I'm working, Hagit will help out at the nursery school where Chloe will be with the little kibbutz kids.'

Hank still said nothing, reached for more pita bread.

'So?' She sipped wine. 'Aren't you going to say anything?'

He shrugged. 'Yes. Good. Decision.' He dug into the cucumber and tomato salad.

That was it? Harper chewed pita, sipped more wine. What was going on with Hank? Was he angry about something? She'd expected him to ask questions, express some interest. Lend some support. But nothing. Maybe he didn't really want her to go.

'Look, Hank, I didn't just unilaterally decide—'

'No.' Or know? 'Think you should go. Agree.'

'But you don't seem enthusiastic. In fact, you seem distant.'

'Sorry.' He took a swig of wine.

'Besides, with all these murders, it's better if I take the baby away for a few days . . .'

'Why?'

'There have been two murders here in two days . . .'

'Murders happen. All over. Even home.'

Yes, she was aware of that, was well experienced with murders back home. 'But they aren't usual here. Inspector Alon's worried there's a serial killer in the shuk.'

'He is?'

Harper hesitated; she'd agreed not to talk about specifics. She lowered her voice. 'There were similarities in the crimes. Symbols were left on both bodies.'

Hank took a sip of wine. 'But men. Were killed. Not. Women. You're not. Killer's. Type.'

Hank was right. Serial killers tended to select victims who shared common profiles, including gender. 'Even so, Alon told us to be cautious. Hagit and I are the only witnesses connected to both murders.'

'Witnesses?'

'Not to the actual crimes, but to events before or after.'

Hank shrugged, swallowed more wine.

'So you're not concerned?'

He looked at her; something sharp glinted in his eyes. 'Just co. Incidence. Hoppa.'

Probably he was right. It was just coincidence. Still, why wasn't Hank more concerned that she'd seen one man right before his murder, and another right after? 'Well, anyway.' She controlled her voice, made it unemotional. 'It won't hurt us to go away for a few days.'

'I agree.' He looked at his wine glass.

'What's wrong, Hank? Is it about me going?'

'No.' He looked up. 'Sorry. Not you.'

She waited. Decided to give him time to explain his moodiness. Ate a piece of eggplant. A dollop of tahini on pita. Waited some more. Still, Hank said nothing. 'If not me,' she finally said, 'then what? The symposium?'

He sighed. Poured more wine. Stared at it. 'Can't tell. You.'

'Well, if you can't tell me about it, please don't bring it to our dinner table.' She regretted it as soon as she'd said it. Hank was troubled about something, not deliberately hiding it from her.

He reached across the table, took her hand. 'You're right.'

'No, I'm not. I'm sorry.'

'Hoppa. Sorry. Don't be.' He squeezed her hand. 'I see. Factions. Alli. Ances. Politics. Finance. But science? Best for en. Vironment? For people? For future? Not so much.' Again, something steely flickered in his eyes. 'Serious problems.'

Harper didn't know what to say. She'd been so focused on the murders and her travel plans that she hadn't thought about Hank or the importance of his work. He was dealing with issues of global impact. And, with his aphasia, he had limited ability to communicate with, let alone to influence other symposium members. His opinions had to be enunciated slowly, carefully written out or filtered through Trent, who didn't always agree with him. Hank couldn't debate, couldn't counter ideas he found erroneous, couldn't express opposition to factions seeking political or economic gain rather than the best interests of the land and population. Clearly, he was frustrated.

And worse, he was burdened. Worried. 'Conflicts. Could be dire. If water. Issues aren't solved.'

Conflicts? As in war? She'd overheard Trent say that one of the participants had already threatened that. The restaurant faded, became a sandy checkpoint. Harper tasted metal, smelled smoke, heard gunfire. Saw a white-hot explosion, felt herself fly. She pulled her hand away from Hank's, picked up her fork and jabbed it into her hand.

'Hoppa?' Hank grabbed the fork.

'Flashback. It's okay.' She closed her eyes, focusing on the pain in her palm. When she looked up, Hank was still watching her.

He took her punctured hand in his, examined it. Kissed it. 'Okay now?'

Yes. Better. She'd aborted the flashback. But the echoes lingered. She felt them in the marrow of her bones; saw them in the periphery of her vision.

Harper's hand disappeared inside Hank's. Buried itself in his grip, felt safe there. He kept talking. Apologizing for alarming her. But going on, anyway. Telling her about the symposium – not about anything secret. But about power and greed influencing research, about trips into the field where they were to examine the river, the sea, proposed pipeline and desalination sites. About possible repercussions of their recommendations.

He was talking in phrases, broken sentences, his words sometimes out of sequence. Harper had no trouble understanding him, but was only half listening to his words. The other half was concentrating on Hank himself, on how well he was doing. A few years ago, his fall from their roof had almost killed him, left him with aphasia, threatened to destroy both his spirit and his career. But now, because of his determination and perseverance, here he was, invited with Trent to this international symposium as an eminent geologist despite his speech problems. Her vision blurred; she blinked away tears. What was wrong with her? She wasn't sentimental. Not a weeper. Needed to get a grip.

'Tensions get. High.'

The waiter served the main course. Harper looked at the platter in front of her. The eye of a crusty black fish looked back.

She turned away, glanced at Hank's plate. His chicken breast had no face.

'Need help. Boning?' Hank grinned.

Harper stiffened, shook her head. She wasn't going to be queasy about food; she was Army. Could survive on bugs if she had to. And she knew how to bone a fish. First, she removed the skin, then ran her knife under the meat above the bones. Felt the fish watching her. Lopped off its head.

Saw the man lying in the shuk, his throat slashed.

Gulped some wine.

'When leaving. For dig?'

'In the morning. About ten.'

His eyes widened, surprised. And something else. Sad? Scared? Before she could figure it out, the look was gone.

'Away how long?'

'Ten days.'

Again, his eyes flickered. 'Seems long.'

Harper's face got hot. 'It was the shortest volunteer session. Most are for a month or more. And I don't have to stay the whole time. I can leave whenever.' Damn. She felt guilty. Missed him already.

'Hoppa. Go. Dig.' He looked into her eyes. 'I'll. Every night call. Okay?'

Of course. Every night. His eyes were dark, fiery. They made her skin tingle. For ten days, she wouldn't see them. She wouldn't fall asleep lulled by his breathing. Wouldn't wake up to his kiss. Lord, why was she going? What had she been thinking? How could she leave this man, even for a few days?

Hank looked away, finished his wine. And Harper reminded herself why she was going: the dig opportunity; the murders. Besides, Hank wouldn't even be around; he'd be off visiting potential pipeline sites. And it was only ten days.

Only?

Harper looked down, regarded her headless, half-boned fish. Damn, her eyes were tearing again. When had she become such a sap? Hank reached over, picked up her plate, swapped it with his. 'Better?'

She laughed, wiping her eyes. 'Yes. Much.'

Back at the hotel, they made love slowly, sweetly, knowing they'd be apart for a while, and then Harper fell asleep against Hank's chest.

In the morning, when she woke up, he was already gone.

Hagit drove the jeep up north, to the fertile Jezreel Valley. Everywhere was lush farmland, rolling green hills. Hagit pointed out landmarks.

'That's Mount Carmel,' she said, pointing to the west. 'North of us is the Lower Galilee and Nazareth. That way is Jordan Valley.' She pointed to the east. 'You know the story of King Saul? That's Mount Gilboa. He committed suicide there instead of falling to the Philistines.'

Harper strained to see it. History, stories of the Bible, the lives of the ancients seemed carved into the land, the hills.

They passed fields of sunflowers, and farm after farm. 'This one is silk and honey,' Hagit told her. 'This is wheat. That one grows cotton.'

Chloe slept most of the way. When she woke up, she called out, 'Meetz?'

Harper smiled. 'Hi, Chloe.'

'Meetz, Mama?' Chloe repeated.

Hagit said something in Hebrew to Chloe, then told Harper, 'She wants her juice.'

'Juice?'

'*Mitz*. It's Hebrew for juice.'

'But she needs to learn English—'

'Just a few words. I already told you.'

'So now I have no idea what she's saying?'

'Why is it a problem for you?'

'Meetz, eeeeeemah,' Chloe persisted.

Hagit laughed. 'Juice, Mommy. She sounds like a little *sabra*.'

Harper's jaw tightened. Hagit was overstepping, taking too much control of her child, excluding her. She pulled the juice bottle from her bag, handed it to Chloe.

'What do you say? To—'

'Dah!' Chloe began drinking.

'She doesn't know the difference,' Hagit said. 'Hebrew. English. It's all just sounds to her. I can teach you, too.'

Harper didn't answer. She wanted to learn, but wouldn't admit it.

Hagit began singing in Hebrew, a peppy song with a haunting melody.

Harper wondered if she was making a mistake, bringing the baby to a kibbutz, leaving her with Hagit for so much of the day. On the other hand, what was the harm in Chloe learning words in another language? Why did it bother Harper so much? Was she too possessive? Jealous?

Harper gazed out the window at the hills. They looked peaceful, welcoming. Even so, Harper felt uneasy. She told herself it was excitement about the dig and anxiety about being away from Hank. Nothing more. Her reaction was normal – she was starting a new endeavor for the first time since Chloe's birth. Of course she was uneasy. But by the end of ten days, she probably wouldn't want to leave.

And by the end of ten days, Chloe probably would be fluent in Hebrew. Wouldn't understand a word of English.

Harper turned to look at her. Chloe made a silly face; Harper mimicked it, their game. Chloe giggled, showing her six teeth, and made another face. Harper imitated that one, too, and again, Chloe shrieked with laughter. Harper reached into the back seat, put her hand on the baby's thigh and squeezed.

'Settle down, you two.' Hagit turned into a narrow driveway lined with pines, blocked by a guarded security fence. 'Behave so you'll make a good impression. We're here. Ramat Goneh, right down this road.'

They had their own bungalow; their hosts called it a chalet. It was up in the hills, on a winding road of similar bungalows overlooking fertile valleys and verdant fields. Mountains towered in the distance. They had a kitchen, two bedrooms. Their own hot tub. A fireplace.

They were assigned a host couple, Adi and Yoshi, a young couple with matching smiles and sparkling eyes. They helped them get settled, then took them on a quick tour. First stop was the nursery school, a vine-covered cottage, its inner walls painted with bright balloons and cartoon characters.

'This is Yael,' Adi introduced a woman holding an infant. 'We both work here, though Yael puts in more hours than I do.' Adi stopped to talk with Yael; Harper wandered around, watching toddlers play in secure areas, finger-painting, looking at picture books, building with blocks.

Yoshi followed her to the window, pointed to a little boy of about three. 'That's our son, Ari.'

Harper saw him, riding a tricycle on the pavement. Other children were on the swings or wading in an inflatable swimming pool. The children seemed happy, safe. Chloe wiggled to get down.

'It's okay. Let her explore,' Adi said. 'She will have a good time.'

A long, toddler-sized table was set with juice and crackers for snack time.

Chloe pointed. 'Eemah? Meetz?'

'Already she's learning Hebrew? She knows Mommy and juice?' Adi smiled. 'She's very smart—'

'Hush.' Hagit scowled and spoke harshly in Hebrew to Adi, ending with 'Kenahara.'

Adi answered in Hebrew, then explained, 'She's afraid of the Evil Eye—'

'I can hear you,' Hagit scolded. 'And you should be afraid, too.'

'It's just an old . . . Yoshi? How do you call it?'

'Superstition,' Yoshi said. 'A *bubbe meise*.'

'Exactly.' Adi's laugh was light, like bells. 'An old wives' tale.'

'Don't be so sure,' Hagit replied. 'You both should know better than to say such things. Are you daring it to find you?'

Chloe freed herself from Harper and ran to the table.

'Meetz?'

'See?' Adi nodded. 'She is already at home. Can she have some snack?'

Chloe drank some juice, ate a cracker, and ran from section to section to see what was going on. She seemed confident, suddenly older and more independent. And she didn't want to leave when Harper lifted her to continue the tour.

'Chloe, will you come back and play?' Adi asked. 'If you want, I'll bring you myself tomorrow.'

Chloe smiled, sucking her fingers.

Harper considered how odd it was: she felt perfectly at ease with this stranger offering to play with her baby. She trusted her even though they'd just met.

Yoshi led them along the main road, looking out over the valley. 'It's the most beautiful part of all Israel,' he said.

A dog ran by. Chloe pointed and grinned, but Harper stiffened.

'Dogs run loose here?'

'Of course. They are free. Dogs. Cats. You'll see them everywhere. They play outside all day, then go home for food.'

'They don't bite?'

'Bite? You mean people? Of course not.'

Hagit lagged behind, made a comment in Hebrew, her voice snippy. Adi answered in the same tone.

Yoshi ignored them both, talking to Harper. 'This kibbutz was settled by survivors of HaShoah, what you call the Holocaust. Settlers came from Poland and Germany, raised their families, grew their own food. Now, many more are living here, but still it's like a big family.'

'And children are our joy.' Adi stepped forward and tweaked Chloe's cheek.

Chloe smiled coyly.

'Come this way.' Yoshi stopped beside some bushes and stepped through them to a mound of stones. 'This is one of our shelters.'

It was? Where? Harper saw no entrance.

Yoshi led them around to the back of the rocks; the entrance was camouflaged, hidden in foliage, not visible from the road. 'It's good to know where it is, even though most likely you won't ever need to go inside.'

Of course they wouldn't. Harper told herself that the tour stop was just routine, like pointing out fire escapes. Nothing to worry about. Still, she took hold of Chloe's leg as they moved on, passing gardens, small homes. The main office was a new building with high windows and lots of light. It contained the meeting hall, which doubled as a theater, and the recreation area, with a gym complete with exercise equipment, volleyball nets, ping-pong tables, and a swimming pool.

After the main building, they stopped at the medical center/ infirmary. Then at two more bomb shelters, concealed within leafy gardens. Yoshi and Adi pointed them out casually, the same way they had the dining hall and the swimming pool. But Harper didn't feel casual about them. She wanted to know more. Had the shelters been used often? If so, why? Was the kibbutz a target for rocket attacks? How big were the shelters? How safe? What provisions were inside? She had lots of questions, but held herself back. She was overreacting; Yoshi had said there would be no need to go inside.

Even so, the shelters were a statement that life here was not always peaceful. That it was necessary to remain on alert, always prepared. Harper recognized the undercurrent of vigilance. Here, she was not the only one perpetually watchful. Here, she would fit right in.

Adi and Yoshi brought them back to their bungalow, made sure Hagit and Harper had their cellphone numbers, said they'd be available to them night or day. Reminded Harper that the dig organizers would be holding a meeting in the main building after dinner.

As they left, Harper thanked them for the tour, and Adi and Chloe exchanged a hug. 'You are such a good girl! All the other kids will love you.'

'Kenahara!' Hagit's skin went gray. 'What is wrong with you?'

Adi's eyes twinkled. 'See you at dinner, Hagit.' And she walked off with Yoshi, waving goodbye.

'Thanks again,' Harper called.

Hagit poked her arm. 'Don't thank them. The Evil Eye already follows you, and now she made it worse—'

'Hagit, stop,' Harper snapped. 'You were rude to them. They were trying to be nice.' She turned to Chloe. 'Come on. Let's get you a bath before dinner.'

'Fine.' Hagit fumed. 'Don't listen to me. Pretend I'm a lunatic—'

'Hagit, can you get her yellow outfit from the suitcase?'

'Ignore me if you want, but sooner or later, you'll see. The Evil Eye is nothing to make light of.'

Harper walked away, feeling the pierce of Hagit's gaze on her back even as she filled the tub.

*   *   *

When Harper arrived at the meeting hall, only about half a dozen chairs were filled. She took a seat near a long-legged woman with golden hair.

'That was something today, wasn't it?' The woman had freckles, a sunburned upturned nose. Prominent cheekbones. She looked athletic. Maybe a runner. 'Hot as Hades. Never gets like that back in Indiana.'

Harper explained that she hadn't been at the dig site yet. Had just arrived that afternoon.

'Really? Well, never mind. You didn't miss much. They just handed out gear and explained what all of it was. Who knew there would be so much stuff? I thought they'd give us a sifter and a shovel, but man, all that equipment could fill my garage. Kneepads. Trowels. Tweezers. Screens. Buckets. Brushes . . . I can't remember all of it. But trust me: tomorrow, don't forget to wear a hat. And sun block.'

Harper smiled. She knew all about the equipment she'd need. 'I'll have to get a kit.'

'I'll show you where. I'm Lynne Watts. That's my husband over there. Peter. The one in the blue shirt.' She pointed to a group of men standing by the door. Peter was tall, wiry, with a dark crew cut and horn-rimmed glasses. 'We're here with our church.'

Harper smiled.

'It's a special mission – just a smattering of us came. The church council – that's twelve, like the apostles. A few other select members. Plus our pastor. We came yesterday, after four days in Jerusalem.'

Harper didn't say that she'd been there, too. In fact, she didn't have time; Lynne Watts kept on talking.

'I'm sure you'll meet our pastor. He's one in a million. A genuine Bible scholar. Inspirational. I'm blessed to be with him here in Megiddo.'

Harper smiled. Nodded. Had nothing to say.

'Oh look, there's Pastor over there.' She pointed to several men standing by the window. One was beefy and taller than the others, had receding ginger hair. Harper had seen him before; he was staying in the bungalow next door to hers. Now that she thought about it, her neighbor looked like a pastor. 'He's the big, handsome one. Those others are council members.' She turned back to Harper. 'Who are you here with?'

Harper hesitated. 'Just me.' She didn't mention Hagit or Chloe. Wasn't sure why.

Lynne eyed her with pity. 'Divorced?'

'Oh no. No. Actually, I just got my degree in archeology. So I'm here for some experience.'

'Really? Wow – a professional! Well, I'm sticking close to you, so someone can tell me what the Sam Hill I'm doing out there.'

Harper smiled, started to respond, but a tanned, silver-haired man stepped to the front of the room, asking everyone to be seated.

'Here we go,' Lynne whispered. 'That's the head honcho.'

'Good evening. For those of you who haven't met me yet, I'm Givon Ben Haim.'

The thirty or so people in the room gave a round of applause. Some whistled and hooted, shouted, 'Yeah.'

Dr Ben Haim smirked and raised his hands, waiting for them to quiet down. 'Okay.' His English was accented. 'I want to formally welcome you to Tel Megiddo South.'

More cheers. More hoots. A whistle.

'I'm glad for your enthusiasm. I welcome it. And I hope it lasts when the work gets hard and the day gets hot. For those of you who are not my students, let me tell you a little about where we are and what we're doing here.'

Harper looked around the room. About a dozen young people, probably his students, sat in the front row, hanging on his words. Responding to everything he said with laughter, comments or applause. Peter Watts and his fellow churchmen sat further back, their backs stiff and bodies alert. The pastor sat with a group at the back of the room.

Dr Ben Haim spoke casually, sitting cross-legged on a table, pointing to easels with maps of the region. He reviewed the progress of digs at Tel Megiddo and Tel Megiddo East, where twenty-six layers of ruins had been excavated since 1903. He talked about the major finds: an altar from the Canaanite period, a grain pit from the Israelite period, stables from the time of Ahab and an intricate water system. He told them about thin carvings on hippopotamus incisors from the Nile, possibly from the time of Ramses III.

Harper listened, enthralled, more eager than ever to get to the site.

'Think he's sexy?' Lynne whispered.

Who? Dr Ben Haim? Actually, he was, in a distinguished kind of way. He was solid, muscled, neither tall nor short. His tan contrasted with his silver hair, made it gleam.

'Because I do,' Lynne went on. 'These swarthy Semitic types stir up my blood.'

Harper said nothing, tried to listen to Ben Haim.

'Not that I'm looking or anything.'

Harper glanced at Lynne. A couple of decades ago, she would have been her high school's Homecoming Queen. A cheerleader. The quarterback's girlfriend. Miss Small Town Indiana or wherever she'd grown up. But now, she was married, traveling with her husband and her church. Why was she fixating on Dr Ben Haim?

Harper tried to forget about Dr Ben Haim's supposed sexiness and listen to his words. He was listing their specific goals for the week, defining the sections of the site, explaining that they would work in pairs, each assigned to a section.

'You'll be my partner.' Lynne nudged Harper's arm. It wasn't a question.

'Next, let's talk about safety. Remember this: We have to protect not only the site and the finds, but also our volunteers. So I'm telling you: be careful. Read your safety manual. Pay attention to it. The equipment can be dangerous. Wear your work gloves, your hats. Sturdy shoes. Don't run. Don't fall into the ditches. And remember. It's Israel. We have all kinds of life here. Spiders. Snakes. Respect them. Don't lift rocks by hand – use a tool. Don't sit down on something until you've had a look underneath. Check your shoes every time before you put your feet in. Understood?'

His students whistled. Others nodded, replied, 'Understood.'

Harper did neither. She was thinking of Iraq. How she'd been warned about snipers and IEDs. Insurgents. But spiders and snakes? No one had thought to mention them. And yet, they'd been there. Like the flies.

'Let's go.' Lynne stood, headed for the front of the room.

Harper joined her in line, waiting for Dr Ben Haim to hand them their assignment. When Harper got to the front, he stood and shook her hand.

'Dr Jennings! Welcome. I was told you'd be joining us. It's a pleasure to have you here.' He asked about her trip and her accommodations, invited her to join him for lunch after work later in the week. Gave her a welcoming embrace as she left.

Lynne walked out of the building with her. She was about three inches taller than Harper and far more striking. 'That dude was into you.'

Harper shook her head. 'He was just being professional. Acknowledging me as a colleague.' She looked over their packet. Handed Lynne her copies of the map and paperwork. 'We're at section thirteen.'

'He'd be too short for me, anyway,' Lynne said. 'But not you.' She paused. 'Harper? Do you believe that things happen for a reason?'

Harper looked up. 'Sorry?'

'Just . . . Maybe you two were meant to meet. Maybe that's why you came here. Now. To this place at this time.'

Harper didn't respond. This woman Lynne seemed kind of wacko; she didn't want to engage. Instead, she concentrated on the map of the site.

'It could be part of God's plan.' Lynne pursed her lips.

God's plan? Harper didn't look up. She located section thirteen.

'Think about it. Maybe that's why you were called to come here—'

'Lynne. I'm married.' Maybe that would end the conversation.

'Really?' Lynne frowned. 'So where's your husband? Are you separated or something?'

What? 'No, he's in Jerusalem. Attending a symposium.' Why was she answering? Hank's location was none of this woman's business.

Lynne looked troubled.

'What's wrong?'

'Nothing. I just – I don't want you to be alone here.'

Why not? 'It's fine. Just ten days. And I'm not alone. Our baby's with me.'

'Your baby? Here?' Lynne's eyes widened.

'With a sitter. Yes.'

'Well.' Lynne looked up at the stars. 'Even so. You're here for a reason. God wanted you to come.'

Harper folded the map, replaced it in the envelope. Wondered how she'd last ten days with Lynne talking nonstop, connecting every other sentence to God.

'It's sure beautiful here, isn't it?' Lynne said.

Harper agreed.

'I didn't imagine it this way. I thought it would be, you know, desert and sandy. But I guess I shouldn't be surprised that God would put beautiful events in a beautiful place—'

'Hey, Lynne. You coming?' Peter called from the street.

'On my way!' Lynne ran off, waving to Harper. 'See you tomorrow, partner!'

Harper watched her scurry down the path to Peter. He held his arm out, wrapped it around Lynne and led her away into the night.

* * *

The next morning, Harper dressed in khaki pants and a long-sleeved white cotton shirt, a wide-rimmed hat to shield her from the sun. She rushed through breakfast, dropped Hagit and Chloe at the nursery, and hurried off with a quick goodbye, both relieved and a little hurt that Chloe seemed oblivious to her departure.

Harper was the first one on the bus that would shuttle them to the site. Dr Ben Haim's students arrived next, filling the back of the bus. Lynne and her husband took a block of seats with others from their church. As the driver pulled out of the kibbutz, their pastor stood and led them in prayer.

'Lord, guide us today as we attempt to do your work. It is your word that we follow. Your will that we seek to fulfill . . .'

Harper tried not to listen. Thought of Hank. Missed him. Pictured Chloe, wondered what she was doing. Imagined her listening to a story. In Hebrew.

Finally, the bus ride ended, and they arrived at Megiddo South. Some structures from the prison were still there – the watchtower loomed over the parking lot as if armed guards were still posted there. Beyond the tower, the dig covered a vast, bare expanse, stripped of topsoil and a few feet of fill, in sharp contrast to the surrounding green hilly fields. The area was divided by string and posts into a grid of five-meter squares, each identified on the map. Paths of wooden scaffolding ran across sections and around the perimeter.

A line of trailers and supply shacks had been set up at the edge of the parking lot. One trailer served as the site office, and there Harper found Josh Kahn, one of Dr Ben Haim's student assistants. Josh fitted her with an equipment kit: two pairs of black leather gloves, white suede gloves, a grapefruit knife, graph paper and pencils, brushes, a trowel, a folding shovel, Ziploc bags, a pick, screens, measuring tape, tweezers, clippers, a level, foil, a folded tarp, a dustpan, nails, a hammer, a camera, dust masks, kneepads, a scale, tablespoons, an air puffer, a refillable water bottle. She asked about dirt buckets, learned they'd already been distributed throughout the site.

Josh guided her to section thirteen, where Lynne was waiting, decked out in hat, sunglasses, kneepads and gloves, her nose covered with zinc oxide.

'Let me show you how to get started,' Josh offered. He took out a trowel, gently digging into the ground, scratching the top exposed stratum of earth. Removing the dirt, straining it through a screen into a nearby bucket. 'You strain to examine the fill.'

Harper watched impatiently. 'We'll manage. Really.'

'But be careful,' Josh said. 'The earth is in layers, or stratifications. You'll be able to see them, the different colors and textures. So you want to dig evenly, going only one layer at a time to preserve context – in other words, to be sure of the exact location of the find. Because the deeper the stratum, the older the find. That's why we remove only one level at a time, to keep things in their own time—'

'She knows all about it, Josh.' Lynne interrupted. 'Harper here has a PhD in archeology. She could probably teach you what to do.'

Josh's mouth opened. 'Oh. You're Dr Jennings? Dr Ben Haim told us you'd be joining us. Sorry. I didn't realize . . .' His face splotched red. Embarrassed. 'Well, nice to meet you. Let me know if you need anything.' He hurried away.

For the next several hours, Harper and Lynne removed dirt from their five-meter section, strained it into buckets to make sure nothing of interest was in there, and dug some more.

And for just about all of those hours, Lynne seemed compelled to talk. She complained about the heat. About how monotonous the work was. About men, marriage. She talked about how she'd met Peter back in college, at Ball State. How they'd had a rough patch when she couldn't get pregnant, but then they'd turned to Pastor Travis and he'd saved their marriage and put them back in touch with God. She talked about how blessed she was to have the pastor in her life. How he'd inspired her and given her new direction. She asked about Harper's marriage.

Harper didn't want to talk about it but, as the day passed, she opened up, sharing memories of meeting Hank in Iraq, when he had been a civilian consultant, she an army officer. He'd offered her a drink, even though she'd been on duty. He'd been confident, brash. Handsome. Her voice thickened, remembering how he'd been then, his smooth words, his easy gait. God, it had been a long time since she'd thought about how he'd been before his accident. She stopped talking, coughing. Not wanting to go on.

'You okay?'

'It's just the dust.' But her voice was unsteady, so she didn't say more.

They repeated the digging pattern, working in rhythm: removing earth, straining it, filling buckets, straining again, digging some more. Lynne went on about her pastor and how he'd changed her life. She talked about how much evil there was in the world – crime, poverty, disease, war. How leaders had risen on false pretences, serving not for good, but for their own interests. How, if you really thought about it, the end of the world seemed inevitable. In fact, that realization was what drew her into her church. Made her want to serve God's purpose in these troubled days.

Harper tried to tune her out. She didn't want to engage in conversation about Lynne's world view or her church. She wanted even less to talk about crime and war, or to theorize about the end of the world. She made no reply, focusing on the joy of being part of a dig. On lifting small bits of ancient earth, sifting them through a screen into a bucket.

Eventually, Lynne stood and stretched, stepped carefully around the perimeter of their section, pulling over an empty bucket. 'I don't get it, Harper. Why would you want to be an archeologist?' she reached for her trowel.

Harper looked up, not sure how to answer.

'I mean,' Lynne laughed, 'your career's always going to be in ruins.'

'Very funny.' Harper smirked, took off her hat, wiped sweat from her forehead. She'd heard the joke before, but chuckled to be polite, relieved that Lynne could talk things other than church.

'But there's good news. The older your husband gets, the more interesting you'll find him.' Lynne grinned wickedly.

Harper groaned. 'So, this is how it's going to be?'

'Sorry. When I told my friends back in Indiana that I was going on a dig, they told me a ton of archeology jokes.'

'I've heard them all.' Harper kept digging.

'So, tell me.' Lynne lowered her voice. 'Is it true archeologists like it dirty?'

Harper rolled her eyes, nodding. 'And we will date anything, even our own mummies. That's because we dig mummies.'

This time, Lynne moaned.

'Also, we cut our hair with Caesars. And, if we don't eat right on digs, we get irregular trowel movements. Trust me, Lynne. I have millions of them – they get worse. Want me to go on?' She put her hat back on, picked up her trowel and began digging again.

'No.' Lynne put her hands up, grinning, warding off more jokes. 'It's enough. But we should write these down and put on a show for the others. We can call it "The Archeology Revue", or – wait for it – "Arty Facts" – get it? Artifacts?'

Harper got it. She stood and sifted dirt through a screen, found nothing, came back and dug some more. The sun was hot, she was sweaty, covered with dirt, and so far, the earth hadn't given up a single find. But, Lord, she was having fun.

Harper didn't even go back to the bungalow to shower. As soon as the bus pulled into the kibbutz, she said goodbye to Lynne and hurried to the nursery. In fourteen months, she hadn't been apart from Chloe for longer than a couple of hours. Had Chloe missed her? Had she been afraid or cried?

From a distance, Harper heard shrieks and giggles, and when she got to the picket fence, she stopped and watched. Chloe was standing in the big inflatable toddler pool, perfectly happy, wearing her pink ruffled bathing suit, pouring cups of water onto a little boy's back. Harper's chest tightened. Chloe had been fine without her. Had played happily with other kids. Had transformed in just a few hours from a baby into a little girl, and at least one little boy seemed entirely at her mercy. Lord.

Hagit and Yael chatted beside the pool. Everything was calm. Harper's presence wasn't required.

'Mama! Eemah!' Chloe spotted her, but continued to pour water onto the boy.

Hagit looked up, seemed startled to see Harper. Glanced at her watch. 'You're here already?'

Harper joined them by the pool, knelt to kiss Chloe. 'How did the day go?'

'How did you expect?' Hagit asked. 'It was fine. You can see for yourself.'

'Chloe made lots of friends,' Yael smiled.

'She's having fun. Go. Relax a while. I'll bring her home later.'

Harper felt dismissed, but didn't want to argue. She gave Chloe another kiss and wandered back out the gate, the sounds of children's laughter fading as she got to her bungalow.

By evening, Harper was restless. She waited for the goodnight call from Hank, but when it came, it didn't calm her. In fact, it upset her even more. Hank's attention was divided because Trent was in the background, interrupting like a pestering child, nagging Hank to get off the phone. They talked for only a few minutes, long enough for her to say that Chloe liked nursery school and that she'd made it through her first day at the dig. She asked if there was any news about the murders in the shuk; he said he hadn't heard anything except that the investigation was ongoing. She asked how his day had been; he gave a vague, clipped response.

'Busy. Went to sea.' Or to see? 'Tired.'

And the call was over. Afterwards, Harper sat outside on the porch, looking at the stars and the dark valley. Then she looked in on Chloe, who clutched her stuffed monkey in her sleep. Hagit was drinking tea, watching Israeli television on the big flat screen. Harper didn't want to watch television. Didn't feel like reading. Finally, too unsettled to sleep, she decided to take a walk.

The air was cool, almost chilly. And the stars so bright, she could see her way even where there were no streetlights. She walked without a destination. Just following the road in the quiet star-filled night. For a while, the only sound she heard was her own footsteps. But then, passing the main office building, through the open windows, she heard a man's voice. She stopped walking and listened.

Yes, someone was speaking in the meeting hall. Was there a kibbutz meeting? Or – uh-oh – a meeting about the dig? Had she missed a memo? She followed the voice, heard it more clearly but couldn't make out the words until she heard a chorus of 'Amen'.

Oh, of course. The church group. They must be having a prayer session. Harper relaxed, kept walking. But the man's voice was so full of vibrato, so pulsing with energy that she had to stop and go close enough to hear it.

'. . . And it will be glorious as promised. It will surpass all your dreams and hopes, will be more passionate than any love you've known, more joyous than any pleasure you've experienced . . .'

'Amen!' voices shouted.

'The Lord has written it in the code that he guided me to decipher, has pledged it to you, the few who have come here with me, to Megiddo . . .'

More cries of 'Amen.'

'It will be here, where I have brought you. All we have to do is follow His word, as He has written it, as I have read to you from His hidden verses. We must bring unto Him—'

'Three lambs,' the voices answered.

'Yes. Three lambs. Symbolizing each of His lineages, sacrificed according to His word, and then, only then, and exactly then on that date which He has written in the code that I have read to you – then will His promise be fulfilled and—'

'The battle in Megiddo will begin and end,' the voices answered.
'And when it is over—'
'We will rise.'
'Yes, we will. We will rise with Him to His holy kingdom—'
'Where we will live forever with the Lord. Amen.' The voices
rang, and a hymn began.

Harper stood transfixed. She hadn't been to church in a while.
But, even when she'd gone, she hadn't heard this kind of preaching.
What was the pastor talking about? Sacrificing lambs? Fighting a
battle here in Megiddo? Rising up to God's kingdom?

God's kingdom, as in heaven? Where dead people went?

Oh Lord. Was this preacher one of those charismatic leaders –
like Jim Jones? He'd been a charismatic. Years ago, he'd made his
entire church kill themselves, promising they'd go to heaven. Some
nine hundred of his followers had died – even children had swallowed poisoned Kool-Aid just because he'd told them to. Was this
another Jim Jones? An end-of-the-world cult leader?

The small congregation was singing an unfamiliar hymn; someone
with a soprano drowned the others out. The voices were strong,
didn't sound suicidal. Harper thought about what the preacher
had actually said. He'd deciphered a code in the Bible. And they had
to make sacrifices so they could go to God's kingdom.

Maybe the pastor was just into Numerology. Wasn't that all about
codes hidden in the Bible? Or maybe he'd been preaching about the
Book of Revelation. Didn't that talk about the end of days? There were
lots of possibilities. Interpreting the Bible didn't make the pastor an
instrument of death and suicide. No. Harper was seeing danger where
there was none. Lynne's pastor had nothing to do with Jim Jones.

Harper stood under the night sky, listening to the little congregation begin another song. 'Amazing Grace' floated out of the building,
up to the stars.

She gazed up, felt small. Humbled. She walked back to her
bungalow, ready to sleep. When she climbed into bed, she was still
humming 'Amazing Grace'.

The killer had gone through the motions of the day, mingling, chatting, eating. But by sundown, the tension had become unbearable.
Every nerve was on fire, every muscle screamed. Relief could come
only from fulfilling the promise, making it right. But how was that
possible? How? Nothing had gone right so far. The assignment was

a shambles. It hadn't been completed, hadn't gone as expected. And failure – well, failure would be catastrophic.

The killer was breathing too hard, sweating. Needed to regain control. Okay. It was best to begin by making peace with the Lord. Admit to Him that mistakes had occurred. Accidents had happened. Unpredictably. It was important to clarify what had happened. The killer knelt, head bowed, and offered a prayer. Apologized. Promised to make adjustments, fulfill the obligation. Prepare His people for what was to come. Make the required sacrifice. Clear the way for what He willed.

Afterwards, the killer washed again to be pure for the task at hand. Scrubbed away dusty traces of the physical world, scraped flesh until bloodstained water circled the drain. And then, cleansed, the killer donned black clothing and stepped into the night, called the assistant, and drove off, passing gates and security stops and miles of highway, to search for a proper lamb.

Finally, in the labyrinth again, while the assistant waited, the killer hunted. The hour was late, the stalls locked. The place almost abandoned. But that was fine. Those still here would be of the final lineage. Would fulfill the triad. Hunkering in shadow, the killer remained alert, ready to strike. The trap was set: a dark string tied tautly across the main path, a line for prey to trip over.

Waiting. Enduring cramps in the legs. Resisting fatigue. Mentally rehearsing the process: seeing the lamb stumbling and falling. Pouncing before it could recover, swinging the blade cleanly and mercifully across its neck while uttering the prayer. And finally, leaving the warning, the mark for all sinners to see.

This time, it would go smoothly, completing the command.

If only the lamb would show itself.

The killer counted seconds, minutes. Began to fear that it was too late, that sunrise was too close.

But, finally, footsteps clacked on the stone walkway, approaching the trap. The killer peered out of the dark corner, watching, gripping the blade. Ready. The prey wore a uniform. A soldier? Maybe security. And it walked with energy, a purpose in mind. The footsteps echoed against metal shutters of the booths. And they came closer. Ten steps away? Eight?

The killer counted down, thighs burning and set to spring, knife ready to slay.

Three steps. Two.

One.

The killer rose to strike, but the security officer walked on. Didn't fall. Didn't stumble. Didn't even break stride.

Stunned, the killer gaped at the empty path, at the broken string. It had been too thin, had snapped. Hadn't brought down the prey.

The killer jumped up and started after him, knife raised. Unwilling to admit defeat, revising the plan, deciding to call out and startle him. To plunge the knife when he turned.

But at the last moment, the killer hesitated. The officer was trained, would reach reflexively for his firearm.

Instead of getting shot, the killer went back to the shadows and tied another string across the path, this time doubling it. Failure was unacceptable; the offering had to be made, the sacrifice completed. And then, the position of honor would be eternal, with passion and joy for all time.

The killer waited, crouched in the darkness. When someone tripped on the string, the killer jumped, raising the knife, reciting the prayer and realized almost too late that it was the assistant coming to say it was time to go. The killer clutched the knife, angrily waiting for the assistant to recover. Neither made mention of how close the assistant had come to death.

Lugging the gear in the hot sun reminded Harper of other lugging, other gear. She rattled it off in her mind: ammunition, rifle, pistol, body armor, helmet, assault pack, food, flashlight, water, batteries, radio, first-aid kit. Eighty pounds, maybe more . . .

But this wasn't Iraq. This land was moist and green. Its air clear and sweet, not heavy with sand and smoke. Not broken by cracks of rifle fire and cries of pain.

Damn. Why was she drifting back to Iraq? Oh, right: the gear. But this gear was trowels and gloves, brushes and screens. Peacetime gear, intended for discovery, not war and destruction. Harper stopped to look out over the site, the expanse of exposed sections, the pits partially dug. She took a deep breath, felt a rush of anticipation. Even working as a menial volunteer was exhilarating. She was reaching into the past. Bringing it back into the light. Who cared about the weight of the gear? She hurried to section thirteen to join Lynne and start working.

Lynne, however, was not as eager to work as Harper. She'd sat with her husband on the bus, and now she stood with him, the pastor and another man at the perimeter.

'Harper,' Lynne called her over. 'Meet my husband, Peter. His dig partner, Lowell Olsen. And our pastor, Ramsey Travis.'

Harper had to put down the gear in order to shake their extended hands, one by one. Peter's was perfunctory, impersonal. Lowell's was eager, damp. And Pastor Travis's was indistinct.

Harper didn't want to stop and chat. She wanted to pick the gear up and go to work. But Lynne went on talking.

'Harper's a real archeologist. She actually knows what she's doing here.'

The others chuckled. Well, everyone but Peter. His eyes were strained, and his smile forced.

'Do you really?' Pastor Travis's broad shoulders towered over her. 'Because our little group, our church members, are just relying on the Lord's guidance. We're here to help Him reveal what He will in His own time. Because time is different to the Lord. If you remember Peter chapter three, verse eight: With the Lord, a day is like a thousand years, and a thousand years are like a day.'

Harper didn't know how to respond. Wasn't even sure what he meant. She thought of his preaching the night before and of Jim Jones' poisoned Kool-Aid.

'Amen,' the others mumbled.

Harper looked at Peter. His skin looked clammy, as if it were melting. And his gaze shifted from Lynne to the ground, avoiding Travis. Lowell, by contrast, kept his eyes fixed on Travis, whose eyes locked with Lynne's.

'So,' Harper finally spoke. 'Lynne? Should we get to work?'

'Oh.' The idea seemed to surprise her. 'Sure.' But she didn't move.

Harper hesitated. Maybe Lynne wanted to finish talking with the others; after all, Harper had interrupted.

'Okay. Well. Nice meeting all of you.' She picked up her gear and moved away. When she looked back a few seconds later, they remained just as she'd left them. Travis said something she couldn't quite hear, and the others proclaimed, 'Amen.'

By the time Lynne arrived at Section thirteen, Harper had already sifted a bucket of earth.

'So. What did you think of him?'

Him? Harper looked up, squinting into the sun.

'Could you sense his power? Just being near him, you can feel it. And I swear, it's like . . . like he can see right through people, into their souls.'

Harper adjusted her hat to shade her eyes.

'Besides which, Pastor's literally a genius. He'll never brag about it, but he knows practically everything there is to know about the Bible. I think he has it memorized, not just in English, but in Latin, too. And I think also – maybe in Greek? Or German? He read the Old Testament in Hebrew.'

So far, Harper hadn't said a word. Lynne didn't seem to notice. She squatted next to Harper, and went on. 'Every morning, he starts our day with an inspirational prayer meeting; every evening, he ends with one.'

Harper kept digging, hoping Lynne would stop gushing. Then she realized Lynne was waiting for a reply. 'That's nice.' She tried not to sound sarcastic.

'Oh, Harper. I get it. You're cynical. A doubter.'

Harper worked her trowel. 'At the moment, I'm a digger. Are you going to help?'

Lynne picked up a folding shovel. 'Sorry. I just get so excited.'

'I can see that.'

'You think it's stupid.' She fumbled with the shovel, trying to open it. 'But you'd change your mind if you knew what Pastor has accomplished.'

Harper continued to dig. Lynne continued to fumble.

'Harper.' Lynne lowered her voice and looked around, making sure no one was within hearing distance. 'Pastor Travis discovered something big. Secret codes in the Bible. And he deciphered them.'

'You mean numerology?'

'No no. It's different. I'm no scholar, but I know this goes way beyond numerology.' She tugged at the shovel, straining to open it.

Harper put down her trowel, reached over and took it. 'Here, let me try.' The shovel was standard military issue. Harper flipped it open and handed it back.

Lynne kept talking. 'The thing is, the messages Travis has found are directly from the Lord, and nobody else has ever read them.'

Harper couldn't take much more of Lynne's chatter. She tried to focus on the earth, on digging. On the heat. On what Hank might be doing, or Chloe. On anything other than Lynne's voice.

'I don't blame you for not believing me. Like I said, I was skeptical, too, until I saw him reveal God's words.'

Harper put down her trowel, picked up her screen, started straining earth into a bucket. Stifled the urge to tell Lynne to shut up.

'See, no one ever saw them before because the Lord's words are buried in text. They go diagonally, backwards, vertically – in all directions within certain sections of the Bible. But hearing them . . . It's like the Lord was talking with Himself about this or that and leaving Himself reminder notes inside the Bible. Like He was intending to revisit and revise His thoughts. And, out of all mankind, Travis is the one who found it'

'Lynne.' Harper was sweating with exertion. She couldn't listen to any more drivel. 'Are you going to do any work today?'

'Of course.' Lynne set the shovel down. Picked up a trowel instead. Began digging. Harper looked into the pit, saw no evidence of relics. No shards. No glass.

'I know I'm boring you, Harper, but I can't help feeling blessed to be here, serving with Travis. He's shown me the purpose of my life. He's revealed what the Lord intends for our church and guided us onto God's path.'

Harper tightened her jaw, fantasized about decking Lynne. If she were unconscious, she'd be quiet and Harper could dig in peace. Instead of knocking her out, though, Harper interrupted. 'Lynne. Please. Can we talk about something besides religion?'

'Sure.' Lynne shifted positions, grinning. 'How about men?'

Harper let out a breath, relieved. 'Fine. What about them?'

'Tell me about your husband.'

She pictured Hank. 'He's great.'

'Handsome?'

Harper pictured broad shoulders, dark eyes. 'Yup.' She examined a pebble too big for the screen.

'Peter's not great looking. He's like a seven. Wouldn't you say?'

No, Harper wouldn't say.

'We've been together forever. Since we were sixteen. We've had our troubles, maybe because we never dated around, I don't know. But Pastor Travis saved our marriage.'

Oh Lord. Did every topic lead to Ramsey Travis?

'Pastor showed us that we're bound through vows before God, and that even though we each have individual work to do for the Lord, we also have a shared purpose as one united being.'

As one being? Really? Harper wiped sweat off her forehead, thought of Hank. She and he were certainly not one being. In fact, they were very separate, distinct beings, and she liked it that way. Again, she saw his dark eyes. His bare chest. His muscled thighs. She clutched her trowel.

Lynne was finally quiet, looking across the site; Harper followed her gaze and saw Peter and Lowell working together. Beyond them, Ramsey Travis was digging with a woman in a blue straw hat. A new partner?

'I've never known anyone like Ramsey.' Lynne sounded dreamy. 'He's so giving and genuinely brilliant . . .'

Harper wondered if the praise would attract the Evil Eye. Maybe she should say Kenahara. But she didn't. She simply continued working. Digging and sifting dirt. She had eight more days there. Eight more days of listening to Lynne? No, she couldn't do it. She'd lose it; she'd snap. Harper had to assert herself. Had to insist that they not talk about religion or Bible codes that only Ramsey Travis could read. The man was just a fraud. Maybe not as sinister as David Koresh or Jim Jones, but a fake just the same.

Feigning a headache for the rest of the morning, Harper managed to quiet Lynne and concentrate on cutting a deeper layer into the ditch. And when, near noon, Dr Hadar stopped by to ask her to join him and Dr Ben Haim for lunch, Harper nearly leapt with joy.

Lunch was pre-packed turkey sandwiches at the dig trailer amid students bustling in and out. But neither the food nor the traffic mattered; Harper savored the chance to spend time alone with the leaders of the dig.

'Do you mind it?' Dr Hadar talked with his mouth full. 'The . . . how do you call it?' He said a word or two in Hebrew to Dr Ben Haim.

'Grunt work,' Dr Ben Haim translated.

Harper assured them that, no, she didn't. In fact, she tended to lose track of time while digging, absorbed in the rhythm of physical work.

'Well, actually, we hope there will be more than digging soon. We think the first real finds should show up any time now.'

They went on about their expectations that the ruins of a third-century town should be discovered shortly. A church and mosaics had already been discovered on the old prison grounds in 2005.

'We'll take you to see it. The mosaic is fifty-four square meters, and it's inscribed with three dedications. One to a Roman officer; one to a woman, and another to "the God Jesus Christ".'

Harper had read about the mosaic. 'I saw photos of it. It's medallion shaped with two fish in the center?'

'Yes. Exquisitely beautiful and intricate. And almost pristine.' Dr Hadar's eyes sparkled.

'And here at Megiddo South, they've found so far the oldest Christian church in Israel.'

'And where there's a church, there are worshippers.'

'So we expect to find outlying structures from that same time. As we go deeper, there should also be Roman era ruins.' They spoke in tandem, almost finishing each other's sentences. Dr Ben Haim reached for a water bottle. Took a drink.

Dr Hadar finished his thought. 'Like an army camp. And a Jewish settlement.'

'But for right now,' Dr Ben Haim leaned forward, elbows on his knees, 'the exciting part for us is to discover more Christian ruins. Think about it: the third century. Not much is known about that early period . . .'

Their excitement was palpable. And contagious. Harper doubted that she'd still be at the site when they unearthed significant structures. But she couldn't help picturing the buried ruins waiting to be uncovered.

A student came over with a question that required attention, and lunch finished abruptly. Harper thanked them and stepped out of the trailer, expecting to work with Lynne for another half hour. But as she headed back to section thirteen, she saw Lynne with a bunch of people gathered in the parking lot where the bus was to pick them up. What were they doing? Why had they finished work early? She walked closer, recognizing the rising timbre of Ramsey Travis's voice emerging from the center of the group. The man was holding a church meeting, preaching, right there in the middle of the dig.

Their heads were bowed. Harper stood beside a trailer where she could watch without being noticed.

'We all know the signs. We've studied them, read them. We know that they are all in place. First: false prophets. Matthew twenty-three, verse five: "For many will come in my name . . . and will mislead many." We've seen this come to pass, haven't we? Those who want to lead, who claim to have direct lines to God, when all they want is to amass fortunes and gain worldly power.'

The group nodded, answered, 'Yes.'

Ramsey went on. 'Second: wars. Matthew twenty-four, verse six:

"And you will be hearing of wars and rumors of wars; see that you are not frightened, for those things must take place" Anybody hear of Iraq? Of Afghanistan? Syria? Iran?'

The crowd responded.

'Tell me if I'm crazy. Because I hear about wars and I hear rumors of wars. I see our nation's armies going off to fight multiple wars. I hear about war all over Africa. Uprisings in the Middle East. Threats of war with North Korea and Iran.'

Again, the group responded, 'That's right.' And, 'For sure.'

Pastor Travis paused to make eye contact with a few of his followers. 'Third: famine and earthquakes. Matthew twenty-four, verse seven: "For nation will rise up against nation . . . and in various places there will be famines and earthquakes." Every day, we read about poverty and children starving. There's a worldwide shortage of food. Isn't that what famine is? Besides that, we're having the strongest earthquakes in history – literally hundreds in any given two-week period. Consider this, friends. Between 1890 and 1900, there was one recorded earthquake – only one. And not just one in California or even in America. One in the *whole world*.'

The group murmured with enthusiasm. Shook their heads. Someone said, 'Praise God.'

A gaggle of Dr Ben Haim's students walked by, discussing something in Hebrew, drowning out the pastor's voice. Harper smiled at them, said, 'Hi.' Pretended to be waiting for the bus, not eavesdropping. But as soon as they passed, she tuned in again.

"'. . . you will be hated by all nations on account of my name.'"

Pastor Travis looked from one face to another. 'Tribulations "on account of my name"? We all know what this means. Christians are under attack these days all over the world. You name it: China. Sudan. North Korea. Russia. Any and all Muslim nations. Even in our own country – we're under attack by those who want to control the schools, the courts, the laws. Make no mistake, it's happened exactly as predicted in Matthew.'

The group's agreements were loud, agitated.

'But wait, I'm not finished. Matthew twenty-three, verse fourteen: "And the gospel of the kingdom shall be preached in the whole world"' He paused, lowering his voice. 'Let me ask you. Is the Gospel preached on television, radio, the internet? Are there missionaries all over the globe? Is the Bible translated into many languages? Has this sign shown itself?'

Voices cried, 'Yes.' Someone called out, 'Thank you, Jesus.'
'Yes, Lord.'
'For sure.'
'It's the truth.'

The group was alive, vibrating, chanting their responses and swaying in rhythm with Pastor Travis's voice, which rose above theirs, compelling them on.

He stopped, waiting for the group to quiet down, dropping his pitch. 'We see the prophecy all around us. In corporate greed and government corruption. In cities of crime and brutality. In neon signs that proclaim our sinful and godless natures, in secular education that leads to promiscuity and false values, in the embracement of homosexuality and the environmental movement—'

Once again, his voice rose, throbbing with vibrato; the group was shouting, raising their hands. Cheering. Chanting, 'Amen,' and, 'Praise God.'

The bus rumbled into the parking lot, past the lookout tower of the old Megiddo prison, spouting exhaust fumes.

Pastor Travis motioned for quiet. 'We have to adjourn until this evening. But I promise you that I've read and understood God's code, and with the council, I will help all of you to comply with his word. For now, my friends, let us join hands here in Megiddo, the place where He in His wisdom has led us for His purpose, and let us pray.'

Harper watched them reach for each other's hands, saw Lynne look around. Felt a jolt as their eyes met.

'Our Father in heaven . . .' Travis began.

Harper felt her face heat up as if she'd been caught spying. She looked away, scooting across the parking lot and onto the bus as the voices called out: 'Your kingdom come, your will be done . . .'

Taking a seat in the back of the bus, she closed her fingers around her *hamsa*, reflexively completing the sentence: 'On earth as it is in Heaven.'

It was a cult. It had to be.

Harper eyed the church members as they climbed onto the bus, looking for wild eyes or dazed expressions. But she saw none. They looked sweaty, a little grimy. They joked with each other, talked about their appetites. Smiled, greeted the driver. Didn't behave like cult members. Not that she knew how cult members behaved.

'How was lunch?' Lynne walked all the way to the back of the bus, plopped into the seat beside her. 'Tell me – what'd they serve?' She opened her backpack, took out a wipe, rubbed her face with it. 'Want one?' She offered one to Harper, who declined, and leaned back in her seat, let out a breath. 'I'm starved, so, tell me. What'd you have?'

'Sandwiches.'

'Just sandwiches? I thought it was going to be a big deal.'

'Well, it was. Spending time with them was—'

'What kind of sandwiches?'

Really? What kind? 'Turkey.'

Lynne raised her eyebrows. 'Yeah? No wine or anything? Any potato salad?'

No wine. No potato salad. Not even pickles. 'But it was fascinating to hear about the dig. They think we'll find structures soon.'

'Good. Because so far, all we got is dirt. Dirt, dirt and more dirt. I feel like it's under my skin. At night, I dream about dirt. Mountains of it.'

Harper smiled. 'So you're having dirty dreams.'

'Seriously. I thought by now we'd at least have found some escape tunnels. You know, from when the place was a prison. But nothing.' Lynne shrugged. 'Well, it doesn't matter. We'll find things or we won't. Either way is fine.'

Really? Harper couldn't imagine being so indifferent.

The bus started up, headed out of the parking lot onto the road.

Harper couldn't help asking: 'So if you don't care about finding stuff, why did you come on a dig?'

Lynne looked blank. 'What?'

'You said you didn't care about finding anything.'

She shrugged. 'I'm here because it's God's will that I should be here – that all of us should be.' She paused. 'Whatever happens in this place will happen because God has declared it. We are just His agents.'

Wow. 'So if we find ruins, it's because God willed it?'

Lynne frowned. 'Sure. That, too.'

That, too?

'Don't you know your Bible, Harper?'

Harper had gone to Sunday school as a child, but her teenage years had been spent with her alcoholic, desperate-not-to-be-single mom, and all structure – including visits to church – had disappeared. Then came college and ROTC, the Army, the war and grad school. Bible study hadn't been a priority.

'Some.'

'Then you should know the significance of this place. Haven't you heard of Armageddon?'

Of course she had. 'As in the end of the world?'

Lynne nodded patiently. 'The end of days, yes. The final battle is to be fought there.'

So?

'Harper, in Hebrew, Armageddon is Har Megiddo.' Lynne waited for the words to sink in.

Wait. Har Megiddo. Like Megiddo? So . . . oh God. They were digging in Armageddon? 'You're kidding. We're there?'

Lynne smiled. 'You're an archeologist. How come you didn't know that?'

Good question. How come? And why hadn't that information been in the printed dig materials?

'It's common knowledge,' Lynne went on. 'It's why Pastor Travis signed us up to work here. So we could be part of it.'

Part of what? 'The end of days?' Harper smirked. 'You think it's coming now?'

Lynne didn't answer. She took a granola bar out of her bag, unwrapped it.

'So you're expecting . . . what? The Messiah to rocket in and fight it out with Satan?' Harper wasn't entirely ignorant of Bible stories. She pulled out another one. 'But wait – before the end, isn't there supposed to be a big war? Between . . . Hold on. I know this.' She closed her eyes, pulling out a distant memory, 'Gog and Magog!' Yes! She'd impressed herself, recalling those names. But as she uttered them, she felt a chill, remembering her younger self being frightened by those unfamiliar sounds that made no sense, like gibberish.

Lynne chewed, nodding. 'The war will come after Satan is thrown into the pit and stays there for a thousand years. But it might not seem that way because, to God, 'a thousand years is as a day, and a day as a thousand years.' So it's not for us even to try to understand the timing of it all.' Lynne reached for her bag, pulled out some aloe, globbed it onto her neck.

'I saw your pastor speaking before.'

'Yeah, I saw you there. No big deal. We were just praying. Reviewing signs of the Apocalypse.'

No big deal? The Apocalypse? Harper nodded as if Lynne made sense and sat back, looking out the window.

The bus roared past a field of sunflowers, an orchard. A truckload of soldiers. Everyone waved. The bus filled with chatter. A few rows up, Lowell dozed beside an attractive woman with red hair. Peter laughed loudly with a man Harper hadn't met. Pastor Travis was plugged into his iPod. Others slept or chatted. No one seemed concerned about the end of the world.

Outside, the sky was cloudless, the fertile fields serene. Harper watched the scenery, trying to put aside her discomfort. Other people's religions were none of her business.

Besides, she was Army. A combat veteran. A survivor. Certainly, she shouldn't be upset by a few syllables. They'd simply been jarred from her memory by talk of the Apocalypse; she should be able to stop repeating them in her head. Gog and Magog didn't exist, let alone have armies that could wage war and end the world. They were nonsense. Meaningless gobbledygook. Not even real words.

Kind of like Megiddo and Armageddon.

By the time Hank called that night, Harper had almost put aside all thought of Armageddon. She was still vaguely troubled by the church group and its focus on the end of the world, but Chloe distracted her with her fascination with the cats and dogs that wandered the kibbutz, her compulsion to chase each of them relentlessly. Hagit was no help, talking nonstop on the phone, her voice low and intense. Harper wondered if something were wrong at home, realized she hadn't learned much about Hagit. Didn't know if she was married or had kids. Didn't know anything, really, except that Hagit believed in the Evil Eye. Wow. Harper felt insensitive, self-absorbed, embarrassed. She resolved to find out more when Hagit got off the phone. After she rescued a kitten's tail from Chloe's eager grasp.

Finally, after dinner, a bath and a story, Chloe fell asleep. Harper joined Hagit on the porch.

'Everything all right?'

Hagit eyed her. 'Why do you ask?'

'No reason. You were on the phone a lot, that's all.'

'It bothers you that I get phone calls? It didn't interfere. You were watching the baby—'

'I didn't say it bothered me. I just asked if everything was—'

'Even if you hadn't been here, I'd have been fine. I can watch her and talk at the same time.'

Oh Lord. How had this become an argument? 'I just wondered if maybe someone at home had a problem. Your family.'

Hagit crossed her arms, sat back. 'Nothing's wrong with my family.'

Okay. 'I just wondered.'

'Of course. It's natural. I'm here with you, watching your baby, so you'd want to know my story. Here it is: my husband is dead. He was killed in the 1973 war.'

'I'm sorry.'

'I never married again; why would I? We have a son, Etan. He and his family – he has three boys – they live near Tel Aviv. They're all fine. I was on the phone for work, not for personal reasons. Anything else you want to know?'

Actually, Harper had wanted to know why Hagit seemed so annoyed, but she was tired, didn't want to start a confrontation. She simply said, 'I'm glad everyone's okay.'

When Harper's phone rang, she was relieved for an excuse to leave Hagit and go inside. It was just after eight, so she didn't expect Hank. It was early for him to call.

'You watched news?' His voice was tight.

The news? 'No. I haven't seen television since I got here. What happened?'

'They caught. Guy.'

What guy?

'From shuk. Killer.'

Oh. That guy. 'Really? Who was it?'

'Im. Migrant. Homeless. From Sudan.'

Really? Harper ran a hand through her hair, confused. 'Are they sure?'

'Found on him. Dead American's. Credit card. He tried using. It.'

So it was a robbery? Was that why he did it? 'He killed them both?'

'Didn't say.'

And if he had, why had he marked the bodies?

'Crazy.' Hank sounded stressed, hurried. 'Inspec. Tor Alon was on news. Said. Big illegal im. Migration. Problem here.'

Harper had heard that thousands of refugees from various African nations were flocking to Israel. Probably many of them were desperate. Possibly one was a killer.

'Wanted you to know. Big relief here.'

'Thanks, Hank.' Harper didn't feel relieved. Too much remained unanswered. 'How's the symposium?' She changed the subject.

'Same.' He didn't elaborate, asked about Chloe, about Harper's day.

Harper didn't mention Lynne or her church; instead, she told him about lunch with Ben Haim and Hadar. About Chloe learning Hebrew. About Hagit being snippy.

When they hung up, Harper lay back on her bed, thinking of Hank, missing him. She closed her eyes. Saw not Hank, but a man lying dead in the shuk, a crescent carved into his forehead. And heard a childlike voice taunt, 'Gog and Magog, Gog and Magog. Gog and Magog.'

The next morning, Lynne was unusually quiet, focused on shoveling and sifting.

After an hour or so, she sat back, leaning against a full bucket, taking a break. Harper joined her, handed her a water bottle. Sat beside her and casually asked, 'So you think the Apocalypse is imminent?'

Lynne laughed. 'You've been thinking about what I said.'

Harper shrugged. Drank water.

'Thing is,' Lynne said as she opened the bottle, 'to you that sounds nuts. It would to most people. But, believe me, Harper, it's not. There's more known about the Apocalypse than you can read in Matthew or Revelation.'

There was? 'Like what?'

Lynne turned to face her. 'You sure you want to know?'

Harper met her eyes. 'Yes.'

'We mostly don't talk to outsiders about it.' She studied Harper. 'But what's the harm – we're partners, after all.' She grinned, looked like a surfer girl. 'See, the Bible is like a history book. Except history books are written after events have happened, and much of the Bible was written before. It tells what will happen – like history written backwards. And the key events that will happen are all there, described in code.'

Harper crossed her legs. 'In code?'

'Yes. Words are made of letters, and letters are associated with numbers that have meaning, and they can be read backwards or diagonally or vertically. People have known that forever.'

Harper felt like she'd fallen into a rabbit hole.

'So, the thing is, in the Bible, God Himself told of events yet to come. He wrote these things in code, and He also coded comments about them.' She leaned closer to Harper, looked around to make sure no one was in hearing distance, lowered her voice. 'Pastor

Travis found and decoded God's notes. He's the first one ever to read God's personal comments.'

Okay. 'What kind of comments?'

'All kinds.' Lynne's eyes drifted. 'Sometimes, He's made notes to Himself to reconsider a decision.' She took a breath, pulled off her work gloves, folded them. 'For example, according to Bible code, God was going to bring the fire from heaven in the Hebrew year 5756.'

Harper said nothing.

'That was coded. It's not even a question – any scholar of numerology will tell you that.'

Of course they would.

'Look, it's common knowledge. By the Christian calendar, the last day of 5756 was September thirteenth, 1996. And guess what? Mossad – Israel's intelligence agency – and its military were on high alert. That proved that even Israel takes Bible code seriously.'

It did?

'But September thirteenth came and went, and nothing happened. Despite what the code said, there was no big fire. No bombs, no conflagration. Nothing. So the code must have been wrong, right?' Lynne took the elastic band out of her ponytail, hung it on her wrist. Combed her fingers through her hair as she talked. 'No. That's the thing. Pastor Travis studied it, and he found that the code had been deciphered correctly, but not completely. They'd missed the hidden commentary. Get this: the code for 5756 also contained the code for,"Will You change it?"'

Wait, what? 'I'm confused.'

'It's all numbers and Hebrew letters in a bunch of different patterns. Way too complicated for my brain. But what I understand is that, thousands of years ago, God pre-wrote history in code. And He coded that there would be worldwide destruction in 1996, but left Himself open to canceling it. Obviously, since it didn't happen, we can assume that's what He decided to do.' She smoothed her hair back and gathered it in her hand, reforming her ponytail.

Harper's mouth was open. She didn't know what to say. Apparently Lynne believed in her preacher's ability to interpret things that hadn't happened.

'Honestly? I didn't believe any of this at first. I thought Pastor Travis was a lunatic. But then, when he was helping us – Pete and me – we began going to his Bible study. And we heard him read dozens of examples – specific events that we'd read about in the paper that were clearly spelled out in the codes and commentaries – including recognizable names and dates. The assassination of that Israeli leader, Yitzhak Rabin? It was coded. The date and even his name. And so was the Gulf War.'

Harper stared, wondered if the second Iraq war had also been coded. Rubbed her scarred leg. Didn't ask.

'These codes tell of things that have either happened or almost happened, like that war in 1996. But when they only almost happen, Pastor finds coded words like, "changed". Or "postponed".'

Harper blinked.

'You think I'm insane.'

Harper didn't answer.

'Well, you'll see. Time will tell. Pastor Travis has discovered secrets about things that are about to occur. And things God wants us to do to prove our faith.'

'Like what?' Drinking poisoned Kool-Aid?

Lynne's gaze wavered. 'We have to comply with His word and expedite His will. Thus, we assure that we will live in His kingdom forever.'

The words didn't seem to be Lynne's. She had to be parroting her pastor. 'So yesterday, when your pastor was talking about the signs of the—'

'Oh. The signs are all in place. Now, we have to prepare. Before the Apocalypse begins, God has encoded exactly what we have to do.' Lynne smiled openly, her skin golden and glowing. 'You know? It's not too late, Harper. You can still join us.'

Harper forced a smile. 'I'm good, thanks.'

'It's a lot to take in, I know. But, for your soul's sake, think about it. God promises eternal life.' She sounded as if she were asking Harper to join her sorority. Lynne stood, stretched. Put her gloves back on, still smiling. 'Time to get back to work.'

Good Lord. Harper got to her feet, staring across the dig at the pit, the scaffolding, the pairs of volunteers. Who were these people? Harmless eccentrics? Religious zealots? And what about Pastor Travis? What was he planning for them? Was it another 'postponed' or 'delayed' conflagration? A self-induced Apocalypse? Or maybe something even worse?

For the rest of the day, Harper studied the others, their interactions, their moods. She'd been trained to spot terrorists or insurgents. People with secrets. People with explosives.

She saw none of the signs, though. No unexplained sweatiness. No blank staring, no intense vigilance or stiffness, no silent mumbling or praying, no restlessness or spaciness or disinterest in material objects. No distracted behavior. Just a bunch of American volunteers, yammering and joking as they did grunt work.

Even so, Harper sensed danger the way she'd sensed the presence of insurgents in Iraq. She felt it in the tightness of her lungs, her stomach. Her skin. Lynne and the others seemed talkative and open, but something hid behind the grins, rumbled below the surface. Something unseen, like a snake under a rock.

When the day ended and the bus finally lumbered back to the kibbutz, Harper hurried to the nursery to check on Chloe and Hagit. Then she hurried to the bungalow, for her laptop.

She couldn't get online. She sat with her computer in the kibbutz's main office where there was supposed to be wireless access. She logged on, but couldn't connect to the Internet. She asked the woman at the front desk for help.

'Internet's down. It happens,' she shrugged. 'Could be back any time.'

But Harper couldn't wait. She wanted to find out who Ramsey Travis was, what qualified him to be a preacher, where he'd come from. Whether he had a criminal record. Why he was in Megiddo. And she could do none of that without the Internet.

To make time pass, she examined the pattern on the tile floor. Got up and looked out the window at the valley. Lost a game of spider solitaire. Then tried to connect again. Still couldn't. Began another game. And heard a familiar voice coming into the lobby, speaking in Hebrew.

Dr Ben Haim was there, talking on the phone.

Harper closed her laptop; it could wait. It was more urgent to tell Dr Ben Haim what was going on at his dig. That a potentially dangerous cult leader had brought his followers there to prepare for Armageddon. For the Apocalypse. She stood to get his attention.

Dr Ben Haim saw her and raised a forefinger, indicating that he'd be off in a minute. That she should wait. Harper sat again, reopened her laptop and tried again for the Internet, but still couldn't get online. Finally, he hung up and walked over to her.

'I'm trying to use the Internet.'

He sat beside her. Too close? 'Good luck. It isn't always easy here. Sometimes it works, sometimes not. You should wait until tomorrow; use the computer at the site. We have better service there.'

His eyes were soft, connected with hers. His hair glistened silver, reflecting the light. Harper edged away.

'I hope you enjoyed our lunch.' Was he flirting? 'Sorry the students interrupted. For some, this is their first dig—'

'Dr Ben Haim,' Harper blurted. She felt clumsy, unsure of his intentions. 'About the dig – there's something I need to tell you.'

'Yes?'

She told him about Ramsey Travis and his followers, that they were preparing for the End of Days. That they believed that only Travis could decode secret messages in the Bible. 'They think the Apocalypse is imminent . . .'

Dr Ben Haim's hand landed firmly on hers, startling her. And he was smiling. 'Dear Dr Jennings. Harper – can we be Harper and Givon?'

Harper nodded, yes. Tried not to stiffen.

'Harper. I'm happy you came to me. It was wise and even very brave.'

Oh dear. How was she going to get his hand off of hers? And why was he saying that she was brave?

'You thought you saw danger, and you acted on it.'

Well, 'acted' was too strong a word. She hadn't actually done anything.

'But, clearly, you are new to our country.'

His hand was warm, meaty. Tanned. Less hairy than Hank's. And it was squeezing hers.

'Yes. But I served in Iraq.' Why had she said that? Was she trying to impress him?

'Really? You were in the war?'

'I was. I am not completely naïve about danger.'

'No, of course not. It was not my intention to imply that you were. What I meant was that this country is not like any other. Certainly not like Iraq. And why is it different? Because this country draws followers of every religion from the whole world. We get everyone: secular, pious, and fanatic. We Israelis even have our own fanatics – have you seen them? They'll spit at you or throw stones if you drive a car or operate an elevator on the Sabbath. Even if you show the skin of your arms. But you know what? It's the beauty of this place. The richness and uniqueness. History, traditions, sacred places and faith. All of it belongs to all of us – even, like it or not, to the fanatics. Here, as nowhere else, we tolerate them. Unless they pose a threat, we let them be.'

Harper felt his breath on her face. He was too close. And he was missing the point. She tried again. 'But Dr Ben Haim – Givon. What if these people do pose a threat? What if they're planning more than a few prayer meetings?'

Ben Haim's eyes probed hers. 'Do you know this? What kind of threat are you talking about? Because if there is one, tell me. In Israel, we take threats very seriously.' He waited for an answer.

Harper didn't know what to say.

'So? Are they planting a bomb? Planning an attack?'

'I don't . . . No. Not that I know of, but . . .'

'Poisoning each other? Planning mass suicide?'

'I thought you ought to know. They believe the end is coming.'

'A lot of people who come here believe the end is coming—'

'But these people think it will happen at your dig.'

Ben Haim frowned, still didn't release her hand.

Harper moved it away. 'Look. I'm sorry if you think I'm over-reacting. Maybe they are just another group of harmless religious kooks. You have more experience than I do. So, if you think it's nothing, just forget it.' She stood. 'Well. Good night. See you tomorrow.' She started for the door, sorry she'd even approached him. He'd completely dismissed her concerns, almost scolded her for bringing them. And what about the way he'd held onto her hand?

'Harper, wait . . .'

Maybe she should keep going, just pretend she hadn't heard him? No, she had to be polite. He was, after all, the head of the dig. A professional colleague. Composing herself, she turned.

'Maybe you'll want this?' Dr Ben Haim's eyes twinkled as he held out her laptop.

Chloe played in her bath, pouring water from colored cups, singing. 'My Im. My Im. My Im.' Harper sat on the side of the tub, sponging her while Hagit washed out Chloe's clothes in the sink.

'Just stay away from them,' Hagit declared.

'I can't. Lynne's my dig partner.'

'So get a new partner.'

'Everyone's assigned.'

'So watch them. Listen to what they're up to.' She carried Chloe's wet clothes to the porch, hung them to dry.

Harper put shampoo in her hands, massaged it into the baby's hair. Put bubbles onto Chloe's nose and stomach. Gave her a handful of suds to play with. Laughed with her when she reached up and plopped suds onto Harper's nose, getting even. How did little Chloe even know about getting even? Was it the nursery? Playing with other, older toddlers? Harper rinsed away the shampoo, wrapped Chloe in a towel, thinking of all the other baths she'd given her – the recent ones, with bubbles, songs and toys, and the early ones, when Harper had been afraid to put even the gentlest soap on the newborn's skin, had worried that the water would give her a chill. Fourteen months? How had they passed so fast? Chloe had six teeth already, was walking, learning to talk. Harper held Chloe on her lap, memorizing the moment. Smelling her curls. Drying her off. Noticing the little *hamsa* around her neck.

Hagit came back in and took out Chloe's pajamas. 'I don't like it.'

It took a moment for Harper to realize what Hagit was talking about. 'Dr Ben Haim is probably right. Probably they're harmless.'

'Probably? You want to stake your life on "probably"?'

Chloe was singing 'My im, my im,' again.

'What's she singing?' Harper fastened the diaper, pulled the pajama top over Chloe's head.

'Water. Mayim.'

A song about water?

'A song from the nursery school.' Hagit began to sing it. 'Mayim mayim mayim mayim, hey, mayim b'sason . . .' Chloe scrambled to join her, beaming and clapping, trying to sing along.

Harper watched as Hagit led her in a circle dance.

'Hey hey hey hey,' they shouted, and Chloe squealed, jumping and clapping.

Harper didn't know the words or the dance. She sat alone until Hagit, winded, had to stop. But Chloe, overtired and – thanks to Hagit – over stimulated, kept shouting and spinning, and tumbling and getting up again.

'So, anyway.' Hagit sat down on the bed, panting and dabbing her forehead. 'I'm serious. You already attracted the Evil Eye, so trouble isn't going to be far away.' Again, she picked up the conversation from before. 'Tomorrow, keep your eyes and your ears open. Watch what's around you.'

'I always do.'

'I've learned something, Harper. Don't assume people are who or what they say. It's not always the truth.'

'Thanks, Hagit.' It was good advice. Harper had learned it, too.

Harper grabbed Chloe, ending her rampage. 'Time for you to settle down. Let's go tuck you in.'

Hagit wasn't finished. 'Be sure you wear your *hamsa*.'

'I will.'

'And say Kenahara. In fact, say plenty of them.'

Chloe leaned against Harper's shoulder, sucking her fingers. 'Hagit? You think these people are really dangerous?'

'Dangerous?' Hagit paused, thinking. 'Maybe. Maybe not.' She went back to the other room, but turned, shaking a finger at Harper. 'But say Kenahara anyway. Just in case. It never hurts.'

The talk with Hank was brief. He was exhausted from visiting potential desalination sites, but Harper wanted his opinion and decided to tell him about her conversation with Lynne.

'She said they're preparing for the Apocalypse.'

'Normal. For cult.'

Was it? Dr Ben Haim had seemed to think so.

'But their leader says he's found secret codes in the Bible, and I think he's having them prepare now for the End of Days . . .'

'Just don't drink. Their Kool-Aid.'

Really? Hank was joking about it? He thought that Jim Jones' mass killings were funny? That it was comical that people blindly followed their leader to their deaths?

'Chloe asleep?'

And now he was just moving on, ignoring the entire topic?

'Yes.' Her answer was clipped.

'Good day?'

'Fine.'

'Hoppa?' Finally, he was getting it. 'What?'

He really didn't know. He sounded drained, half-asleep. Was she really going to start an argument?

'Cult?' So he knew what was wrong.

'We'll talk about it another time, Hank. You're tired.'

'Hoppa. Here. All kinds come. Normal.'

Again, he agreed with Ben Haim. Probably she should relax.

'Okay? You?'

She said she was fine, told him she loved him. They said good night.

Harper didn't feel like going to bed, felt unsettled. She went to the next room, saw Hagit sleeping. Thought about trying again to get online. Doing some research on Ramsey Travis and his church.

Quietly, she wrote a note for Hagit, picked up her laptop and tiptoed to the door. She was on the porch, about to step onto the path, when she heard a wail. A cat in heat, or maybe hurt?

'Oh, Ramsey!'

It wasn't a cat. The wailer was a woman.

Instinctively, Harper ducked into the shadows and peered towards the voice. Next door, light spilled out from a window onto the porch of Ramsey Travis's bungalow. A couple stood silhouetted, locked in an embrace. Kissing, groping. Harper stepped deeper into the shadows, not wanting to spy. Unable to look away. Even in the dimness, she thought she recognized the woman, her long legs, straight blonde hair. Was it Lynne? No, it couldn't be. Harper squinted into the darkness, trying to see.

Finally, the woman broke away from the man and stepped into the starlight, and Harper saw her clearly. No mistake.

'Trust me, Ramsey.' Lynne's voice was husky. 'You have my word.'

Travis came after her, gripped her hands, 'Are you sure? Because the ninth is the twenty-sixth . . .'

'I told you. I'll do it.'

Do what? And the ninth was the twenty-sixth? What the hell did that mean?

Travis pulled her back for a final, lingering kiss, and then, abruptly, released her. Lynne turned and walked away. Right toward Harper.

Harper backed against the wall, not moving, not making a sound. Lynne passed without seeing her, and Harper looked back at the porch, at the tall beefy man with receding hair. Ramsey Travis.

Who was he really? What was he planning? All Harper knew for sure was that he'd been kissing Lynne and making her wail like a wounded animal. And that he'd sent her back to her husband.

As soon as Travis went back into his bungalow, Harper hurried down the path to the main road. The main office was empty except for a security officer and the guy at the desk. She bought a Coke from the machine and tried to log on to the Internet, but the whole time, she was replaying the scene she'd just witnessed, trying to process it.

Lynne had said the pastor had counseled her and helped save her marriage. It wasn't much of a stretch to think that Travis would have used Lynne's vulnerability and trust to seduce her. What a hypocrite, preaching God's word while practicing adultery with his followers. Harper ached to get online and find out more about this guy. Ramsey Travis. Where had he come from? What was in his past?

The screen said: 'Internet Explorer cannot display the web page.' Damn.

Again, Harper replayed the scene on the porch. What was it that Travis wanted Lynne to do? Was it to tell Peter about their relationship? Maybe. But what about 'the ninth is the twenty-sixth'? What did that mean? Bible code? Harper had no idea. Could make no sense of it.

She tried another browser. Mozilla. No luck.

'Miss, you need some help?' The guy at the desk was watching her.

'I'm trying to get online . . .'

'To send an email? Or make a reservation? I can help you . . .'

How? Did he have Internet? Harper stood, went to the desk. The guy's nametag had a name both in Hebrew and English: Schmuel. 'Are you connected?'

'Me?' He and the security officer exchanged glances and laughed. 'Not now. Sometime tonight, though, it will happen. Usually about two or three a.m. But maybe earlier. Maybe in an hour. Look, when it happens, I can make a reservation for you. Or send a message – anything you want.'

Actually, anything except what she wanted. Harper thanked him and explained that he couldn't help; she was trying to do research. She picked up her laptop, deposited her Coke bottle in the recycling can, and headed out. At the door, she stopped, turned back.

'Schmuel? Let me ask you. Does this make any sense to you? The ninth is the twenty-sixth?'

Then Schmuel blinked, said something in Hebrew to the guard who said something back. Schmuel shrugged.

'Maybe he's right. He thinks it's about the ninth of Av.'

Harper didn't understand.

'The ninth of Av,' Schmuel repeated. 'Tisha B'Av. He thinks it comes this year on July twenty-sixth. In a few days.'

She still didn't. 'What's the ninth of Av?'

The guard smirked, made a comment in Hebrew.

'For the Jews,' Schmuel explained, 'it's a serious day. A day of mourning. Very holy.'

The guard interjected something. Schmuel nodded.

'It marks the destruction of the Temple. First by the Babylonians, later by the Romans. We are supposed to fast and pray – not just for the Temples any more, but for all misfortunes and injustices. It's a day to remember the tragedies of ages. But not to worry. We'll still have service for you that day. Anything you want, as usual.'

Harper thanked him and the guard, and started back to the bungalow. The whole way home, she kept replaying Lynne's uninhibited moans as she clutched Ramsey Travis. Why, in the midst of a passionate embrace, would Lynne and Travis be concerned with a Jewish holy day? And why would they care that it fell on July twenty-sixth?

The next morning, Harper studied Lynne for signs of her affair. She looked for feigned cheeriness, for fatigue. For glances that wandered toward the pastor. For shifting eyes and guarded conversation. But she found nothing; Lynne was her usual chatty self. She walked to their section arm in arm with Peter, gave him a smooch when they separated. Seemed completely open and innocent with her freckled tan and wide blue eyes.

Harper told herself it was none of her business. If Lynne wanted to cheat on her husband, even with the pastor who had counseled them, it was entirely Lynne's decision. Hell, she'd only met these people three days ago; what did she care what they did? Maybe the entire church believed in open marriage. Maybe they were all sleeping with each other. Maybe Peter knew and didn't care. Maybe Peter was also having sex with him. It wasn't her problem. She should just butt out.

'So. Have a nice night last night?' She emptied dirt into a bucket and watched Lynne's reaction, which was none.

'I did. You?'

Harper made her voice casual. 'I couldn't sleep. So I went for a walk at about . . .' What time had it been? 'About midnight.'

Lynne looked up, frowning. 'What kept you up? The baby?'

'No, she was sleeping.'

'Oh, I bet I know why you were up. You miss your hubby.'

Her 'hubby'?

'Well, here's what I would do. Have a little drinkie. Some wine right before bed.'

'Good idea. You're right – I don't like sleeping without Hank.' Maybe if she revealed things about her marriage, Lynne would reciprocate.

In fact, Lynne nodded. 'I know what you mean.'

Harper stopped listening, stuck her trowel into the dirt. Thought of another approach. 'You know what? My bungalow is right next to your pastor's.'

'Yeah?' If she was worried that Harper might have seen her, Lynne didn't let on. 'Nice location. Ours is down the hill – closer to the restaurant.' She reached for a screen. 'Think anyone'll find anything today?'

Harper adjusted her hat. There had to be a way to make Lynne reveal something. Maybe just getting her to talk about Travis? 'So I was thinking about what you said about your pastor. That he could see people's souls . . .'

'Yeah, he's amazing.' Lynne sifted dirt, smeared some on her forehead as she wiped away sweat. 'He understands people. What's inside them. What each one is capable of. He's truly a man of God.' Lynne's face glowed as if reflecting holy light.

'So is he married?' Harper watched Lynne's face for a blush. A tightened jaw. A twitch.

But all Lynne did was smile. 'Oh, you bet. Ramsey Travis is married to his church.'

Of course he was. A complete saint. And he had Lynne brainwashed. She apparently felt no guilt or conflict about canoodling with Pastor Travis; he'd probably convinced her that having sex with him was a way of serving God. Still, Harper wanted to hear more.

'So what's he learned from those codes?'

'Oh.' Lynne took a drink from her water bottle. She waved to Lowell a few sections over. 'Hey, Lowell. When you dig to China, you can stop.'

'Got my chopsticks ready,' Lowell called back.

'What exactly did you want to know?'

'I don't know. Just some more examples.'

Lynne shook dirt off her trowel and beamed at Harper. 'I'm so glad you asked. Really. I have a feeling about you. I mean it. Ever since we met, I've sensed that you should join us. So, let me tell you about Pastor's discoveries. Of course, there are too many examples to give right here and now. What have I already told you? About Yitzhak Rabin? And also the first Gulf War. Okay. Here's another one.'

While they dug, Lynne told Harper about Prime Minister Bibi Netanyahu's near assassination. The codes had said that it was supposed to have occurred in Amman in July, 1996, and that his death was to have triggered an atomic war.

'Obviously, it didn't happen.' Lynne sat on a bucket to take a break. 'But here's the thing: Netanyahu was *scheduled* to go to Amman in July of '96 to meet with King Hussein. Check if you want – it's historical fact. At the last minute, Hussein canceled. So the assassination never happened; the war never got triggered.'

'You're going to tell me that Hussein canceled because God wanted him to?'

'I am. God's decision to change His plan is written in the code. In fact, I know some of the exact words. The code specifically says, "Bibi", his actual name. And "July to Amman". Then it says "murdered", and "his soul was cut off", and "death", along with the date, "the ninth of Av, 5756" and the question: "Will you change it?" And then it gives the answer: "Delayed."'

Wait. 'Did you say the ninth of Av?'

'That's the date given in the code. It's a holy day marking the destruction of the First and Second Jewish Temples. And it's also the date the final war was supposed to begin. But God delayed it. In fact, Netanyahu went in August instead, so he wasn't killed and the war was avoided. At least, that time.'

Harper removed her work gloves, closed her eyes, rubbed them. None of this made sense. Lynne looked like a damned cheerleader, had a Midwestern accent and freckles, wore a Cubs hat. And she discussed atomic wars and the end of the world as easily and breezily as she might a backyard barbecue.

'I know. It's mind-boggling. You should talk to Pastor Travis. He'll give you more examples. But the most amazing part is that all the codes were written thousands of years ago. Like I told you, God wrote history backwards, telling what was to come. But He left Himself choices. He gave several dates when conflagrations could begin. But so far, for every conflagration date, there's been a code that says, "I will delay the war", or "I changed it". It's amazing, isn't it? And Pastor has deciphered it.'

Harper's mind was still fixed on the ninth of Av. July twenty-sixth was just three days away. It couldn't be a coincidence that the pastor had planned the trip to include that date. 'So do all the codes have to do with destruction? With, you know, the end . . .'

'The End of Days? Good question. I don't really know the answer. All I know is that Pastor Travis wants us to prepare. So far, the conflagrations have been postponed. They were written to occur in 1996, 2006, and again in 2010 – I'm sure there are other dates, too.

All of those were "Delayed". But the codes also indicate the date when all God's delaying will end and the conflagration will actually begin. Pastor Travis knows when that is. He says it will be soon. And when the date arrives, the action will start right here, in Megiddo.'

Oh God. The pastor had brought his followers there for Armageddon – the end of the world. Ramsey Travis believed it would start right where they were digging, in three days, on July twenty-sixth. The ninth of Av.

Harper had to know for sure. 'So that's why you're here. For the action?' She thought again of Jim Jones and his suicidal followers.

Lynne didn't answer. She might have, but from across the site, Josh shouted from section nine, 'Dr Hadar! Dr Ben Haim!'

Volunteers ran toward the voice, a bell rang, and people hollered and hooted.

Harper was on her feet, hurrying toward the commotion before she realized what had happened: Josh and his partner had uncovered something.

It was a wall. A row of large square stones.

The excitement was palpable. Dr Hadar gathered everyone together, passed out cups of wine, led a prayer and made a toast to the discovery. The rest of the afternoon was spent gently brushing away dirt, clearing off the surface of the wall, and removing earth around it to reveal more of the structure. Harper and Lynne were able to join Dr Ben Haim's students in the effort, clearing earth from the wall and sifting for shards or other relics.

Harper became immersed in the work. Her hands almost shook as she brushed off the wall. She imagined the people who'd used this building – what had it been? Clearly, it had been a place worthy of solid construction, surviving as a structure for almost two millennia.

Dr Ben Haim and Dr Hadar were involved in the process, supervising the volunteers, conferring with students, consulting computer programs. Harper didn't notice the heat or the time; didn't think about anything but the dig until, abruptly, the work day ended, and she was on the bus with the others, heading back to the kibbutz.

Even then, her thoughts remained fixed on the discovery and the promise of the site. But when she saw Ramsey Travis lean across the aisle to whisper into Lynne's ear, images of antiquities were replaced by those of the night before: Lynne clutching the pastor, kissing him desperately. Assuring him, 'I'll do it.'

Do what?

And Travis reminding her, 'The ninth is the twenty-sixth.'

He'd meant the ninth of Av. The date on which Jews mourned destruction. And the date on which, according to Travis, God had scheduled, postponed and rescheduled a conflagration to begin the end of days, right there in Megiddo.

The ninth of Av would fall on July twenty-sixth.

Harper watched Travis sit back in his seat. He wasn't doing anything remarkable, was just relaxing, looking out the window. Even so, there was something intangibly menacing, something too self-assured about him. Harper was absolutely sure: Travis was preparing for the End of Days to happen in just three days, on July twenty-sixth. But she had no idea what he intended to do.

Travis dozed, one arm hanging into the aisle. He didn't look much like a man preparing for the end of the world.

Maybe she was mistaken. Like Dr Ben Haim had said, end-of-the-world cults popped up in Israel frequently. Most were harmless. Travis probably had a big feast planned, or an all-night prayer vigil. Nothing more.

The bus rumbled on. Harper studied Travis as if somehow she'd be able to see his thoughts, but all she saw was his receding ginger hairline. She sat sideways to see him better. Her mind rattled phrases, repeating them in an endless loop. 'The ninth is the twenty-sixth.' 'I'll do it.' 'Armageddon is Har Meggido.' 'Gog and Magog.' 'Will you delay it?' 'The ninth is the twenty-sixth.'

She rubbed her temples, turned to look out the window at the lush, hilly countryside and was reassured by its stillness. How ridiculous she was, reacting so seriously. She needed to get a grip, enjoy her time in Israel. The land was calm; the sun was bright. Nothing was going to happen in three days – certainly not the end of the world.

By the time she got off the bus, though, her wariness had grown. The stillness of the hills seemed not peaceful but ominous. The sunshine was too stark. She started for the nursery, but stopped. She should talk to Dr Ben Haim again. Or Dr Hadar. Should let them know about the pastor's specific focus on the ninth of Av. Just in case. Maybe they would be at the kibbutz office. She stopped there, didn't see them.

A young, pregnant woman whose nametag said 'Noa' was working at the desk. 'They aren't back yet.'

Harper bit her lip. Of course they weren't back. Not after their first major find today. They'd probably stay at the site until nightfall.

'It's an emergency?' Noa watched Harper. 'I can reach them if it's urgent.'

Was it? Harper wasn't sure. But probably the dig leaders wouldn't think it was. In fact, they'd be annoyed at the interruption – Dr Ben Haim had already told her to forget about the church group. And he'd be more than a little irritated if she bothered him again with another far-fetched warning about the End of Days.

The woman was watching her, waiting for a reply.

Harper took a breath. 'No, thank you. It's not urgent.'

July twenty-sixth was, after all, three whole days away, and she had nothing concrete to present. She stepped out of the office into the harsh, glaring light. Stopped. Went back in and wrote the same note to both dig leaders, asking each to contact her when they had a moment. She reread the message, thought it sounded too casual. Threw it out. Rewrote it, adding a congratulatory opening about the find, then saying that she had something unrelated that she needed to discuss. Fine. It even sounded somewhat professional.

On her way to the nursery, Harper squinted. Even with sunglasses, the angle, the brightness felt wrong. The sun seemed intense, almost hostile. She took a breath. Made herself slow down. What was wrong with her? There was no problem with the sun or the light; the problem was with her – her unease about Pastor Travis. She needed to stop. To pretend that she didn't know anything about them or their codes; that she wasn't disturbed by Travis's calm, self-assurance, his booming voice and blindly adoring followers.

But she couldn't. She had to know: who was Ramsey Travis? What about him drew such loyalty? Where had he come from? Was he really a scholar? With all the excitement at the dig, she'd completely forgotten to use the computers there and look him up. And now that a structure had been uncovered, the computers would be in constant use. Maybe she'd talk to Hank, ask him to do some research. Because the twenty-sixth was coming . . .

In fact, what was she thinking? Why didn't she just take Chloe and leave? Not risk being around for Travis's version of the Apocalypse, whatever it was.

She approached the nursery, deciding that, yes, they would leave. Nothing was worth endangering Chloe. At the gate, she heard the children singing. Not the 'mayim' song. This one had 'Shalom' in it

– finally, a word she understood. It meant goodbye, hello, and peace. She walked into the cottage, nearly tripping on a cat, and stood at the door. The children were sitting in a circle, their faces earnest, their voices sweet. Harper looked at them, one by one. Among them, she spotted the little boy who'd played with Chloe in the swimming pool. Adi's son, Ari. A little girl with pigtails who was holding Chloe's hand. And Chloe, who was trying in vain to sing the words like the older children. Their voices flowed lighter than air, and their little bodies swayed side to side with the beat, together, as one.

No. Harper couldn't take Chloe and run. Couldn't take off and leave the other children unprotected.

Like it or not, she had no choice. They had to stay.

The killer walked alone. The sun was low above the horizon, the air crisp, finally cooling. People were preparing supper or still at work, not out and about. A good time to plan, to prepare for all the possible snags. Because, clearly, snags had arisen before.

'Stop,' the killer said out loud. Going over the past was useless. What had happened was done. The victims had run, had ended up in the wrong territory, but that had been unforeseeable and nobody's fault. Bottom line was that they had both been offered. A Christian and a Muslim. Now all that remained was a Jew, the trigger that would spark suspicions, stirring hostilities among those three groups in an area already simmering with tension. And, as God intended, those hostilities would ignite further violence, incite mobs, elicit a chain of escalating and expanding conflicts until, finally, the ultimate battle of fire.

Heat coursed through the killer. Frightening heat, but also arousing. Dangerous, like playing with explosives. Or explosive sex. Yes, it was like sex – driving, sweaty, breathless, powerful. Building in intensity, in anticipation. The killer stopped, thinking of the night before. The melding of souls, the rapture of skin joining skin. But no. It wasn't the time to think of flesh. Focus had to be on the next step, no distractions – not even nerves. Nerves were nothing to dwell on. The body was connected to the spirit and the mind. So the roiling of a belly, the searing of a stomach, the racing of a pulse – these were signs that the body was preparing for action, nothing more. This time, the mission would succeed, clean and sleek. The target would be worthy. And the strike would come swiftly, unex-pectedly, allowing no time for reaction. Death would come before the victim had even realized that he'd been slashed.

And then, the sacrifice would be finished. The reward would be bestowed.

The killer smiled. Stopped to pet a dog. Felt simultaneous humility and pride, eagerness and dread.

By the end of the night, preparations would be complete. The future would be sealed. Everything would change with the carving of a star.

Hagit fixed Chloe a snack of juice and chunks of apple and banana. Harper didn't join them. She sat in the bedroom, thinking about how to foil Travis's plan, whatever it was. Maybe she could expose him as a fraud. Maybe reveal some dark secret from his past. Or she could expose his affair with Lynne. But that seemed low; Lynne's love life wasn't her business. Best would be to find out what Travis was planning and prevent it. Maybe she could attend prayer meetings? Talk to him personally – pretend to be a convert? Spy on him?

In the next room, Hagit was singing the Shalom song, Chloe trying to join her.

'What do the words mean?' Harper called.

Hagit stopped singing. 'It's just a song.' She started singing again.

Really? Hagit wasn't going to tell her? Harper strode into the next room, interrupting. 'Hagit. You're teaching my child a song. I want to know what it means.'

'She's just a baby. What's the difference?'

'I asked you what it means.' Harper used her lieutenant's voice. Commanding and harsh.

Chloe dissolved into tears.

'It's all right, *tinoket.*'

'Tinoket?'

Hagit turned to Harper, facing her. 'It means baby. You made her cry. What's wrong with you?'

With *her*? 'I asked a simple question.' Chloe was wailing. Harper picked her up, kissed her. Told her everything was okay.

Hagit glared, hands on hips. 'She was fine. Happy and eating. Now look . . .'

'All you had to do was answer me—'

'Am I your servant? Must I bow to you?'

Okay. This was out of hand. Harper took a deep, assertive breath. 'I'm Chloe's mother, Hagit. I want to know what she's learning.

'If you don't like what she's learning, take her home. If you don't trust me to care for her, then you stay with her all day. Do it your-self.' Hagit spun around and headed for her closet, started pulling clothes out, spouting Hebrew.

Chloe sniffled, her eyes on Hagit.

Harper was speechless. How had the conversation gotten so heated? What kind of mother was she, making her baby cry? And now what was she supposed to do? Just let Hagit storm out? Certainly, she wasn't going to beg her to stay; she could manage without her. Chloe could still go to the nursery: none of the other children had their own personal sitters.

But Chloe had become attached to Hagit.

And, in a way, despite the gruffness, so had she.

Hagit folded her nightgowns. Her skirts.

Harper looked out the window, saw Ramsey Travis's bungalow.

Maybe they should all leave. Maybe she should take Chloe and follow Hagit.

She thought of the children at the nursery. And of the dig. The exhilaration at the site. The promise of discovery.

'Hagit, wait.' She followed her. 'I don't know why we're arguing . . .'

'Why? I'll tell you why. Because you're always with the comments. Always with the questions. You don't trust me.'

'Of course I trust you. I wouldn't leave Chloe with you if I didn't.'

'Then why so many questions?' Her hands were on her hips again.

Chloe's chin quivered. Harper smoothed her curls, didn't remember asking Hagit a lot of questions. Even so, what if she did? She was the mother here. And the employer – well, not really. The government had hired Hagit. But still, she outranked the babysitter, didn't she? She should be able to ask as much as she wanted.

Hagit packed her socks.

'Hagit. Please. Let's have a cup of coffee and talk. Let's not fight.'

Hagit stopped folding clothes, looked at Chloe, then at her suit-case, then back at Chloe. 'You make the coffee,' she said as she reached for Chloe.

Harper watched Chloe wrap her arms around Hagit's neck and felt a pang. Then she went to the cabinet for the Nescafe.

'Milk, no sugar.' Hagit put Chloe back at the table so she could finish her snack and resumed singing. It was the same song as before, the same haunting melody, but this time, in English. 'Peace, my friends, peace, my friends. Peace. Peace. Until we meet again, until we meet again. Peace. Peace.'

Chloe munched an apple chunk. And Harper stood in the kitchenette, humming along with the mournful turn, gazing out the window at the bungalow next door.

Peace had been restored long before Hank called. Harper asked him to Google Ramsey Travis. 'I'd do it myself but I can't get online here.'

'Hoppa. Very busy here. No time.' He sounded cranky and tired.

'It'll just take a minute to look him up. He's from Indiana.'

'Why?' His tone changed, concerned now. 'What. Happened?'

'Nothing.' Not yet, anyway. 'I told you. He says the world's about to end. I want to find out how crazy he really is.'

'But Ben Haim. Said he's. Not dangerous.'

'Hank, please. Can you do this one thing? Look him up?'

With a long sigh, Hank agreed.

Harper asked about the symposium, but Hank changed the subject, asked about Chloe, about the dig, and then they said good night.

After the call, Harper plugged her cell phone in to recharge and pulled off her T-shirt. Before she could step out of her shorts, her cell phone rang.

It was Hank.

The only record Google had of Ramsey Travis was as pastor of the Word of the Lord Church in a small town south of Muncie, Indiana. Travis had been there for at least three years. There was no other information about him.

Harper sat on the bed. 'Nothing about any articles he'd written? Or academic degrees?'

'No.'

'How about other churches he's led? Or other work he's done – you know, in business?' She tossed her shorts into the laundry.

'Hoppa. Told you. No.' Hank sounded impatient. 'But. Listen. First, I punched in. Wrong name.'

So?

'Put first name Travis. Found guy. Travis Ramsey.'

'And?'

'This guy. Did. Six years. In Illinois. For man. Slaughter.'

Harper was on her feet at the window, looking out at Travis's bungalow. 'Hank. Do you think it's . . .?'

'Could be. Don't know.'

'Was there a photo?'

'No. Just news story. Picture only of vic. Tim.'

'Who did he kill?'

'Hoppa. Calm down. Killer was a minor. Happened. Twenty-nine years ago.'

'Who?'

'And could. Have been. Accident.'

'*Who?*' Why wouldn't he tell her?

Hank paused. 'His father.'

His father? Good God. 'Did the article give a motive? What else did it say?'

Another pause. 'Not much.'

Why was he being so difficult? 'Hank, what aren't you telling me?'

'Might be not same. Guy, Hoppa.'

'I know.'

'Don't get crazy.'

Of course she wouldn't, unless he kept stalling. 'Hank. Tell me.'

'The father.' He took a breath. 'Was strict.'

And?

'And. A Pente. Costal. Minister.'

Damn. Travis Ramsey had to be Ramsey Travis. It would have been too great a coincidence – a charismatic preacher and the son of a Pentecostal minister whose names were the reverse of each other? And, if the patricidal Travis Ramsey had been a teenager twenty-nine years ago, he'd be in his forties now. Just like Ramsey Travis.

No question. It was the same guy.

Harper asked more questions. Where was the mother? How had the man died? Hank didn't have answers, had seen just a couple of Google entries based on articles from an old newspaper in southern Illinois.

He sounded tentative. 'Hoppa. Might be him.'

Seriously? Of course it was.

'Come back. Don't stay there. Don't like this.'

Harper didn't like it either. 'I can't just leave these people at his mercy, Hank. If Travis has some crazy plan—'

'Not you have to save everyone. Need to take Chloe. And go.'

'But what if . . .?' Harper closed her eyes, saw an explosion, heard men scream, felt her body fly onto a burnt-out car. No. Hank was right: protecting everyone wasn't her job; she wasn't in the military any more. Couldn't risk endangering her child.

'Okay.' She ran a hand through her hair.

'Okay?' Clearly, he hadn't expected her to agree.

'Give me a day or two—'

'Hoppa. Why a day or two?'

'To finish up—'

'Why not tomorrow?'

'Nothing will happen for a few days, not 'til the twenty-sixth.'

'You don't know . . .'

'I'm positive. And if I see anything suspicious before then, we'll high-tail it out of here. I promise.'

He was seething. She could hear it. Could almost see steam coming from the phone.

'We're safe. The kibbutz has security. And I've got my eye on Travis. Besides, I'm Army, remember? I've taken down dudes a lot tougher than this guy. I can take care of myself. And of Chloe. Trust me.'

When he finally spoke, Hank's voice was flat. 'Hope for all our. Sakes. You are right, Hoppa. Come back as soon. As you can.'

After they hung up, Harper thought of calling him back, but had nothing else to say.

Besides, whatever Travis had planned for his followers wasn't supposed to happen until the twenty-sixth. And when it happened, it would probably affect only them; there was no reason to think the kibbutz or others at the dig would be involved.

Then again, they might. After all, the end of the world could require a fairly massive incident. Harper paced around the bungalow, decided that she felt guilty because Hank was angry, not because she'd done anything wrong. She checked on Chloe, went back to the sitting room. Finally, stood at the window, staring at Travis's bungalow. Wondering if it contained evidence of what Travis was preparing.

The place was completely dark. Probably no one was there. Maybe the porch door was unlocked? She looked at her phone to check the time. Not late – just after ten. Pastor Travis was probably out tending his flock.

Hagit had dozed off in front of the television. Harper went back to her room and pulled her clothes back on. She wouldn't be gone long, so she didn't bother to leave a note before she went outside.

*   *   *

Harper moved quietly down the steps of her porch, along the path, toward the pastor's bungalow. Once she got inside, she'd have to make sure that it was empty, that he and his roommate hadn't just gone to sleep early like Hagit. If they were home and caught her there, what would she say?

Okay. She could say that she'd gotten confused – mistaken their place for her own. That would work if she acted real embarrassed and stupid. But probably, she wouldn't have to. Probably, they weren't home.

Barefoot, Harper crept along the dark path connecting her bungalow to Travis's. Lord. What was wrong with her? What had happened to all her experience and training? She'd gone out completely unprepared. Didn't have a flashlight. Or even her phone. Damn. She'd left it in her room. So there she was, creeping up blindly to a possible murderer's porch with no phone and nothing to defend herself, not even a nail file.

Never mind. She'd only be there for a minute. Two, max. If she saw anything resembling a bomb or wires or poison or ammunition – anything remotely hinting of impending death or murder, she'd skedaddle back to her place and call the authorities.

Harper stepped on a pebble, winced. Kept going, silently, steadily. Like a shadow, she glided to the steps of the porch, climbed the first step. Paused. Continued to the second. Paused.

'Can I help you?'

Startled, she tottered backward. Caught hold of the railing. The voice had come suddenly, from nowhere.

'Miss?' It was a man's voice, wheezy. From the darkest corner of the porch.

Harper froze, didn't answer.

He emerged from the blackness, a stout man with short legs. 'Looking for Pastor?'

She could see him now, his outline. Let out a breath. Feigned girlishness. 'Oh, my. I didn't see you . . .' She giggled, as if embarrassed.

'Sorry. Didn't mean to scare you. I'm just sitting, enjoying the night air.' He laughed, wheezing. 'Pastor's at a council meeting. Should be back any minute.' He paused, tilted his head. 'I don't think we've met. Harold Wade.' He held out his hand.

Harper could barely see it in the dark but managed to shake it. 'Harper Jennings. From next door. I was just—'

'Pastor'll be here soon. Come have a rocking chair. Sit with me while you wait.' He took her elbow.

'Thanks, but I can't. I just came by to see if you had any milk.' It was the first thing that came to mind.

'Milk?' He let go of her arm.

'We're out. My daughter's having trouble sleeping—'

'Your daughter?'

'She's fourteen and a half months old.' Why was she telling him that?

'Oh, a baby? Well, sorry. We've got coffee and some sodas. No milk.'

'Of course. Well. Thanks anyway.' Harper apologized for disturbing him, wished him a good night and hurried away before he could say anything else.

Back in her bungalow, Harper let herself breathe. The television was on; Hagit sound asleep. But Harper couldn't think of sleep. She paced. Where was Travis's council meeting being held? What were they doing there? She chewed her lip, heard Hank urging her to leave the dig and come back to Jerusalem. Insisting that it wasn't her job to protect everyone, just her baby and herself.

She looked in on Chloe. The baby sprawled belly up, arms open wide, trusting the universe. Her tummy rising and falling with each breath. Harper thought she could stand there all night, watching her golden baby.

Instead, she lightly touched Chloe's cheek, then switched gears, grabbed her phone and flashlight, looked around for a weapon. Found a stuffed monkey. A bottle of baby shampoo. A picture book. Finally, she tucked a kitchen knife into her pocket and headed back out into the darkness, walking away from Travis's place, keeping out of sight of Harold Wade.

She made a loop around the bungalows, taking the path to the parking area behind them, then crossing back to the main path. She continued past the darkened nursery, the closed restaurant, toward the main office building.

Harper stopped in the shadows near the entrance. The lights were on, but the building was open round the clock, so lights didn't mean much. The only way to find out if they were there was to go inside.

Schmuel was at the front desk. He looked up.

'Are you online?' Not that it mattered; she'd already found out about Travis.

'No, just doing scheduling. But I can try . . .'

'No, don't bother.' She smiled. 'I just wondered.'

Harper wandered across the open lobby, past the soda machines, travel brochures, big-screen television, small offices and storage rooms, all the way to the far wall lined with windows. She stood for a moment, disappointed. No sign of Travis. Sighing, she turned to go. Stopped at a sitting area near the television. Off to her left, behind a closed door, someone was talking.

Harper glanced back at Schmuel. His attention was on his work. She stepped closer to the door. Closer. Listening.

'. . . in just two days.' It was a man's voice. Didn't sound like Travis.

'You act like this is news to you. You've known about this for months.' This one sounded more like Travis. Commanding. Resonant.

'But it isn't as simple as you make it sound . . .'

'Simple? I never said it would be simple. Nor did the Lord. Is proof of our faith supposed to be—?'

'They didn't mean it like that, Pastor.' Harper thought she recognized Peter Watts' voice. 'They meant there were unforeseen obstacles.'

'Obstacles?'

'Yes.'

Harper looked back at the desk, edged closer to the door.

'Okay, explain that to the Lord. 'Sorry, Lord. You offered me eternal life and a chance to bask in Your glory. But no thanks. I'll have to pass; there were obstacles."

'Amen,' someone said.

'Pastor,' Peter began.

'No! No more excuses.' Travis's voice rumbled like distant thunder.

'Sorry, Ramsey. I have to agree with Peter.' Another voice. A third man. 'The Lord is all-powerful.'

'Your point?'

Harper wished she could see through the door.

'Well, that is my point. He's all-powerful. He can do whatever He wants. He created the universe. He can destroy it whenever He wants, with or without our offerings. What we do doesn't matter. Why are we so brazen as to think He requires help from us?'

Silence followed. Harper waited for Ramsey Travis's reaction to this challenge. Travis would expect complete allegiance from his followers. But someone was openly challenging – even contradicting him. She stood beside the door and pressed her body against the wall, expecting all hell to break out on the other side.

When he finally spoke, though, Travis didn't sound enraged. He sounded sad. 'This is a difficult moment for me, council members. As you know, Brother Lowell has been a long-time trusted advisor to me and our church. He's been as my right hand. But now, Brother Lowell has lost his way. He is questioning the Lord's own written words, rejecting the Lord Himself. I'm disheartened, Brother Lowell. Your loss of faith saddens me.'

A few people said, 'Amen,' as Lowell began to defend himself. 'I never rejected the Lord—'

'Lowell,' another voice interrupted. A woman. 'Pastor Travis has read God's code. It's not up to us to question what God wrote or try to figure out the logic of it. We aren't equipped to understand God—'

'Amen!'

'All we can do is obey Him.'

'Amen.'

'It grieves me, Lowell.' Travis took command. 'But I see no alternative. As of this moment, you are stripped of your position as council prelate.'

'Ramsey, you're taking my comments way too seriously—'

'As all of you know, this is a critical time for our church. We have no time for disbelievers.'

'Fine. You don't have to demote me. I quit the position – and the council. But never accuse me of doubting the Lord. All I said was that we were foolish if we believe that the Lord needs anything from us. Our offerings aren't necessary—'

'Our offerings aren't necessary?' Travis roared. 'Our offerings, Brother Lowell, prove our allegiance and our pure unquestioning absolute obedience to the Lord. They are a symbol of our faith. How can you lose sight of that now, on the eve of our fulfillment?'

Lots of 'Amens'.

'And now, as you are no longer a member of the council, I must ask you—'

'Don't bother,' Lowell barked. 'I'm leaving.'

Oh dear. Harper scooted away from the door, made it to the soda machine and pretended to be buying a drink just in time for the door to swing open. Lowell strode past her, his eyes filled with tears.

* * *

Harper waited until Lowell was out of the building before she strolled back and leaned against the wall beside the door. Listening.

There was clapping. And then someone said, 'Thank you, Pastor Travis. I won't let you down.'

'Frank, Frank, Frank, it isn't about letting *me* down. This is all about the Lord. It's about not letting *Him* down.'

Several people said, 'Amen.'

'Thank you all for putting your trust in me. I'm honored to be the new prelate. Especially now, when our task is so urgent. We're almost there: our teams need to finish preparing. And we need the third lamb to complete the triad. That shouldn't be difficult, by the way. They're all around, and we just need one.'

Just one what?

Somebody called out, 'That's for sure.' Harper heard laughter.

'So my first obligation as prelate is to assure that we move ahead swiftly. Let's finish our work here.'

Voices yelled, 'Amen!' A round of applause and hoots.

'Quiet down,' Travis said. While the others cheered, he sounded grave. 'I appreciate your enthusiasm, but we have more business.' He paused. 'Before we proceed, I must share my concerns about the effectiveness of the Offerings Committee.'

The Offerings Committee? Really?

'Let's review. As Frank said, three lambs were to be sacrificed.' Travis's voice reverberated. 'Three. In specified locations near the Temple, before the ninth of Av. Correct?'

Someone said, 'Correct.'

'So what happened? What was it about those instructions that confused you?'

'We weren't confused,' a new voice answered. 'But the shuk was crowded and it was hard to get around. We got lost.'

Wait. The shuk? In Jerusalem?

'And now we're far away. It takes half the night just to get there—'

'Are you honestly saying that you value a night's sleep more than you value the Lord?'

'Amen,' someone said.

Travis's voice was scalding. 'He has required three small sacrifices of us. His code has spelled out what to do, where and when to do it. And it says what we will receive in return.' His pitch was rising.

'Yes. We've tried to do what He asks. We tried to make the third—'

'Tried? You *tried?*' Travis cried out. He lowered his voice, kept talking.

Harper heard a low rumble of words, couldn't make them out until Travis raised his voice again, blasting like a thunderclap.

'Three! Not two. Not *almost* sacrificed. Not *tried* to sacrifice. Did Abraham say it would be too hard to sacrifice his own son, Isaac? Did Noah say it would be too hard to build the ark? Did Jesus say, sorry, it would be too hard to die on the cross? Their tasks were far more difficult than yours, but they did what He asked because of their faith in Him. And now, the Lord has asked us simply to give him three lambs. If we do this, and only if we do this, His promise will begin.'

More shouts of 'Amen' all around.

'Time is short and failure is not an option. I'm making another personnel change. I was hasty in giving the honor of making the offerings. Obviously, the agent I entrusted wasn't qualified—'

A high-pitched gasp. 'Ramsey? What are you saying?'

'No more interruptions.' His voice was a knife. 'The agent failed to execute the Lord's instructions. I am therefore reassigning the task to another council member: Peter Watts.'

'To Peter?' The question was drowned out by clapping and congratulatory comments.

'Peter, do you accept this task?'

'Well,' Peter stammered. 'Pastor, honestly? It seems kind of . . . Well, never mind. I do. Of course I accept.' He sounded choked up.

'We can rely on you?'

'Yes. Completely.'

'We can stake our souls on your word?'

A slight pause. 'You can. Yes.'

'We have two days, Peter. Our last chance. You realize that?'

'I do.'

'God's will be done.' Travis took a breath. 'Let us remember Peter three, verses one to eighteen: "But the day of the Lord will come like a thief. The heavens will disappear with a roar, the elements will be destroyed by fire, and the earth and everything in it will be laid bare."'

Voices chimed, 'Amen.'

Maybe Travis lowered his voice again. Maybe the room was silent. But Harper couldn't hear anything. She stood there, replaying what she'd just heard, trying to make sense of it.

A promise would be fulfilled only after three lambs were sacrificed. What promise? That the skies would disappear and the earth be laid bare? That promise? The end-of-the-world promise? Harper rubbed her eyes, her mind replaying what Travis had said earlier, that three lambs were to be sacrificed near the Temple; that two lambs had already been offered there.

In the shuk.

Harper saw the body of a slaughtered young man, a crescent carved into his forehead. She recalled the other murder victim: the American tourist. Inspector Alon had said that he'd been marked with a cross. Two murders in the shuk, both with slashed throats, both marked with religious symbols. Both committed in the few days she'd been in Jerusalem – when the church group had also been there. A ripple of alarm ran along Harper's arms, down her back.

'Lambs' didn't really mean *lambs*. It meant living sacrifices. Slaughtered men.

Harper ran a hand through her hair, shook her head. No. Impossible. The church group had extreme beliefs and their pastor was a manipulative adulterer. But adultery and religious fervor were a long way from murder.

Then again, Travis might have killed his own father. Might be unfazed by spilling blood.

Behind the door, chairs scraped the floor. The meeting must be finishing up. Voices joined together, reciting, 'Our Father in heaven, hallowed be Thy name . . .'

Harper scurried away, but not before the door opened and Peter walked out with another man.

Peter looked at her, startled.

Smile, Harper told herself. She forced her lips to curl. 'Hey, Peter.' She tried to sound breezy, as if she'd heard nothing. As if, even at this moment, she didn't hear voices from the next room declaring, 'On earth as it is in heaven.'

Peter's companion eyed her.

'I thought there might be a movie playing tonight . . .'

'Don't know. Why don't you ask him?' Peter nodded toward Schmuel.

'Good idea.' She started toward the desk. But not before Peter checked his watch.

'A little late for a movie, isn't it?'

It was, yes. More than a little. Harper kept walking. 'Is it?'

Stupid response. Peter's friend was openly staring.

Harper stopped. 'So if not a movie, what brought you guys here tonight?' Good. She'd turned it around, acted ignorant.

'Church meeting,' Peter said. 'Meet our new prelate, Frank.'

Harper managed a smile, said it was nice to meet him, returned his direct stare, wished them a good night. And walked directly to the exit.

As the door closed behind her, she looked back through the window. A red-haired woman hurried to exit the meeting room, followed by Travis. Others were straggling out. Frank and Peter stood with their heads together, looking somber, deep in conversation.

The killer lingered in the meeting room, unable to breathe. The air wouldn't come in, got stuck halfway down.

It wasn't fair, wasn't right. The way Travis had spoken to them, his ragged, furious tone. The fire in his eyes, the icy blame he cast in front of the others. The killer's jaw clenched at the injustice, stomach wrenching at the shame.

And Travis's voice echoed, over and over: 'I'm assigning it to another council member: Peter Watts.'

Insult of insults. Travis had done it purposely, had planned it. Had kept it secret as a punishing humiliation.

And he'd refused to listen. Had shown no allegiance, no loyalty. No connection to those who'd already devoted themselves to him and the codes, had already committed murder for him. The killer remembered the first lamb, the shock of blood spurting out, spattering the plastic coat, sounding like rain. The man's eyes wide with surprise, his mouth open and silent. The soul that floated from his body as a gift to the Lord. The assistant, carving the cross into the flesh because the killer hadn't been able to move, had been overcome, sobbing. Trembling with awe.

What was the point of remembering this? Travis didn't appreciate what they'd done. Had shamed when he should have honored them. The killer's stomach cramped, twisting at the wrongness of it, the betrayal. The unbearable injustice.

And what had Travis been thinking? Peter Watts? He wouldn't be able to kill. Wasn't steely or decisive enough. But wait. Maybe there was a way to redemption – the final sacrifice had to be made swiftly – faster than swiftly. And if the killer were to complete it before Peter, Travis would see which of them was truly devoted, reliable, and strong enough to fulfill God's command.

The killer left the office building, walked alone through darkness, mind skittering from thought to thought. Going back to the Old City was preferable but not practical. It took too much time. Plus, when they'd tried it, they'd nearly been caught early in the morning – surely, the Lord wouldn't require that it be done in the Old City, as long as the triad was complete.

The original plan had been to offer them all in the shuk: the Arab in the Jewish section, the Christian in the Arab section, the Jew in the Christian section, connecting the triad of God's children, the circle of faith. It had sounded simple. But the Arab had stampeded into the Christian section, messing up the design. And the Jew had refused to die in any section, had escaped entirely.

Surely, though, God would accept the final sacrifice even if it happened on an uncoded altar. An altered altar. The killer chuckled at the wordplay. And felt better, ready to go on.

Travis had been so quick to judge, to dole out wrath. But, in the end, who was Travis? Wasn't God their only judge? And certainly God was loving, would reward their effort, forgive their mistakes. Wouldn't He?

The killer stopped outside a cottage and gazed up at the sky. Was God watching? Now? At this very moment? Was His grace beaming down like a father's hand through the night sky? The killer waited for a sign, felt a breeze dance by. Was that God's gentle touch? Oh, and a star – the one just beyond that cluster – twinkling brightly. God was sending a message of light, of encouragement. The killer stood, lonely under the heavens, thanking God for love and forgiveness. Weeping openly, letting tears fall to the ground.

Forget Peter Watts. By the ninth of Av, the killer would find the final lamb that would spark the conflagration. Christians would turn against Arabs who would turn against Jews who would turn against Christians. Gog would rise up against Magog, and the Lord's glorious flames would rage across the region and the world.

Harper called Hank, got his voicemail. Voicemail? Why wasn't he picking up? Was he already asleep? She pictured him sleeping. Missed him, the warm smell of his skin. Best not to think about that. Better to decide what to do about doomsday.

Damn. Why hadn't Hank picked up his phone? She needed his advice. Okay, who else could she call? Inspector Alon? Or Dr Hadar? What would she say? That Ramsey Travis had just ordered another sacrifice? That the church council was planning a murder like the two they'd already committed in the shuk? That Peter Watts was supposed to commit it? She pictured Alon's reaction. He would remind her that an arrest had already been made for the murder of the American. And he'd ask for evidence that backed up her claims.

Okay. Evidence. Did she have any? She replayed what she'd heard at the meeting. They'd talked about the shuk, but Travis used words like 'offerings' and 'lambs'. He'd never actually mentioned killing humans. So, even if she'd taped the meeting – which, of course, she hadn't – she wouldn't have proof.

Harper looked out the window at Travis's cottage. Stars lit the path, the bungalows, the sculpted hills beyond. The night was quiet, undisturbed. Harper paced. Checked on Chloe. Opened a kitchen cabinet, not sure what she was looking for, and closed it. Opened the mini fridge. Stared at a bottle of apple juice. Closed it. Finally, she brushed her teeth and got into bed. Tossed and rearranged her pillows. Got up. Thought of trying Hank again. Decided not to; what could Hank do? Nothing. And what would he say? Obviously, he'd say she should pack up and haul her ass back to Jerusalem.

Maybe she should.

Again, she walked to the window. Pastor Travis stood outside his bungalow, talking with a woman. Lynne? Too dark to tell. But Travis was facing Harper's window. Could he see her, watching him? Harper slid sideways, out of sight, and watched the two separate. Travis went inside; the woman walked away. No passionate kisses this time. Maybe she wasn't Lynne . . .

'So where were you?'

Harper wheeled around. Hagit pulled on a robe.

'You're up?' Stupid question.

'What are you doing? Spying on the neighbors? See anything interesting?' Hagit joined her, peered out the window. Seeing no one out there, she eyed Harper. 'What's going on? Tell me.' It was more a command than a request.

Harper thought for a moment, decided that telling Hagit wouldn't hurt. So she did. She told her everything – that Ramsey Travis might be a killer named Travis Ramsey, that he'd already ordered two sacrifices in the shuk that she thought were the murders that had happened there. That he'd ordered a third sacrifice to take place within the next two days, and that Peter Watts had been put in charge of it. Listening to herself, she realized that she sounded kind of crazy. And that, despite her aroused suspicions and strong instincts, she might have misinterpreted everything. Might be completely wrong.

When Harper finished, Hagit didn't comment. She sat quietly. Then, pulling off her robe, she went to her room. 'Get the baby. She'll go with us.'

What? 'Go where?'

But she didn't wait for Hagit to answer. Harper obeyed as she would a superior officer, without delay. Gently, trying not to awaken her, she lifted Chloe and carried her to the porch. She was lowering the stroller's back and arranging Chloe under a blanket when Hagit stepped out, dressed in a T-shirt, khaki pants and sneakers. Did she plan to go hiking?

'We'll find Yoshi or his friend Gal. They'll decide what to do.'

Harper carried the stroller down the porch steps, began pushing it along the path.

'Trouble is,' Hagit went on, 'if your suspicions are right, we have no proof of anything. And we have no idea who they are going to target or where.'

'The authorities can watch Peter Watts, though. They can stop him.'

Hagit grunted, a sound of semi-agreement. And of authority. Where had her attitude come from? Increasingly, Hagit had seemed . . . Harper didn't like the word insubordinate, but that's what it amounted to. Hagit worked for Harper, not the other way around. She was the babysitter, a fiftyish, rather short, plump woman, yet she was talking to Harper as if she outranked her. For now, though, Harper wasn't going to call her on it. In fact, she felt relieved to have someone else take charge.

'We'll go to the office.' Hagit turned. 'They'll call Gal.'

Fine. But then what? Would Gal confront Travis or Peter Watts? Order them to leave? Would he be able to prevent another murder?

Chloe slept soundly as they approached the office building. Inside, Schmuel was still at the front desk, staring at his computer screen. Maybe it was finally online? Hagit held the door while Harper pushed the stroller inside, then spoke to him in Hebrew. Schmuel stood, his face reddening. Was he embarrassed? Alarmed? He mumbled something and reached for a phone. Punched in a number. Handed it to Hagit, who spoke sharply when someone answered. She was still on the phone when the door flew open and Yoshi rushed in, shouting Hebrew words. Stumbling. Falling.

Bleeding.

Even before Schmuel or Hagit could react, Harper went into combat mode, assessing the wild eyes, bloody shirt. The knife clutched in Yoshi's hand. She moved reflexively as trained, jumping to his side, taking away the knife. Ripping away his shirt, finding the deep and gaping gash beneath his arm. Pulling the blanket from Chloe's stroller, bunching it up, pressing it against the wound. Controlling the gush. Trying to ignore the flashback to other wounds – a leg in the street, a boy with no face, buzzing flies . . . No. This was not war, not Iraq. She needed to stay in the present. Focus on this man, this wound. Harper concentrated on Yoshi's eyes, bringing herself back to the moment, all the while pressing on his chest, telling him he'd be all right. Telling herself the same thing.

Hagit and Schmuel crowded around Yoshi, asking questions. Yoshi gave broken, urgent responses, none of which Harper understood. And then others arrived. A medical team, security officers, kibbutz officials. Harper stepped back, letting the medics take over. Gal appeared, and Adi, who knelt beside Yoshi, gripping his hand, touching his face, her chin quivering. Hagit spoke to Gal, who asked Yoshi more questions. Yoshi talked to him, wincing as his wound was cleaned, as something from a vial was injected. As a young woman stitched up the gash.

'They're not taking him to a hospital?' Harper asked Hagit, who shrugged.

'There's no need. The kibbutz is self-sufficient. Besides, the wound isn't so serious.'

Not serious? Harper had seen Yoshi's ribs.

Hagit bent over the stroller, checking on Chloe.

'Hagit. What was he saying? Did he say what happened to him?'

Hagit straightened, looking at her. 'What do you think happened? He was stabbed.' She turned away.

Harper grabbed her arm. 'Hagit. Tell me what he said. Did he see who did it? Was it Peter Watts?'

Hagit lifted her chin, waiting for Harper to let go of her. Then she let out a breath. 'The person wore a ski mask. He couldn't see who it was.'

'But what did he tell you?'

'Nothing. Just that the person was medium sized. Thin and fit. Strong.'

Peter Watts was thin. But he was tall, not of medium height. And kind of saggy, not fit and strong.

Then again, Yoshi might be in shock, might not be remembering accurately.

'Whoever it was, he picked the wrong one with Yoshi. After he was cut, Yoshi took away the attacker's knife and went after him. Almost caught him. Yoshi is a good fighter – he was a sergeant in the army.'

Harper nodded. Saw another sergeant, a checkpoint, an explosion . . .

'Anyway, Yoshi can't identify him.'

Yoshi's eyes looked glazed, probably from a painkiller.

'All he remembers is someone flying at him out of nowhere, feeling the knife plunge into him and thinking it was the end of the world.'

The police were from the Northern district. Mefake'ah Ben Baruch, a beefy inspector with a ruddy face, brought three men with him. While the others talked to Gal, Harper rushed over and asked if he spoke English.

'Of course.' His eyebrows rose. 'Why? What do you have to tell me?'

She took him aside and told him about Peter Watts. That he might be the one who stabbed Yoshi.

'Yes, okay. And who are you?'

Oh. Right. He didn't know her. Harper began to introduce herself, but Hagit interrupted with a rapid stream of Hebrew. Ben Baruch listened, but kept his eyes on Harper. Was Hagit talking about her? What was she saying?

Harper tapped Hagit's arm. 'What are you telling him?'

Hagit ignored her.

'Hagit. Tell him about Ramsey Travis and the church.'

But Gal walked up, interrupting Hagit, apparently annoyed by Harper's intrusion. Pointing at Yoshi and Adi. Gesturing as if to indicate the entire kibbutz. The medical staff gathered around them, and Schmuel. A man ran in wearing only underwear, his wife following with his pants. He seemed puzzled and worried until he saw Yoshi and his bandages; then, he began yelling at Gal and the police – at everyone. Security officers huddled with a bunch of able-bodied men and women near the front desk.

In all the commotion, no one was looking for Peter Watts. In fact, no one seemed to be doing anything. Harper didn't need to understand the language to recognize concern, anger and fear. Someone needed to take control, organize the scene, calm people down. It wasn't Ben

Baruch who did it, though; it was Gal. He stood on a chair, made calming gestures and spoke in a soft, steady voice. Adi remained beside Yoshi; her voice was ragged as she interrupted, shouting something; Gal answered slowly, gently. His voice seemed to lull the group enough that, finally, Ben Baruch took over.

'What's going on?' Harper asked Hagit.

She made her usual shrug. 'Nothing. Just kibbutzniks.'

As if that made sense. 'What about them?' Harper held onto the stroller, rolled it back and forth, amazed that Chloe was sleeping through the noise.

'It's nothing. They assume it's a terrorist.'

That was *nothing*?

'They think it was an infiltration from the border by who knows how many or from which countries. They want all the children taken to the bunkers and everyone to take weapons. And they want the army to send support. That's all.'

Oh.

'But Gal told them it's not an infiltration, at least not by a group. It's just one person.'

Finally, everyone was quiet enough for the police to question witnesses. 'Hagit. Why don't they talk to Peter Watts?' Harper urged.

Hagit put a hand up. 'Never mind.'

What? 'It's important . . .'

'They already did it.'

Really? So fast? 'And?'

'And he has an alibi. He was with others from the church. What's it called, a prelate? He was there. And Mrs Watts says both men were with her in the bungalow at the time of the attack.'

Well, of course she did. What else would Lynne say? That Peter had gone out and she had no idea where? Or that he'd been trying to slaughter someone so their pastor could bring on the end of the world?

'So they're just leaving it at that? He says he didn't do it, so he must not have?' Harper looked across the crowd at Ben Baruch. Was he so easily manipulated?

'They have no evidence that the man did anything—'

'But Hagit. Don't you see? They believe that they need to kill a third person. They've already killed a Christian and a Muslim in the shuk. But they still need to kill a Jew—'

'So you said. Why again?' Hagit crossed her arms, one eyebrow raised.

'Travis called it "God's triad". A circle connecting all of God's children – something like that. But now that Yoshi escaped, there's a problem—'

'A problem? How, if he escaped?'

Why didn't Hagit get it? 'The problem is that Yoshi didn't die.' Harper paused, waiting for her words to sink in. 'They still need their third offering, Hagit. They have to kill someone else.'

For a nanosecond, Hagit's eyes flamed. Then she put her round hand onto the handle of the stroller, covering Harper's. 'Let it be, Harper. You're here as a tourist.' She nodded at the police. 'This isn't their first ride on the train. Let them do their jobs.'

Harper sputtered. Let it be? She asked Hagit how she was supposed to do that when nobody seemed to comprehend the imminence of the threat. She wanted to do some investigating. Stop by Peter and Lynne's bungalow. Drop in on Pastor Travis. Call Dr Hadar and Dr Ben Haim and ask them to arrange a meeting of everyone working on the dig.

Hagit would let her do none of these things. 'Listen to me, Harper. I can't let you start trouble.'

What? 'You're here to babysit, Hagit. You're not in charge of my decisions.'

Hagit lowered her voice. 'Okay. I'll tell you. It isn't just Chloe I'm here to watch.' She headed out of the building.

'Wait. What did you just say?' Harper chased after her, pushing the stroller.

Hagit said nothing, kept walking. Out the front door, onto the path.

'Look, Hagit.' Harper caught up with her. 'We can't just let this go. Someone from that church group is going to try again to kill somebody – and soon.'

'This is not your country, Harper.' Hagit's tone was curt. Like a warning. 'Leave it alone.' She turned and went back into the bungalow.

Harper felt like a prisoner. And Hagit seemed to be her guard, always just a step away. Shadowing her as she put Chloe back in her crib. Waiting for her to go to bed, refusing to sleep until Harper did.

'Why don't you turn in?' Harper finally asked. 'The baby will be up in a few hours. You'll be tired.'

'So? I'll be tired. There are worse things.'

'It feels like you're stalking me.'

'Because I am.'

'Well, stop. It's annoying.'

'You should thank me instead of being annoyed.' Hagit sat on the sofa, letting out a sigh.

'Hagit. Please. Go to bed. I can take care of myself.'

'Maybe you can. But maybe that's not why I'm watching you. Maybe I'm making sure you stay out of trouble.'

Really? 'There's plenty of trouble around here, but it's not because of me—'

'Tell me the truth. If I go to bed, tell me you won't go out and start playing detective? You won't go bother the people in the next bungalow? The pastor? His followers? Tell me.'

Harper didn't answer. Did want to lie. Was aching to talk to Peter Watts.

'See? That's why I'm watching you. So you might as well give up and sleep. In five hours, you have to go to the dig.'

The dig. She hadn't even thought about it.

'Here. I'll make us some tea, and then we'll sleep.' Hagit stood and went to the stove, took out tea bags. 'You should be glad I'm here, Harper. At least I'm on your side, not like the other one watching you.'

The other one?

'I told you it would follow, and look. It has.' Hagit pour water into the pot, dried her hands. 'You shake your head, but I tell you again. Kenahara, never underestimate the power of the Evil Eye.'

Hagit was pouring tea when they heard voices next door. Harper turned out the lights and went to the window.

'What are you doing? I'll scald myself in the dark!' Hagit cried.

'Shh. Come look.' Harper looked out. Inspector Ben Baruch and his officers were standing on Travis's front porch. Travis's booming voice invited them inside.

'What are you looking at?' Hagit taunted. 'It's nothing. The police are just following up.'

'Maybe they'll find something.'

Hagit brought her a mug of tea. 'They won't find anything. Sit. Drink.'

Harper took a sip of fragrant, honeyed tea, thanked Hagit. Stayed riveted at the window until, some twenty minutes later, the police left.

When she finally went to bed, she kept replaying moments, reruns of the night. Lowell bursting out of the council meeting, having been expelled. Travis naming Peter Watts head of an Offerings Committee. Yoshi stumbling into the office building, collapsing from a knife wound. Ben Baruch not listening to her warning. It seemed that she had just dozed off when Chloe began jabbering in the crib. Chirping happily, repeating syllables, listing names. 'Eemah, Adi. Geet. Mama. Dada.'

Speaking of Dada, Harper still wanted to talk to him. She sat up, reached for her cell phone to check the time. Just after six. Hank should be up, or just getting up.

He answered on the first ring. Wide awake. Alert, as if expecting the call.

'Hoppa?' He sounded surprised. Who else would call at six a.m.?

'Everything all right?'

'Sure. Yes. What's up?'

Harper hesitated. Hank was edgy, talking too fast. 'Are you in a hurry?'

'Not hurry. Just . . . Yes. Can't talk now.'

Harper ran a hand through her hair. Why couldn't he talk? And if he couldn't now, when could he?

It must be the symposium. 'You're okay?'

'Fine,' Hank snapped. 'Hoppa, what?'

Chloe held up her stuffed monkey, squealing, 'Mama, Dada. Adi, Geet.'

'Why can't you talk?'

'Hoppa. Just . . . something came up. Tell me. Why. Calling?'

Damn. She needed to talk to him, but not in a rush. What was so important that he couldn't take a few minutes at six effing o'clock in the morning for a phone call? 'Things are happening here.' How could she explain quickly? 'Bottom line: I think you were right. I should bring Chloe back to Jerusalem—'

'No. Don't.'

What?

'Not right now.'

'Hank. Excuse me for being confused, but yesterday, you said we should come back.'

'Changed. Mind.'

'Listen. Ramsey Travis – or Travis Ramsey – his church is planning to kill somebody. They've already stabbed someone, and—'

'Hoppa.' Hank took a breath. 'How do. You. Know this?'

'How do I know? I heard them planning it.'

A voice in the crib sang, 'Ma yim, ma yim. Mitz. Mitz. Mitz.'

Hank paused. 'You heard them? How?'

'How is not the point. I'm telling you there's a murderer here—'

'Calm down.'

Really? 'No. I will not calm down.' In fact, she got out of bed, started pacing.

'Eema. Geet. Adi. Mama.'

'What's the story, Hank? First, you want us to come back, and now, when I say I'm coming, you want us to stay? What the hell?'

'Dada. Eemah.'

'Sorry.' He sighed. Then his tone changed. Became soothing. 'Tell me what. Happened.'

Harper's nostrils flared. She steadied her voice so she'd sound less emotional. 'Here's the situation. The church council met last night and planned a sacrifice. Right after that, Yoshi – a man who lives here – was stabbed—'

'Police there?'

What? 'Yes. Of course.'

'Then they'll solve. You'll be. Safe.'

Really? 'Hank. I'm not worried about that. I can keep myself and Chloe safe. I just don't think it's a good idea to stay under these circumstances. Believe me. Travis is planning something, and I don't want to be around when it comes down.'

'Eemah. EEMAH.' Chloe was getting impatient, her singsong becoming a complaint. Harper went to the crib; Chloe scrambled to her feet, reached for her.

'But dig. What about?'

Oh, the dig. The wall they'd unearthed. The excitement – the hunger to discover more. She lifted Chloe, grabbed a fresh diaper, carried her to the bed. 'The dig will survive without me.' She unfastened Chloe's onesy.

'But. Just found ruins. Can't leave now.'

What was going on?

'I think you. Should stay longer. Good for you, your career.'

'My career? What part of "there's a killer here" don't you understand?'

'Police will find. Don't lose this oppor. Tunity. Can't run away.'

Harper was speechless. Run away? Harper never ran away from anything. In fact, she'd been accused of seeking out danger and trouble, never backing down. She simmered silently as she changed Chloe's diaper, dressed her in a monkey T-shirt and pair of shorts.

Chloe chanted, 'Eemah! Geet! Eemah! Geet!'

'Not talking to me?'

She said nothing.

'Hoppa, give dig another. Couple days. Then, if you still want. Come back.' Voices shouted in the background. Not in English. 'Sorry, must go. I love you.'

After the call, Harper brushed Chloe's six teeth, combed out her curls, kissed her tummy. She followed their routine, but she couldn't shake her feeling that something was wrong with Hank. Why had he been in such a rush at six a.m.? What could be going on so early? Why had he sounded so edgy?

Harper pictured him in the hotel suite. Wearing a towel, fresh from the shower. And a woman – a naked woman, rubbing his back while he was on the phone. Her chest tightened. Could that be it?

No, of course not. She shoved the woman out of the hotel room. Slammed the door.

But why had Hank been so abrupt? Why had he changed his mind about her leaving Megiddo?

Chloe beamed as Harper finally set her down to let her run around. 'Geet?' she asked.

Good question. Where was Hagit? Harper looked out of the bedroom.

Hagit was on the phone at the breakfast table, brows furrowed, talking in a low voice.

'Geet!' Chloe shrieked and ran to her.

Hagit ended the call too quickly, smiling too broadly and trying too hard to act normal, as if she'd been caught doing something wrong.

The kibbutz was on alert. Two security guards stopped at the bungalow, part of a door-to-door check, making sure everyone was all right, asking if anything unusual had happened during the night, looking around for hidden weapons or culprits. Men and women carrying firearms patrolled the streets and pathways. Gal and another man stopped and questioned everyone as they entered the restaurant building.

Harper watched it all through a haze of sleeplessness. At breakfast, she asked Hagit, 'Is this normal?' She cut up an egg and some fruit for Chloe.

'Of course it's not normal. It's a reaction. Remember, they think it was a terrorist.' Hagit swallowed coffee. 'They will take precautions.'

'And if they don't find the guy?'

'They will. And if they don't, they'll keep looking until they do.'

'I was thinking we should take Chloe back to Jerusalem—'

'No.'

No? 'Excuse me?' Hagit had reacted just like Hank. Definitively telling Harper not to leave. Why? And beyond that, Hagit was the babysitter. How did she feel entitled to tell Harper what to do?

'I think you should stay.' Hagit looked away, gave a chunk of sweet roll to Chloe. 'What do you say, Chloe? To—'

'Dah!' Chloe grabbed the roll, squishing it.

Hagit wiped Chloe's mouth.

'But why?' Harper pressed. 'Why should we stay?'

Hagit made her customary shrug. 'Why should we? Why shouldn't we? There's no reason to leave. You still have the dig. It's why you came. The authorities here have matters under control. So, why rush off?'

'Hank said I should wait a day or two.'

'He's smart, your husband.'

What was going on? Why was Hagit so determined to stay? Unless . . . Wait . . . Had Hagit talked to Hank? Were they conspiring to keep her there? It seemed that way.

But why would they do that? Unless . . . Were they hiding something?

No, ridiculous. She was imagining things. Needed sleep.

Across the restaurant, church members began to arrive. Lowell was first to the buffet. He looked pasty and haggard. Frank was next, all hale and energetic, greeting Lowell with a smile and a back slap as if he hadn't just replaced him as church prelate.

Pastor Travis and his roommate, Harold, joined them with broad smiles and loud cheery comments about the beauty of the morning and the grace of the Lord. A few women whom Harper hadn't met got in line, a few men. A sultry redhead. And Peter and Lynne.

'You're staring,' Hagit chided.

Harper turned to her. 'What of it?'

'You won't find anything out that way. It's not what you can see that you need to watch. It's what you can't see.'

Did that make sense? Harper's gaze returned to Lynne and Peter. Did Peter have any wounds or bruises? Did he look as if he'd been in a fight? She couldn't tell. But he seemed bedraggled, as if he, too, had been awake all night.

Lynne must have sensed her gaze. A plateful of food in one hand, coffee cup in another, she turned, saw Harper across the room. 'Morning,' she grinned as if nothing were wrong.

'Geet. Down?' Chloe was finished eating.

Harper took a last gulp of coffee as Hagit cleaned Chloe's hands and face and lifted her into the stroller, ready to go to the nursery.

On the way, they passed scampering dogs. Wandering cats. A boy kicking a soccer ball. And three pairs of guards, youthful and alert, carrying rifles.

Dr Ben Haim condensed the work area. Harper and Lynne joined others digging close to the find. He believed the wall would have structural counterparts close by. The sun glared even early in the morning; Harper's overtired head throbbed from the brightness. She put on her sunglasses, and the world took on a golden tint. Even Lynne looked a little bit orange as Harper studied her for signs of stress or concern.

But Lynne showed signs of neither. She was her talkative self, cheerily chatting about how accustomed she'd become to eating salad with every meal, even breakfast.

Lynne's cheeriness irritated Harper. Didn't Lynne care that her husband had been questioned by police? Wasn't she even a little concerned about the stabbing? Maybe she was overcompensating, pretending, but even so, Harper couldn't stand the lilt of Lynne's voice and called her away. 'Come help me get more buckets.'

Lynne glanced at the stack of buckets near the perimeter. 'I think there are plenty.'

Harper tilted her head, stared at her until Lynne understood.

'Oh. Yes. More buckets.' She made her way around the other volunteers and joined Harper. 'What's up?'

Harper didn't answer right away. She walked toward the supply trailer, waiting until they were a distance from the pit.

'Are you okay, Harper?'

Was she? 'I'm fine.'

'Then why did you . . .?'

'Lynne, did the police come to your bungalow last night?'

'Oh, that?' Lynne seemed unconcerned. 'Yeah, they sure did. They kept us up half the night.'

'Aren't you worried?'

Lynne frowned, confused. 'Should I be?'

Harper stopped walking. 'Lynne. A man was stabbed last night. The police thought Peter might have done it . . .'

'I know. Isn't that crazy?' Lynne's eyes widened. She smirked, shaking her head. 'Peter? Stabbing someone? Peter couldn't stab a watermelon. He faints when he gets a blood test—'

'But the police must have had reason to talk to him.' She didn't mention that she'd given them the reason.

Lynne looked around, lowered her voice. 'Look. Apparently, somebody told the cops to look at Peter because Pastor Travis had asked Peter to make a sacrifice for the church.' She emphasized 'somebody' as if she knew it was Harper. Did she?

'And?' Harper kept her face blank, gave away nothing. 'Is that true? I mean about the sacrifice?'

'Yes, it's true. Pastor asked Peter to make an offering, and Peter was honored to accept the responsibility.'

'What kind of offering?'

Lynne rolled her eyes. 'Do we really have to go into all this?'

'I'm trying to understand . . .'

'Look. I told you about the Bible code. Pastor says the code tells us to make three sacrifices by the ninth of Av. He put a couple of people in charge of them, and they did two of them, but there were complications. Nobody's fault, but still. Anyway, last night, pastor assigned the last sacrifice to somebody else. And that was Peter.'

'What kind of sacrifices?'

'What? Oh, just the usual. Throwing a couple of virgins into boiling oil.' Lynne smiled.

Harper didn't.

'Come on. Why are you so serious?'

Harper watched her for a moment, deciding how much to tell her.

'Harper? You're looking pretty scary.'

'It's time we talk.' Harper found two buckets, turned them over. Sat on one, motioned for Lynne to sit on the other.

Lynne seemed baffled, a little alarmed. 'What's going on?'

Harper leaned forward, looked Lynne in the eye. 'Your pastor?'

She didn't know exactly how to put it. 'He might not be who he says he is. I think he's got a criminal past.'

'No way.' Lynne started to stand, but Harper put a hand on her arm.

'Hear me out. I think his real name isn't Ramsey Travis; I think it's Travis Ramsey. Travis Ramsey is an ex-con who murdered his own father.'

Lynne shook her head.

'And that's not all, Lynne. I think he's planning to kill again. In fact, I think he's planning to kill you.'

'Me?' Lynne gasped.

'Not just you. All of you. Your whole church group.'

Lynne crossed her arms and stood. 'Harper. I don't know where you're getting this. But you are way out there. I mean, way, way—'

'I hope you're right.' Harper looked up at her. 'But honestly, I don't think so. Look, Lynne. Travis has been telling you that the ninth of Av will start the battle, bring on the Rapture or whatever—'

'He only tells us what God has written.'

Harper stood and faced her. 'Lynne, Travis isn't the first preacher to lead his followers to destruction. Don't you see? What's he going to do when his big battle doesn't start?'

'But it will.'

'Haven't you ever heard of Jim Jones? The guy who poisoned all his followers with Kool-Aid? Or the Heaven's Gate sect? Their leader was a guy named Applewhite, and Applewhite convinced his followers to kill themselves in order to achieve salvation—'

'Harper, stop.' Lynne put her hands up. 'That's got nothing to do with us. You probably mean well, but you're completely off base. Ramsey Travis isn't like that. Believe me, I know him.'

Harper pictured the couple groping on the porch.

'He would never hurt me or any of us. He loves us.' Lynne smiled warmly. 'I get it, Harper. Your issues with Travis. Your suspicions. They all come back to the same thing. Faith. You don't believe.'

Harper opened her mouth to answer, but Lynne stopped her.

'No. I understand. I told you, at first, I didn't believe either. I had to be shown. Travis had to translate codes written three thousand years ago, codes that specifically identify events that have taken place now, in our lifetimes. I've told you about some. But there are many others, with dates, places – I began to understand that the codes are accurate. They're for real. And guess what? World War Three is in there, too. It begins here, in Megiddo, on the ninth of Av.' In the bright sun, Lynne's blonde hair glowed, looked like a halo.

Harper didn't know what to say. Lynne had just said that a world-wide disaster was coming in a couple of days, and she seemed pleased by it.

'Harper, I never knew anything before I met Ramsey Travis. I was all caught up in petty stuff. Problems with Peter. Problems with getting pregnant. Problems with money or gossip or jealousy or ego. Pastor showed me to see beyond all that. He read me God's word. And he taught me real love.'

Real love? Again, Harper saw Travis and Lynne on the porch. Obviously, Lynne was infatuated, brainwashed. Still, Harper had to try.

'Lynne. Please. Try to think objectively—'

'Harper. Don't criticize. You just don't get it.'

Harper had encountered true believers before. People completely committed, blindly devoted to a cause or a leader, even willing to kill or die for them. An Iraqi woman popped to mind, smiling at her before detonating the bomb inside her robe. Harper saw a flash of white, felt the blast, but made a fist, digging her fingernails into her palm, refusing the flashback.

'Please, Lynne. You're an intelligent person. Can't you see that you're being manipulated?'

Again, Lynne smiled. 'Peter, chapter three, verses one to eighteen, warns that in the last days, "scoffers will come". You're a scoffer, Harper. But the ninth of Av is just a couple of days away. You'll see . . .'

'What will I see? The Apocalypse? The end of the world? Because, really, if you're so sure it's coming, why are you here at the dig? Why bother? Why not eat gobs of fattening food, get drunk, have sex and party for a couple of days?'

Lynne reached out, put her hand on Harper's. Her voice was slow and patient, as if talking to a child. 'I've been chosen, Harper. I'm one of the few who's been blessed enough to do God's work until the final day.'

Harper sat watching as Lynne stood. Saying nothing as she began to walk away. How had Lynne fallen under Travis's control? Was it just sex? Had he drugged or hypnotized her? And what about the others? Peter, for example. Did he know about his wife's affair? Did he care? Had Travis hypnotized all of them?

Lynne stopped walking and wheeled around, beaming. 'Harper, I have an idea. I know you don't understand, but I can see that you're trying. It's not too late.'

What?

Lynne ran back to her, grabbed her hands. 'You can still find out the truth. Will you? Meet with Pastor Travis. Listen to him read the Bible and translate the code. There's still time. Once you understand, you can join us. You and your baby – you can both be saved.'

Harper saw the light in Lynne's eyes, her sincerity. Her pure, unbreakable belief. What would happen to her when the ninth of Av came and went without incident?

Harper thought for only a moment. 'Okay.'

'Okay? Really? You'll do it?' Lynne jumped up, grinning, laughing. Clapping her hands like a cheerleader. Talking about setting up a meeting with Ramsey Travis.

On the way back to the dig, Harper felt like an undercover investigator. Lynne had given her a chance to infiltrate the church, find out more about their sacrifices. She'd have to move quickly, though. She had just two days to meet with Ramsey Travis, to find out what he envisioned for the ninth of Av.

And, somehow, before he could do any harm, to stop it.

A section of wall about six meters long and a meter deep had been cleared. Harper sifted excavated dirt, thinking about Travis, not paying much attention to the chatter of the volunteers. Gradually, though, she realized that they were talking about Yoshi, the stabbing at the kibbutz.

'I think it was personal,' a church member commented. 'Somebody with a grudge against him.'

'Maybe he was messing around,' the redhead said. 'You know, doing the wrong man's wife—'

'Come on, Marlene. Why do you assume it was a jealous husband?' This came from Peter. 'It could have been a woman. Maybe he dumped her and she got mad.'

Someone said she'd heard the attacker might be a terrorist. Someone else said that, no, they'd overheard a policeman say it was someone on the kibbutz.

None of them mentioned sacrifice or Bible codes.

Harper didn't enter the conversation. She sifted dirt, recalled Yoshi running into the office, the gushing of his wound, the smell of blood. But then the blood wasn't Yoshi's any more; it was a soldier's. A mere boy with gray eyes and a missing right arm. She pressed and pressed, climbed onto his shoulder to use her body weight, but the blood kept coming, a torrent from too many wounds that she didn't have enough hands for and she told him to be calm, that he'd make it and yelled, 'Medic,' but his eyes glazed and he was gone.

Harper blinked, looked around. Saw no blood on her clothing or her hands. No dead boy. No war. She took a deep breath. She was at the dig, not in Iraq. And she was strangling her straining tray. Collecting herself, she casually took stock of the people nearby. Lowell and Peter worked near her and Lynne. Frank, Harold, Travis and the redheaded Marlene were working with the students, digging out the wall. Dr Hadar was supervising them. No one was staring at her. Thank God. Apparently, she hadn't acted out the flashback. She tightened her jaw, relieved, and focused on the dirt. A stubborn clod in the middle of the screen wouldn't break down.

Harper pressed on it gently with her glove, felt a crusty layer crumble and give way. But the clump underneath resisted. It was firm, three or four centimeters in diameter. Maybe a stone? Or a shard of Roman glass? She got a brush out of her kit, gently scraped away dust. Held the lump in her glove. Rolled it. Brushed it again, felt dirt give way in the middle. Odd. She worked her finger gently around the center, and more bits fell away. Then more, until the core was hollow.

Hollow?

Harper's mouth was dry. Her breath quick. This wasn't, couldn't be a rock. Probably wasn't glass, either. She should bring it to Dr Hadar. But she didn't, not yet. She took a tiny pick from her kit. Poked the thing gently, afraid to think that it could be anything significant. Unable to consider that it wasn't. And finally, when the dirt was off, before she shared it with anyone, she examined it from all angles, turning it, marveling at its greenish pocked texture, its underlying metallic sheen, blunt squared top, simple structure. She guessed it was Roman. Maybe a soldier's? She pictured it on his finger as he marched through ancient Megiddo. Didn't hear Lynne talking to her.

'. . . what are you doing? What have you got?'

And was a little annoyed when, before she was ready and without her permission, Lynne started shouting, telling everyone to come look: Harper had found a ring.

It was a small find, but Dr Hadar reveled in it. He agreed that the ring had probably belonged to a regular soldier in the Roman army, circa AD 300. Not an uncommon relic. But, since it was nearly time to wrap up for the day, he celebrated the progress on the wall and the new find by bringing out sparkling wine and paper cups. Something was said in Hebrew, probably a blessing, and everyone toasted the ring, the wall, the volunteer team, and their work at the site.

Harper smiled and quietly sipped her wine, but inside, she was somersaulting on top of the supply trailer. Doing the chachacha around the perimeter of the dig. She was sizzling, too hot to touch, an actual archeologist. She'd moved from books, papers, assistant-ships and internships and finally made her own find – her first ever. She wanted to giggle. She wanted to call Hank. She'd unearthed the ring of a Roman soldier, and she felt personally connected to him, as if she'd rescued a remnant of his life, restoring it to light and air and the world of the living.

Harper was energized. She took a seat by herself on the bus, and during the drive back to the kibbutz, kept reliving the process of uncovering the ring. The gradual revealing of texture and shape. She wondered if it had been by itself. Maybe it hadn't been – maybe it was just the first part of a bigger find. A trove of jewelry, maybe. Or military artifacts. Lord. Was it possible that the site would turn into a major excavation? She rested her head back, closed her eyes, spent the ride savoring her excitement. This was why she'd come. This was what she'd been hoping to experience.

Her mood stayed with her for the entire ride. It probably would have lasted longer, but as they pulled into the parking area, she spotted Inspector Ben Baruch. He was waiting to greet the bus, wearing a dark frown.

The killer watched Travis, waiting to catch him alone. Surely, if he heard a rational argument, he would reconsider. Would see that Peter was a dismal choice and reverse his decision.

'Ramsey,' the killer whispered. 'Got a minute?'

Travis looked toward the voice, tilted his head. Peered through the bushes. 'What are you doing in there?'

Was he serious? They needed to talk privately. The bunker entrance was perfect. 'Come here. I need to talk where no one can hear us.'

'Why?' Travis looked around to see if anyone was watching, finally ducked through the bushes to the camouflaged doorway. 'Look, if this is about the other night – my decision is final.'

'Ramsey, please. Just hear what I have to say. I've been completely devoted, done everything you've asked. Including the first two offerings—'

'I wouldn't brag about those. They were an abomination.'

The killer grimaced. Took a breath. 'I explained what happened. None of that was my fault—'

'Oh, cut the crap.' Travis put a hand up for silence. Lowered his voice. 'Tell me, was that you, last night? The stabbing? It was, wasn't it?'

The killer fidgeted. Damn. The conversation wasn't going as planned. 'I thought I could complete—'

'You thought? Who told you to think? I specifically took the assignment away from you.' Spit flew out of his mouth. 'Do you have a clue what you've done? You've brought the Israeli police – their Internal Security ministry down on us. Inspector Ben Baruch is on my back, watching my every move, tailing me like I'm a criminal. He stopped me when I got off the bus. Wants to talk to me after lunch. Do you think I need that? Now?'

The killer looked at the bunker door, took a deep breath. Ramsey wasn't being fair. It had been unfortunate that the third offering had gotten away. But if he hadn't – if the sacrifice had been completed – Ramsey would have been jubilant. The police presence would have been irrelevant. 'At least I tried. I have the stomach and the determination. Peter's done nothing. Come on, Ramsey. I'm asking you for one more chance.'

The muscles of Ramsey's jaw rippled. 'Don't beg.'

'But why Peter? What makes you think—?'

'I honored him as a reward for his loyalty and faithfulness—'

'Bullshit. I've been loyal and faithful, too.'

Travis took in air and faced the killer, his voice low and ominous. 'How dare you question me? Your weakness of will and poverty of judgment have repeatedly imperiled our purpose . . .'

What? 'No—'

'Your failures have disappointed – no, they've repulsed me and I daresay the Lord Himself.' His words rumbled from his chest. 'If I were you, instead of groveling for yet another chance to fail and destroying whatever final modicum of dignity and hope for salvation I had left, I'd use my last days to seclude myself, fast and pray for mercy.' His gaze froze the killer for a moment, and then he simply turned and walked away.

'Ramsey, no, wait.' The killer reeled, stricken, finally recovered enough to speak, but too late, in too small a voice.

Mefake'ah Ben Baruch approached Pastor Travis as he exited the bus, spoke for a moment. Harper messed with her supply kit, pretending to be looking for something. When Travis walked off, Harper waited at the edge of the parking area to see if anyone else had lingered. But people had trailed off, going home to shower before lunch. Ben Baruch stood alone, watching her dawdle near a cluster of pine trees. He didn't speak. Didn't move.

When she thought the others were gone, Harper picked up her kit and walked over to him.

He greeted her by name, asked how she was.

She couldn't help it, and told him about the ring she'd found.

He congratulated her, said something about the present day being just another layer, built on top of those who'd lived before. His eyes never left hers. They probed, not unkindly, but precisely and firmly. Never smiled, even when his mouth did.

'Why don't you tell me what's on your mind?' he said.

Harper stood tall. 'It's the church group, sir. I'm convinced that they're behind Yoshi's stabbing.'

He waited for a noisy jeep to drive by. Then he said, 'And you think this because . . .'

'Travis has them believing that the Apocalypse will begin on the ninth of Av.'

'And?' He sounded unsurprised.

'And they believe that they have to make three sacrifices before then. Apparently, Travis says there's a code in the Bible that orders them to kill three lambs, but I don't believe they are actually killing lambs – I think they are sacrificing innocent people, starting with those two murdered men in the shuk in Jerusalem.' She was talking too fast, made herself pause. Wondered if he believed her.

'You've shared your concerns before, Mrs Jennings.'

'And did you follow up? Because, sir, believe me, these people are planning a third sacrifice. Yoshi didn't die. So they still need a third victim. And they need it quickly; the ninth of Av is the day after tomorrow.'

Ben Baruch took a breath. Crossed his arms.

'Mrs Jennings, I hear that you've been playing detective.'

What? Who'd told him that? 'I'm not sure what you mean.'

'I believe you know exactly what I mean.' He eyed her.

Obviously, he knew something. Maybe from Hagit? Well, she had no reason to deny it – or to apologize. 'Well, do you expect me to sit by and watch while people get killed?'

'Not at all. You need to help us. First, by telling us what you know. Then by letting us do our jobs.' He put a hand on her shoulder. 'You mean well, but you need to keep away from the investigation.'

'But what's Travis going to do when the Apocalypse doesn't come? What if he's planning to hurt his followers?'

'Trust me.' His hand tightened its grip. A warning? 'This is not the first lunatic to bring his followers to Israel. We know how to—'

'But did you know that Ramsey Travis might be a murderer named Travis Ramsey? Might have killed his own father?' Harper interrupted.

Ben Baruch removed his hand and moved closer so that his face was right above Harper's, looking down. His breath annoyed her cheeks. 'What I'm telling you is for your own sake, Mrs Jennings. Stay away from it. Understand me?'

Harper returned his gaze, didn't blink. 'I do.'

He moved away. 'Be assured, I will meet with Pastor Travis in a few minutes. Also, Peter Watts and other key members of the group are being watched. Nobody is going to have a chance to kill anyone.'

Harper nodded, a little relieved. At least the police were aware of the danger.

'But remember this: so far, there is not a shred of evidence to link any of these people to the killings in the shuk—'

'What about the symbols carved into the bodies? They represent two religions. And Yoshi – his religion would have been the third . . .'

She stopped because his eyes narrowed. 'How do you know about any carvings?'

She explained that she'd seen one of the bodies; that Inspector Alon in Jerusalem had told her about the other.

Baruch raised a disapproving eyebrow. 'As I said. We have nothing to dispute the church's claim that their sacrifices are merely symbolic acts involving spilt wine.'

What? 'Then who stabbed Yoshi?'

Ben Baruch looked over her head toward the kibbutz buildings. 'Go have your lunch.' His tone was abrupt. 'Leave police work to the police.' He started to walk away.

Harper went after him, opened her mouth to say more, but stopped when she saw the set of his jaw. She knew that look, had seen it in the military on superior officers. It meant 'Dismissed.'

There was no point in saying anything else; Ben Baruch wasn't listening.

Police were all over the place. Some were easier to spot than others, but the killer knew they were there. Could feel their eyes. They were in the restaurant building, trying to look casual, blending into the buffet line. But they had weapons. Didn't they realize that everyone could see their weapons? Not that regular kibbutzniks didn't carry them – even the older kids carried rifles or pistols now that the place was on high alert.

Police kept close to Travis, who didn't seem to notice. Didn't feel the glide of stealthy gazes. The brush of casual glances from all angles, at all times. They were on Frank, too, probably because of his prelate status. One was sitting with Lowell because he might bear a grudge. Another with Peter because he was the new golden boy. They knew who was who in the church leadership.

Of which the killer had been a part until recently.

Did they know that? Were they watching? The killer moved to the corner of the dining room. Checked to see if anyone's gaze moved there, too. Waited to feel a tingle of suspicion.

Felt nothing. Well, except fury. Ramsey's words reverberated like heavy bronze gongs: 'If I were you, I'd fast and pray for mercy.' Really? The killer seethed, had no more reason to atone than anyone else at the table. Actually had less. Ramsey had made a mistake, a big one. Would soon understand how big. The killer picked up a plate, piled on brisket, potatoes, green beans, cucumber and tomato salad, beets, corn, hummus, pita bread – as much food as the plate could hold and then stacked some more on top, and took a seat directly across from Ramsey, chewing big fat forkfuls. Letting

Ramsey see how little effect his words had had. How confident and resilient the killer could be.

Ramsey, of course, pretended to pay no attention. He avoided eye contact; spoke to the council as if the killer were not present. As if police were not surrounding them. Ramsey chatted as if he had no cares. He ate as if he had no reason to hurry.

But he had just thirty-six hours. That was all.

By contrast, Peter looked terrified. His skin was sickly yellow, and he picked at his food, chewed a mouthful of brisket forty or more times before forcing it down. The others questioned him. 'So, got plans for later, Peter?'

'Made a choice yet?'

Peter hunkered down. 'It's under control.' His fork trembled in his hand.

'We're all counting on you, Watts,' Ramsey beamed. 'I have complete faith in you.'

'I won't let you down.' Peter bounced his knee; his thigh accidentally brushed the killer's.

'Peter, if you need help, let me know.' The words flew out of the killer's mouth on their own, unintended.

For a moment, everyone froze. Then they went back to eating as if the killer hadn't spoken.

Cowards. Weaklings. The killer had completed two sacrifices and attempted a third. What had they done – any of them? Other than the assistant, none of them had contributed a single breath of effort to follow the instructions in the code. Yet they would judge someone who had? They were hypocrites, kissing up to Ramsey. The killer ate in a frenzy of rage, stuffed down wads of food, not caring what kind, barely bothering to chew. Glaring at Travis.

Francine, a bovine churchwoman, came over with a tray. She'd never been on the council. What made her think she could join their table?

The tray was laden with desserts. 'I thought you'd enjoy these.' Her grin was devilish. 'After all, after the ninth, we won't have to worry about our waistlines anymore, will we, Pastor?'

'Gluttony is a sin, Francine,' he frowned.

Francine's hand went to her mouth. 'Oh, I didn't mean—'

'Then again,' Travis grinned, 'I guess the Lord won't mind if we make an exception to celebrate His word.' He reached for a strawberry tart. 'Let Peter choose next.'

Peter froze, staring at the tray as if it held writhing snakes.

'Thank you, Francine, dear,' Travis went on. 'That was very thoughtful.' He reached out and patted her plump hand.

The killer swallowed a forkful of green beans, watching the red splotches emerging on Francine's fat neck, the heat radiating from her bosom in reaction to Travis's touch. And thinking that Peter, the sorry wimp, might very well lose his lunch.

Chloe tottered along the path ahead of Harper. Ahead of them, Travis and his entourage approached his bungalow. The pastor was deep in conversation, but saw Chloe take a tumble and rushed over to help her up.

'It's okay,' Harper told him, hurrying over, grabbing Chloe's hand. 'She falls every three or four steps.'

Travis looked at Harper, didn't smile. 'You're the lady who found the ring. Very exciting.'

She nodded. 'I'm Harper Jennings. We're in the bungalow next door.'

His chin and eyebrows rose. 'Ramsey Travis. Delighted.' He nodded goodbye. Joined his companions and led them into his bungalow.

Harper followed, noticed that his windows were open. Maybe she could hear what they were saying.

Except that Chloe was with her. And Chloe wouldn't stand patiently under a window and let Harper eavesdrop.

Unless she was busy. Harper reached into her bag for something to amuse Chloe. Dug through diapers, packets of wipes, bottles and sippy cups, and finally found a small cardboard picture book.

'Chloe.' She sat on the grass beside Travis's bungalow, under an open window. 'Let's read.' Her voice was a whisper.

Chloe climbed onto Harper's lap, ready for a story.

Harper heard Travis. 'We don't have much time.'

Chloe pointed at a picture of a dog. 'Woof.' She carefully turned the cardboard page.

'By now, everybody should be organized.'

'All three groups are fully prepared.'

'Because, as we've said, we can't expect a passive response. Outsiders aren't likely to sit back and . . . what they don't understand.' Some phrases were muffled. 'We've got to expect . . . reaction to . . . events.'

'Oink,' Chloe declared, then she pointed to a cow. 'Moo.'

'Very good,' Harper spoke softly, kissed Chloe's head.

Chloe turned another page. Saw a cat.

'What's this kitty say?' Harper asked.

'So all sectors are set to go. Ishmael?'

'Meow.'

'Ishmael is all set. We just need to pile in and go.'

'Isaac?' Travis again.

'Ready.'

'And Jesus?' Travis again.

'Cluck.' Chloe pointed at a chicken.

'The Jesus committee is proud to announce that we are completely prepared to act in accordance with the Lord's will.'

'Good. Then all we need is the third lamb, and the rest is up to the Lord.'

Voices said, 'Amen.'

The next picture was of a horse. Chloe blinked at it, sucking her fingers.

Harper whinnied softly. 'A horse says nei-ei-igh.'

Chloe giggled. 'Nei-ei-eigh.'

'Any questions or new business?'

'I have a question.' It sounded like Peter. 'What about the unexpected?'

'The unexpected?' Travis laughed. 'Trust me. To everyone but our church, all of the Lord's plan will be unexpected.'

The others laughed.

Chloe had trouble turning the page. Juice must have spilled on the book, sticking the pages together.

'You guys think it's funny? What if they stop us? What if the starters can't get to their positions? What if something we haven't thought of goes wrong?'

Silence.

Gently, Harper pulled the pages apart, trying not to damage the pictures. Listening.

'Peter.' Travis spoke patiently, but his voice was tight. 'Focus. Finding the third lamb is your only concern. That and only that. Do your work, and let others do theirs. Don't question the Lord's plan.'

Voices said, 'Amen.'

The new picture was a lion. Chloe took a deep breath and, from the depths of her little belly, let out an ear-shattering roar.

Harper froze.

The men stopped talking. For a moment, nothing moved. Even the air hung suspended. And then, chairs scraped the floor. Voices overlapped. Shoes scuffled.

Oh God. They were coming.

'Chloe, we have to go.' Harper swept Chloe up in her arms, hopped to her feet, grabbed her bag. As she started back toward her bungalow, a man stuck his head out Travis's window.

'Harper?' It was Harold. He turned to someone behind him. 'It's that woman from next door.' Looking back at Harper, he called, 'What are you doing out there?'

Travis and Frank had come out the front door, were rounding the side of the building.

'Nothing. Why?' She tried to sound breezy.

'Eemah!' Chloe yelled, pushed at Harper, trying to get down.

Travis and Frank stopped a yard away. Eyed her warily.

'What's wrong? You guys look upset.' Harper feigned confusion. 'Oh, did you hear her roar? Did she scare you?' She forced a laugh. 'She's fine. Chloe was just being a lion.'

'Eemah. Down.' Chloe wiggled.

Travis's lips curled, showed his teeth. 'We thought someone was hurt. In fact, she screamed so loud, it sounded like she was there in the room with us.'

Harper smiled, nodding. 'Well, she was pretty loud.'

The men didn't move. Kept watching Harper and Chloe.

Harper tilted her head. 'Gentlemen? Everything okay?'

Chloe whined. 'Go. Down.'

Harper held her tighter, ready to run.

Peter came around the house, joining them. 'Everything okay?'

Travis and Frank exchanged glances, looked back at Harper.

'Fine.' Travis still didn't move his gaze. 'Just a baby playing. No big deal.'

Harper picked up her bag, made her voice cheery as she said goodbye. Made her legs move slowly as she walked away, as if she hadn't heard anything. As if she weren't the least alarmed. Chloe kept yelling, 'Down,' or 'Momma,' or 'Eemah,' but Harper hung onto her, insisting that it was time to go inside.

And they almost made it. Just steps away from their porch, a hand grabbed Harper's shoulder.

Reflexively, she spun around, shielding Chloe with her body while slamming her right fist out hard. Into Frank's belly.

He went down, winded, groaning, curling and cradling his midsection. Harper dashed Chloe into the bungalow, thrust her and her bag at Hagit, who scowled, said, 'What's wrong?' and followed Harper back outside.

Frank was still on the path, stunned. He cringed as Harper approached. 'What the hell?' He coughed, climbing slowly to his feet. She offered a hand; he refused it.

'Why'd you follow me home?' she demanded.

'Pastor sent me over.' Frank held his belly.

Pastor sent him? Damn. So he knew. They all knew she'd heard them talking. Frank must have been sent to warn her. Or find out what she knew. Or make sure she didn't tell anyone. Best to play dumb.

'Sorry. But you came up behind me and I just . . . it was a reflex. I didn't mean to hurt you.'

'You're crazy.' He glared over his shoulder as he walked away.

Hagit was in the doorway, holding Chloe. 'What happened? Who was that man?'

Harper didn't answer. Now that he was gone, she was shaken. What had he intended to do? What would have happened if she hadn't taken him down? And now that she had, what would Travis do? She stood watching until Frank was inside Travis's bungalow.

'Eemah?'

'Are you coming in?' Hagit asked.

Harper turned to go inside and saw Chloe's book on the ground, open to the picture of the cat. How had it gotten there? Unless . . . Oh Lord. Had she left it next door?

Had Travis found it?

And sent Frank to bring it back?

Mortified, Harper ran into the bungalow. Frank must have come to return it. Must have dropped it when he fell.

Chloe had been bathed and tucked in. Hagit was crocheting, sitting with Harper in the common area between their bedrooms, watching an old episode of *Law and Order*, in English with Hebrew subtitles.

Harper stared at the screen without seeing it. It was July twenty-fourth, less than thirty hours until the ninth of Av. She knew now that Travis had three groups: Isaac, Ishmael and Jesus. All were ready for whatever they were supposed to do, presumably on the ninth.

But what were they planning? All she knew was that 'outsiders' wouldn't like it.

'You're quiet.' Hagit glanced up from her crocheting. 'Something's bothering you.' Not a question.

Harper didn't want to go through it. And didn't want Hagit to tell her to stop investigating Travis.

'What happened to the man outside? You didn't tell me.'

'I guess he fell.'

Hagit nodded. 'I was watching out the window.'

Harper faced her. 'If you saw what happened, why did you ask?'

'You lied.' She continued crocheting, hands moving steadily.

'Yes. I lied.'

'Why?'

Why? 'Is that important?'

'Of course. A lie is a barrier. A wall between people. I want to know why you'd build one between us.' Hagit was round and middle-aged, looked like everyone's favorite auntie. Wasn't.

'I don't intend to.'

'Then why the lie?'

'Because it's easier than telling you the truth.' Harper stood, went to the kitchenette, opened the fridge. Found the same juice and apple that she'd found last time. Closed it. 'I don't want to go through the whole story.'

'So go through it anyway.' Hagit watched her, hands still working, deft and spider-like.

Harper considered it, decided she might as well. She told her what she'd overheard. Explained that, when Frank came after her, she'd thought he intended to harm her and had stopped him before he could.

'So. You meddled with these people. And now you've got their attention.'

'Someone has to find out what they're up to . . .'

'And that someone should be you?' Hagit put down her yarn. 'You've talked to the authorities. And to me. Why don't you trust us?'

'Because no one I've talked to seems the least bit concerned about what Travis is planning. Not the police, not the dig organizers, not Hank and not you. Everyone seems completely comfortable that they're preparing for the world to end Thursday.'

Hagit shrugged. 'You worry too much.'

The news came on. Hagit turned to watch, distracted. Harper glanced at the screen. Images of an airport. Some official leaving or arriving. Couldn't understand the Hebrew. Again, Harper thought of taking Chloe and going back to Jerusalem no matter what Hank said. The television showed a shoreline. A dark and muddy beach. A map, indicating receding waters. The Dead Sea? Was this a story about the symposium?

'Hagit? What are they saying?'

The images were of a limousine now. Men getting out. Wait – one of them was Trent? Hagit changed the channel.

'Wait. Go back. That was about the symposium – I saw Trent . . .' Harper went for the remote control, but Hagit scooped it up.

Harper held her hand out, but Hagit wouldn't give it up. 'It was nothing. Just a mention—'

'Give me the remote, Hagit. I want to see—'

'They were just showing about the symposium—'

'Well, I'd like to see it. Maybe Hank will be on.' What was Hagit thinking? 'Put it back on.'

'Fine.' She fumbled with the remote buttons. Put on the wrong channel. Twice. By the time she found the news, the anchor was back on the screen; coverage of the symposium story was over.

'What did they say?'

'Nothing. They were just telling about it, saying what it is.' Hagit picked up her yarn again.

Harper watched Hagit, saw the tightening of her jaw, the determination in her shoulders. Oh God.

'What happened, Hagit? Tell me. Is Hank all right? Did something happen?'

'Nothing happened. It was only a story.'

'If it was only a story, why wouldn't you want to watch it?' Harper insisted.

'Because I already know about it.' Hagit glanced up, scolding. 'Since when do I have to explain every little thing I do? What's the matter with you?'

Harper didn't answer. She went to her bedroom, not knowing what Hagit was hiding or why. But she'd felt the barrier, bumped an invisible wall. Recognized the unmistakable presence of a lie.

Hank picked up on the first ring.

'Hi.'

'Hoppa? One sec.' He covered the mouthpiece and talked to someone. 'Can't talk. Long.'

'Okay. I called because there was a story on the news. About the symposium . . .'

'Oh.' A cautious tone. 'You saw it?'

'No. Just a glimpse. Hagit turned it off.'

'Oh.'

Oh? 'So that was cool. Are you famous?'

A hesitation. Or was it? 'Don't know. Didn't. See it. Busy.' He was breathing into the phone. Rapidly.

She missed him, wanted to see him. Pictured him in his hotel room, barefoot, shirt off. 'Hank, I want to come back—'

'But you said you'd wait. A few days.'

'I know. But these people – Travis's church is planning something, and—'

'Hoppa. We. Talked about this. Before.' He sounded annoyed. 'We. Agreed. You'd stay—'

'Well, guess what? I'm changing my mind. I overheard them. They're dividing into three groups, each going to a different location. And they're planning for the world to end on Thursday.'

'And?'

'What do you mean, "and"?'

'This is. Tuesday only.'

What? 'So you want me to stay until Thursday to find out how big their bombs are?'

'Hoppa. Stop. You don't know—'

'But I'm pretty damned sure. Hank, these people have killed two people, almost three. They're planning another murder and something big – maybe mass killings—'

'Can you prove?'

'You don't believe me?'

'Calm. Down.'

'I will not calm down. Nobody's listening to me.'

Chloe stirred in her crib; Harper was being too loud. Didn't want to wake her. Hagit was still crocheting in the sitting area. Harper had no privacy and finally walked outside onto the porch.

Hank was talking, reassuring her. 'Police listened. Security listened. I listened. Everybody. Listened.'

'Bullshit. You all dismissed—'

'No. We listened. Now. You. Need to trust.'

Trust? She sat on the steps, looked up at the stars. Didn't see God up there, arming troops for Armageddon.

'What did you hear. Them say?'

Harper told him that they'd said they were ready. That outsiders would resist what they had planned. That they needed another sacrifice.

She realized that nothing she'd heard was specific.

Or incriminating.

'Hoppa. If I thought. You. Were in danger. I'd run. To get you. But I think you're safe. At dig.'

How could he be sure? Why was she the only one concerned?

Hank reminded her that she was surrounded by experienced security personnel, soldiers and police – much more protection than she'd have in Jerusalem. And that she owed herself the chance to work on the dig. He wouldn't hang up until she promised to stay.

When they hung up, Harper sat on the porch, wondering why everyone thought she was overreacting. Had motherhood distorted her perceptions, exaggerating her sense of danger? Were Travis and his church just harmless religious kooks and Yoshi's stabbing an unrelated incident?

The night was crisp and chilly. Refreshing. The sky clear. Harper lingered, sorting her thoughts. She wasn't sure how long she'd been there when the door to Travis's bungalow opened and a couple stepped out.

In the light of the stars, she watched them pressing their bodies together. Damn. Harper couldn't look away. She wondered again if Peter knew about Lynne's affair, whether it upset him. Finally, the woman broke away and stepped off the porch and Harper realized that Peter shouldn't be concerned. Even in the dim light of the night sky, Harper could see Marlene's long red hair.

The next morning, when the bus dropped the volunteers off in the Megiddo south parking lot, Harper noticed Peter standing by himself.

'Aren't you coming?'

'Forgot my kit. I guess I'll just go back to the kibbutz.'

He didn't look well. Skin was clammy, yellowish. Probably he was worried about the sacrifice, or the end of the world. 'Feeling okay?'

His eyes were hollow. 'Sure. Just stupid. How could I forget my kit?'

'I'm sure they have spare tools. Come on. No sense wasting a whole day.'

'No, don't bother . . .'

'It's no bother.'

He hung back for a moment. Finally followed Harper to the trailer office, where he got a bucket filled with tools, but they couldn't find extra work gloves. No problem; Harper had a spare pair. She dug them out of her kit, gave them to Peter, and they joined the others. Lynne was waiting on the path.

'Got everything?' She smirked at him.

Peter nodded, said nothing.

'Oh, shucks,' Lynne stamped a foot. 'I forgot a water bottle. Peter, will you be an angel and go get me one? I'll watch your stuff.'

Peter dumped his kit and started back to the trailer.

'Go on ahead, Harper. I'll catch up.'

Harper was glad to go ahead. She couldn't wait to get back to the spot where she'd found the ring. When she got to the wall, she saw Frank and Pastor Travis, Marlene working beside them, her red hair spilling out of her work hat.

The day was breezy, the sky dotted with puffy clouds. Harper was sifting fill from the section adjacent to the wall when Lynne joined her.

'Sometimes the Lord tests me,' she said.

Harper thought she was referring to the pastor, his dalliance with Marlene. 'Something wrong?' Harper asked.

Lynne gazed across the site, toward Travis. 'Nothing the Lord won't help me handle.'

'You look tired.'

Lynne shrugged. No chatter. She sifted dirt, her eyes on Travis, who never even glanced her way.

Harper examined pebbles. If Travis had dumped her for Marlene, maybe Lynne's loyalty would be shaken. Maybe she'd be angry.

Maybe angry enough to discuss Travis's plans?

'So have you talked to Pastor Travis about me?'

Lynne blinked. 'What?'

'Remember? You were going to ask him if I could join . . .'

'Oh, no. Sorry. He's been busy.'

'Because you said I'd have to join by the ninth of Av – isn't that tomorrow?'

'Sundown tomorrow. I haven't had a chance to talk to him. Pastor's been sequestered with the church council. Their meeting lasted all night.'

Really? Is that what he'd told her? Had Lynne believed him?

'A council meeting?' Harper smirked. 'That's not what we call it back home.'

Lynne looked up. 'Excuse me?'

'I mean unless the council is a curvy redhead.'

'What?'

'That's who he was with last night. I saw them.'

Lynne's eyes narrowed. 'Marlene must have needed spiritual counseling.'

Harper laughed. 'Is that Bible code for getting it on?'

'No way. He wouldn't.' Lynne's grip tightened on the handle of her trowel.

'Why? What's the problem?' Harper pretended to be clueless. 'You said he wasn't married.'

'But Marlene is.' Lynne shoved the trowel into the ground, cut a chunk of clay. 'And Pastor's been seeing someone – a woman in the church.' Her chin wobbled ever so slightly. 'Trust me, if she were to find out, he'd have a problem.' She slapped the clump into a bucket.

Harper winced. 'I guess it would be awkward.'

'Are you kidding? He was with Marlene?' Lynne stabbed the ground again. Were her eyes tearing? She sniffed. Wiped her nose with her sleeve.

'Well, who knows?' Harper kept at it. 'Maybe his other thing ended. Maybe the other woman—'

'Believe me, I'd know. It's not ended.'

Harper stopped sifting and wiped her forehead with her glove, leaving a smudge. 'Sounds to me like your pastor's a womanizer—'

'No, he's not. You don't even know him. Besides, how can you be sure he was even the guy you saw? It was dark, wasn't it? It could have been anyone in the council . . .'

'It was Travis.' Harper kept calm. Added more dirt to her sieve.

'Because,' Lynne came closer, insisting, 'see, I know him. We got close when he was counseling me. Counseling Peter and me about our marriage.'

Harper said nothing. She picked up a small clod of clay, examined it.

'I know he wouldn't cheat.'

Harper was about to reply, but the clay distracted her. Its shape and weight were wrong, didn't feel like just earth. Had she found something? Another ring or maybe a shard of Roman glass? She brushed it, gently removing dirt.

'Besides, Pastor would never be interested in Marlene. She's a spiritual lightweight. And she didn't fulfill her assignment—'

An ear-bending howl interrupted them. For a long moment, it hung in the air, suspended and palpable, and then people called out in Hebrew, scurrying from all directions toward the exposed wall.

Harper didn't scurry. She didn't move. She was stunned by the impact, the loud blast of an explosion. Soldiers ran past her, dodging sniper fire as they hurried to rescue survivors. She tried to move and help them, but couldn't feel her legs. Couldn't see her patrol. Could only watch from the top of the burnt-out car on which she'd landed. Oh God. Where was her patrol?

'Harper.' Someone grabbed her arm, pulling.

Harper reached for her weapon.

'Come on. Something's happened.'

It was a blonde woman, tugging at her. Jabbering. Grabbing her weapon.

'Leave your trowel.'

Trowel? What? Oh God. Harper bit her lip until it bled, struggling to come back to the present. The dusty battle of her flashback faded, and she followed Lynne along the path to the crowd of volunteers. Hushed voices floated past.

'. . . said it was a deathstalker . . .'

'A what?'

'A scorpion . . . yellow . . . deadliest venom . . .'

'Is he dead?'

And then the crowd opened, arms grabbing Lynne and pulling her forward, Harper holding onto her arm. Hands touched Lynne's shoulders. 'We're praying for him,' someone said. Whispers brushed Harper's face, pieces of ideas. And then they came to an open space. A couple of soldiers crouched, working on a man who was writhing and moaning. Dr Hadar was beside them, urging the man to be still, to stop moving. Students gawked. Dr Ben Haim paced in a small circle, occasionally waving at the crowd to back away.

Lynne seemed confused. 'What happened? Who's hurt?'

Harper put an arm around Lynne's waist, steadying her. On the ground beside the man were some work gloves. She recognized her spare pair.

The soldiers packed Peter's hand and arm in ice and elevated it to slow the flow of venom. Lynne held his unbitten hand, praying until Travis came over and touched her shoulder. Their eyes locked and their gazes connected even as the medics rushed Peter to a nearby army base to receive anti-venom.

Dr Hadar offered Lynne a ride to the base, but she hesitated. Said she couldn't bear to go there and see him in so much pain. Pastor Travis intervened, offering to pray with her and accompany her to the base.

Lynne gripped Harper's arm, overwhelmed, unsure what to do.

Dr Hadar urged her to go. He spoke frankly. 'It's a bad creature, the yellow scorpion.'

Lynne sniffed, closed her eyes, indicating that she understood: Peter might die.

'Your husband – he has no heart problems?'

Lynne shook her head no. 'Why?'

'I'll be honest. If his heart is strong, the bite won't kill him. But he will be so miserable, he'll wish it would.'

Harper tightened her grip on Lynne.

Dr Hadar went on. 'The yellow scorpion lives all over the Middle East. I've learned about the effects. At the very least, he'll have a raging pulse, severe muscle cramps, intense pain. The venom is a cocktail of neurotoxins. And the biggest danger, as I said, will be to his heart. The anti-venom will help, but while he's ill, his wife should be there. As soon as you are able, you should go.'

Lynne's skin seemed translucent. The veins in her forehead pulsed. She said nothing.

'For now, sit down,' Dr Hadar told her. 'Or lie down in the trailer. Drink some water. Go. You look pale.'

'No. I'm okay. I just need to pray with Pastor.'

Dr Hadar nodded. 'Of course.' He waved a student over, asked him to set up some folding chairs for Lynne and Pastor Travis.

Harper watched them walk away, confused. She turned to Dr Hadar. 'But how could it happen? He was covered in protective clothing.'

Hadar frowned, rubbed his face. 'The clothing is not the problem. He was bitten on the hand.'

His hand? 'But I lent him gloves. Wasn't he wearing them?'

'In this case, it would have been better if he hadn't been.'

Harper didn't understand. She tilted her head.

'That's how it happened. The scorpion was hiding there. Inside his glove.'

Oh God. In his glove? One that Harper had given him?

'But how could it get in there?'

Hadar shrugged. 'These creatures like cool dark places. My guess is that it crawled.'

Harper felt the blood drain from her head.

'Are you all right?' Dr Hadar put a hand on her shoulder.

Volunteers crowded around, asking questions. Dr Ben Haim stood on an overturned bucket, motioning for them to settle down.

'The gloves . . .' Harper began.

'What?' Dr Hadar couldn't hear. People were shouting.

Dr Ben Haim waved to Dr Hadar to join him. Hadar excused himself, jumped up onto a bucket and let out a piercing whistle. 'We'll answer everyone's questions, one at a time.'

And then, little by little, the crowd heard about the yellow scorpion, its nickname of deathstalker. Its intense complex venom. The likelihood that Peter would survive. Dr Ben Haim, frustrated and concerned, scolded everyone, reminded them that they'd been explicitly warned to check under stones and woodpiles, inside their clothing before putting it on. That an incident like this should never have happened. Someone in the crowd yelled, 'You told us to check our shoes, clothes and hats, but you never mentioned work gloves.'

Ben Haim rolled his eyes and began to answer that he hadn't told the heckler to wipe his ass, either, but Dr Hadar cut him off.

Harper couldn't listen. She was focused on only one fact: the work glove containing the scorpion was hers. Peter Watts had been bitten because she'd lent him that glove. She thought back to the morning, to putting on her gloves. She'd checked hers before slipping her hands inside. Had looked in and shaken them out. She did it automatically; her stint in Iraq had taught her never to step or reach into anything – garments included – before checking. So if she'd kept the pair that she'd given to Peter instead of those now on her hands, she would have found the scorpion.

Unless it had crawled up inside a finger. In which case, she'd have been bitten. And she, not Peter would be writhing in pain.

Or dead.

Oh God.

Harper wandered away from the others. She should have checked the gloves before lending them. Should have reminded Peter to check them. She walked along the path toward the office trailer, noticed Lynne and Pastor Travis walking ahead of her. Travis had an arm around Lynne's shoulder, and his head tilted toward hers, deep in conversation. Maybe the pastor wasn't completely self-serving. Maybe he was actually comforting her.

Or maybe they were comforting each other. After all, they'd been having an affair, at least until last night. What if one or both of them had tried to get rid of Peter so they could be together, had planted the spider in the glove . . .

No. That was ridiculous. First of all, they both believed the world was going to end at sundown the next day; why kill one of their own now? Besides, neither of them could have foreseen that Peter would forget his kit, much less that he'd borrow a pair of Harper's gloves.

Damn.

Harper ran a hand through her hair, took a breath. And stopped walking. If someone had planted that scorpion in her glove, the intended target must not have been Peter.

Had someone tried to kill her? She looked around the site. No one was watching her. She had no enemies there. Nor did Peter. No one had tried to kill either of them. The creature had simply wandered into the glove, seeking a cozy spot. The bite was an accident, nobody's fault.

On the other hand, what were the chances of a scorpion finding her glove on its own? And right after two murders and a stabbing, all in the space of a few days. Harper wasn't sure how the scorpion was involved, but she was almost sure that it was connected to Travis and his group. Too many people had been hurt or killed, and no one was stopping them. She scanned the site, unwilling to be passive. Dr Hadar was talking with some students and volunteers. As soon as he was finished, Harper was going to take him aside.

After a while, the killer moved away, watching Pastor Travis move among the stunned volunteers, the shaken church members. They clustered together like a mindless herd. Never mind. The killer wanted a moment alone to evaluate this unexpected turn of events. What had gone wrong this time? Why was God constantly thwarting the killer's efforts? Was it personal? Did God intend to make everything so difficult?

Wait. Maybe it wasn't God who was ruining everything. Maybe it was Satan, interfering with God's plan by preventing the killer's work.

The killer contemplated that possibility. Couldn't be sure, because the scorpion hadn't actually been part of God's coded plan. But, either way, whether due to God or Satan, once again, despite the killer's detailed diligence and infinite care, events had unpredictably and uncontrollably gone wrong. Peter was at a military base, getting anti-venom, and Harper Jennings was still around, snooping and prying, talking to the authorities. Trying to interfere with the pastor's church and God's coded instructions.

The woman just plain knew too much. Asked too many questions, hung around council meetings, spied on Ramsey. The scorpion had been hiding under a rock. Had slipped easily out of the jar into a glove in Harper's kit. Who could have guessed that Harper would give the glove to Peter? No one; it had to be the work of Satan.

But Peter was tall and big. Strong enough to survive the venom. Not like Harper. What was she – five foot three? Tiny. The death-stalker's bite would have killed her and put an end to her prying. And no one would have suspected a thing; it would have been a terrible accident. Tragic. Perfect.

Except it hadn't worked. What had been the chances that, on the very day that the scorpion had been securely deposited into Harper's glove, Peter would forget his own? And even then, who could have imagined that, of all the people on the dig, he would borrow a pair from Harper? Why not from some student or a dig official? And even on the small chance that he borrowed spare gloves from her, who would guess that she'd give him the ones with the scorpion? And why did every single thing the killer tried to do go wrong?

The killer took a deep breath, needed to calm down. The others were all gathered around the excavated wall, uncertain what to do next. Well, they had no idea what uncertainty really felt like. What hell it was. To be uncertain about Ramsey, about how to win back his love and approval. To be uncertain about how to succeed in doing God's work. And to be uncertain about why so many honest efforts ended up in failure and shame. The lambs in the shuk running away. The Hebrew lamb – they called him Yoshi – striking back?

Someone walked by, asked the killer a question. 'You all right?' Something like that.

The killer tried to stop panting. 'Yes. I'm good,' the killer answered and strolled down the path a little further.

But the killer wasn't good at all. The killer was sulking. Ramsey had been cold and dismissive, had stripped away everything, had given the final sacrificial honor to Peter, who was laughably, pathetically inept.

Not to mention half dead from the scorpion bite, barely able to breathe, let alone perform a sacrifice.

Which meant – which had to mean – that Ramsey would reinstate the killer. No one else was even close to qualified. The killer had experience. And time was short: they had until sundown the next day.

A wave of elation, of perfect clarity washed over the killer. Everything made sense. It all fit together: The reason Peter had forgotten his kit and taken Harper's gloves, the reason he'd been bitten and struck down – it hadn't been chance at all. Every step. Each event had been ordained and orchestrated by God Himself.

God Himself had willed the killer to perform the final sacrifice.

And woe unto anyone who got in the way.

Dr Hadar listened to Harper with a poker face. No reaction at all, even when she explained that Peter had been wearing her gloves, that someone had probably put the scorpion in them deliberately, trying to kill her and make it look like an accident. That someone in the church was trying to stop her from preventing their next murder and the terrible catastrophe they were planning for the next evening.

She was about halfway through her story when she realized that Hadar wasn't listening. He was watching the students at work in the pit near the wall.

'Hannah,' he interrupted Harper, shouting something in Hebrew.

Harper followed his gaze, saw a young woman stumble over a crooked plank, almost falling into the ditch.

Hannah laughed and yelled back, 'Todah.'

Hadar turned back to Harper. 'Yes, well, I have to get back.' He started to step away, but Harper stopped him.

'Just give me a minute.' She rushed through her thoughts again, sounding disjointed, even a little paranoid. But Hadar was in a hurry. She had to be quick, so she skimmed over details, merely reminding him that Pastor Travis's church believed that the battle of Armageddon was going to start the next day at sundown. That a murder was going to be attempted – that they'd already tried to kill Yoshi. She was about to talk about the three groups planning something violent when Hadar cut her off.

'You'll have to excuse me, Dr Jennings. You've said all this before. But with all due respect, I have work to do.' Abruptly, he started away.

Harper went after him. 'Dr Hadar, I'm telling you that this whole site is in danger, that someone tried to murder me, that someone else might die, and you're too busy to—'

'Yes, exactly. I am too busy.' His eyebrows raised. 'I've heard what you've had to say. And I've told you not to worry. I understand you're upset about today. Why don't you go back to the kibbutz and rest? Take a day off. A van is going back in a few minutes. I'll arrange for you to be on it.'

Harper opened her mouth to insist that he take her seriously, but she stopped herself. She had no credibility. She was just a volunteer; Dr Hadar was the boss. And he obviously thought she was nuts.

As he walked away, students descended on him. Harper went back to her section, saw the small clump of dirt she'd left on the screen when Peter had screamed. She stared at it, not seeing it, replaying the agonizing pain of his scream, unable to get back to work. Dr Hadar was right. She should go back to the kibbutz, forget about dirt and ruins for the day. After all, someone from the church had tried to kill her, and would likely try again.

The van was filled to capacity. Lynne was there, wide-eyed, clinging to Travis's hand. Marlene sat behind them, watching, listening, Frank beside her. Lowell sat in front of them. Harold was in the back. Others from the church filled the rest of the seats.

Harper looked for a vacant spot, saw one beside a plump woman with a perm. On the way, she stopped to talk to Lynne.

'Are you all right?' Stupid question. How could she be?

Lynne sat stiff, answered slowly. 'Everything will be okay.'

Her pupils were dilated. Her reaction slow. 'I should be with him, I know I should. But I can't bear seeing him—'

'It's okay.'

Lynne stared into space.

'He's in good hands. Right now, Peter doesn't know who's there and who isn't, and he won't remember anything.' Travis squeezed her hand.

Harper blinked, saw Hank falling off the roof, hitting his head. Lying unconscious, not knowing she was there. She dug her nails into her palm, but the flashback wouldn't go away. Hank reappeared on the roof, fixing it, slipping. Falling. Hitting his head . . . Oh God.

'He was screaming. His eyes were rolling, and his tongue . . . I couldn't watch. I can't.'

Harper saw herself running across the yard, kneeling beside Hank. She saw his battered head, grabbed his hand and held onto it, wouldn't let go even as the EMTs took him onto the ambulance. Even at the hospital. The doctor insisted, 'You need to let go, Mrs Jennings. We need to take him to surgery.' Harper felt Hank's limp hand, squeezed it. Felt its absence after she released it. Orderlies rolled Hank's gurney away, and she couldn't breathe, felt hollow, as if they'd taken her heart.

'You'd do no good by being there, Lynne,' Pastor Travis said. 'Peter's delirious. And he'd want you to do what's right for you.'

'He'll be okay,' Frank joined in. 'They said it shouldn't be fatal.'

Lynne's skin got grayer.

Hank was on the roof again. Harper pressed her nails deeper, breaking skin.

'You'll be with him when it counts.' Marlene leaned forward, poking her head between Lynne and Travis. 'First, you need to take care of yourself. Like on an airplane when you put on your oxygen mask before you help others.'

Lynne didn't respond.

The driver climbed in and started the engine. Time for Harper to take a seat. She reminded herself that Hank's accident had happened a few years ago and, except for aphasia and a slight limp, he'd recovered completely. He was in Jerusalem, not a hospital. But Harper still felt the warmth of his hand. The sticky blood on her skin . . . No. She was in Israel, on a dig. Without bloodstains. Hank was fine. Peter would be, too.

Dr Ben Haim called to the driver to stop and ran up to the van. He climbed on, announcing that he'd just now talked to the doctor at the army base. Peter would be taken to the medical center at Kibbutz Golen in a few hours. He was still in pain, in and out of consciousness, but so far, he was responding well to the anti-venom.

Harper looked at the passengers around her, wondering if one of them had planted the scorpion. Could it have been Travis? Unlikely; Travis never did anything himself. But he might have encouraged one of his followers to kill her. Was someone eyeing her now, disappointed to see her alive? She scanned the group. Problem was, she sensed a threat everywhere, from no one in particular. Finally, she settled into her seat and looked beyond the woman next to her. Tried to see out the window, to concentrate on green hills and fertile valleys. But Harper saw the scenery only sporadically; mostly, she saw Hank on the roof, fixing loose shingles. Slipping. Sliding. Falling. Again. And again.

When it was finally possible, after lunch, the killer took the pastor aside. They took a walk to the highest point of the kibbutz, stood in the breeze, looking out at green fields and hills.

The killer waited for a moment, then took a breath, recited practiced lines. 'Things have changed now. Peter's out of commission.'

'I'm aware.'

'So, let me take care of the sacrifice.'

The pastor rolled his eyes. 'Really? This is what you wanted to talk about? I should have known. Short answer: no.' He started to walk away.

The killer was at his heels. 'But I'm the only one with experience—'

'We have limited time.' He wheeled around, put up a hand as if halting the idea. 'Too much is at stake. We can't afford another screw up—'

'I won't screw up.' Why was Ramsey still assigning blame? Why couldn't he understand that nobody had been at fault?

Travis looked out over the hills. 'Fact is I've already assigned it.'

What? Already? 'To who? Is it Frank? Lowell?' Couldn't be Harold . . .

'You don't need to know. The fewer who know, the better. Too many eyes are on us – largely because of your mistakes.' He checked his watch. 'Let's head back. It's time for the prayer group.' He started back down the hill.

'No. Ramsey, wait.' The killer hurried after him. 'Give me a chance to redeem myself. Please . . .'

'I believe we've already discussed this matter. I see no reason to revisit my decision. You had your chance. You failed and, in failing, you jeopardized our hopes of fulfilling the code. No. If you want redemption, don't come to me. It's out of my hands. The only one who can help you is God.' He turned and strode away.

The killer didn't move. Stayed there, back straight, jaw tight, throat thick and choked. Feeling wobbly, as if the earth were trembling. As if there were nothing to hold on to. How could Ramsey leave like that? Without a hopeful word, a reassuring embrace? Supposedly he loved everyone in the church; helped them in times of need. Was leading them to salvation and eternal life.

But the killer stood alone. Unloved. Rejected.

And then the realization hit: it wasn't the killer who was at fault. It was Ramsey Travis. Truth was, he was only human, had human frailties. He wanted so desperately to fulfill the instructions in the code – was so close to accomplishing God's requirements that he was blind to anything else, including anyone who got hurt on the way. Though he didn't know it, Ramsey needed the killer's loyalty and help more than ever.

In the end, God would recognize the truth, reward devotion, forgive minor errors. In a little more than a day, Pastor Travis would see how well the killer's efforts had pleased the Lord and would bask in the glory.

Meantime, there was a third lamb to sacrifice – quickly, before Lowell or Frank or whichever council member had been assigned made their move. This time, the killer would find one weaker than that Yoshi. Less agile. The Lord would accept a sincere offering, even if it weren't a perfect specimen. The main thing was to complete the triad by sacrificing one of Isaac's people.

It shouldn't be difficult; Jews were everywhere. It was just a matter of picking the right one.

When she got back to the kibbutz, Harper didn't stop in at the nursery to see Chloe and Hagit. She went straight to the bungalow to start packing. Her mind was made up; she wasn't going to discuss her decision with Hank or anyone else. Wasn't going to listen to more lame reasons for her to stay. The dig, the opportunity to participate in the excavation of Megiddo South, was simply not worth risking her life and Chloe's safety. And, even if Peter's bite had been an accident – which she was certain it wasn't – she didn't want to be there with Chloe when Travis and his church members unleashed whatever they'd planned to bring on the end of days.

She pulled her shorts, jeans and T-shirts out of the closet, stuffed them into her duffle bag. Rolled up a skirt, a sweatshirt, a sundress. Threw in her underwear, flip flops, sneakers. A nightgown. Opened the drawer with Chloe's clothes. Blinked. Except for a few pairs of socks and a stack of diapers, it was empty. She looked in the bathroom, checked Hagit's room. Saw no baby clothes. Where were all Chloe's things?

The laundry bag. Harper looked. Found only her own dirty clothes.

Damn. Harper looked under the bed. Then slumped onto it, baffled. Maybe Hagit was doing the laundry?

Well, never mind. They'd just get Chloe's clothes out of the washing machine and transport them wet, in a plastic bag. They'd dry the load in Jerusalem. Meantime, she had to go tell Hagit to get her things together. And go to the office to arrange transportation.

Harper hurried out of the bungalow along the path toward the school. They'd leave before dinner. By bedtime, they'd be in Jerusalem. She'd be with Hank, would sleep beside him. She smiled, picturing it, as she passed Ramsey Travis's bungalow. And felt someone watching her. Lowell was sitting on Travis's porch, alone, his face sullen.

Harper kept going, spurred on by the uneasy ripple dancing along the back of her neck.

The killer didn't hurry. Moved at a steady, careful pace all the way down the hill. Timing was critical. But so was the choice. Maybe the lamb should be someone who'd insulted the church, who'd talked to police. Someone who'd been unfriendly, standoffish. Or who'd interfered with the last attempt to find a lamb – like that guy Gal. Except, no. Gal was too strong. Maybe that young woman Adi, who'd taken them on a tour when they first arrived. Or her friend, Yael.

The killer walked and thought. Considered the boy who worked the desk in the main office. Decided, no, he could easily sound an alarm. Thought about the staff at the restaurant, but they worked as a group. It might be hard to isolate one. The killer kicked a pebble, frustrated. The fact was that most of the people who lived at the kibbutz didn't cross paths with the dig volunteers. How was the killer to get one alone without knowing where to look?

But defeat was not an option. There had to be a way to please Travis and do God's work. And then, boom: the killer knew. The face of the lamb appeared like a vision. She was older, kind of chunky and out of shape; it wouldn't take much effort to overcome her. She'd be alone when Harper took her baby out for a walk. What was her name? Hag-something. Hagit! That was it. Yes. Hagit would be the final lamb. She was perfect.

The sounds of children playing skittered through the air, as light as butterfly wings, as ticklish as the breeze. Harper steeled herself, bracing for Hagit's protests. Ready to fend off her resistance. She simply didn't care what Hagit might say. She and Chloe were going to leave with or without her. The same instincts that had kept her alive in Iraq were ordering her to grab her baby and go. No argument by a babysitter was going to stop her.

Maybe they wouldn't even get the baby's laundry; she could buy more clothes in Jerusalem. Her biggest concern was transportation. Could she rent a car? If not, she could pay someone to drive them. Maybe Gal would do it.

Coming up the hill to the nursery, she saw Harold and a couple of other church members lingering near the fence. What were they doing there? Her spine jangled a warning. Harper checked them out, saw no weapons. She kept walking, nodded a greeting. All three nodded back, identical expressions on their faces. What was that expression? Watchfulness? Uneasiness? Alarm? Never mind. She had no time, kept moving.

The man beside Harold stepped forward, silently blocking her way. She was about to ask what he wanted when, beyond him, the gate to the nursery swung open. Three people stepped out. Frank, Travis and, in between them, wearing a grimace, Hagit.

The killer knew where to find the lamb: the nursery school. Hagit would be there with Harper's kid. This time the plan would work. The killer would go in with a message, saying that Harper wanted Hagit to meet her. That she'd sent the killer to get her. Hagit would go willingly, would suspect nothing. Would have no chance to resist. Would be the third sacrifice.

The killer felt light, weightless, ran as if not touching the ground. Stopped along the way at the bungalow to take the knife from the satchel. Concealed it in a waistband. Hummed Amazing Grace on the way to the nursery, picturing the final sacrifice. The completion of the instructions. The adherence to the code. Travis would beam with appreciation, would open his arms, and they would stand together in glory for all time. What would it look like, feel like, to have their souls rise? To receive eternal life? To face the Rapture?

What would it be like to meet the Lord?

The nursery was just up the hill. The killer clung to the hidden knife, smiling, anticipating glory. But then the gate swung open. The killer stopped, stunned as if sucker-punched, gaping. Wailing aloud, 'Nooo!' as Frank and Travis emerged and led the lamb away.

Harper bulldozed forward, but Harold and the others closed in.

'Just a second, Harper,' Harold smiled. 'I don't think you've met Jimmy Thomson—'

One of the men snickered at her. Harper ignored him, swiveling to get around them. But Jimmy stepped sideways, stopping her, putting an outstretched hand on her arm.

Reflexively, she grabbed his wrist. Before he understood what was happening, his arm was bent and pinned tightly behind his back. Jimmy bent over, groaning.

The others froze for a moment, gaping. Regrouping. Reasoning that Harper was still outnumbered. There was no way she could twist all their arms at once. Harold moved slowly to her rear; the other man went to her left.

'If either of you comes closer,' Harper warned, 'I'll break Jimmy's arm, and then I'll crush at least one of your jaws.'

They paused. Looked at each other, then at Harper, sizing up the threat from this short petite sprite. Meantime, Harper glanced up the path, saw Hagit hanging back, walking reluctantly. Travis and Frank tugged at her, urging her along. Where were all the security officers? The groundskeepers? Anyone could see that the men were forcing Hagit to go with them. And why didn't Hagit call out for help? Why didn't she scream?

The short-lived standoff was coming to an end. Harold nodded to the other guy, and both took a wary step forward. Harper kept her word, raised her knee, snapped down, felt the cracking of bone, heard a howl as Jimmy collapsed. In the same move, she spun around, landing her fist squarely on the jaw behind her. Felt it cave on impact. Before the guy hit the ground, she drew her fist back and pivoted to face Harold, who backed away, hands raised.

'Okay. No problem.'

Men were moaning. Harper stepped toward Harold, ready to strike. She met his eyes, said nothing.

Harold turned and ran.

Harper looked up the path for Hagit, saw her disappearing into some hedges with Travis and Frank. Oh God. Where were they going? With a surge of adrenalin, she took off after them, running to catch up. The war injury in her left leg throbbed; her knee threatened to buckle. And her wrist and knuckles stung; she hadn't cold-cocked anyone in a long time and hadn't positioned her hand quite right. But Harper sped, trying to catch up. It was almost the ninth of Av. And she was pretty sure that Travis had been looking for his third sacrifice.

The killer watched in disbelief. Travis? Travis had taken the third lamb. The killer's jaw tensed, grasping the facts: Travis was going to make the sacrifice by himself. Personally.

But why? Was he so hungry for God's approval that he would deny anyone else a chance for glory? Wasn't it enough that Travis had decoded God's instructions? That he had led them to Megiddo?

The killer watched the entourage climbing the hill – Travis, Frank and the offering, followed by Harper. And how about Harper? She'd just about made Harold wet his pants in fear. Snapped Jimmy's arm like a twig; smashed Wendell's face. Now, they rolled around moaning on the ground while other council members rushed out of the nursery school, coming to their rescue.

'What happened?' A council member named Stephen helped Jimmy to his feet.

Jimmy wailed. 'My arm . . .'

Wait.

What were council members doing in the nursery school?

It had to be about Hagit. Probably they'd stayed there to make sure nobody called for help.

'Just go ahead and do it!' Jimmy bellowed. He tottered, seemed unable to stand.

'Sorry, Jimmy. I'm supposed to wait. Nobody does anything unless Travis calls in an order.'

Wendell whimpered when they lifted him. Blood gurgled from his mouth.

'But look what she did – you've got to . . .'

'Jimmy, I'm not authorized to kill—'

'An eye for an eye! An arm for an arm.'

'—without authorization.'

What were they talking about? Did Jimmy want them to kill Harper?

'Fine. I'll do it myself.' Jimmy thrust himself toward the nursery, holding his dangling and twisted arm. 'Which one is hers?'

Hers? Oh dear. He was talking about Harper's baby. She was in the nursery school.

'Stop.' Stephen pulled Jimmy's intact arm. 'You could ruin everything. It's just a matter of hours, and then none of this will matter.'

The killer stayed hidden, watching Stephen calm Jimmy. Wondering which other council members were guarding the nursery. What they'd been ordered to do if Hagit refused to cooperate. Someone must have called for help; kibbutz medics arrived to deal with the injured men. The killer heard Stephen apologize for them, explaining that they'd been in a fistfight. That they'd caused each other's wounds. Jimmy glared and fumed. Wendell spit blood.

The killer looked beyond them, watching Harper disappear up the hill behind Travis. And, making a wide path around the others, followed quickly, undetected.

If not for the breeze, Harper would have missed the spot, would have run right past. The bushes moved, though, as if to show her the narrow path where she'd last seen Hagit. It was familiar; she'd been there before. On her first day at the kibbutz. On the tour.

If not for the tour, she wouldn't have understood where they'd gone. But she remembered the entrance concealed in the rocks, and she hurried through the shrubbery, easily locating the bunker door.

It was steel. Camouflaged to match the bushes and rocks. Positioned low, away from the road. And closed.

Harper put a hand on the lever that would open it. Slowly, steadily, she pushed it down and pulled on the door. The door didn't budge. Damn. Was it locked? They'd locked it? She had no time to go for help – Travis might be killing Hagit that very moment. Might have already killed her. Harper looked around for help, saw no one. Where was all the kibbutz security? And what about Harold? He'd probably run off to gather a posse of church members. She peered over the hedges. The path was empty: so far, no one was chasing her. She tried the door again, pulled. Then shoved. The door swung forward, into the bunker.

Harper listened, heard Travis's voice rising from below. Quietly stepped inside. The door clanged closed behind her, shutting out the sunlight. She stiffened, not breathing, waiting for Travis to respond to the sound. But Travis was still talking, hadn't heard the door. Harper stood still, engulfed in darkness, hoping that her eyes would adjust. That she was in time to rescue Hagit. That she'd figure out a way to do so.

Carefully, she put a hand out, felt empty air. She extended a foot, tested the ground. Took a tentative step, another. Gradually, her eyes adjusted. By the time she got to the turn and the staircase leading underground, candlelight leaked from below, letting her see well enough to make out dim shapes. And by the time she descended the steps, the light was bright enough to reveal Hagit across the room, tied to a table, her forehead bleeding. And Travis standing beside her, holding a large gleaming knife above her throat.

Harper glanced left and right, saw no one, steeled herself and charged, pouncing, flying at Travis with arms extended. She was almost on him when something slammed her from behind. And she went down.

The bed was cold, hard and sheetless. Not a bed? Harper opened an eye, realized she was on flat concrete. Concrete with a golden flicker. She blinked. Focused. Saw that the flicker was a candle.

A candle?

Pain wracked her skull. She tried to get up, couldn't move her hands. What had happened? Oh God – she remembered. Flying. The explosion, the hot white blast. The thunk of landing on a burnt-out car. The confusion. But wait . . . She wasn't on a car. She was on a concrete floor. Why couldn't she get up? Where was she?

She tried again, couldn't separate her hands or feet. Felt the restriction – rope? Probably rope. Yes. Her hands were tied. She lay still, wondering if anyone were watching her. Peeking out of one eye, not seeing much beyond the candle near her head. Hearing a woman scolding.

'. . . promise, you will have the wrath of God on you. You'll regret . . .' She stopped abruptly, her words muffled. Hagit? And then Harper remembered: she was in the bunker. She'd followed Travis and Frank there. They'd taken Hagit. They were going to kill her.

'And it shall be as promised in Matthew twenty-four, verse seven: "For nation will rise against nation, and kingdom against kingdom."' Travis's voice paused, then continued in a language she didn't understand. Greek? Hebrew? Prayers over Hagit, his intended sacrifice.

Harper needed to stop them. She twisted her wrists until she felt some slack in the rope, and bent her wrists, working the bindings, tugging. Chafing her skin. Accidentally pulling the wrong way and tightening the binding. Starting over, loosening it again. Listening to Travis, racing against his blessings. Yanking, wriggling her hands until, finally, she eased them out of the loops of rope.

Rubbing her raw wrists, she sat up and turned her head. Too fast. The walls began spinning. And so did the elephants.

Elephants?

Yes. And giraffes. And zebras. And monkeys. All in pairs, all around her, all tottering onto the ark.

Harper closed her eyes. Reasoned that she'd been knocked out. Had a head wound. Her balance was off. She needed to steady herself. She held the wall and opened her eyes again.

A monkey stared back at her from the mural, swaying slightly.

Harper leaned against the ark, balancing. Aware that Hagit could die while she wobbled there, watching the parade of animals.

In the next room, Travis was still preaching. 'As written in Peter chapter three, verses one to eighteen: "But the day of the Lord will come like a Thief. The heavens will disappear with a roar, the elements will be destroyed by fire, and the earth and everything in it will be laid bare." So it is that we lay the groundwork for our Father as he directed in his code, preparing the hearth for his flames.'

Someone said, 'Amen.'

Hagit grumbled something unintelligible. At least she was still alive.

Harper reached down, untying her feet. She didn't try to stand. She rolled onto her stomach, looked around, and crawled on her belly to the doorway. In the next room, the walls were lined with cots, sofas and shelves of supplies and canned food. At the far end, candles encircled the table where Hagit lay bound. Travis and Frank stood at her head. Two other men at her feet. Harper leaned through the doorway, saw no one else. Just the four.

Quickly, silently, she got to her feet, testing her balance, steadying her breath. Figuring out how to proceed. But before she could decide, Travis raised his sparkling knife and paused, ready to thrust it into Hagit's throat.

Reflexively, as if it were a grenade, Harper grabbed the candle beside her and threw it at Travis's hand.

*   *   *

It missed. Sailed past his hand, grazing his head as it smacked the wall. But it served its purpose, distracting Travis and the others. Postponing the slash of the knife. While the men were momentarily confused, locating and identifying the flying object, Harper took a running start. By the time they turned to trace its source, she'd built enough momentum to leap around the table and pounce onto Pastor Travis, knocking the knife from his hand. It skittered across the floor, and Harper dove for it, but couldn't get to it before all four men dove for her. Harper managed to poke an eye and knee a groin, but the mass of four men constrained her. She lay on the floor, helpless, four men seated in a row along her back. Crushing her. The one on her calves sent pain up her left leg, and she couldn't breathe under the weight of the one crushing her lungs. Was it Frank? Anyway, she had no choice. Had to lie still, waiting for them to get off.

'How'd she get loose?' panted the one on her legs. 'I thought you tied her—'

'Where's the knife?' Travis snapped. Harper felt his weight shift, starting to get up and look.

But before he could, with a cracking thunk and a deep grunt, Frank's body slumped onto her shoulders. Instantly, the others were on their feet, scrambling. Harper rolled out from under Frank, saw Hagit, her face bloodied and wrists still tied in front of her, raised high, her hands gripping an industrial-sized can of apple sauce. Ready to strike another head.

Before the men could corral Hagit, Harper was up, dividing their attention. One of the churchmen came at her; she lunged, thrusting her fist hard into his larynx, feeling it smash. He was still falling when the next man came for her. She positioned her head and shoulders, braced her body and rammed his gut, using his own mass against him. He staggered, reeling. Harper regained her balance and was drawing back onto her stronger leg, preparing to slam him when she heard a sharp crack. The man's eyes rolled up as he fell, and another apple sauce can clattered to the floor.

Harper pivoted, fists ready. But no one confronted her. She counted three bodies, all limp. At least one – the larynx guy – was dead. She'd crushed his throat. Killed him. Somewhere in the distance, gunfire rumbled. Smoke billowed. A woman became a hot blast of white . . .

'Untie my hands.' It was an order.

And it snapped Harper back to the present. She untied Hagit's hands, but was concerned about her wound. 'Your head . . .'

'I'm fine. Let's go.' Hagit wiped blood from her eyes, pushed Harper toward the door.

But Harper didn't move. She looked around, trying to find Travis's knife. Saw shelves of food and paper goods, medical supplies and candles. Bright colored walls with happy animals, marching two by two.

No knife.

'What are you waiting for? Let's move.' Again, that military tone.

'Where's Travis?'

'Where do you think? He ran. As soon as the first one fell, he took off.'

Hagit pulled up the hem of her skirt, wiped blood off her face. Harper saw the wound on her forehead. It was the shape of a Star of David, cut into her skin.

The killer walked up and down the path, searching. People didn't just disappear, and yet there was no sign of Harper or the others. Where had they gone? Travis, Frank, Hagit and Harper had gone up this path and simply vanished. But that wasn't possible. Four people simply couldn't vanish.

The killer walked all the way up the hill, to the highest spot of the kibbutz. The lookout point. Saw no sign of any of them. In fact, the entire kibbutz looked abandoned. Almost nobody walked on the pathways; no cars pulled in or out of the gate. Maybe everyone was home, preparing for the ninth of Av? Yes, probably. Cooking big dinners for the night before their fast.

Well, good. Let them eat a big dinner. After all, it would be their last, if God accepted the final lamb.

The killer came back down the hill, stopping at the spot where Harper had disappeared. Nothing was there. No buildings. No cars. Just a huge boulder surrounded by hedges.

Wait. That boulder was abnormally large, wasn't it? Jutting out of nowhere. The killer stopped, stared into the hedges. Saw footprints, the ground pounded flat beside the rock. Of course. It was one of the bunkers. Perfect. An isolated, soundproof location. Travis had taken Hagit there.

And might have already made the sacrifice.

The killer stopped breathing. Felt a stab of fear. If the offering had been made, hope was lost. The killer would never be redeemed. Would never regain Travis's approval or earn a position of glory.

Darkness coursed through the killer, cold and dreadful with the threat of endlessness.

But someone was coming. Flip flops clopped up the path. The killer dashed into the bushes, squatted, hiding. And whirled around when a door opened in the rock.

Travis bolted out, his face hard and white as alabaster. His hands gripping a knife.

Hagit wobbled and stumbled, but held onto Harper's arm, dragging herself out of the bunker.

'I need your phone,' Hagit said.

'I didn't bring it.'

Hagit tsked.

'You need to stay here.' Harper led her to a patch of grass. 'I'll go call for help.'

'No time. I'm going after him—'

'Hagit. You're in no condition—'

'I've been hurt worse and never stopped.' She slumped onto the ground.

Harper knelt beside her. Examined the gushing cut on her forehead, a wet red clump of hair on the side of her head. An eye was swollen almost shut, and the cheek beneath was scraped and puffy. Bastards had beaten her.

'I'll be faster without you—'

'Listen.' Hagit's fingers dug into Harper's arm. She spoke quickly. 'You should know. I was Mossad. Retired, but they called me back for this. To protect you during the symposium—'

'You were Mossad?'

'They must have found out I was watching them, so they took me. But listen, you have to get to the nursery.'

The nursery?

'They left people there, waiting for a call. If I resisted – if I gave them any trouble . . . Harper, go. The children . . .'

Chloe?

Harper didn't wait to hear more. She ran.

Behind her, Hagit tried to get up, held her head and teetered. 'Wait! Find Gal. Tell him I told you. He'll catch Travis.'

Harper burst out of the bushes, didn't expect someone to be standing right beside them. Smacked into the guy, sent him sprawling, flip flops flying. Harper didn't stop, but glanced back.

Lowell was on his butt, perplexed and irate. 'What's wrong with you?' he sputtered. 'Look where you're going!'

His voice was lost among the rifle fire and screams of wounded men that chased Harper down the hill. And a white-hot explosion; a boy in the street, his face blown away. She ran past her flashbacks, ignoring them, lungs raw, leg raging, fists clenched and ready to take out anyone in her way.

Travis bolted down the hill as if chased by Satan himself.

'Hey!' The killer called to him.

Travis turned toward the voice, raised the knife, his eyes wild as a cornered dog's.

'Did you do it?'

Travis saw the killer and lowered the knife, but kept going. Didn't answer.

The killer hurried to catch up. 'The third lamb – did you get it done?'

Travis was panting.

'You didn't, did you? I can tell.' The killer ran alongside him, mouth opened in disbelief. Travis had failed? How was it possible? 'What happened?'

'Shut up,' Travis snapped.

'Ramsey – tell me where she is. There's still time.'

Travis didn't answer. He quickened his pace, took a short cut through a garden.

The killer tried to keep up, grabbing the opportunity, pausing to gulp air between phrases. 'It must be mortifying for you . . . having condemned others like me . . . for failure, only to fail yourself . . . I understand. Believe me.'

Travis headed across a driveway.

'Where are you going?'

His eyes darted toward the bungalows, then the parking lot. 'They'll be looking for me.' He stopped, deciding which way to run.

'Ramsey. Let me help.' The killer grabbed his shoulder. 'Don't you get it? There was a reason you couldn't do the offering. You weren't meant to—'

'Shh. Listen.' Ramsey raised a hand. A siren blared nearby. He took off running again, paused, doubled back toward the medical center.

The killer blocked his way. 'You're our leader. Our prophet. Our teacher. Your hands aren't meant to be bloodied.'

Travis panted, met the killer's eyes. 'Get out of my way . . .'

'No. Listen to me. Go to my bungalow and wait there.'

Travis looked over his shoulder, off to the sides.

'It's not the ninth yet, Ramsey.' The killer spoke softly. 'Trust me. Go wait in my bungalow. I'll take care of it.'

Travis hesitated. Sweat trickled down his forehead. He chewed his lip. When he answered, his chin quivered. 'Thank you.'

The killer took his hand, squeezed it. And hurried off, elated, light-hearted. With one more sacrifice, the conflagration would begin; heaven would come to earth. And, for eternity, Travis would be grateful.

Harper ran, her heart pounding Chloe's name. God. If they touched her – if they even came close to her . . . White heat blasted, sent Harper flying. No, she commanded herself. Keep going. It isn't real. It's just the past. But she felt the force, the burning gusts. It's not here, she insisted, and she sped on, spurred by Hagit's urgent words: 'The children.' Lord. The children. They would be safe. Had to be safe. But Hagit. She'd been Mossad? Assigned to protect her? Why? A woman stood in the road, reached into her robe, smiled, and blew up the checkpoint. Ignore her. She's in the past. And so is the sniper fire. Keep going. Don't give in to the flashbacks. Breathe. Stay in the present. But wait . . . what had Lowell been doing there? Guarding the bunker? Why would he after Travis had publicly fired and humiliated him? Oh God. Was Chloe okay? Were the others? Was Adi there? Or Yael? Harper's lungs were raw, her gut wrenched with rage. Up ahead, Hank fell from the roof, slamming his head. No. She ran, felt searing pain in her leg, focused on the pain. The moment. The path down the hill. She cut across a garden, behind a cottage. Around the fence to the nursery, up to the gate.

Children's voices rang out. Shouts, squeals, chatter. Noise.

Harper didn't stop; she ripped the gate open and flew across the playground, past the empty baby pool, the abandoned tricycles. Nobody was outside. Where were the church members? Inside? Slowly, deliberately, she opened the door, knees bent, ready to pounce. Hugging the wall, she crept inside and peered into the classroom.

Saw no church members. Not one. Just busy children, gathered into three groups. One working with wet clay. Another pasting torn papers onto poster board. And Chloe – Chloe was in the third group, finger-painting. Thank God. Harper dashed over to her, chin trembling. Chloe looked up and reached for her. 'Eemah!'

Harper grabbed her, held her too long and too tight, savoring first the hug, then the squirming to get free, caring not at all that her face and clothing were smeared generously with globs of cobalt blue.

If they'd been in danger, no one in the nursery had had any idea. They'd seen some commotion outside earlier; two church members had apparently been in a fight. But nobody had bothered them. No one from the church had come inside. So when Harper barged in and began barking orders, everyone was confused.

'Yael,' Harper snapped. 'Call for a medic. Send them to the bunker up the hill.'

Yael looked from Harper to Adi, hesitant. Not moving.

'Now, Yael. Hagit's up there, hurt.'

'Hagit?' Yael seemed unable to process the news.

'What happened?' Adi's brows furrowed. 'Hagit went off with that pastor—'

A little boy interrupted, crying. Speaking in Hebrew, pointing to a clay creation, somehow smashed. Yael kissed his tears and helped him fix it, not missing a beat of conversation.

'A guy named Frank,' Adi explained. 'He said Hagit had to help with a project for his church. We thought it was odd, but he talked to her for a minute, and then Hagit went along with them—'

Still, no one was getting help. 'She needs a medic,' Harper repeated. 'Go. Call.'

The boy was in Yael's arms still, holding his lopsided clay pot. But she took her phone from her pocket, punched in a number.

'Oh God.' Adi put a hand on her cheek. 'What did they do to her?'

Harper didn't answer. 'Call Gal, have him come here.' She was operating on automatic, wishing she'd brought her cell. 'And the police.'

Children scurried around the room, happy and unsupervised, hands covered with clay or paste or paint. Adi nodded, wide-eyed, and went for her phone.

It was taking too long. With every minute, Travis had more opportunity to kill someone, more chance to escape. Harper watched the clock, unable to sit passively. Thinking. If I were Travis, where would I go? How would I trap a victim?

Obviously, his bungalow would be searched. In fact, police would go through the rooms of every church member, every dig volunteer. Kibbutz security officers would examine every building, every bunker. If he were still on the kibbutz, Travis would be found within the hour.

But what if he'd already managed to get away?

He hadn't, she told herself. Megiddo was where he wanted to be. Where he believed God had ordered him to be. So where was he hiding?

Adi kept asking questions. What had happened to Harper's wrists? Why was there blood on her? What had the men done to Hagit? But Harper dodged, said she'd explain when the police and Gal got there. Meantime, she couldn't stay still. She paced, watching Chloe slap finger paint onto wet paper, unable to separate from her, yet unable to stay in the nursery while Travis was roaming free, likely to kill someone. Maybe she should just take Chloe, find a ride, and escape to Jerusalem where they'd be safe. Even before she finished the thought, she rejected it. She remembered the murders in the shuk. And Travis, holding a knife to Hagit's throat. No, Harper couldn't just take off and let a murderer strike.

But neither could she sit idle. 'Yael,' she called. 'Where is Gal?'

She shrugged. 'He's coming. He'll be here any minute.'

But it had already been ten. Ten long, irretrievable minutes. A medical jeep had driven up the hill for Hagit, hadn't come down. Why was everything moving so slowly? And where was Travis? She thought about the Bible code. The belief that the end was coming, that the battle would begin there, in Megiddo, the next day.

And then it seemed obvious. She was sure she knew where Travis had gone. If she hurried, she could stop him.

Harper went to Chloe, pulled her close, took a deep whiff of shampoo, paint, something sweet, something dusty. Chloe complained, wiggled to get on with her art.

'I'll be back soon,' Harper kissed her, hoped she was telling the truth.

But Chloe was busy with the yellow paint, didn't look up.

Adi stood at the window, looking out. 'The police should be here by now.'

'Tell them to look for Pastor Travis.' Harper rushed past her, toward the door.

'Wait. You're going? But you said you needed to talk to Gal—'

'I do. I will. There's no time now.' She headed out the door, calling over her shoulder. 'Adi. Tell them there are men in the bunker – they might need doctors.'

Adi followed her, called, 'Might?'

'I mean they will, if they're alive,' Harper yelled back and hurried down the path.

The jeep was an unexpected piece of luck. It was idling right outside the office when Harper got there. She'd planned to go inside and try to rent or borrow a car. If no cars were available, she'd ask for a ride. If that failed, she'd call Dr Ben Haim or Dr Hadar. But all that would take time. And she didn't have time. If she was right, a life was already in danger. Might already have been taken. So, without a heartbeat of hesitation, she jumped into the jeep, put it in gear and drove to the kibbutz exit. Security recognized the jeep, opened the gate. And Harper was on her way to Megiddo South.

She expected to be followed. Technically, she'd stolen the vehicle. The guard at the gate would say someone – a short-haired blonde – had driven it out. They'd soon realize who that was and put out an alert, so she wouldn't have much time. She pushed down on the gas, shifted gears, felt the engine surge. Checked the rear-view mirror, saw nobody. Had to get to the dig before they caught up with her. She passed a caravan of trucks loaded with soldiers. A bus full of tourists. No cops. Nobody chasing her. She knew the way to Megiddo South, but the trip seemed longer than usual. Had she made a wrong turn? Oh God, was she lost? The hills, the fields all looked identical. And meantime, where was Travis? What was he doing? Had he recruited more help? Taken someone from the dig – maybe one of the students? Was he, even now, cutting a mark into a forehead or slashing a throat?

Harper pressed the pedal, roaring down the road in the little jeep. And finally, ahead, she saw the tower of the abandoned prison. The trailers that served as dig offices. The parking lot for Megiddo South. And in it, four identical Toyotas, parked in a row.

Had Travis driven one of those cars? Harper pulled the jeep up beside them, got out and looked inside each of them. They were impeccably clean, uncluttered. Rentals? Rented by the dig? Or by Travis's followers?

Her leg throbbed, but she scurried to the trailers, edging around them, listening, looking. Finding no one.

But Travis had to be here. Harper looked behind her, up ahead. The site was perfectly still, silent as time.

Travis might be hiding, watching her. He'd be desperate. Harper needed a weapon; she crept into the supply shed, grabbed a hammer, a pick.

Slowly, she moved around the trailers, peering into windows. Finding an empty bunk bed, tables covered with computers, printouts, maps, file boxes, tools, sodas, water bottles. But no Travis. She hunkered beside a generator, holding still, a predator waiting for its prey to reveal itself. But around her, nothing moved, just an occasional hollow breeze. She got up and searched the site, crossing scaffolds, looking into pits, tracing the perimeter, hearing only her sneakers on the ground, the rustle of her clothing, the sound of her breath.

The rest was silence.

But somebody must be here. Those four cars in the parking lot hadn't driven there themselves. Harper rotated a full circle, saw no sign of Travis. She retraced her steps, returning to the parking lot, accepting that she'd been wrong. Travis wasn't at the dig. She was the only living creature there. All alone. A chill skittered up her neck; a ripple of warning. Wait – were those footsteps behind her? She whirled, gripping the pick, saw an empty expanse of parking lot, the abandoned prison tower. Letting out a breath, she kept walking. Told herself she was imagining the faint shoveling sounds; nobody was in the pit. But when voices flitted by, too faint to understand, Harper pivoted, poised to strike.

And found empty air.

Air and stillness. The voices faded like the breeze. The site was deserted except, perhaps, for recently released spirits of the dead, unearthed by the dig. Maybe they were toying with her. But no one else was there; work had stopped early in anticipation of the fast day. And there was no sign of Travis, no evidence that he was trying to make a sacrifice at Megiddo, the location mentioned in the Bible.

Harper looked one more time across the site; saw the excavation, the top of the ancient wall. Raw, newly exposed earth and rock. Bare scaffolds. Ropes swinging in the breeze. Stark shadows.

Lots of shadows.

Which meant it was late in the afternoon. Probably around four o'clock.

And there were only about eight hours until the ninth of Av.

She was wasting time. Had to get back to the kibbutz and help them search there for Travis – assuming they hadn't already found him. She hopped back into the jeep. Pulling out of the parking lot, she glanced at the row of parked cars. Wondered again what they were doing there, who'd left them there. Four brand new Corollas. Never mind.

When she pulled into the kibbutz, the guard directed her to the side of the road, removed her from the jeep and escorted her to a building near the gate. Harper tried to talk to him, but he didn't understand English. Or didn't want to talk to her. He led her to a room with cinder block walls painted a shade of avocado green that reminded Harper of Chloe's finger painting, its mixture of yellow and blue. The room had a grate over the window, was furnished with several folding chairs, a table bolted to the floor. Nothing else.

Harper sat. Ran a hand through her hair. Reasoned that she had some explaining to do, but that she'd be all right once the authorities understood what had happened. What her military background was. What she'd been trying to do. Meantime, she wondered what had happened in the hour since she'd left. Had they found Travis? Rounded up his followers? Was Hagit all right? And Chloe . . . She closed her eyes, remembering her scent. Were the children safe? Hot rage pulsed through her, thinking of the council members, their threats. She stood. Went to the window, noted the iron bars. No way she could climb out; in fact, she couldn't even really see out with all the crud and dust on the pane. Damn. She should have brought her phone. Called Hank, let him know what was going on. She was in a damned holding cell – how long had she been there? Had it been minutes? Half an hour? How long would she have to wait? She paced, recycling her questions. Sat again. Stood again. Wanted to scream, pound on the walls.

Finally, the door opened, and Gal came in.

'Thank God,' she stood. 'Gal, can I go now?'

Gal took a seat. Didn't indicate that she'd be leaving.

'Have they found Travis?'

He watched her. 'I think you have things to tell me,' he said.

And she did. Harper told him everything. About the men she'd followed to the bunker, their attempt to kill Hagit as a sacrifice. Their threat to harm the children if Hagit resisted. She told him about the confrontation and Travis's escape, her mistaken notion that he'd fled to the dig, and the likelihood that, even now, he and the other church leaders would try to kill someone before the ninth of Av.

Gal watched her, unsurprised. He crossed his legs. 'So the two men who are dead, Harper. You killed them?'

The question startled her. 'We . . . Wait. Two men?' She'd been sure only of one. Unless Hagit had killed someone with that can of apple sauce? 'I had no choice. They'd have killed Hagit . . .'

'You'll have to explain it to the police.' He seemed cold. Unfriendly.

Harper was impatient. 'Of course. But remember, I told the police what the church was up to, and they didn't believe me. I told Dr Ben Haim, Dr Hadar. No one listened—'

'Maybe people listened. Maybe they didn't tell you.'

Really? 'Well, if they listened, why didn't they protect Hagit? Never mind. It doesn't matter. Because now, the ninth of Av is just a few hours away. If we don't stop Travis before then, someone else will die.'

Gal didn't move. His gaze remained steady.

'Gal? Listen to me. They won't stop – they believe they're doing God's will . . .'

'I understand. But you've already done too much. You need to talk to the authorities. And then stay out of it.'

'Talk can wait. If Yael or Adi will watch Chloe, I can help . . .'

'This is not your country—'

'Neither was Iraq, but I still tried my best—'

'And you've killed people here.' Gal's eyes flared.

Harper closed her mouth, swallowed. Surely, they wouldn't blame her for the deaths. She'd been rescuing a citizen – a former Mossad agent. 'Someone else will die, Gal.'

Gal's eyes still didn't waver. 'We've been watching these people. We know they are planning something for tomorrow. Because of who you are – who your husband is – because of that situation, you are being treated with special . . . consideration. You have stirred up trouble, made it worse. Another person would be in jail for what you've done. I realize your intention is to be helpful, but rest assured: this problem is not on your shoulders. Do you understand?' He watched her, waiting.

Harper felt her face get hot. She'd killed two men? 'I do.'

'Good.' He stood. 'I'll take you to your daughter. You can visit

Hagit if you wish. Talk to the police. But nothing else. I warn you: do not get any more involved.'

His tone was final. He gave her shoulder a restrained squeeze before he took her arm. Harper went along, mentally arguing, uttering not a word.

The search for Travis wasn't going well. His bungalow held only Harold, who swore he hadn't seen him and had no idea where he was. In fact, no one did. Church members, bereft at his disappearance, had not all been accounted for. Those who'd been located were confined to their bungalows, pending investigation of the bunker incident. Security officers, soldiers and police moved all over the kibbutz, disrupting evening meals and preparations for the upcoming fast day, warning people to stay together, not to go out alone. Looking for Travis and the few missing followers.

Not finding them.

Harper stood in the waiting room of the medical center, rocking Chloe's stroller back and forth. She couldn't relax. Too much adrenalin in her system. Gal had refused to let her join the search, had even gone to her bungalow and confiscated her passport and phone. Had left her here, pushing Chloe's stroller in circles around the waiting room, staring at the door, hoping a doctor would come tell her how Hagit was.

She checked the clock on the wall. Five twenty-five. Where were the doctors? She'd been here for forty minutes. Had talked to Inspector Ben Baruch, had walked the circumference of the room a hundred times. Had wanted to call Hank, but Gal had her phone. Why had Gal taken it? Who was he afraid she'd call? Harper checked Chloe, who napped soundly after a day of hard playing. Lord, why was no one in the waiting room?

Harper turned the stroller around, pushed it toward the window. Told herself that Hagit was tough, that she'd be fine. But how badly hurt had she been? She'd been dizzy, her eye blackened, forehead cut. Harper reversed her direction and headed back toward the door. Why wouldn't the police let her help? She was wasting time there, waiting, doing nothing. The ninth of Av was six hours away. Travis and his people would make a desperate last effort at a sacrifice. She wanted to assist the search, but Inspector Ben Baruch had scolded her like an angry schoolteacher. 'I don't give, as you say, a rat's ass what war you fought or what you're intentions are.'

She'd asked for her passport, her phone.

He'd looked at her eyes. 'I think not. Not until this mess is sorted out. And meantime, you are to keep out of it. Completely out of it. Understood?'

Why did everyone ask her that?

'Understood.' But she didn't understand, not really. With her training and experience, she could be an asset to them.

She turned the stroller around, frustrated. Breathing too fast. Deciding she'd waited long enough. She stepped to the door to the treatment rooms, opened it a crack. Peeked inside, saw a hallway with several rooms. Heard Mozart playing, saw no one. Propped the door open with Chloe's stroller and went into the hallway. Looked into the first room. Saw Jimmy, his arm in a plaster cast, staring at a ceiling fan. Frank was in the bed opposite, his skull wrapped in gauze.

Oh dear. She dashed away before either noticed her, continued down the hall. Wondered where the other men were. That one guy, Wendell – she'd broken his jaw. They'd have to wire him. She looked into the next room.

'Why are you sneaking? You look like a thief.' Hagit was sitting up in bed, holding a cup of something. Her forehead was pasted together with butterfly bandages.

'You're all right?' Harper let out a breath she hadn't known she'd been holding.

'Me? Of course. Where's the baby?'

Harper glanced back at the stroller. 'Here. She's sleeping.' Harper ran a hand through her hair. 'Damn. I've been so worried. There's no one to get information from . . .'

'They're a little busy here. Somebody went on a rampage and broke a ton of bones. And this isn't exactly a New York City hospital. It's a small staff here.'

Harper wasn't appeased. 'Hagit, Frank and another one of Travis's followers are in the next room. Nobody's even watching them. Those guys tried to kill you—'

'Believe me. They're harmless now. Police are stationed outside and they're checking on me. Besides, those two next door are no danger any more, and I think a couple of others are waiting for surgery. You did some damage.' She smiled.

Harper swallowed, recalling the snapping sound of Jimmy's arm. The crushing of his companion's throat. She looked around, checked Chloe again. 'So, are you in pain?'

Hagit smirked. 'I have a concussion. A cracked cheekbone. A black eye. An etching in my forehead. Of course I'm in pain.'

Harper nodded. For a moment they were both silent.

'So I guess that means you can't babysit Chloe tonight?'

Hagit nodded. 'See? I've been too good to you. Now, I take off one night, and you're helpless.'

Another pause.

'It's too quiet here, Hagit. I don't like it. You should have a guard.'

'They put guards outside, didn't you see?'

'But that's outside.'

'The nurses are here. Remember, we were all in the army.'

'But the nurses are busy. You said it yourself.'

'I have an alarm button.'

More silence.

'They took my phone. Can I borrow yours to call Hank?'

Hagit blinked a few times. 'The battery's dead. I need to recharge it.'

'I'll take it back to the bungalow. I can recharge it—'

'But it's with my things. Somewhere. I don't know where they put them.'

Harper watched her, saw Hagit's eyes shift. Was she lying? Why would she lie about her phone? And why wouldn't anyone let her make a call? Were they afraid she'd cause trouble – call the embassy or something? Or . . . were they trying to prevent her from calling Hank? Why would they? Oh God. Had something happened to him?

No, ridiculous. Nothing had happened to him. If something had, they wouldn't hide it from her. The police – hell, the government would have told her. She was being paranoid, imagining problems as if she didn't already have enough. Even so, she wondered: if Hagit didn't have the phone, how could she know the battery was dead?

'Go. I've had enough conversation.'

Harper gave her a careful hug, promised she'd be back in the morning. In the hall, she glanced into the room across the hall. Peter Watts was in there, still limp and ghastly pale; a nurse checked his blood pressure. Harper was considering going in to wish him well when Hagit called, 'One more thing.'

Harper turned. Hagit had hobbled out of bed and had made it to the doorway. She held the wall for support, curled a forefinger, motioning Harper to come close.

'What are you doing? You need to be in bed.'

Hagit stared at Harper's throat, nodding. 'Okay. You're wearing it. Remember. The baby, too. Both of you. Wear your *hamsas*. Promise.'

The nurse looked out at them.

'Go lie down,' Harper shooed her.

'Promise me.'

The nurse looked up; Peter Watts turned a wan face their way.

Hagit didn't move. 'Well?'

'I promise.'

Only then would Hagit turn around and, refusing help, make her way back to bed.

Two soldiers stood guard outside the medical center. Across the road, Lowell sprawled on a bench. As Harper approached, he called to her.

'Wait. Stop. They let you out?'

She glanced at him, said nothing. Pushed the stroller forward.

'I heard about you. You're a killer.' He pointed at her. 'And Pastor Travis – you tried to kill him, too.' He started to get up, lost his balance. Sat again. 'You belong in jail.'

Harper swallowed her temper. Lowell was an outcast, bitter and obviously drunk. She ignored him, continued on her way.

'You'll answer for your sins,' Lowell called. 'Sooner than later.'

She kept walking, her jaw tightening.

'Thou shalt not kill, sinner! You'll burn in hell.'

She pushed the baby across the street, wishing more people were around so she could get lost in a crowd.

'Ignore me, but you'll be judged.' He was shouting now, and he'd made it to his feet. 'That's right – judged by the Lord Almighty, God Himself . . .'

Harper didn't have to, but she turned up a side path to get out of Lowell's line of sight. Why hadn't he been sequestered like the other members of the church? Was he one of the few who hadn't been accounted for? Hadn't the soldiers on guard noticed him?

Never mind. She had more important problems. And Lowell had stopped hollering. In fact, the only sounds she heard were the stroller's wheels rolling and creaking along the ground. Except for Lowell and the security guards on patrol, the streets were empty. The kibbutz was unnaturally quiet, like a lull before a storm.

*   *   *

The first thing she had to do was dump the stroller. It was so damned bulky and awkward. She'd resurrect the sling; whatever was coming, Harper would have Chloe wrapped against her body where she'd be able to protect her. She spread the cloth onto the bed. Changed Chloe's diaper without waking her. Sat for a moment, planning what to do next.

With Hagit hurt and the kibbutz locked down tight, nobody was coming or going, complicating Harper's plans for returning to Jerusalem. She peered out the window at Travis's bungalow, at the valley beyond, wondering where he was. The sun hung low near the horizon. Sunset would bring the fast day of the ninth of Av – and he would try to make the third sacrifice by then. Another two hours, at most.

Unless Travis was following the Christian calendar. In that case, the holiday wouldn't begin at sunset; it would wait until midnight, the start of July twenty-sixth.

Either way, there wasn't much time.

Harper's stomach rumbled, reminding her that she hadn't eaten all day, that she should have something. But she couldn't stop to eat, not now. First, she had to get to a phone and call Hank, let him know what was happening. And then, even though it irked her to leave with Travis on the loose, she had to convince Gal or Ben Baruch to let her get the hell out of there. Except, wait. She couldn't leave without Hagit. She'd go get her as soon as she'd talked to Hank.

Harper lifted Chloe, whose eyes fluttered open and closed again, and set her on the fabric between the half-packed duffle bags on the bed. As she'd done hundreds of times, she pulled the sling onto her back, holding Chloe by tugging on both ends of the cloth, crossing them over her breasts, tying them behind her under Chloe's bottom, pulling them around her waist and tying them again, securing Chloe onto her back. Chloe's head sagged against her; her legs dangled, relaxed.

Then, arming herself with a baby bottle full of juice and a spare diaper, Harper disobeyed both Gal and Inspector Ben Baruch by leaving her bungalow and set out to find a phone.

Schmuel was nervous. He talked too fast, too loud.

'The phone?' he repeated, bug-eyed, as if he didn't know what the word meant.

'I need to call Jerusalem.'

'I'm not sure that it's possible.'

'I'll pay if there are charges—'

'I don't know. I'll have to ask. There are restrictions now.'

'Fine. I understand,' Harper smiled, made it open and warm. 'Go ask. I'll wait.'

Schmuel looked at the closed door behind him. Looked back at the phone on the desk, then at Harper. He didn't trust her.

'While you check, okay if I get something to eat?' She wandered off toward the vending machines, eyed bags of chips, cookies, chunks of halvah. When he thought she was busy with food, Schmuel slipped into the back room.

And Harper darted back to the desk. Quickly, she picked up the phone, punched in the number to Hank's cell. Waited. Watched the door. Why was she so nervous? If they found her on the phone, what would they do? Scold her? But the call took forever to go through. Finally, it began ringing. And each ring lasted an eternity. Finally, Hank answered: 'Hi.'

Harper burst out, 'Thank God, Hank. Listen, something's—'

But Hank's voice continued. 'This is Hank Jennings. Leave a message at the tone . . .'

Harper's mouth dropped. She froze for a moment, felt lost. Told herself to get a grip. Hank was simply attending a meeting, taking a nap, having a cocktail or a shower. It was no big deal. She ended the call, leaving no message. Schmuel would be back any second. She'd ask him about transportation to Jerusalem. If not tonight, then tomorrow. Maybe she could rent a car or could catch a bus.

Except that she was supposed to be staying in her bungalow. And no one was leaving the kibbutz. And even if they were, there would be no bus service or rental transactions on the ninth of Av. Damn. She looked at the phone, realized that, even if Hank were busy, she might still be able to reach him through Trent. The office door was still closed. No sign of Schmuel. Fingers jittery, she placed the call, waited for it to go through. But it didn't; instead, she heard a series of electronic tones, followed by a computerized voice speaking Hebrew. Probably, she'd misdialed. She tried again, watching the door. Same thing. It made no sense. What was wrong with Trent's phone?

She hung up just as the office door opened and Schmuel came out, eyeing her. Suspicious. 'Sorry.'

'What?'

'I can't let you use the phone. Only officials can use our phone to call outside the kibbutz right now. Security restrictions.' He frowned. 'Don't you have a private phone? A cell?'

Harper's face heated up. Did he know it had been confiscated? 'Yeah, but I lost it, and I'm supposed to check in with my husband.' She faked a ditsy smile.

He sat at his desk, crossed his arms. 'I don't know what to tell you. Borrow one? This one won't be available for a while.'

Harper thanked him. Charged a granola bar and a lemon soda. Ate them as she walked to the medical center.

Stop it, she told herself. Trent might have dropped his phone in the swimming pool. It might have simply been a dud – after all, their phones were temporary, assigned by the symposium. Trent's might have been defective, out of order. Not everything was a crisis.

Or maybe something was wrong. Hadn't she seen Trent on television—on the news? And Hagit had suddenly changed the channel. Why? Had something happened to Trent? To the symposium?

To Hank?

Harper had a chill, saw him fall from the roof.

No. Nothing had happened; she'd talked to him after the television broadcast. He'd been fine.

She kept walking, Chloe's legs dangling, bumping the backs of her thighs. It was getting late. Dinner was being served in the restaurant, and the sun was almost to the horizon.

Security officers stopped her, asked where she was headed. 'It's a situation,' one explained. 'I need to ask you.'

Harper's stomach growled. 'Dinner.' It made sense.

'Are you with the church?'

'No. The dig.'

'You're a student or a volunteer?'

'A volunteer.' She told them her name.

They glanced at each other, then looked back at her. 'You?' one asked.

'Really?' the other seemed amazed.

The taller one shrugged. 'So small? You must be stronger than you look.'

'Anyway, you're a celebrity,' the other one grinned. 'You rescued an Israeli.'

Harper smiled. At least somebody appreciated her.

They nodded her on, and Harper continued along the path, thinking about Hank and Trent, Hagit and Travis, and hoping that somehow she'd be able to get hold of a car to drive to Jerusalem. She went to the restaurant, intending to grab some food from the buffet and take it along, but the aroma of dinner awakened Chloe, who clearly wanted to eat.

Even with the clock ticking to Armageddon, Harper had to stop and get dinner for her daughter. She hurried into the dining hall, thinking that if all soldiers were mothers, wars would have to be fought between meals and after bedtime, with breaks for diaper changes. The room was full. Travis's church members sat together, watched by armed soldiers. Harper found a table in the corner, untied her sling, sat Chloe in a high chair, fixed two plates. Pasta salad, fruit, cut-up chicken. Yogurt. Hummus. Pita. Tomato and cucumber salad. Chloe stuffed food into her mouth, jabbering.

'Geet?'

Oh dear. Chloe wanted to know where Hagit was. 'She's taking a nap.'

'Geet?' Chloe repeated. Sensing Harper's hesitation. 'Geet.' She stopped eating.

Harper held out a piece of chicken, but Chloe frowned. 'Geet!'

'We'll see Hagit after dinner.'

Chloe seemed satisfied, stuffed the chicken into her mouth. Minutes passed while Harper wolfed down some food and, when Chloe was finished, she used the table to fasten her into the sling again, refilled the juice bottle and grabbed a banana and cookies for later. Then she hurried out, determined to find Travis before nightfall.

The security guards were like herding dogs, keeping everyone in a bunch like sheep. But the killer was no sheep. Couldn't stand being around the others any more. Couldn't stand the sound of Harold's voice, or the smell of so many variations of toilet water. Couldn't listen to their insipid whispered conversations. What should they wear when meeting the Lord? Was it better to bow or kneel in front of God? Would they still have their bodies or just be spirits? Would everyone be the same age?

Idiots. How would it be possible to spend eternity with them?

As if eternity were even possible any more. The ninth of Av was upon them.

And where was Travis? He hadn't listened. Hadn't hidden in the bungalow and waited. What could possibly have taken him away from his followers at this critical point? The only sensible answer was that he was off trying to make the final sacrifice on his own. That had to be it. Travis wouldn't give up on fulfilling God's requirements.

No, Travis wouldn't give up. And neither would the killer. Guards watched everyone in the dining hall, but the killer kept a distance, sitting alone, invisibly edging to the hallway.

And now outside, the killer moved through shadows towards the medical center, becoming one with the dusk. It should be simple, really, to complete the sacrifice that Travis had bollixed up. To fix his mistakes. The only obstacle was that the lamb was heavily guarded, allowed no unapproved visitors. But the killer would slide by, get inside the medical center, grab a scalpel from the supply closet. And, while the staff was busy with an emergency elsewhere, complete the ritual.

Travis would be forever grateful.

Sundown was minutes away. The killer approached the medical center. The breeze had died down; the air was almost perfectly still. It was as if God Himself were watching, holding His breath.

'Harper!' Lynne ran up the path to catch her.

Harper slowed, waited for Lynne. What was Lynne doing out on the street alone? Wasn't she supposed to stay with the other church members?

'It's so good to see someone other than church members. It's been crazy.' Lynne was breathless, dressed in black leggings, a black long-sleeved tee. She tickled Chloe's dangling feet, got a smile. 'First, they made us stay in our bungalows. But they couldn't watch all the bungalows, and some of us were unaccounted for. So they gathered us all together in the restaurant and now, we have to stay there or in the meeting hall until further notice.'

'So what are you doing out here?' Harper stopped, looked at her.

'I've got permission. To go see Peter.'

Oh. Of course. Harper stepped around a parked jeep. Nodded back when the security guards waved at her. 'How's he doing?'

'Fine.' She shook her head. 'No. That's what I tell people, but he's not fine. His heart was stressed. He's having a hard time getting his energy back. Stupid scorpion.' She sounded hollow.

Harper remembered the weeks of Hank lying in the hospital. Her own voice must have sounded like Lynne's: empty and far away.

'Harper, listen. Everyone's heard about what happened in that bunker. With your babysitter and Pastor Travis. I want you to know. Most of us were completely flabbergasted. We had no idea what was going on. And, Harper, I don't blame you one bit for what you did. You were right when you tried to warn me about Pastor Travis. But even still, a human sacrifice? It's hard to believe.'

Harper didn't answer, just kept walking.

'But if it's true about the sacrifice – and everyone's saying it is – then whatever you did, they had it coming. I heard you took down four of them, single-handed.'

Chloe began singing the *mayim* song.

'Actually, in a way, I'm glad something like this happened.' Lynne was out of breath, walking fast to keep up. 'It opened my eyes. It showed who Travis really is, how he's led us astray, off the path to salvation. I still believe in God's word, but we were supposed to sacrifice lambs, not people. That had to be Travis's interpretation, don't you think?' She put a hand on her forehead as if it ached. 'It's like he had me – had all of us under a spell. He convinced me to commit adultery with him. And he lied to me about other women. But worst of all, he misled the church. He used his charisma to manipulate us. For all we know, everything he preached – everything – the codes, the prophecies – maybe it's all hooey. Harper, I'm so angry . . .'

'Do you have any idea where he is?'

'Travis?' Lynne's eyebrows went up. 'Me?' She shook her head. 'But I bet Marlene does. The redhead. Ask her, if you can find her. She's his latest . . . disciple. Dumb as cauliflower. Even now, wherever she is, she hasn't a clue that he's using her.'

They turned onto the road to the medical center.

'You're going this way, too?'

'Visiting Hagit.'

'Geet?' Chloe stopped singing, echoed. 'Geet! Geet!'

'Hagit is your sitter? Poor thing. How is she?'

Chloe reached up, grabbed onto Harper's hair, kicking, singing. 'Geet, eemah. Geet. Geet.'

Harper reached back and grabbed Chloe's legs, squeezed them to stop the kicking. Never really answered because she saw Lowell, huddling on a bench across from the medical center.

Lynne saw him, too. 'Hey, Lowell. What're you doing over there? Everyone's supposed to be in the restaurant, together . . .'

Lowell spotted them, jumped to his feet and dashed into the bushes. Harper started after him, Chloe clutching her head, Lynne following. But Lowell was nowhere. Not in the bushes. Not in the road on the other side. Lowell was gone.

'Where'd he go?' Lynne frowned, looked up and down the empty road. 'He must be here somewhere.'

Harper had no idea, but she wasn't going to get distracted by searching for Lowell. Travis was the one she wanted. She turned, walked back through the bushes.

'That was weird.' Lynne kept talking. 'They haven't found some of the members – Marlene included, by the way. But Lowell? He was right there in the open. Why didn't they make him join the rest of us?'

Harper thought she knew. 'Wasn't he kicked out of the church?'

'What makes you think that?' Lynne's eyes widened. 'Did someone tell you?'

Harper kept walking.

'Because, no. Lowell wasn't kicked out of the church, just out of the council. He's still a member of the church.'

Harper was about to suggest that Lowell might not consider himself a member, but security guards stopped them outside the medical center, checking for weapons. Harper asked if they'd seen the man sitting across the way, on the bench.

'Lowell,' the shorter one nodded. 'Why?'

'He's in our group,' Lynne said. 'Our church. Why isn't he being confined like everyone else?'

The guard bristled. 'We're aware of him. Don't be concerned.'

'Really? You're aware of him?' Lynne scoffed. 'So I guess you're also aware that he just ran off through those bushes and disappeared?'

The guard looked past her, across the road. Saw the empty bench. Glanced at his partner, who said something into his radio. 'He'll turn up. Don't be concerned.' He opened the door, admitting them into the center.

In the waiting room, Lynne touched Harper's arm. 'Harper, I need to say this: Thank you. For telling me the truth about Travis. I didn't believe you, but now I see that you were right. Once this is over, I'm going to tell him what I think of him, what a fake he is. And then I'm starting fresh. I still have Peter. And God.'

Harper wasn't sure how to respond. Lynne's eyes were too bright, and she sounded too cheerful. 'I'm glad for you, Lynne.'

'GEET!' Chloe shrieked, slamming her legs into the back of Harper's thighs. 'GEET!'

Harper spoke over her shoulder, reminding Chloe about the concept of 'inside voice'.

'Down? See Geet,' Chloe said softly.

Fine. Harper's leg was sore, and the extra weight of carrying Chloe was aggravating it. She knelt and untied the sling, releasing Chloe onto a chair, rolling the fabric up, stuffing it into her shoulder bag. By the time they were ready and Chloe had quieted down, Lynne had disappeared through the door to the patient rooms.

Holding Chloe's hand, Harper entered the hallway leading to Hagit's room. Lynne's voice flitted past them, cheerfully telling Peter that he looked better. That his coloring was good.

Chloe tugged at Harper's hand, trying to get free. Apparently, the long corridor was an invitation to run. Harper knelt to meet Chloe at eye level, explaining that this wasn't a place to play. People were here because they were sick or hurt, and they needed to rest. Chloe's eyes got big. She sucked a few fingers. Harper tussled her hair, kissed her. Led her to Hagit's room.

Hagit was sound asleep, snoring.

Chloe whispered, 'Shh.'

Behind them the door swung open. Lowell's mouth opened in surprise.

'Lowell?'

'Sorry,' he stammered. 'Wrong room.' He backed up a step, reached for the door.

But, in an eye blink, Harper was ahead of him, blocking his way.

'How did you get past the security guards?'

'No one was at the door. I just walked in.'

What? No one was guarding the building? 'What are you doing here?'

He didn't answer.

'Eemah,' Chloe came over, grabbed her leg.

'Tell me.' Harper's voice was low, threatening. 'What do you want with Hagit?'

'Nothing. Like I said . . .'

'Eemah,' Chloe repeated, louder.

'Were you planning to help Travis?' She took a step closer, pointing a finger at his chest. 'Trying to finish what he screwed up – that final sacrifice? That would get you back into your pastor's favor, wouldn't it? Even get you back on the council.'

Lowell's eyebrows rose; he shook his head, kept backing away from her until he was flat against the wall.

'How were you going to do it?'

'Do what?' His hands went up, defensively.

'EEMAH!' Chloe shouted.

'Just a second, sweetie.' Harper glanced down to quiet her.

Lowell used that moment, flung his body forward to get to the door, bumping Harper, knocking Chloe onto the floor. Chloe was stunned, but Harper wheeled around, pouncing, taking him down. As he fell, he crashed into a table, sent a bedpan clattering to the floor. Chloe howled.

Harper was on Lowell, whispering into his ear. 'You sonofabitch. You're not going to hurt anyone.'

'I wasn't trying to.'

'What's the trouble? Come here, darling.'

Harper looked up. Hagit was squatting beside Chloe, comforting her; Chloe was breathless, gaping at Harper, at Lowell.

Great, Harper thought. She'd traumatized her baby. 'It's okay, Chloe,' she cooed, tried to sound convincing. Lowell twisted, trying to roll over; she shoved her fist into the small of his back. 'Mommy's going to take this man to see the nice policemen. It'll just take a minute. You stay here with Hagit, okay?'

'No!'

But Hagit had already taken Chloe's hand and was leading her to the bed. 'I want to show you something. Look what my bed can do.' She pushed a button, and the foot of the bed rose up. 'You want a ride?'

Chloe nodded, enthralled.

Lowell kept protesting and whining, but Harper ignored him, straddling him while she unfastened his belt and used it to bind his hands. Then she pulled him to his feet, shoved him into the hall, through the door. They were crossing the waiting room when an alarm went off. A nurse shouted in Hebrew. The front door opened and the guards ran in.

Harper shoved Lowell toward them. 'I found this man in Hagit's room—'

Lowell shouted, 'This woman assaulted me!'

But they kept running past Lowell, past Harper, through the door to the patient rooms. Oh God. What had happened? Chloe was back there, and Hagit . . .

She whirled around, following the guards, yanking Lowell by the shirt.

Lowell let out a breath. 'Please. Untie me.'

Harper dragged him back to the door, opened it a crack. Saw two nurses running with a cart. A medic yelling. Everyone, even the guards, were rushing into a patient's room.

The room belonging to Peter Watts.

'I swear. I wasn't going to hurt her.' Lowell was almost crying. 'Please let me go.'

Harper wasn't paying attention. She watched the corridor, listened to orders being given in a foreign tongue. Recognized the emergency. The coordination, the reflexive responses. Felt sand on her skin, heard the buzzing of flies. The moans of the wounded.

'I was in the wrong room. I wasn't there to see your friend. I was there to see Peter – I swear.'

Wait. Peter? 'Why?'

'Why?'

'Why do you want to see Peter? Why did you go to all the trouble of sneaking past the guards? What was so important?'

Lowell closed his eyes. Shook his head. 'Let me go. Please.'

'Tell me.'

He opened his eyes. 'I've been on the outs with the pastor and the council.'

'I know.'

'I was steamed at the whole bunch of them. So I did some poking around.'

'And?'

And I found something I thought Peter should know.' Lowell met her eyes, lowered his voice. 'His wife has been having an affair with Travis.'

Harper rolled her eyes.

'His wife thinks Travis is in love with her. And that he'd marry her if not for Peter.'

The tingle of warning began on her neck even before she fully comprehended what he was saying.

'So Peter's wife, she decided to get rid of the problem. Lynne put that scorpion in his glove—'

'That's crap. Why would she think it would bite Peter? Those were my gloves.' The tingle moved down her back, refusing to be dismissed. 'I lent them to Peter at the site. She couldn't have known he'd be wearing them.'

Lowell shook his head. 'She did it. I know she did.'

The tingle penetrated her skin, got to her gut. 'How do you know?'

Lowell shrugged. 'This is church business. Pastor dismissed me, and I wanted to know why. Somebody had to have pushed him to do it. Somebody who resented my place at his side. So I studied up on people who might have coveted my spot, and I found out the affair. And when Peter had that accident, I nosed around and guess what? She planted the scorpion. The proof was in her dig kit.'

How could he know that? 'What proof?'

'Nothing much. Just a small jar with air holes poked into the top.'

Oh. Harper pictured Lynne, spilling the scorpion from the jar into the glove.

'That's why I came here. To warn Peter that his wife tried to kill him. And that she might try again—'

By the time he finished his sentence, Harper was on her feet, running down the hall, oblivious to the voice trailing after her, calling, 'Wait! Come back. Untie me!'

A crowd was in Peter's room, surrounding his bed. A doctor barked orders. Nurses scurried to obey. Guards watched, rapt, ready to assist. But, oddly, one person was missing: Lynne.

Harper took a second look. Lynne had to be there; Harper had seen her going in just moments ago and hadn't seen her come out.

Maybe Lynne was standing in the corner, out of the doctor's way. Harper poked her head into the room, looked around. No Lynne.

Lord. Could Lowell have been right? Had Lynne put the scorpion in Peter's glove and come here to finish him off? Harper gestured to a guard, trying to get his attention, to ask if he'd seen Lynne. But before he responded, she realized that, if both guards were here with Peter, they weren't at their posts. And Hagit was unprotected.

Harper flew. Hagit's room was just across the hall, but the hall seemed elastic, stretching, expanding as she ran. Hagit had been chosen as the third lamb. Travis had tried to kill her. It was almost the ninth of Av, and Hagit was alone.

Harper propelled herself forward, leaping the final few steps, sliding across the tiled floor, flinging open the door to Hagit's room. Seeing Hagit in bed, her arms crossed over the sheets, her jaw set in anger.

And Lynne standing beside her, pressing a scalpel to her throat.

Everyone froze.

'Lynne, stop.' Harper used a soothing tone, slowly scanned the room for Chloe; didn't see her. Felt her stomach twist. Oh God. Where was she? 'It's too late. There's no point in killing Hagit—'

'It's not too late. And nobody else can do it – not even Ramsey. Just me.'

'It won't do you any good. Travis doesn't care about you; he's moved on.'

'What?'

'He's in love with someone else.' Harper scanned the room, couldn't find Chloe.

Lynne scoffed. 'With Marlene? That airhead? He'll be bored in five minutes. That woman – she was supposed to be my assistant but she was useless. No, I'm the only woman strong enough for him. And after I sacrifice the third lamb – on my own, without Marlene tagging along – he'll see that. The conflagration will begin, and Ramsey and I will have eternity—'

'Oh, please, Lynne. You don't believe that crap. He's conned all of you. Nothing's going to happen.'

'You're wrong.' Lynne spoke through her teeth. 'You're not a believer. Stay out of it.'

Under the sheet, Hagit's belly wiggled. Oh Lord. Chloe was in there. Harper wanted to charge, knock the blade from Lynne's hand, take her down, but she forced herself to stay still and take a breath. Hagit could die with a flick of Lynne's wrist. And Chloe wasn't far from the blade.

'There's more at stake here than just a life, Harper. This woman was chosen for the final sacrifice. Ramsey himself picked her out. I have to complete it for the sake of salvation—'

'What happened to Peter?' Harper interrupted. Changed the subject.

Lynne frowned. 'Peter's dead.'

Hagit's belly moved again. Harper tried to divert Lynne's attention. 'Dead? No – he made it. They're attending to him now . . .'

'You're lying. Don't mess with me, Harper.'

'I'm not lying. They got there in time and saved him. He's going to be fine.' Harper took a small step toward the bed.

Lynne shook her head, insistent. 'No. He can't be. I gave him mega doses of epinephrine.' She blinked rapidly, gazing at the door. 'What are they doing, zapping his heart?'

'Come, see for yourself.' Harper moved closer.

'Oh, aren't you clever. Sorry. Can't join you. I have business here.' She pushed the scalpel into Hagit's neck, drew blood. Started uttering the Lord's Prayer.

Hagit shuddered, made no sound, watched Harper steadily, as if assuring her that Chloe was safe. She hugged the sheets to her belly.

'Wait, Lynne. Stop.' Harper kept moving, was almost to the bed. 'They're looking for you. They know what you did to Peter—'

'Why do you keep talking about Peter? Peter's gone. The wimp couldn't even get it up. Was I supposed to be celibate? Forever? Because that's what we're talking about. The code promises eternity – that is, if I finish the third offering.' She smiled, but her mouth was distorted. More a grimace than a grin. She turned her attention back to Hagit, steadied herself, repositioned the scalpel, continued the prayer.

Harper swung her arm out and sent the IV pole clattering to the floor.

Lynne looked up, startled.

Hagit reached up and grabbed Lynne's wrist, twisting it until she dropped the scalpel, enduring punches from Lynne's other fist while Harper raced around the bed, dove at Lynne's knees and pulled her to the floor. Pinned her there. Saw the scalpel lying loose beside the bed.

'Hagit,' Harper breathed. 'Is Chloe all right?'

Hagit lowered the sheet. Chloe was lying on her belly, sucking her fingers, fast asleep.

But Lynne wasn't finished. The doctor declared Peter dead about the same time Harper yelled for the guards. Harper stayed on top of Lynne, holding her down until they came in. When the guards were in the room, she shifted her weight and got off, expecting Lynne to lie still and surrender, outnumbered.

But as soon as Harper moved, Lynne's arm darted out, grabbing the scalpel, raising it to Harper's thigh, right at her femoral artery.

Climbing to her feet, she wrapped an arm around Harper's neck and held the blade to her throat. The guards aimed their weapons, ready to fire. Lynne slouched behind Harper, using her as a shield.

'Don't be stupid,' one guard said. 'We will shoot you.'

'Be quiet,' Lynne snapped. 'Not a word. I swear I'll cut her.'

'If you cut her, you will die, too.'

Harper tried to pull away; Lynne tightened her arm, choking her. Harper's mind raced, considering her options. She could reach up, grab Lynne's head and twist. Or jab her eyes. Or use a foot to trip her. Or twist around and simply punch her out. But each of those alternatives would only work if Lynne didn't react by slashing her throat. Meantime, Lynne was edging around the room, the wall to her back, Harper blocking her from the guards and their weapons. Hagit sat alert, cradling little Chloe. Harper looked at Chloe and rage coursed through her veins. She had no choice, had to obey her instincts. On the count of three, she would throw her head back, slam Lynne in the face and duck, giving the guards a clear shot.

One. Harper counted, taking a step with Lynne, feeling sharp thin steel against her neck. Wondering if she'd survive or die right here while Chloe slept, never again to hear her little girl laugh or see her run. Well, at least they were in a medical facility; maybe the staff would save her before she bled out. Two. Lynne pulled her toward the door. They moved in sync, matching steps like partners in a grim waltz. Just as Harper got to three, Lynne backed through the doorway and, with a low grunt, thrust Harper forward.

Harper fell forward, heard the door slam.

The guards shouted Hebrew commands, jumping over Harper as she got to her feet. They pulled the door open and ran into the hall, stumbling over a man with his hands bound behind his back. Lowell asked for help as they shoved him aside, one going in each direction, rifles raised, checking the rooms.

'Untie me,' Lowell called to Harper, but she ignored him, followed the guards. Saw a nurse in the hall, hurrying to see what the commotion was. An orderly pushing a gurney. No sign of Lynne. Harper ran to the waiting room, Lowell trailing after her. She looked out the front door. One of the guards was ahead of her, checking the street. No Lynne. Harper stopped and wheeled around: if she and the guards were out looking for Lynne, Hagit had to be, once again, unattended.

*   *   *

Oh God. Maybe that had been Lynne's plan – to distract them so they'd leave Hagit long enough for Lynne to kill her. Harper cursed herself for being so gullible. Her leg throbbed and her lungs burned as she dashed back into the center, through the waiting room, down the hall to Hagit's room, dreading what she might find. Flinging the door open.

Almost crashing into Hagit. She was carrying Chloe and Harper's bag, apparently leaving.

'What are you doing?' Harper panted.

'It's too crazy here,' Hagit declared. 'We'll be at the bungalow.'

'No.' Harper still had not caught her breath. 'Hagit. You're not going anywhere. You're hurt.'

'I'm not going to get better here.'

Harper looked into the hall. Saw a guard on his phone, holding Lowell by his collar, the nurse standing there with her hands on her hips. 'Don't leave yet. Wait here for me.' She started to leave. Stopped in the hall to look back.

Hagit was heading into the hallway, following her.

'Hagit. I mean it. We'll go but not yet.' Harper watched until Hagit turned back and the door closed. She had no time to argue. Lynne was still there, still determined to finish the sacrifice. But where? Harper went down the hall, looked in on Jimmy and Frank. Jimmy's eyes widened and his good hand clung to his sheets when she walked in. Frank was asleep. She hurried on. Checked the rooms, one by one. Saw Wendell with his jaw wired. Peter's body, lying under a sheet.

The guards were talking at the end of the hall. Apparently, they hadn't found her either.

Damn. Harper wanted to shake the guards. If they had protected Hagit, none of this would have happened. But yelling at them would accomplish nothing. Police reinforcements were arriving. The building would be searched, and Lynne would be found. Meantime, while the guards were busy talking with the police, she took off with Hagit and Chloe, walking out right through the front door of the medical center.

'Hey,' one of the guards shouted. 'Wait.'

Hagit turned to yell at them, argued in Hebrew.

The group approached them, scolding Hagit. Waving their arms.

Hagit put her hands on her hips and said something that quieted them.

A policeman replied angrily and walked off. The guards muttered to each other.

Hagit held onto Harper's arm for support; Chloe clung to her neck, half asleep. With the guards trailing after them, the three headed back to the bungalow to collect their things. They would not spend another night at the kibbutz, would take off and hit the road, even if she had to steal another car.

Lynne held her breath, not daring to move. Waiting for the consternation to stop. What had gone wrong? She'd almost done it – almost killed the lamb. She would have, too, if not for Harper Jennings.

That woman. So clean looking. Such an open, fresh face. Who'd have suspected the evil that lay beneath? Harper had pretended to be her friend – even to be interested in the church. And Lynne had welcomed her, had divulged confidential information, hoping to help Harper join them, earn God's grace, attain eternal life. But Lynne had been fooled. Conned. Harper had hidden her true intention. All along, she'd been planning to prevent the final sacrifice. Clearly, she was an agent of Satan. How else would she have known to show up at that very moment, just as Lynne had been about to slaughter the lamb, preventing her from meeting God's coded requirements?

Harper Jennings. Lynne repeated the name to herself like a chant, pumping herself for revenge. But first, she had to get out of this stinking bed and away from the medical center. She lay still as death, staring into the fabric covering her face. Waiting.

Nearby, men shouted in Hebrew. Shoes pounded against the tile floor. Stopped. Were they at the door? In the room? Would they find her?

Lynne didn't breathe. In a moment, the footsteps began again, moving away. She let out a breath. Inhaled. Felt ill. The bed still smelled of him, his sickly sweat. His weakness. She prayed to God that they'd stop looking for her soon so she could sneak out of the building and try once more to do His work. And that, in the meantime, nobody who looked in Peter's room would know that his body had already been taken away.

The sun was setting; the path to the bungalow was shadowy and quiet. According to the Hebrew calendar, the ninth of Av was about to begin. As she walked, Chloe secured in the sling, Harper scanned the valley, the hills. Saw no signs of a conflagration. Heard no thunderous explosions that would end the world. The green fields and gently sloping hills sat serene and still as if prepared for a holy day.

But the calm didn't relax her. She was in combat mode, her senses alert. Hagit leaned on her for support, still weak and unbalanced, moving slowly. When they got to the bungalow, Harper made Hagit lie down and put Chloe in her crib so she could finish packing.

'Tell me where your things are.' She grabbed Hagit's suitcase but, exhausted from the walk, Hagit had already fallen asleep. Harper dashed around, emptying Hagit's closet and tossing clothes and toiletries into the bag. She gathered the rest of her own clothes and shoved them into her duffle. Glanced around to see if she'd forgotten anything. Decided that, if she had, it didn't matter. Clothes were replaceable. She was ready to go, but Hagit and Chloe were asleep. She stood at the door, figuring out what to do next.

And remembered she hadn't talked to Hank. Needed to let him know they were coming back tonight. She grabbed Hagit's phone, called. Got his voice mail. Her stomach cramped. Why hadn't she been able to reach him in over a day? Why hadn't he called?

She needed to let it go. He was busy. Nothing was wrong. But her clenched stomach insisted otherwise. She left a message, asking him to call Hagit's phone. Adding that it was urgent. Then she sat down, trying to convince herself that there was simply a problem with Hank's phone. The battery had run out. Or he'd forgotten to turn it on. Or dropped it in the Dead Sea. She stared at Hagit's phone, telling her stomach to quiet down, but the clench tightened, became a wrenching twist. Her hands were unsteady as she tried Trent's number. And when the call didn't go through and an electronic voice began speaking Hebrew, she froze, not even breathing.

Harper stood, ran a hand through her hair. What the hell? Why were neither of them answering? She set the phone on the counter, chewed her lip, told herself to keep moving, not to take the time to worry. Harper picked up the bags, moved them to the porch. Realized that she couldn't carry everything, would need a cart. Or no, she could leave the bags until she got a vehicle, then pick them up along with Chloe and Hagit. In fact, the bags didn't matter – she could leave them behind. What mattered was getting Hagit and Chloe away, safe from Lynne and Travis and the rest of their crazy flock. She was wasting time, needed to find a ride or a car, but how? She couldn't leave Hagit and Chloe alone, felt off balance . . .

Oh God. She was standing in the middle of the bungalow, turning in circles. Panicking.

Panicking? Harper Jennings never panicked. She reacted to threats and danger reflexively, without self-doubt or intellectualization. She'd been trained to respond quickly, efficiently and effectively in emergencies of all kinds. So why was she running around her room, rotating like a spitted chicken?

Her head pounded. She shivered.

Harper stood beside Chloe, settling herself by matching the baby's steady breath. She made herself hold still, massaged her temples. Tried to understand her reaction. She'd been surrounded by dangerous, misguided people before, had managed to stay grounded in literally hundreds of life-threatening situations. So it wasn't, couldn't be Travis or Lynne or the church group that was unsettling her. What then was it? Why were her senses malfunctioning, sending her in random unfocused directions?

Harper sat again, took a long deep breath. Relaxed her shoulders, her neck. Untensed her back. Closed her eyes.

And saw Hank, falling from the roof. Hank lying unconscious, his head smashed on one side.

Oh God.

Harper couldn't breathe. She knew. Without any proof, without being told. She wasn't sure what it was or why no one had told her, but she was certain. Something had happened to Hank.

Finally, the place was quiet. Lynne counted to five hundred, heard nothing. No voices. No footsteps. Soon, someone would come to clean the room; she couldn't hang around. Slowly, she lowered the sheet, peeked out. The room was darkness and silence.

She counted some more, listening. Hearing no one. She took a breath, sat up, got out of the bed. Crept to the hall, ready to finish her work. Who cared if they caught her? The conflagration would begin after the sacrifice, and she'd be blessed with eternal life. No earthly chains would hold her.

The hall was empty. Lynne dashed across into Hagit's room. Opened the door and entered in one swift move. Blinked in disbelief, her hands tightening into fists.

Harper Jennings, she sneered. Harper Jennings. Harper Jennings had taken the lamb.

*   *   *

'Hagit,' Harper repeated, gently shaking Hagit's shoulder.

When Hagit's eyes opened, they appeared glazed and unfocused. Then she bolted upright, glaring at Harper with accusing eyes. Finally, she relaxed.

'I have to leave you and Chloe here while I find us a ride.'

Hagit seemed puzzled. 'A ride?'

'To Jerusalem.'

Hagit started to sit up. 'You're not serious.'

'I think you'll be okay for a few minutes. Those two guards should still be outside. I called Adi to ask her to stay with you, but no one answered—'

'It's the holiday. They're all in shul. At services. But Harper, we can't go to Jerusalem. Not just all of a sudden.'

'Why not?'

Hagit opened her mouth, closed it. Said nothing.

Harper wanted to insist that Hagit explain. Why couldn't they go to Jerusalem? What did Hagit mean? Did she know something about Hank and Trent? Harper stopped herself, not wanting to take the time. Not sure she could bear to hear the answer. She bit her lip.

'Keep the curtains closed and the door locked.'

'I know what to do. But listen to me. We should stay here—'

'So someone can finally kill you?'

'The guards are out there. No one will bother me.'

'Should I take Chloe? Are you well enough to watch her?'

Hagit's eyes narrowed. 'I was Mossad.'

Harper went to the crib, touched Chloe's curls, leaned over to kiss her, inhaled her scent. Then she ran to the door.

On the way out, closing the door, she saw the guards standing on the path. And beyond them, a man carrying something bulky near Travis's bungalow, cloaked by the dusk.

Without a sound, Lynne crept down the hall, wondering how she'd get past the police. She moved swiftly, soundlessly. Cracking the door to the waiting room, she expected to see guards and braced herself for a confrontation. But the waiting room was empty.

Lynne released a breath. Kept moving. The guards, the police – they had to be outside.

She stood at the entrance, peering out into the dusk. Police cars, a coroner's van were parked near the rear of the building. No one was guarding the front door.

Had they stopped looking for her? Did they think she'd already left the building? And where was Hagit?

Lynne opened the door just wide enough to slide through, then slipped out, hugging the wall, staying in shadows. At the end of the medical center, she ran.

Harper Jennings had taken her lamb. But Lynne wasn't going to give up, not after going this far. There was still time. The ninth of Av was just beginning. She could still complete the directions in God's code.

Then again, there might be security around the lamb. She'd have to find a way to get past them. And past Harper Jennings, the agent of Satan who wanted to obstruct God's own plan.

Lynne walked quickly, silently, senses alert. Her jaw tightened. Harper was pure evil. Once she got rid of her, no other obstacle would block her. She'd have no problem performing the sacrifice.

Travis Ramsey smiled even though his load was backbreaking and his muscles screamed. He couldn't help it. He'd spent the last hours scurrying around, dodging those hunting for him, pilfering or siphoning off what he needed, compiling it behind his bungalow under a tarp. It had been embarrassingly easy; no one had been looking for him in the open, near pumps or sheds; he'd been hiding under a hat and sunglasses, in plain sight. But it was neither their fault nor to his credit that he hadn't been found. The real reason that he'd eluded them was that God had cloaked him from sight. God wanted him to succeed. Of that, he was certain. Any doubts had been dispelled as he'd spent days reading and rereading, studying his notes, re-examining the codes, making sure his translations were accurate. Searching for a mistake, double checking, triple checking for a misinterpretation or an amendment – because, after all, God had changed His mind before.

But Travis had found only the original code, calling for the blood of three lambs: one of Isaac, one of Ishmael, one of Jesus. 'By fire,' it said, and, 'I will begin the conflagration,' and it had identified this day of this year in this place, Megiddo.

So it had been written. So it would be done. And he, Travis Ramsey, concealed from those who would interfere, would set it off.

'Wipe that shit-eating grin off your face.'

Damn. He'd thought he'd gotten rid of that voice, but now, after all this time, it surfaced again. He kept trudging along the road, shaking his head as if he could make the voice fall out.

'You think God picked you? Hah! Why would He do that?' the voice went on. 'You're nobody. You're just a messed up kid who can't tell when his socks are inside out.'

Ramsey refused to acknowledge the taunts. He kept going, hauling the heavy bags up the path. Keeping his mind on the task of God's work.

'What, you think you're special? You're the product of fornication and lust, born in sin like the rest of us. Repent.'

Why was the voice coming back – why now? He tried to shut it out, but it persisted. Memories rose up, and his father came at him, holding his belt. 'Stop your ninny-blasted crying. You think I like this? I'm doing it for you, for your sorry-ass soul. Pain is part of atonement for your sins. Take the beating willingly and beg for more. It's your only chance for redemption.'

Ignore it, Travis told himself. Think about fulfilling the code.

'Where do you think you're going? You think God's made you His agent? What would God want with a maggot like you? You're delusional. You're hearing the Devil. Pray for forgiveness!'

'Go away,' he told the voice. How many times, in how many ways did he have to stifle it? He'd been chosen by the Lord to do this work. What difference did it make what a pathetic dead old preacher thought?

'Get on your knees, Travis,' the voice said. 'You've let Satan feed you lies. Repent.'

'Shut up!' Ramsey growled, startling himself with his fury. Okay, enough. He had to stop the voice. Ramsey stiffened, closing his eyes, recollecting the first time he'd stopped that infernal voice. The wrench swinging, the stains spattering his father's sofa cushions, carpet, walls. And then the sweet silence.

Ramsey opened his eyes, listened. The voice was gone again.

He resumed walking. His muscles throbbed. The hill seemed steeper than usual because of the weight of the bags.

Harper strained to see the man. Could he be Travis? Would he be stupid enough to go back to his bungalow and risk being caught? And what was he carrying? Where was he going? She should alert the guards. But that would distract them from watching Hagit. It would be better to follow him and find out who he was. Why make a fuss if it wasn't even Travis?

She held back for a moment, trying to avoid the guards. But they spotted her, recognized her. Gestured for her to come closer.

'And now where are you going?'

Damn. 'Just to the office.'

'The office? Why?'

Oh God. While they were talking, the man was getting away. 'To make arrangements for a car.'

'A car.' The guards smirked at each other. 'Tonight? It's a holiday. The office is closed. The main building is being used for prayer.'

Damn. How would she get a car? Meantime, she'd lost sight of the man. Had to get past these guys.

And then it occurred to her: she would lie.

Her attitude changed. She smiled. 'Well, in that case, I'd like to attend the service.' There. Did they believe her? Had she sounded convincing?

'Are you Jewish?'

Harper hesitated. 'No, just interested in religion.'

She wasn't dressed appropriately for a religious service. But she fingered her *hamsa* under the streetlight, hoping they'd see it.

'Okay.' The bigger one shrugged. 'The service just started at sundown. You didn't miss much.'

Harper thanked them and hurried up the path, looking for the man who might be Travis. Hoping she hadn't lost him. She moved quietly through the shadows, listening, watching, but the path ahead was empty. Not a soul was out walking. Church members were still being confined to the restaurant building; kibbutz residents were attending prayer services in the main building. That didn't leave many people to go strolling in the dark – just security personnel, Harper, and a man carrying a burly load. Harper hurried along until, finally, up ahead, she spotted a figure hobbling through the darkness, carrying a big sack. Near the center of the kibbutz, he passed beneath a streetlight, and Harper was certain.

Even from behind, she knew. She'd found Travis. She turned, looking for police or security, saw hedges, parked vehicles. A stray cat. Nobody.

Harper kept following him. This time, he wouldn't escape.

Travis looked at the stars. He'd done it. He himself, alone. He had been generous to share the glory, but foolish to think others were gifted enough to comply. The women Lynne and Marlene were worthy concubines but inept executioners. And Peter had been felled by a scorpion, the Devil attempting to foil God's plan.

So it had fallen to him alone to fulfill the commands that he alone had read and understood. And when he'd done his part, the four teams would spread out as planned, lighting four matches in the powder keg, igniting the tinder box of the Middle East, spreading flames from Megiddo to the ends of the earth, consuming the followers of Isaac, Ishmael and Jesus alike. The conflagration would swell, swallowing everything and everyone from Gog to Magog.

Travis stood tall, fluttery and lighthearted as he opened a can of kerosene – or maybe gasoline? Acetone? He'd filled so many containers, couldn't remember which was which. Chemicals had come from sheds and gas tanks and pumps and maintenance stations, and now he poured them freely in a fragrant soup of flame enhancers.

"'But the day of the Lord will come like a thief,'" he quoted Peter as he christened the walls. "'The heavens will disappear with a roar, the elements will be destroyed by fire, and the earth and everything in it will be laid bare.'" Travis splashed liquids, prancing giddily in the mud, anticipating the consternation, the conflagration, the celebration, the glorious conflagration that he, Travis Ramsey, was about to ignite for the Lord.

And then, from nowhere, a banshee rammed him, baring her teeth.

Harper followed Travis as he left the path, circling around to the rear of the main building. Silence was more difficult back there. The ground was gravelly; she had to time her movement with his, synchronizing their footsteps. She approached the rear of the building, careful to keep her distance. Smelling a familiar odor.

Harper stopped, recognizing it, her chest tight, unable to breathe. Men were screaming, guns popping. Flies buzzing . . . No. She pinched her arm hard, bringing her attention back to the moment, stifling the flashback. Then she continued after Travis.

With each step, the smell got stronger. Harper told herself to ignore it. It wasn't real. It was a symptom of her Post Traumatic Stress Disorder, just like the cracks of sniper fire, the screams of the wounded, the coating of sand on her skin. It was all illusion, a wound in her mind. She bit her lip and pinched herself again, banishing the images and sounds of war, but the smell wouldn't fade, persisted even when the other sensations faded. Odd.

Unless . . . maybe it wasn't a flashback.

Maybe it was real.

Harper stopped on the gravel, smelling accelerant. Hearing liquid splashing.

Oh God.

She ran ahead, no longer trying to muffle her footsteps. Almost tripped over an empty gas can on the path. Paused to listen. Heard more splashing up ahead. Understood what Travis had been carrying and what he was doing with it.

His code. He'd said it called for triad of sacrifice – a Christian, a Muslim and a Jew. Travis was trying to complete the triad – but not by killing just one Jew. He was planning to slaughter everyone attending the service.

Harper had no time. Travis had already poured cans of accelerant behind the building, onto its walls. Any second, the place would be ablaze. She paused to plan her move while the spatter of fluid continued ahead of her – maybe forty feet away? No, less. Thirty? Travis was coming closer. Doubling back? Making sure he'd poured enough to make the fire inextinguishable? Or maybe ensuring that he had a safe escape route.

Finally, the splashing stopped. An empty container flew into the bushes, discarded, maybe twenty feet away. Any second, Travis would light a match and start the fire. Harper took a deep breath and took off, darting through the bushes, hurtling onto his back, knocking him to the ground. In the dim light, she saw the cigarette lighter fly from his hand, heard it land with a splatter.

'No!' he roared, rolling and wriggling to get her off of him, reaching blindly into puddles of accelerant to retrieve the lighter.

But Harper wouldn't let up. She straddled his belly, grabbed at his arms. 'Enough. It's done.' Her strength surprised her; her body moved on its own, machine-like. Weapon-like.

Travis stretched his fingers, searching for the lighter. 'Get off me.' He bucked.

Harper drew her fist back, rammed it into his jaw.

Travis caved but didn't black out. He spit out a tooth. 'Foolish woman! You don't understand what you're interfering with.'

'Sorry. Armageddon isn't happening today.'

In the starlight, his eyes gleamed. 'No. You're wrong. It was in the codes. On this date, the conflagration will begin. The fire was proclaimed by God—'

'Maybe He changed His mind again.'

Travis blinked. 'What did you say? You know about the codes? How?' He lay back, sputtering. 'Lynne? You were her dig partner. That blabbering cow will never earn eternal life.'

'Well, she'll earn life anyway. She's killed three people.'

'Three?' Travis's eyebrows lifted. 'So she succeeded? She slaughtered the final lamb?'

'She killed her husband.'

'What? Peter's dead?' He squirmed, tried to sit up.

'Quit wiggling. You're done.'

Travis lay back. 'Well, no matter. Peter was a true follower; after the conflagration, he'll receive his reward.'

'Except that there will be no conflagration.'

Travis turned his head toward the nearby pool of chemicals, and Harper realized that she couldn't hold him down forever, had nothing to bind him with and no phone to call for help. Her only option was to knock him out. Damn. Her knuckles already throbbed, bruised and raw from all the punches she'd thrown lately. Never mind. She released his wrist, made a fist, drew her arm back, and flew backward, stunned, as Travis bolted up, slamming her with his forehead.

Dizzily, Harper dug her knees into his ribs, still grasping one of his wrists. He twisted, punching with his free arm, digging his leg into her thigh to roll over and get free. Harper's weak left leg folded and, for a few moments, they lay side-by-side, grunting and struggling beside puddles of accelerant. Harper's arm was twisted, about to snap; she couldn't hang on. Travis pulled away, crawling through the puddles, groping for the lighter. Harper reached out and grabbed his ankles, yanked them back. Heard a splat as he landed on his belly. A squish as he slid, searching in the puddles. An exuberant cry.

Damn. Harper couldn't see it, but she knew he'd found the lighter. She heard Travis slog to his feet and realized that she couldn't stop him. It was too late.

Travis looked up and saw God's face smiling down at him from the dark sky.

'I've been waiting.' God didn't say it out loud; He transmitted His message directly to Travis's brain. 'You alone have deciphered my codes and understood my intentions. You will be rewarded. Now, it is time. Let the conflagration begin.'

'Thy will be done.' Travis lifted the lighter, stepped back from the puddles of fuel and recited a blessing. Then he flicked the lighter.

With one great whoosh, all the air was gone, the earth's entire atmosphere sucked away while a rainbow of color – of blues and oranges, reds, purples and golds – all in one wrapped around him, swirling in a raging cyclone, and the earth rolled and spun in a torrent of heat so powerful that his mind couldn't grasp it. A roar torpedoed through him, a swollen scream so large that it must have come from all of humanity. Travis couldn't move, overwhelmed by awe. The code had been right and, this time, God had not delayed it. Because of him, God's words had come to be. Soon, the Lord would call him to His side. Any moment, he would receive his eternal reward.

Travis watched the conflagration. It was the end of the world. From somewhere in the flames, a voice called: 'Travis!'

Was it the Lord? Travis used his last strength to answer.

And the voice commanded. 'Get on your knees, boy. Take the pain and beg for more. Repent.'

As everything around him burned, Travis sank to his knees before the Lord.

In the bright night, Harper saw Travis look up to the sky and smile. He held the lighter in his hand, lifted it and uttered, 'Thy will be done.'

Then he stepped back, distancing himself from the puddles of fuel, ready to toss the lighter and ignite the buildings, completing the sacrifice. And, unless she moved away fast, as close as she was to the accelerant, Harper would be engulfed in the flames.

Harper tried to get up, but her legs wouldn't obey. Her skull was rattling, her entire body sore. While Travis recited a blessing, she got to her hands and knees, began crawling away from the puddles. Her hands clawed grass and dirt; her left knee screamed with pain. She had to hurry, had to stand. Managed to lift her torso, then a thigh. Planted her right foot on the ground. Tottered on her weak left knee, pushing with her right foot and struggling to her feet. Travis was silent, his blessing complete. Harper heard a click and leapt, diving as far as she could, sliding onto gravel, propelled by a harsh whoosh. For an instant, she lay still, waiting for a burst of light and heat, and when she felt the blast, she scrambled further, driven by an ear-shattering howl. Harper kept moving until, certain that she was clear of the blast, she stopped and looked back, preparing to have to rescue people from a building being consumed by fire.

But the building wasn't burning. Travis had flicked the lighter, but before he could throw it into his pools of accelerant, the chemicals coating his skin and soaking his clothes had ignited. Harper gaped, helpless, as she watched him stumble to his knees, crackling, consumed in a ball of hungry yellow flame.

Lynne couldn't afford to mess up again. She needed to eliminate Harper Jennings. Then she could perform the final sacrifice without obstruction.

Now that the sun was down, it was easy to sneak around the kibbutz. Men were on patrol, but it wasn't hard to avoid them by crouching in bushes, behind cottages. Until now, she hadn't noticed how many hiding places the kibbutz had; there were hundreds. With the foliage, camouflaged bunkers, storage huts, vehicles and cottages, cover could be found everywhere, especially in the dark.

Lynne felt calm. Confident. She was in no rush as she moved toward Harper's bungalow. She stopped to pet a cat. To admire the starry sky. And, as she approached the path to Harper's, she stopped again, to watch Harper talking to the guards.

Wait. Harper was leaving the bungalow. Which meant Hagit was unprotected? Lynne swallowed air, not believing her luck. She stepped closer, trying to be invisible, straining to hear them.

'I'd like to attend the service,' Harper said.

What? She wanted to pray? The guard told her that the service had just started, that she wouldn't have missed much. And Harper hurried away. Lynne eyed Harper, then the bungalow. Now was her chance. She scurried down the hill, making no sound.

But the guards moved closer to Harper's bungalow, took a position at the porch. They'd see Lynne if she approached, hear her if she broke a back window. She had no chance. Her head throbbed. How was it possible? Harper Jennings had once again kept her from the lamb. Lynne's eyes narrowed; her jaw clenched. 'Harper Jennings,' she whispered, repeating the name like a curse, looking up the path.

Harper was already out of sight, but Lynne knew where she was headed: worship was being held at the main building. And Harper was alone, unprotected, unsuspecting.

Lynne moved back up the hill, out of sight of the guards. She hurried behind the bungalows, parallel to the path Harper was taking. Rushing. Seeing security guards posted outside the building. Hiding in the cluster of trees across the road, watching the entrance, the pathway. Waiting for Harper.

And waiting.

But Harper didn't appear.

Lynne told herself that she'd been walking faster than Harper, had gotten there first. But after a few minutes, she realized that Harper must have lied to the guards. That she hadn't been going to worship at all. So, where had she really been going?

In a heartbeat, Lynne knew. She knew with absolute certainty. Harper had been going to meet Travis.

How obvious. How come she hadn't seen it before? Harper was helping him. Without help, how could Travis have eluded the authorities? He couldn't have. Yet somehow, he'd not been seen since Harper had barged into the bunker and prevented the sacrifice.

Of course. Now, everything was clear. Lynne smirked, shaking her head. What a blind fool she'd been, not seeing it before. Wasn't it odd that Travis had been the only one to escape the bunker? Wasn't it a big coincidence that Harper had let him go and that now, while he was missing, she'd made up a lie about where she was going alone in the night?

Lynne's chest tightened, thinking of Travis, aching for him. Picturing him with Harper, their bodies entangled. The harlot. Harper had wanted him, just like Marlene had. Just like Evelyn and Jenna and Bethany had. Women were always trying to take him from her.

But not this time. Not now.

Not Harper Jennings.

Lynne waited in the trees, trying to figure out where a viper like Harper would arrange to meet Travis. Obviously, not the restaurant or the medical center. Not here at the main building or back in the bungalows. So, where?

Maybe up at the top of the hill? That lookout point with a view of the whole valley. Yes, it would be deserted tonight. They would have gone up there for their tryst. Lynne moved out of the trees. Avoiding the path and the view of the guards, she headed to the back of the building. From there, she'd scoot around to parallel the main road up the hill.

As she approached the back of the building, though, she slowed, smelling something pungent. Gasoline? Kerosene? Smoke? And something rank and sharp. Burning meat?

Lynne shivered, suddenly clammy, and her limbs were heavy, resisting movement. What was wrong? Was she having a stroke? No.

She persisted, inching ahead, taking baby steps. Breathing in short shallow spurts. Trying to ignore the smell.

At the corner of the building, she peeked around, saw a bundle of something burning, flames licking it like a ravenous beast. Beyond it, her face lit by the fire, Harper Jennings stood frozen, face contorted, mouth open in a silent scream.

Harper needed a shower. Had to wash off the smell. It seemed to have penetrated her skin, her mind. Might be in her blood.

Shivering, she closed her eyes. Felt the thud of landing on a burnt-out car, and shook her head, no, she wasn't on a car. She was outside the main building of the kibbutz, under a blanket, waiting for the firefighters to clean up Travis's chemicals. But she couldn't get warm, couldn't shake the damned smell. Fuel. Burnt flesh. Death. And images kept reappearing, changing: Travis, his hand raised, ready to throw the lighter. Then the whoosh, the scream. And Travis shifted, became the woman in Iraq approaching the checkpoint. Her smile. A hot whoosh, the sense of being lifted by a blazing rolling ball. Flying, crashing onto a car . . . Stop, she told herself. She was not in Iraq, had not just seen her patrol blown up by a suicide bomber. She had to stay in the present. Take a shower. Get rid of the damned smell. But there was Travis again, raising the lighter.

'. . . look you over.'

Someone was talking. Harper opened her eyes, saw Adi crouching beside her, Gal by her side. How long had they been there? Could they take her to get a shower?

Inspector Ben Baruch walked over, frowning. He addressed Gal in Hebrew, and Gal answered with a shrug.

'I told you,' Harper told Ben Baruch. 'Travis was going to kill someone by the ninth of Av.'

Ben Baruch nodded. 'So you did.'

'I think you're in shock.' Adi's voice was soft, cottony. She smelled like vanilla.

'Someone has to go to my bungalow.' Harper took Adi's hand. 'Tell Hagit I'll be back as soon as I get a car.'

'A car,' Adi repeated.

Harper nodded. 'Yes.' She looked at Ben Baruch who was talking in a low voice with Gal. 'We're going back to Jerusalem.'

'To Jerusalem.'

'Shh. Don't tell them,' Harper cautioned. 'We're leaving tonight. I just need to get a car.'

'Okay. It's okay.' Adi stroked Harper's head. 'Let's get you looked at by the doctor, and then we'll see—'

'No, I don't need a doctor, just a car . . .' Harper tried to stand but sharp pain shot up her left leg, jolted through her hip, along her spine. She sat again, trying to figure out why she was so sore. To remember why she had to leave. What was so urgent? She closed her eyes to think; Travis held up the lighter, paused. Click. Whoosh. Scream.

She opened her eyes. Men were carrying a body bag to a van. Maybe a coroner's van. Was there a coroner on the kibbutz? A morgue? Probably they'd take Travis to a city – maybe to Jerusalem? Maybe she and Chloe could ride along? But she had to go get Chloe. And Hagit. Had to hurry. Damn. Harper's mind felt muddled. Maybe inhaling the chemicals had poisoned her.

Adi and Ben Baruch were talking in Hebrew.

'Can I go?' she interrupted.

'Go?' Adi met her eyes.

Gal's mouth opened. 'What? Are you crazy?'

'I need to get Chloe—'

'Look, you're injured. Plus, it's still not safe. The guards reported a woman running away. A blonde woman. Probably it was Lynne Watts.'

'What?' Harper pictured Lynne's freckles, felt a blade at her throat.

Had Lynne been there? Had she seen Travis – the man she adored and idolized, the man for whom she'd killed her husband and two other men – had she seen him burn to death? Oh God. Where was she? What would she do?

Harper's hand went to her throat, rubbed away the memory of steel.

'Mrs Jennings.' Inspector Ben Baruch stepped closer. 'Tell us what happened here tonight.'

Harper wondered why he didn't understand. Why none of them did. It was pointless to go over what had happened. They had to find Lynne. And she had to get to Jerusalem, to find Hank. Had to leave now.

She eyed the coroner's van. There would be plenty of room.

'What were you doing here?' Ben Baruch asked.

Harper could tell from his tone that he would insist on hearing

everything. That he wouldn't let her leave. A medic came over, sat
beside her, flashed a light in her eyes.

'What happened?' Ben Baruch repeated.

And so she told him what had happened, as simply as she could.
Travis had burned up before her eyes, and she'd done nothing, not
one thing to help him. Hadn't even tried.

Lynne couldn't move. Couldn't breathe. Her entire being was a
bleeding gaping wound.

Ramsey . . .

His name reverberated in her head. Ramsey. The firmness of his
hand on her breast, the hunger of his lips pressing hers. She wanted
to scream his name, to chase after the medics and rip open the body
bag, rescue him. Bring him back.

She closed her eyes, clawed at them, unable to stop seeing the
flame, reliving the shock of identifying the shape it was devouring.
Not a pile of trash or a bundle of waste. No. A man.

And then, reflected in the flickering light, she'd seen Harper.

And she'd known.

Her legs had caved. She'd sunk to the ground, tearing at her hair,
her ears. She wasn't sure what had made the sounds in her head.
Had she screamed? Wailed? Never mind. It didn't matter. She'd
coiled up like a fetus, mirroring Travis's curled frame, rocking.
Wrenching. Consumed with pain.

This couldn't be. Couldn't be. Couldn't. Be.

Not after everything she'd gone through, everything she'd done
to please him. Not when they were almost at the end, just one small
sacrifice away from salvation. Lynne opened her eyes again and
stared, unable to look away. Thought of killing someone, anyone
at the kibbutz, completing the sacrifice for Travis's sake. Except
that, now, what was the point? Even if she completed the triad,
slaughtering the third lamb—Even if God's coded instructions led
to the battle of Armageddon, what good was it? How could she
endure eternal life without Travis by her side?

She couldn't. She didn't want to live another minute without him,
let alone forever.

It wasn't fair. Maybe . . . Would God bring him back anyway?
Weren't all true followers supposed to be rewarded? Of course they
were. But . . . Oh dear. If Travis would be brought back, wouldn't
Peter as well? No. He couldn't be. Nothing – no one – would keep

her from Travis. And anyway, she didn't know who'd get eternal life and who wouldn't. Only Travis knew that.

But Travis was gone. The flames had consumed him, melted him into a huddled mound. Firefighters had arrived. Who'd called them? Satan's number-one ally? Where was she? Lynne looked around for Harper, couldn't see her. A team spread foam over the clump that had been Travis and lifted him into a body bag. While others examined the ground and the building, Lynne lay flat, shivering in the shrubbery.

Ramsey. Holding her belly, she kept whispering his name. And finally, he answered her. As clearly as if he were sitting beside her, she heard him speak. But this time, he didn't scold or berate her. This time, he praised her as the only one he could count on. He told her he'd been wrong to doubt her, called her his true love and eternal soul mate. He reminded her she didn't have to mourn him, promised that, after the conflagration, his soul would be called back to join with hers. And then, when she stopped sniffling and shaking, he told her precisely what he wanted her to do.

Finally, the questions stopped. The doctor patched Harper up and told her that her body was badly bruised, as if she didn't already know. Soldiers drove her back to the bungalow, escorted her inside.

When she saw her, Hagit's mouth opened and her hand went to her heart.

Harper hadn't looked in the mirror yet. She touched her face. Gauze pads were taped to her cheek. The skin on her chin was raw and sticky. There was a lump on her forehead.

'Travis is dead,' she told Hagit.

Hagit stood. 'I know. Adi telephoned.'

The soldiers were double-checking the bungalow, making sure it was safe. Hagit waited until they finished. Watched them go outside and station themselves on the porch.

'Tell me the truth,' Hagit eyed her. 'You killed him?'

'No.' Harper began trembling again. 'But I didn't save him.'

'Adi said he burned. What happened?'

'I saw him pour the fuel. We fought. And he lit his lighter . . .' She heard the whoosh, the scream.

'Go. Wash it all away.' Hagit hobbled over, guided her to the shower. Turned on the water. Helped her undress. Let out a gasp when she saw the bruises on Harper's legs and arms. 'My God. You're purple.'

Harper stood under the shower, letting hot water stream over her, cleaning her stinging wounds, trying to scrub away memories. She shampooed her hair, rinsed, shampooed again. Yearned for Hank, thought maybe he'd be near his phone now. Got out of the shower and grabbed a towel, borrowed Hagit's phone to call him.

His voice mail answered. This time, she wasn't surprised. She stood at Chloe's crib, body aching, figuring out how to get to Jerusalem.

She still smelled accelerant. Impossible. None of it had actually been on her skin. And yet, the odor remained. She went to the mirror, looked at herself. Damn. Raw scratches and scrapes all over her face. She peeled off wet gauze, saw a raw red patch of deep abrasions on her cheek. Same on her forearms from sliding on gravel.

Hagit came into the bedroom, her forehead still bandaged, her eye still black. Losing prizefighters looked better than they did.

'Here. Let me help.' Hagit taped on fresh gauze. 'Go. Lie down. You're going to hurt in the morning.'

But Harper had no intention of resting. Wrapped in a towel, she went to the porch, nodded to the soldiers, retrieved her duffle bag.

'What are you doing?' Hagit scowled.

Harper opened the bag, pulled out a pair of jeans, a fresh T-shirt. 'Getting dressed,' Harper said. 'We're going to Jerusalem.'

'Now? Not tonight . . .'

'Yes, now, tonight.' She stepped into her jeans.

'But Travis is dead. The army is guarding us. It's safe to stay and sleep . . .'

'I haven't been able to reach Hank. Or Trent. Something's wrong—'

'Why do you assume something's wrong?'

'It's been two days—'

'You've been through a lot, so you're thinking the worst. They're busy, that's all. Wait until morning.'

Harper eased her T-shirt over her head. 'No. I feel it. I have to go.'

Hagit sighed, looked away.

'What?' Harper eyed her. Stepped closer. 'You know something.'

Hagit looked away.

'You do. You know something. Tell me . . .'

'What I know is: you should rest.'

Harper grabbed Hagit's arm. 'What's happened? Tell me. Is Hank all right?' She was strangling the skin above Hagit's elbow.

Hagit looked at her evenly, devoid of emotion. 'Okay. I'll tell you. You'll find out soon anyway.' She paused. Took a breath. 'There has been an incident.'

An incident?

'What does that mean?' Harper tightened her grip.

'With the symposium. It's almost resolved. It will be over any time now.'

Harper listened, her head becoming light, bloodless. The room began to twirl.

She heard Hagit's voice from a great distance, as if it was calling from far across the checkpoint, drowned out by explosions and rifle fire. She strained to make sense of Hagit's words, to ignore the intrusion of Travis and his lighter, disregard the whoosh, the spine-jangling scream.

When Hagit finished, Harper understood only that she had to get to Jerusalem, that the ride had been arranged. She waded through detached limbs, past a boy with no face, around the bombed-out buildings, hurrying but moving slowly as if through gelatin. As soon as she was dressed, she got Chloe, carried her outside without waking her, still hearing distant rifle fire, smelling smoke and fumes.

Hagit was ahead of her, on the phone, speaking Hebrew. The soldiers were waiting in the jeep; they'd already loaded the bags.

The soldiers blocked Harper's door. Lynne went around behind the bungalow, looking for a way in. Thinking about creating a diversion – maybe breaking a window in the rear of Harper's cottage. Or maybe next door at Travis's. Then, when the soldiers went to investigate, she'd storm into Harper's place, cut her throat, sacrifice the lamb, and run back out into the night. Not a bad plan.

She crawled around, looking for rocks heavy enough to break panes of glass, small enough to lift and throw. Wasn't sure what that meant, had no experience breaking windows. But Travis's spirit urged her on. She lifted a baseball-sized rock, decided it wasn't solid enough. Crawled some more. A stray cat wandered over, nuzzled her, let out a long bellowing meow. Lynne froze, listening for the soldiers. But they didn't respond. Of course not. They wouldn't react to a stupid cat. She was too jittery. Needed to calm herself. To remember Travis's promise.

They would be together forever, as soulmates.

She lifted another rock. Perfect. It would take both hands to throw it, but if she put her body weight into it and stood close enough, it would shatter the glass. She was sure. Lynne stood silently, carrying the rock. And heard the bungalow door slam. A woman, chattering in Hebrew.

She hurried around the side of the bungalow, keeping close to the wall. A car engine started up. Harper climbed in to the soldiers' jeep, carrying her baby, sitting next to Hagit.

Lynne stood paralyzed, astounded, her vision blurred by tears of fury. She heard Harper ask, 'They'll take us straight to Jerusalem? To the King Saul?'

She couldn't hear Hagit's answer. As the jeep pulled away, she stepped back and hurled the rock at a window. It made a bang, but didn't even crack the glass.

Lynne roared, ran at the pane, pounded it with her fists, remembering Travis in flames, burning like a martyr or a saint. Like Joan of Arc. And here she was, not even able to break a window. Failing again, letting him down. Slowly, she sunk to her knees. Maybe she should use the knife on her own body, joining Travis in the hereafter.

She lay back on the ground. Looked up at the stars. Realized Travis and the Lord were watching her. Felt ashamed. She dried her eyes, wiped her nose. Thought back to Harper climbing onto the jeep and hopped to her feet, finally understanding.

None of what had happened had been an accident or failure. It had all been part of God's will. In fact, God Himself was guiding her through Travis, as his disciple, showing her how to follow His coded instructions. Comprehending the importance of her new role, she stood tall, confident. She was God's warrior, prepared for battle. She hurried, aware of her time constraints; the ninth of Av had already begun. But the Lord and his prophet Travis had told her what to do, and Harper had told her where to do it.

For most of the ride, Harper was too angry to talk. She held onto Chloe, staring out the window, not seeing the night. All she saw was Hank. Hank, dressed in a white polo shirt, cargo pants and flip flops, a gunshot wound oozing on his shoulder. Or his arms bound behind him, eyes swollen shut, mouth bloody from beatings.

Or lying on a carpet, staring at the wall, dead.

No. Not dead. No, not not not not. Her chest burned and she tried to erase that image, reject the possibility, but the more she fought it, the more it persisted. Hank's body kept popping to mind, lifeless, the spark gone from his eyes. His hands limp. Harper's throat thickened. Her mouth went dry. Oh God. He couldn't be dead. But there he was again, lying on a carpet. Had he been shot? Stabbed? It didn't matter; dead was dead. A host of dead bodies paraded through her mind. The Iraqi boy with no face; Evan, a fraternity boy from Cornell. Zina, her classmate. Graham, her student. Her entire check-point patrol – bodies flashed by in a medley, and somehow, though they'd died in different ways, they all looked the same, shared the same final indifference. But Hank? No. Hank couldn't be one of them, couldn't be dead. She'd have known. She'd have felt it. Her heart would have stopped; she'd have gone cold.

Hagit was talking to her, but Harper wasn't paying attention. Had no use for a person who'd kept the truth from her, who'd conspired with others and lied, preventing her from being with her husband. She clung to Chloe, saw Hank in the darkness, on the side of the road. Tied to a chair, his eyes beaten closed. Or a gunshot wound in his shoulder.

Or lying on a carpet . . . No.

She had to stop. Had to focus. Had to figure out what she'd do when they got to Jerusalem. They'd want her to stay away. But there was no way. She would have to leave the baby with Hagit. Hagit the secret-keeper, Hagit the liar, Hagit the betrayer. She had no choice. She would wander off, casually. Find a way into the hotel. A way around the military. Maybe she'd have to ambush a soldier, steal a weapon, a uniform. Make the soldier tell her exactly where the hostages were being held. What floor, what rooms. And then knock the soldier out. Yes, so he wouldn't interfere. And then she'd penetrate the perimeter, get inside the hotel. Proceed to the location where Hank and the others were being held. And go in . . .

Hagit kept pushing on her arm. Yammering. 'You can't ignore me forever. What I have to say is important.'

Hank was sitting beside Trent. In a row of hostages, all tied together. Scientists from all over the world. And the captors didn't expect her – she imagined them young, wiry, shiny-eyed. Lethal. Surprised when she opened fire.

'Okay, so ignore me. But I'll tell you anyway. When we get there, you are to go where they tell you and stay there. The call I got just confirmed the exchange for the morning. Once the prisoners are released and the kidnappers allowed to leave, your husband and the others will be freed.'

Harper kept shooting. The three who'd been standing against the wall were down; two others had pivoted and opened fire on the hostages. One shot at her. She felt the hits in her thigh, her torso, but kept firing, aiming, even as her body sank. She hit a man shooting the hostages; his head exploded.

'As far as we know, the hostages are unharmed. There were cameras and microphones in the conference room, but the kidnappers disabled them. But remember, they have no reason to hurt anyone. In fact, they let one go because he's diabetic. Harper, are you listening?'

She shot the other man, but not before he'd hit some of the scientists. Harper was caught up in screams of pain, smells of rifle fire. She was on the floor, now, aiming at the hostage-taker who'd shot her. Realizing, as she fired, it was a woman. Young, beautiful, her eyes ablaze. Harper saw Pastor Travis burning in them, consumed in their fire as the eyes closed in death.

'Be that way. Pretend to ignore me. This attitude is exactly why we thought it best not to tell you. We know who you are. We know your background, your past. You are headstrong and stubborn. We knew you would have gotten involved and interfered with a peaceful settlement. It was not just for your own safety, but for the safety of the symposium members that we kept you away.'

Harper heard Hagit vaguely, like a dog barking down the block. She saw herself lying on a carpet, quickly losing blood. Hank was sitting on a chair across the room, wearing a white polo shirt and cargo pants. His hands were bound behind him, his mouth bloody and eyes swollen shut.

Dr Ben Haim wasn't religious, had no interest in attending shul for the holiday, wasn't planning to fast. In fact, he was munching a handful of sugared almonds as he left his bungalow on his way to his car, about to drive home to Herzliya. He hadn't seen his wife or kids in three weeks because he hadn't wanted to leave the dig. Didn't want to now, either, but, with the holiday, he might as well. Fieldwork would be stopped for the day. And, with all the craziness – those volunteers from America killing people and waiting for the end of the world, and the kibbutz being overrun with soldiers and police – he didn't know when it would start again. He might as well go home. He could catch up on paperwork there.

That was, if Sima would let him.

Sima. He thought about her as he loaded the car. He wasn't eager to see her. She would be angry, was always angry. The apartment would be a mess, an expression of her anger. And she would be decked out in some expensive new outfit, something she'd bought to punish him for being away. At least he would have a chance to see the children. Little Aviva and Moshe. He smiled, thinking of them, and climbed into the driver's seat, started the car. And yelped when he looked in the rear-view mirror.

'Keep driving.'

Ben Haim opened his mouth, couldn't find his voice. Didn't have words.

The woman held up a knife. Was she going to kill him?

'Don't be afraid.'

He stared at the mirror, at the tear-smeared face of the woman in the back seat. She looked familiar – long blonde hair, but in the dim light, it was hard to see her face.

'Drive.'

His hands were unsteady, clinging to the steering wheel. He backed up slowly, considering his options. Should he open the door and run for it? Lean on the horn? Drive to an army jeep? Crash into a tree?

'If you help me, I won't hurt you.' She wiped tears with the back of a hand, positioning the knife behind his ear. 'But if you don't, I'll cut your neck open. If you try to run or call for help, you'll die. If I were you, I wouldn't even think of it.'

'What do you want?' His voice was feeble.

'A ride to the dig.'

To the dig? 'But nobody's there. It's closed for the holiday . . .'

The knife pricked the back of his ear. 'Don't talk, Dr Ben Haim. Just drive.'

Ben Haim touched his ear, felt for blood. Pulled out of his parking area onto the main road of the kibbutz. He looked into the rear-view mirror again, recognized the woman. She was one of the volunteers, part of that crazy sect.

'When we get to the security gate, I'll be under your laundry bag. But the knife will be at your spine.'

Ben Haim felt it puncturing his seatback when he stopped at the gate. The guard recognized him, chatted, looked into the windows, finally said, 'Shalom,' and opened the gate.

Ben Haim drove through, wondering if he was making a grave mistake. This woman was the follower of a fanatic. Once they got to the dig, she might kill him anyway. And what did she want at the dig now, at night on a holiday? The shock of finding her in his car was wearing off; he began thinking more clearly.

'What will you do at the site?'

'Not your concern.'

'Of course it's my concern. It's taken years to get this project underway, and we're beginning to make progress—'

'I don't care about your stupid dig.'

She didn't? 'Then why are we going there?'

He watched her in the mirror. She sniffled, watching the road, the windows. Agitated. Not focusing on him. He could swerve, knock her off balance, and as she recovered, he could open the door and jump . . .

'Don't you know what's happened?'

'You mean at the kibbutz? I heard about a fight in a bunker. Your pastor apparently tried to kill a woman, and two men were killed—'

'Did you know the pastor's dead?'

He hadn't known that.

'He burned to death.'

'What? No, I didn't know.' Ben Haim had heard the fire alarm, wondered what had happened. Whether anyone else had been hurt. 'That's terrible.'

She sniffed. 'I was his assistant. He left some supplies at the site.'

'Supplies?' Ben Haim considered slamming on the brakes, jumping out when she fell backwards. He watched her in the mirror, smearing away tears. She looked fragile, maybe broken. Not like a killer.

He drove more calmly, finally turning into the parking lot of the old Megiddo prison. Saw some cars parked there. Wait. Were other people there?

'Drop me over by those rental cars.'

'Those are yours?'

'The church rented them.' She paused. 'The Lord promises us eternal glory if we complete three sacrifices by the ninth of Av.'

'That's today.'

'We are to offer a Muslim, a Christian and a Jew.'

'What?'

'I've done the first two. Pastor tried the Jew and failed.'

Ben Haim pulled over to the rentals and stopped the car. The knife pressed the back of his neck. He stiffened. 'I have children.'

'All God's children will rise and share His glory.' She opened the door, put one foot out and leaned forward, reaching the knife around to his throat. When she slashed at him, Ben Haim grabbed her arm, twisted it and tossed her out of the car. His back door was open, flapping as he stepped on the gas. He looked back, saw Lynne sprawled on the ground beside the rental cars. She was still clutching the knife, but her head was bent, and she sobbed, thwarted again.

The hotel was closed off. Police cars with flashing lights blocked the road. Harper sat in the back of the jeep, scanning the area. The intersection was lined with camera crews, police, soldiers, military vehicles, ambulances. The entire hotel and street around it were lit up, glowing in the night. The soldiers who'd driven them to Jerusalem pulled as close to the hotel as they could, spoke in Hebrew to each other, commenting on the scene.

Everyone – the whole world – must have known about the hostage situation. But Harper hadn't even suspected. She wanted to thrash Hagit, to blacken her other eye. How could she have kept the truth from her, hiding from her the fact that Hank had been kidnapped? That seven of the symposium attendees had been taken prisoner in the hotel? How long had Hagit known? And why had she agreed to keep such a terrible secret? Harper had saved her life – at the very least, Hagit owed her honesty, didn't she?

Harper's jaw ached from clenching her teeth. She glared at Hagit, fists itching to deck her. Saw a haggard, gray-haired lady with a bandaged neck and forehead.

'You're angry.'

How perceptive of her.

Hagit shrugged. 'I don't blame you. But it was decided to keep you uninformed as long as possible. To keep you from getting involved.'

It was decided? 'Who decided? Your government? Who gave them the right to decide what I know about my husband—?'

'No, it wasn't the government.' Hagit watched her with tired, sympathetic eyes.

Then who?

'Harper. It was your husband. He asked that you not be told.'

What? Not possible. Why would Hank ask that? 'How? If he's a prisoner, how could he manage to ask anything?'

'When they were taken, he still had a phone. He made a call to Inspector Alon. That's how.'

Harper felt slapped. Hank had had his phone, had called the police. But, instead of asking them to contact her and bring her back, he'd asked them to keep her uninformed?

'He wanted you to stay where you were. To be safe. Not to worry.'

Harper looked out the window at the hotel.

'That was, after all, the whole point of you going in the first place.'

Wait, what? Harper's chest tightened. 'What are you talking about?'

Hagit sighed. 'There was intelligence. Reports that the symposium might be targeted—'

'Who are they? What do they want?'

'They're terrorists. What do terrorists ever want? They want to terrorize. In this case, they want to disrupt international cooperation. To punish Arab countries for cooperating with Israel, even as regards something as critical as water. And they want to use the opportunity to free some fellow terrorists from prison.'

Harper's hands were icy. The lights and barricade went all the way around the hotel. No way she could penetrate. Unless there was an underground entrance. But the guards weren't fools; they would have them covered, too. Damn. What could she do? There had to be a way in.

Finally, she looked at Hagit. 'The truth. Are they alive?'

Hagit reached out, put her hand on Harper's. 'We have been assured, but we have no proof. Without the internal cameras working, we don't know. But we'll find out soon. The exchange is soon. Set for two a.m.'

'What time is it?'

Hagit asked the driver; he answered in Hebrew.

'Almost time.' Hagit looked out the side of the jeep at the sky. 'The helicopter should be here.'

Helicopter?

'With the prisoners.'

'I thought Israel doesn't negotiate with terrorists.'

Hagit sighed. 'It isn't just us. Jordanian, French and Egyptian delegates were taken. There is pressure to get them back alive.'

Harper closed her eyes, trying to absorb all the information. Her chest was raw, her legs numb from sitting still with Chloe's weight on her lap.

'Look. It was hard for me not to tell you. But it was for the best.'

The soldiers turned to Hagit, jabbering, nodding at the sky. Harper heard the distant chop of a helicopter. Oh God. Her skin prickled, alert. What if something went wrong? Where was Hank? Was he alive? Again, she saw him, his bloodstained polo shirt.

'How's the exchange supposed to happen? When will they release the prisoners?'

Hagit looked away. 'I don't know the details. They know what they're doing, though. Trust them.'

Like hell. 'Tell me.'

The helicopter hovered overhead, drowning out their voices. Hagit had to shout.

'The helicopter can't land on this hotel. So it's landing a block down. On an office building.'

And?

'This is their demand: the street is to be empty. No army, no police. The kidnappers will drive the hostages to that office building in armored cars. They will release them only when they find their demands have been met, and then they will take off in the helicopter.'

'How do they know they won't get shot down?'

Hagit's face told her the answer. Of course: they would take a hostage with them. Maybe several.

And then, when they were safely away, they'd kill them.

The helicopter stayed over the street, waiting as a pair of black limousines penetrated the blockade, drove to the front door of the hotel.

Harper sat up, not breathing, throat clenched. The street was empty, just as the kidnappers had demanded. Soldiers, officials stood around the perimeter, armed but helpless. Harper saw people beginning to file out of the hotel. Were these the hostages? She watched for Hank. Didn't see him. Couldn't wait any more. Couldn't sit. In a heartbeat, she thrust sleeping Chloe onto Hagit's lap.

'Hold her for a minute,' she shouted over the helicopter's engine.

Before Hagit could respond, Harper opened the door and hopped out of the jeep, standing where she could see the front of the hotel. Their driver climbed out, joining her, his hand near his weapon.

'Harper,' Hagit yelled out the window. 'Don't be stupid—'

'I need to watch for Hank.'

Up ahead, across the street, men were getting into the limousines. In a moment, they'd drive off. Where were Trent and Hank? She squinted into the lights and, for the briefest moment, glimpsed Hank. He was wearing a white polo and cargo pants, and he lowered his head, climbing into the second limo.

Harper's knees threatened to give way. She grabbed onto the soldier's arm, biting her lip to stifle a wail. The limo doors closed, engines started and, as Harper's eyes filled with angry tears, the cars blurred and pulled out of the driveway, heading up the street.

Helpless, Harper stood in the street beside the jeep, watching the second limo, aware of Hank, each heartbeat, each breath. Was he thinking of her now? Did he know she was there? The limo proceeded slowly, steadily. Coming closer. Looking larger.

Police, soldiers, everyone stood silent, rapt as the limos approached. The helicopter moved, finally, heading for a nearby rooftop. Dimly, Harper became aware of voices. People shouting in a side street, but she paid no notice, kept her eyes on the limos, watching for Hank until, behind her, she heard a sharp metallic crash.

Harper pivoted, saw a smashed ambulance, a broken barricade. A couple of soldiers running, weapons raised. And a car careening up the street – not a limo or security vehicle, not military. A new Corolla.

Around her, police and soldiers remained focused on the hostages, the helicopter. But the Corolla was barreling ahead, accelerating, on a collision course with the limousines. Harper didn't think; she just reacted, grabbing the soldier beside her, pulling out his gun. Raising it, aiming, shoving him away when he fought her for it. Aiming again while he and others finally saw the car. Seeing it change direction, steer right towards her, just heartbeats away. Steadying her stance, inhaling, Harper glimpsed the driver's face. Saw that it wasn't one of the kidnappers. And fired anyway.

From then on, it was a jumble. The recoil of her gun. The firing of many others. The screech of the car veering out of control. A thick weight knocking Harper's back, pushing her away. A crack like the sky shattering. The shaking of the earth. Harper pictured Chloe and Hank and, as the night around her erupted in flame, she thought that Travis had been right. It was the end of the world.

* * *

Don't cry, Lynne comforted herself. Don't fall apart. Ben Haim didn't matter. There would be other chances. Meantime, she had to keep going. She got up, brushed herself off. Headed for the rental cars.

There was one for each sector. But with the rest of the church being loaded onto buses and taken away, the designated drivers wouldn't be around. She didn't know who besides herself was free. Had they ever found Marlene? Was Lowell still loose? What about the guys in the medical center? Were they still there? Never mind. It didn't matter. None of it mattered. All that mattered was finishing the sacrifice. She would do it, still had time.

Her hands were dirty, two – no, three nails broken. Blood crusted around one of them. Her fingers were unsteady. She needed to pray. Please, Lord, give me strength. Guide me to fulfill Your wishes . . .

She stopped, mid-prayer, unable to finish. Angry. What kind of God was she working for? Travis had led his people across the world, had devoted himself to obeying God's coded word. And look what had happened. Couldn't an all-powerful Lord cut them a single break? So far, at every attempt, they'd confronted obstacles. Been stifled. People had died. Travis . . . Travis had died. What kind of a twisted freaking cold-hearted God would permit that? She stopped, stared up at heaven and let out a bellow. A howl.

But what was she to do? She couldn't just walk away. Had to finish it so Travis could come back. So they could be together.

But what about Peter? What if he came back, too? It wouldn't happen, she decided. But if it did, Ramsey would simply explain that he and she were soul mates. That God Himself had paired them. And Peter would buzz off. Lord, guide me, she whispered. Lord, give me strength.

Tears blurred her vision. She smeared them across her face, deciding which car to take. Were they all the same? She hadn't paid attention, hadn't been assigned to this phase of the plan. If she relaxed and opened her mind, Travis's spirit would guide her to the right one. She took a breath, straightened her spine, closed her eyes. Waited for a sign. Thought of the number three, like the trinity. Like the triad of lambs. Headed for the third car from the left. Stopped. Reconsidered. She was in Israel; Hebrew was read right to left. Maybe she should take the third car from the right. Why was every single little step so complicated? What difference did it make which car she used? It didn't. She could take any of them and it would be fine. She opened the door to the third car from the right, found the keys under the seat, found the phone, punched in the number pasted to it, started the engine, pulled out of the parking lot.

The whole way to Jerusalem, she sang hymns. Once there, she used her GPS to find the hotel and even then got lost. Jerusalem was a maze. Street names changed randomly. Roads wound into each other. Finally, she found the hotel . . . But something was going on there. The road was blocked. Maybe because of the holiday? She'd heard you weren't supposed to drive in Jerusalem on holidays. She'd heard people had been spat at, that cars had been stoned. But this looked different. The street ahead was bright with huge lights. She pulled up as close as she could. A guard stepped over to her car.

'It's a detour,' he barked. 'Go back and around.' His English was good. He pointed to show her the way.

Lynne nodded, thanked him. Before she turned the car around, though, she looked up and down the road. The spotlights were aimed across the street, onto the King Saul Hotel, the very place she'd been headed. That couldn't be a coincidence.

What was going on?

'Go,' the guard waved her on. 'Move away from the area.'

She grabbed the steering wheel. 'On my way.' She made herself smile, pulled away a few yards to satisfy him, then stopped, looking back.

Across the street, a pair of black limousines pulled out of the King Saul driveway, moving slowly like a funeral.

A circle of police and army personnel watched from the perimeter. Lynne scanned their vehicles, looking for a weak link. Decided that the ambulance ahead was good enough. As was the present moment.

With a cry of, 'Thy will be done,' Lynne picked up the cell phone with one hand, made a screeching U-turn with the other and floored the gas pedal. She was aware of the guard's yelling, but sped forward, bracing for impact with the ambulance blocking her way, exulting in the collision and speeding on. As the car lurched, she pressed her foot down on the pedal, and looked at the perimeter, the crowd facing the limousines . . . Wait.

No way. Was that her?

She looked again. And laughed out loud.

Her chest pounded. Holy Lord. Truly, Harper Jennings' presence was a sign, a gift from God. 'Thank you,' she shouted. 'Thank you!' She adjusted her steering to hit Harper head on, and kept going even when Harper raised a weapon. Even as bullets shattered her window and blood spurted from her body, Lynne remained certain that she was finally succeeding and, in one stroke, avenging Travis's death and completing the third sacrifice. That she and Travis would rise and be rewarded.

Her foot slipped off the gas pedal, her bloodied hand off the steering wheel. Fading, she praised God and Travis and used her last burst of energy to push the 'send' button. For the briefest of moments, she saw heaven. It was bright pure white.

Harper opened her eyes and, once again, knew she was in Iraq. A bomb had gone off; she'd flown into the air and landed on a burnt-out car. She knew before she tried that she'd be unable to move her legs. Or to feel them. Or to hear. She would be deaf and numb, like always. But where were the others? The rest of her patrol? They'd been standing at the checkpoint. A car had driven up, not slowing. And at the same time, a woman had been crossing the street, had turned and smiled, had reached inside her robe . . . Harper couldn't remember the next part. Couldn't hear. Couldn't feel. She turned her head, looking for her patrol. Saw blazing white light. Flames. Closed her eyes.

When she opened them again, she was moving. Being carried – on a stretcher? Passing flashing lights, ambulances, people scurrying. A burnt-out limo. She tried to speak, but couldn't form words.

Inside the ambulance, someone, a man in uniform was messing with her. Attaching her to a tube. But where was her patrol?

She had to find out. Had to ask. 'What happened?'

The man's lips moved. She didn't hear what he said. He closed the ambulance doors. Feeling the rumble of movement, Harper closed her eyes.

She didn't open them again until late on the tenth of Av.

When she did, Hagit was sitting beside her, crocheting. 'So, you're up?' She stood. 'Good. I'll tell them.'

Harper blinked. 'Wait. Where am I?' Her words were slurred. Her mouth was dry. Tasted metallic. She looked around, saw IV tubes, an ECG monitor. Oh God. What had happened? Where was Chloe? Hank? She lifted her head, twisted, trying to sit up.

'Don't even think about it.' Hagit scowled. 'Settle down. I'm going for the nurse.'

'Chloe?' Harper rasped.

'Chloe's fine.' Hagit moved toward the door.

'Where . . .?' It took all her energy to speak.

'Don't worry. I'll be right back.'

'Hank?'

Hagit was almost out the door, but she stopped, turned around. Her expression had softened. 'You don't remember anything?'

Harper shivered. What had happened? She closed her eyes, trying to recall. Saw bright light and smelled flames. Oh God. 'Where's Hank?'

Hagit stepped back to the bed, put a hand on Harper's shoulder. 'The doctors will tell you everything.'

'No. You tell me. Now.'

Hagit sighed. 'That woman from the dig. The one who tried to kill me?'

Lynne. What about her?

'She showed up here.' Hagit told her that Lynne had driven to Jerusalem in a car fitted as a bomb. That Travis's group had managed to make several of them and parked them at the dig.

At the dig? Car bombs? Harper closed her eyes, saw four brand-new rented Corollas parked in a row. Damn.

'But why did she come here?' Harper felt dizzy, unfocused.

Hagit shrugged. 'Who knows? Maybe to make more sacrifices. Maybe to kill you.'

'Me?' Harper lifted a hand to her chest. Stared at it. It was covered with gauze.

'It can't be a coincidence that she brought the bomb to the hotel where you'd be staying. Face it. She blamed you for Travis's death and, as long as she was setting off a bomb, she might as well get revenge.'

Harper heard a click, saw Travis disappear in flames. How could Lynne blame her for that? 'She's dead?'

'She is.'

Harper closed her eyes.

'Shhh.' Hagit stroked Harper's head. 'It could have been much worse.'

What? 'Hagit. Tell me.'

'Okay. I'll tell you. Lynne Watts is dead. But her bomb didn't blow up the hotel or any other building because of you. You stopped her.'

'I did?' Harper tried to remember.

'You and the soldiers. You shot her with a gun you took from our escort.' Hagit paused. 'You don't remember? Really?'

She'd stolen a gun? When?

'You shot the bomber before she could get in position, just seconds after she crossed the barricade.'

Harper saw snapshots: lights glaring on an empty street. A limousine. She tried to remember more. Couldn't.

'But you were too close to the bomb. You have burns.'

Harper looked at the bandages covering her arms, her right hand. There had been an explosion. A fire.

She'd killed Lynne.

'The explosion would have been a big tragedy if not for you and those soldiers. As it was, instead of blowing up a hotel, she made a hole in the street and destroyed a limousine.'

A what? Harper closed her eyes, saw a limousine . . .

Hank's limousine.

Harper's throat closed. Ice sliced through her chest. She couldn't speak. Hank – Hank had been in a limousine. Was Hagit preparing to tell her that he'd been killed? Oh God. Hank. His sparkling eyes, his broad grin . . . He couldn't be dead. Could he?

Hagit was still talking. '. . . killed four of the kidnappers, a French geologist, an Egyptian hydrologist and an Israeli driver.'

What? Harper tried to breathe. 'Hank?' Her voice was faint.

'Hank was in the second limousine.'

So what did that mean? That he was alive?

Hagit sighed. 'The explosion threw it across the street, onto its side. A chunk of the blown-up car flew onto the soldier who tackled you. He saved you. You should send him chocolates.'

A soldier had saved her? What about Hank? Why wouldn't Hagit just tell her? Was she deliberately stalling? Putting off telling her that Hank was dead?

'Hank?'

'Hank?' Hagit seemed irritated. 'I already told you. He was in the second car. In that car, they all lived.'

No, she hadn't told her. Or had she? Harper wasn't sure, couldn't remember. Her thoughts were jumbled. She saw a car speeding toward her. Then nothing. Just a disconnected image. She tried to absorb the news. She'd shot Lynne. And Lynne had blown up a limousine full of kidnappers and scientists.

But Hank had survived. Where was he? And what about Trent? Was he okay?

'Now, I'm going for the nurse.' Hagit headed for the door.

Harper lay back, wondering why Hank wasn't with her in the hospital room. Where was Chloe? Questions swirled and mixed together until she couldn't remember what they were. Couldn't keep track of them. Her eyelids drifted down and, as she dozed off, she thought she heard a voice calling her name. Insisting that she'd been awake just a moment ago.

The next day passed in a fog of heavy medication, sleep and dreamy impressions. Harper didn't have much pain. Once, she felt Hank's lips on her mouth. She heard him whisper that she'd be fine, that she was a hero. That Chloe missed her so she should hurry up and get well. She heard these things clearly, but when she managed to open her eyes, he wasn't there.

On the second day, pain woke her up. Her medications had been reduced, so she was more alert, able to stay awake. Hank was there, his back to her, talking to someone. Inspector Alon?

She tried to hear them. Alon said something about debriefing. About coming back.

Harper got out of bed for the first time in two days, wobbled on her way to the bathroom. Saw herself in the mirror for the first time, too, and gasped at her appearance. One side of her face was mottled and crusty, like the top of a crème brûlée. Her scrapes and scratches had been seared away. Her eyebrows were gone. So was a patch of hair over her right temple. Oh God. She looked ghastly.

'You are. Beautiful.' Hank had come into the bathroom, stood behind her. Ever so gently, he put his arms around her waist, kissed her neck. His gentleness triggered tears. 'They said. You won't scar.'

Wait. Something was wrong. 'What did you say?'

'The doctors. Said. Your arms and hand might scar a little. You have some third degree burns there. But not your face.'

Harper gaped.

'You'll be okay.'

'Hank?' It was all she could manage to say.

'What? What's wrong?'

'You got hit on the head?'

'Just a bump.'

She put a hand to her mouth, another to his chest. Was it her imagination? Was he talking more clearly? A tear trickled over her crusty skin.

'Are you in pain?' His brows furrowed.

She shook her head.

'Then what?'

'Nothing. Just you. I missed you.'

Gently, he kissed an uninjured ear. 'I missed you, too.'

'Hank. Do you realize? You're talking better.' Tears kept coming.

'No. I don't think so.' He hesitated. 'Am I?' His mouth opened. He stood, scratched his head. 'Do you really think so?'

Harper didn't answer. Her hands were wrapped in gauze; she used it to dab away another tear.

Hank's speech was almost normal, and nobody knew why. The doctors said it was unusual, but not unheard of, for aphasia sufferers to spontaneously improve. They theorized the injury to his head might have affected the change. They were fascinated, wanted to run tests.

Harper's delight about Hank's speech was dulled when Inspector Alon reappeared. He brought a box of halvah, but his manner was somber.

'You should be in serious trouble.' He sat opposite her in the visitors' lounge. 'You assaulted a soldier and took his weapon. But as it is, four kidnappers were killed and the rest are in custody. The prisoners for the exchange are back in prison. All but three captive symposium members and the limo driver were rescued. The woman you shot intended to cause a disaster, but unintentionally, her bomb thwarted the terrorists and saved many more lives than it took.' He didn't smile.

Harper didn't either. In fact, she glared. 'Why didn't you tell me about the hostage situation? I had a right to know that my husband was in danger—'

'Mrs Jennings.' Alon shook his head. 'Keeping you uninformed was not an easy decision, but we thought it best to honor your husband's request and protect you from the truth for a while. You and your child were safe, guarded by experienced agents—'

'You mean Hagit? Some agent. She was captured and almost killed – I had to save her.'

'It wasn't just Hagit alone. We were focused on the symposium situation, but we also had people watching the rest of the country, including the small religious sect. Bringing you here would only have complicated matters—'

'My husband's life was at stake. Even if he asked you to hide that from me, I had a right to know.'

'I'm sorry, but you didn't. This is our country, our security, our decisions. We needed to minimize publicity as well as threat. To communicate only as needed. Let me ask you: if we had told you what was happening, what would you have done?'

Harper let out a breath. She got his point.

'You and I both know you'd have gotten involved and drawn attention to the situation. In fact, as soon as you found out, you ran here like a bat out of hell with no concern for consequences.'

'Maybe I wouldn't have if you'd included me in your plans from the beginning.'

Alon leaned forward, elbows on knees. 'Mrs Jennings. We have quite well trained defense and anti-terrorist forces here. Even with your military background and good intentions, let me remind you again: in this country, you are merely a tourist.'

Harper stiffened. Fuming.

'In fact,' Alon sat back, crossing his legs, 'after killing two men, stealing a jeep and confiscating a soldier's weapon, if not for my intervention, you'd be in a different hospital. In prison, pending evaluation of your case.'

Harper crossed her arms, remembering her burns only when deep slow pain rolled through them. Cautiously, wincing, she uncrossed them, and looked at the window, saying nothing.

Hank joined them, bringing coffee.

'What did the doctors say?' Harper had trouble taking the cup, couldn't hold it, so she pretended she didn't want any. 'No thanks.'

Hank set her cup on an end table. 'They don't know what to think. They're baffled. And cautious.' He sat beside Harper, touched her less wounded shoulder. 'But we'll talk about it later. I don't mean to interrupt your conversation.'

Harper stared at him, dumbfounded that Hank had just articulated those sentences. Maybe she was dreaming? Or in a coma?

But Inspector Alon seemed real enough. He went on, updating them. The symposium had been put on hold, due to the violence. Relations with Jordan, Egypt, Germany and France hadn't been helped by the incident, but, in actuality, everyone was thankful that more hadn't died. And the important work would continue, perhaps with some of the same participants, within the year.

As to Travis's followers, Jimmy, Wendell, Marlene, Lowell, Frank and Harold and the rest of the church council had been arrested.

His other followers had been unaware of the human sacrifices, had been appalled when Travis had died attempting arson and mass murder. After being questioned, they'd been shipped home.

The council members, hoping to obtain clemency, had talked nonstop about Travis's discovery, translation and interpretation of the Bible code. They'd confirmed that the code had called for the sacrifice of a Christian, a Muslim and a Jew. That Lynne, with Marlene's help, had conducted the first two offerings in the Jerusalem shuk, but because she'd messed up the locations, the third had been assigned to Peter Watts. When he'd become incapacitated, Travis had taken on the responsibility himself.

'And tried to sacrifice Hagit,' Harper added.

'He would have if not for you.' Alon sipped coffee.

The council had also revealed Travis's plans for the car bombs. He'd intended to explode them at designated points in Jerusalem and Tel Aviv, near Gaza and Megiddo to spark God's final conflagration.

'We knew about Ramsey Travis and his church. We'd gathered intelligence; the group had been assessed but, this time, we underestimated the threat. Until the incident with Hagit, we wrongly thought of Travis as a standard-issue, basically harmless fanatic. You were right, Mrs Jennings. We arrested the wrong man for the murder of the American in the shuk.'

Harper closed her eyes, saw Travis crumble to the ground, consumed by flames. She took a breath, said nothing.

Hank asked about the status of the dig, and Alon told them it was back in operation with a new staff of volunteer college students from all over the world.

A policeman came in, whispered something to Inspector Alon.

'It seems that I have to go.' He finished his coffee and stood. 'I wish you a quick recovery, and a safe return home.' He met Harper's eyes for a long moment, shook Hank's hand, and took his leave.

Hank started to say something, but was interrupted by cheery voices from the hallway. Adi, Yoshi, Gal and Yael rushed in, jabbering and carefully hugging, their arms laden with sunflowers and baskets of spiced nuts and fresh fruit. As he greeted her, Gal handed Harper an envelope containing a cell phone and passport.

With his right arm in a cast, Trent had trouble pouring a drink. But he managed. He seemed reluctant to go to his own room, still shaken and unwilling to be alone.

Chloe shrieked and ran across the room, crashing into his legs, causing his Scotch to splash onto the carpet. Hank scooped her up, carried her like a sack of laundry to the bedroom.

'Need help?' He'd already packed, was ready to go. His only significant injury had been to his head; he had a colorful bump and some staples on his scalp.

'No, almost done.' It wasn't easy packing with bandaged hands, but Hagit was doing the folding. Harper missed her already. Wasn't sure how she'd manage to say goodbye.

'Remember, you'll Skype with me,' Hagit told her. 'You'll let me know you got home all right. And I'll teach more songs to Chloe.'

Harper nodded. 'What will you do with yourself? You'll be bored without us . . .'

'No, she'll be relieved.' Hank grinned.

'Geet!' Chloe reached for her.

'What are you talking about?' Hagit stopped folding, took Chloe from Hank, kissed her. 'I already have my next assignment. I start before your plane takes off.'

'Really?' Harper doubted it. Hagit had barely recovered from her injuries. Still had a bright red scar on her forehead, a greenish yellow hue around her eye.

'Doing what?' Hank handed a stack of t-shirts to Harper. 'More babysitting?'

'You know I can't tell you. I'm a secret agent.'

'I thought you were retired.'

Hagit smirked. 'And I thought you were smart enough to recognize a lie.'

Harper met her eyes. Saw a glint. Were Hagit's eyes tearing?

'Okay. That's the end of packing. Now, I have to go.' Hagit gave Chloe a squeeze. Handed her back to Hank. Kissed him on both cheeks. Took Harper's less burned hand, kissed her less burned cheek. 'Take care of yourself, Harper. And your family. I wish you well.'

Harper wasn't prepared, hadn't expected Hagit to leave so abruptly. She tried to collect thoughts. What could she say? She held Hagit's hand, met her eyes. 'Thank you.' The words seemed lame.

'Don't forget to wear your *hamsa*. Hang one in your house . . .'

'Hagit, still with the *hamsas*? After all that's happened? The *hamsas* didn't protect us—'

'Of course they did.'

'Yours didn't help you. Travis nearly killed you—'

'Nearly. I'm still here, aren't I?'

Harper sputtered. 'What about me? The explosion almost—'

'Yes, almost. What's wrong with you?' Hagit shook a finger, scolding. 'Can't you see what would have happened if you hadn't been protected? The Evil Eye is watching. It follows you. Remember. Wear your *hamsa*.'

Harper couldn't help smiling.

'Why are you smiling? It's not a joke. Wear it. Promise me.'

She lost the smile, made a somber face. 'I promise.'

'Good. Have a safe trip home. Shalom.' She turned to go.

'Shalom,' Hank repeated.

Shalom? Really? Harper's throat thickened. She held onto Hank's arm, walking Hagit to the door. Chloe began repeating 'Shalom', singing bits of the goodbye song she'd learned in the nursery. Trent stood and held up his drink, toasting as Hagit walked by, wishing her well. Hank opened the door; Harper gave one last gentle hug.

And then, the door closed. Chloe kept singing, but Hagit was gone.

Harper blinked away another tear.

'You okay?' Hank watched her. Chloe squirmed; he set her down to scramble around.

Harper sniffed, composed herself. Nodded. Of course she was okay.

'We have a few hours. Why don't you rest?'

Harper thought about it, realized she had an errand to run. 'No, let's go to the shuk.'

'The shuk?' Hank looked doubtful, eyeing her bandages.

'For souvenirs.'

Trent volunteered to watch Chloe. So, twenty minutes later, Hank and Harper were in the shuk, walking slowly past booths selling rugs, jewelry, water pipes, clothing, spices, nuts, flowers and fruit.

Vendors called to them, offering bargains and treasures.

Finally, Harper stopped at a display of *hamsas*.

'I'll give you a special price, to show my wishes for you to heal.' The vendor eyed Harper's bandages. 'Three bracelets, ten shekels.'

'No, that's too much—'

'Okay, I want you to be happy. For you, I'll give three bracelets for eight.'

They haggled, quibbled, finally reached an agreement. Hank

didn't have cash, so he used his credit card to buy fifteen *hamsas*: six key chains, six charm bracelets, three pendants, for a total of two hundred shekels, somewhere over sixty dollars.

Finally, for the last time, they left the shuk. Back at the hotel, they collected Trent and Chloe. Harper tried to put their purchases into their carry-ons but the bag of *hamsas* slipped out of her bandaged hands. Picking them up, she looked at the receipt.

'Damn.'

'What?'

'Didn't we agree on two hundred shekels? Look at this.'

Hank looked. In loopy scrawled numerals, the receipt said three hundred.

His eyebrows raised. He shifted Chloe to his other arm. 'Son of a gun. Ahmed soaked us.'

'What time is it?' Harper started for the door. 'Let's go back—'

'Harper, relax. We got taken.'

'So, let's get untaken.' Harper stuffed the *hamsas* into her bag. 'I don't like being a chump. Let's go straighten that guy out.'

Hank smiled. 'You're real intimidating with your bandages.'

'Come on, Hank, it's not right—he probably cheats unsuspecting tourists all the time.'

Hank nodded. 'I bet he does.' Setting Chloe down, he wrapped Harper in his arms. Harper smelled his shaving cream. Suddenly, settling things with the vendor didn't seem all that important. What mattered was her family, her friends. And, if those *hamsas* could keep them safe, then they'd be well worth the extra money. Not that she believed that Evil Eye nonsense.

But wearing the *hamsas* wouldn't hurt.